Hannah's Reach

S0-BEF-388

Hannah's Reach

By Eileen Snow

With the creative collaboration of Jane Bennion

© 2007 Eileen Snow

Copyright 2007 by Eileen H. Snow. All rights reserved. Printed in the USA. No part of this book may be reproduced or used in any manner without the written permission of the author except for brief citations used for articles or reviews. For more information visit Hannahsreach.com.

First Edition

Cover Artwork by Rachel Jackson. Cover Design by Scott Snow of Royter/Snow Design

ISBN # 0-9777913-1-9   New Hope Publications

Library of Congress Cataloging in application.

Dedicated to and inspired by...

the Dee and Shellie Doman family,
the Wayne and KaLee Harper family,
the Robert and Mary Judd family
and all the other kind souls who see children
not only as our most important responsibilities
but also as our most precious gifts.

and

To Nixmary

Suffer the Children
By Eileen Snow

Suffer the children to come.
Show them all they have inside to give,
That there's a reason why they live.
Help them to understand,
That they are a part of a plan.
Suffer them to come, for of such is the kingdom.

(chorus)
Oh lift them high upon your shoulders.
And let them fly on eagle's wings.
Let them soar to get a heaven's view
For they too, are heavenly things.

Suffer the Children to stay
Innocent and pure as they come to earth.
Untouched and holy as the day of their birth.
With heavenly light in their eyes,
Strangers to guile and to lies.
Suffer them to stay,
For that is their Father's way.

(repeat the chorus)
Take the ragged make them whole.
Replace the trust that someone stole.
A life that's shattered love makes new
And lets the face of God shine through.

Suffer the children who hurt.
Bring them to His wounded feet to kneel
And He their wounded hearts will heal.
Give them a place that is safe and warm—
With a loving face and an open arm.
Suffer them to come
For of such is the kingdom.
Oh lift them high, let them soar and fly
with you in the kingdom.

2006

PROLOGUE

The beat-up Oldsmobile backed full-throttle out of the gated driveway skidding into a perfect 360-degree donut on the snow-covered road. The slightly high driver cackled with glee as he spun the wheel one-handed to drive away. The other hand held a fistful of cash. Carlos tossed it blissfully into the air, rammed the gearshift into drive, stomped on the accelerator for a few seconds and then slammed on the brakes as he cranked the wheel to re-experience the spin. It was 2:00 a.m. on a deserted road and who was going to care? The little passenger in the backseat was not amused. She was terrified and let out a wail.

"I hope she's not going to do that all the way down I-95," Patti said after a noisy few minutes.

He rolled his eyes. "I'm sure I'm not going to drive like that on 95, now, am I? She'll settle down." She wailed again louder. "She'd better!" He yelled it over the seat, lifting the back of his hand threateningly.

"She's already upset so take it easy, okay?"

"Oh yeah. We must remember she's precious cargo." He looked down at the stacks of crisp cash sitting on the seat between them and let out a satisfied sigh. He laid his hand on a stack of hundreds and said, "She's going to bring us a lot more than this before we're through."

Patti turned to the backseat and tried to quiet the distraught nineteen-month-old with a cookie. "You'll be okay. Right, Sweetheart?"

The offering was batted across the car and the ear-piercing siren of a scream continued.

"I don't know if I can stand to listen to this racket very long when I'm trying to drive in the snow. She makes me nervous. Make her shut up!"

"Oh, Carlito, mi amor, tranquilo." Patti put out her joint and climbed awkwardly over the back of her seat. She fiddled with the belts and buckles and after some struggle; the child was in her arms. The little face was red and blotchy from crying and a large stalactite of mucous was hanging down almost to Patti's thigh. The baby was nearly hyperventilating in her sobs.

"Oh, gross!" Carlos whined, glancing over his shoulder to the backseat.

"So why are you complaining? I'm the one dealing with it." Patti wiped the little runny nose with a Winnie the Pooh shirt from the child's bag. She was rocking the baby and gently rubbing her back.

"It wasn't supposed to happen this way. She was gonna be out of our hands by now. We keep the money; they keep her. She was supposed to be a nice little Christmas present, but—"

"It just didn't work out that way, did it? But we got the money, even more than when we started. Do you think we should keep her, Carlos? She's so sweet and so cute, when she's not hysterical, that is."

"Oh yeah, we're keepin' her alright. Not gonna let an opportunity like this pass us by."

"That New York witch! How could she be so cold?" Patti was having some success in comforting the baby now. She'd found a bottle with some cinnamon sugar water in it. "Her loss is our gain."

"We'll just keep gaining and she'll keep losing." Carlos almost laughed. "You'll be a great mother, high all the time."

"I could cut back on the dope. I think I could be a mother. How hard can it be? It's the right thing to do."

"Besides, we promised her. Didn't we?" Carlos said, dripping with sarcasm.

The baby was settling down, cuddling against Patti's chest. After the three days she had spent with this child, Patti had really come to care about her. After a few minutes of quiet she said, "But Carlos, she deserves better than us."

"So what do you suggest? —Maybe we dump her someplace or... hey! Maybe we could sell her to one of those lawyers who sort'a sells babies. They gotta buy 'em from somewhere, ya' know."

"They only buy and sell babies who are as white as the snow that you are drivin' in and in case you never looked, she's no Blanca Nieves. Selling her! How could you even think of such a thing?" A little sweaty head drooped onto Patti's shoulder. "Oh Carlito, she's hugging me. She's going to sleep now."

Soon, Patti nodded off as well.

By first light they had reached the Maryland state line and traffic had begun to increase. It was early in the morning and the rats had awakened for another day's race. By the time Carlos reached the Washington Beltway the snow had nearly stopped and the traffic was bumper to bumper –even on Christmas Eve.

"Patti, wake up!" Carlito practically shouted. "Put the kid in the seat thing and come up here and drive. We're not gettin' nowhere. You can sit in park as well as I can and I gotta get some sleep. I had some beer and some cocaine and I can't stay awake."

"Oh, Honey, she's asleep. If I move her it'll wake her up and she'll start screamin' again."

"So be careful. She's really out of it so if you are slow and gentle she'll stay asleep. Slow and gentle." Suddenly Carlos sounded like the parenting voice of authority.

"Oh Carlito! She's so precious when she's asleep and..." she registered what he'd just offered. "See? You'll be a good daddy."

"Patti, just get up here."

"Just listen. A little while ago she lifted up her little face and said 'Mama? Mama?' And so then I held her close and she went back to sleep. It was so tender."

"So?"

"You told the woman you needed money to take care of her. So we have to do it; we have to take good care of her."

"Oh we will!" The wheels had been turning in Carlos' head and he was tapping the steering wheel. "We'll take *real* good care of her and milk this for all it's worth. Maybe there's a little gold mine there in the backseat. I'm seeing all kinds of angles here. I know a guy back in Miami who takes kids and takes these pictures...he makes more money than God, himself." He laughed loudly.

"No, Carlos! We're supposed to take care of her, love her."

"Don't worry. They don't really hurt 'em or anything. Just... you know... But I'm too tired to think about it right now. Just put her down and get up here."

"Fine! I'll drive," Patti answered angrily. The baby didn't wake when Patti gently put her back in her car seat. Patti reversed her earlier acrobatic move and bounded ungracefully into the front seat.

"You coulda got out and come around. The car is in park and I coulda just moved over." Carlos said.

"Now you can get out and I can move over!" Patti snapped back.

"Fine! I don't care. What's your problem?"

"You! What's yours?"

"Nothin'."

Patti slid into the driver's seat and Carlos slammed the door after he climbed into the passenger side.

"Stupid woman. I get us more money than you have ever seen in your life and you go nuts on me. We are talkin' lotsa money here."

"Just shut up and go to sleep like you said you would. And I won't say a word, trust me."

"And don' draw attention to us, got it? Just drive normal. Act normal."

"—Like I'm going to speed in this traffic and with your crack pipe and my grass in here... Besides, nobody is looking for us, are they?"

"No, not yet anyway." Carlos sounded concerned for the first time. "I was just thinking that if he found out, we might have a problem."

"He has no idea, none at all."

"You're right; he doesn't know and she sure isn't gonna tell him. There's nothing to worry about so I'm going to put my head back and sleep." Carlos gradually drifted down into the profound sleep of the truly wasted.

The ribbon of highway known as I-95 wound south warming with each state line. Carlos slept soundly for hours, occasionally snoring and twitching. Patti drove on, and stopped now and then for gas and snacks for her and her *Angelita Linda*, the baby. Linda means lovely and this little girl certainly was that. Patti could feel herself becoming fonder of her with every passing hour. For most of the last three days she had been very little trouble. Carlos couldn't be serious about letting that...man... do anything to her. Why couldn't they keep her? Maybe that would be the *right* thing to do.

She fought with herself for the next several hours. It all played out in vivid scenarios in her mind: her wishes, Margarita's wishes, what was best for the baby. Keeping her would make them stop the drugs. Maybe Patti just needed a good reason to get clean and here was as good a reason as she would ever find.

With all this money, Carlos could stop dealing and they could live decently, downright respectably like other people. He wouldn't need to do anything else for more money. Patti mentally built the house and the neighborhood where they could settle down. They could get married and be a real family.

"We could have another kid or two of our own and one of those big yellow dogs and a yard with a barbeque and everything." She told Carlos in her mind. "We could have a life, Carlito, a real life." She was pleading now.

She looked over at him asleep against the car door and then down at the drug paraphernalia on the floor and saw things in the stark light of reality. She toyed with the idea of just taking Linda and disappearing with her and of course, some of the cash. But that would get complicated and she knew he'd come after them for the money.

She knew about his temper and that he was capable of violence. She had witnessed a horrible and tragic scene brought on by Carlos and his dealing. He had never hurt her; she'd only seen his violence directed at others, but he had threatened her with a beating several times when he was stoned. She could leave the money with him and just take the little girl. She could only imagine what an out of control, drug-crazed Carlos could do to a helpless little child. Linda would only be a pawn in his next scam. Patti had always imagined herself able to reform Carlos and sometimes she could almost see, deep inside of him, the Carlos that Margarita believed in. –But to risk the child's well being on him? The whole thing made her so uneasy.

Unconsciously, she reached for another joint and then caught herself.

"Who am I kidding?" She said aloud. "What a joke. Sure. I can be Betty Crocker and Carlito can be Father of the Year."

She gave in and smoked the marijuana and softly cried knowing that things would never really change because Carlos would not change. If she stayed with Carlos, she would not change either. The little dream world she had created dimmed from her mind. She looked back at Linda and heaved a long sigh of genuine sadness and regret. She drove on searching for an answer, praying for an answer...a way to protect her little angel and herself.

Somewhere in North Carolina, a sign on the side of the highway caught her attention. It read, "St. Thomas Aquinas Convent. Little Sisters of the Poor."

With hardly a thought, Patti took the exit and followed the narrow road back into some rolling hills. Nestled among the trees was a beautiful little Catholic church surrounded by some small rectangular buildings that Patti guessed were the sisters' sleeping quarters. She parked behind some trees and quietly got out; Carlos didn't even stir. She tiptoed toward the church. There seemed to be no one at all around and Patti wondered if they had run out of people to be nuns and had closed up shop. It was so silent that it startled her when the organ sounded and the sisters in the chapel began to sing. She stood for a moment and listened to them sing a Christmas hymn and thought they sounded like the heavenly choir must have when Jesus was born. It was beautiful and peaceful and joyful. "Angels we have heard on high..." It was their Christmas mass.

When Patti returned to the car, Linda was playing happily with the little stuffed dog that Patti had bought her at a truck stop. Her man was snoring, obviously sound asleep. Patti opened the back door and released the belts that fastened the infant seat to the car. She lifted the seat and the child out onto the trunk. Then she reached inside and grabbed a Nikon camera from the floor of the car and put the strap around her neck. Photography was the one thing that she shared with her father and for years she had never gone anywhere without a camera. Carlos had managed to steal this one for her. She also removed a baby blanket and Linda's diaper bag. She took some of the rubber-banded bundles of cash from the front seat. There were stacks of tens, twenties, fifties and hundreds, nearly sixty-five thousand dollars. She counted out $10,000 in one hundred dollar bill stacks and tucked them into the Minnie Mouse bag. *This could help care for Linda and other children too. It's her money, really.*

"You deserve more than this, my love, but you understand that this is the best thing, don't you? Carlos and me, we're no good for you. But I wish that I could keep you; I know that I could love you. I wish we could be a family. I'm just afraid of what kind of life you'd have with us. No good honey. But someone will love you, and take care of you and everything will be wonderful for you real soon. Real soon, Sweetie." Patti whispered.

She took some baby wipes from the bag and wiped down the car seat, the bag and even the money in the small stack.

Inside the bag was a picture of poor, beautiful Margarita. She had given it to Patti a few months before. Patti wrote on it, "Por mi angelita Linda, con amor, Mami. I will be with you always." Then she took the cross pendant with the daisy on it from around her own neck and wrapped the chain around the photo, cleaning it off as best she could. She closed up the bag and put the strap over her other shoulder. With two wipes in her hands, she lifted the car seat from the trunk and crept behind the trees toward the church. Looking around in all directions, she saw no one. The nuns were chanting the Lord's Prayer and Patti recited along from distant childhood memory.

"I'm trying to deliver you from evil, my little love," Patti said.

She placed the child, still in the seat, with the diaper bag, just inside the vestibule near the Holy Water. She pulled out her camera, turned on the flash and quickly and yet skillfully snapped a couple of photos.

"These are to remember you by."

At the instant that Patti took the photos, Linda raised her little arms, begging to be picked up, to be held, pleading to be loved. The image was stored in the camera and locked in Patti's memory. She would never forget her perfect milk-chocolate complexion, adorable baby teeth smile and the heartbreaking longing in those hazel eyes. Linda's chubby little hands held Patti's face as she kissed the child's forehead in farewell. "Adios, mi Linda."

Patti couldn't stop the tears as she crouched low and crept silently away. She had almost reached the car when she heard the nuns begin to sing, "Away in a Manger." The child, too, began to cry.

When Patti would stop for gas just inside South Carolina, Carlos would finally wake from his long winter's nap. There would be hell to pay. "She's my blood! I decide what happens to her. I'm the man," he'd holler. He would be furious. –Not for leaving the child so much as leaving the money and his easy ticket to so much more.

CHAPTER 1

The snowflakes floated like lacey fairies in the Manhattan air. The bitter cold was somehow lessened by the warmth of Christmas all around. Strings of white twinkle lights glittered everywhere and strains of carols and the bells of Salvation Army ringers could be heard floating on the cold but gentle wind. The store windows invited each passerby into a holiday fantasyland and some stood mesmerized, unable to simply walk on and miss the magic. Olivia Thomas could easily walk on and smiled to herself as she hurried home to her apartment on W. 83rd Street. She smiled, not in response to the spirit around her, but instead she smiled an almost mocking smile. Livy was an executive in a toy company and the Christmas season always represented the culmination of months and months of work and preparation and usually paid off handsomely in a large fourth quarter bonus. Many of these haggard shoppers were helping to swell that lovely bonus and she knew that she should really be thanking them and not judging them.

But she really didn't get it. Every year she would see the quarterly reports and the actual numbers of dollars spent on the toys and games from her company and other gift companies and was amazed. She observed all the foods and wines and holiday apparel and all the useless gifts of every variety. Who in the world would really want a fruitcake or worse, a chiapet? Heaven forbid. It was as if there was some kind of Yuletide gas in the air and Livy was the only one with a protective mask. On they went, these robots of Christmas—must buy, must give, must spend, must eat, and must rush. On and on it goes and so her bonus grows. And so, Livy smiled to herself.

Earlier in the season, the day after Thanksgiving to be exact, she had felt just a touch of what she thought Christmas spirit might feel like. Her boss had given her the dreaded PR assignment of delivering some of the company toys to kids in some kind of interim care shelter. A couple of photographers and an in-house reporter of sorts accompanied her. It felt less than genuine, very contrived. *JOY'S TOYS cares and we have pictures to prove it.* Photos of the event were immediately published in the New York Post in what looked like an article but was really paid advertising.

The shelter was for kids between foster situations or those recently removed from their homes and waiting to be assigned to foster families for the first time. A few older ones were there on their way to juvenile detention. What did Christmas mean to all of them? Wasn't it just another occasion to keenly feel unwanted, forgotten, unloved and so different from other, "regular," kids? It was uncomfortable, even painful for Livy to be there.

But she would play her role and do this part of her job superbly like she handled the rest of her duties. She sat in an overstuffed chair surrounded by beautifully wrapped packages. She picked up the first one and read the name on the tag. "This is for Sasha, straight from Santa's workshop! Where is Sasha?"

A little brown skinned girl who looked barely three shyly came forward. She had wild hair and wore a tattered little romper. She reached for the package and shook it. She wasn't sure what to do with it. Livy realized that she had possibly never received a pretty, wrapped present before.

A young man with Downs's syndrome appeared from the crowd to help her open it. He was dressed as an elf. He seemed a bit too old to be in the shelter so Livy guessed that he must be a volunteer. She hoped he was a volunteer and not just some unfortunate soul who'd wandered in off the street.

The gift was a teddy bear dressed for ballet.

"A dancing bear for a dancing girl!" the elf said.

He lifted Sasha high in the air and made a clumsy little twirl. She glee-fully hugged the toy tightly and gave the young man a hug too. He then helped Livy pass out the gifts to the rest of the younger children. The little ones were completely oblivious to his handicap. Some of the young teens headed for juvenile detention made cracks about him, but he didn't seem to hear them or pay them any attention. His focus was entirely on bringing joy to those little ones. They readily climbed onto his lap and embraced him. They ate up his affection and friendly laugh like a starving stray devours scraps from anyone who will offer. He was so excited for them, so delighted to help open each package and to see what magical item lay waiting inside. The children got more of their joy and thrill from this boy and the happiness he showed for them than from the gifts themselves. Livy felt warm inside like she had just sipped a wonderful, soothing cup of peppermint tea. There was just the slightest tingle of gooseflesh down her arms and she felt a lump in her throat.

The handicapped volunteer looked up and caught Livy watching him. He smiled a loving smile and said, "Thank you." He walked over to her and gave her a hug and she stiffened. The young man drew back and looked intensely at Livy. He seemed to think he recognized her. "You're my best friend. I knew it was you. You're here! Jesus knew you'd come. He loves you. Thank you for coming." With that he happily went back to playing with the children and their gifts. Every once in a while he would look up at her and something in his smile stirred a hidden place within…like a distant memory or some vaguely familiar feeling.

It was strange. As a rule, she was not comfortable with children and even less so with the mentally handicapped talking about Jesus, but there on that day, she had felt something warm and sweet and wonderful. Was that what Christmas was supposed to feel like? Suddenly, fleetingly, a Christmas that was "strictly business" was not enough and an old familiar longing returned. But that was weeks ago and now, on December 21st, the feeling was gone, thankfully.

She pulled her coat tighter around her as the damp air chilled her to the very bone. Livy, an exotic African-American beauty, was tall and thin and getting to the bone didn't take the frigid wind much effort at all. At last she reached the steps of her apartment building. As with most evenings recently, it was the new late shift doorman, Bryan Kimball, who was on duty.

"Hello, Ms. Thomas," Bryan called out in greeting. "Yet another late night? I guess this is the season when you'll work the hardest and the latest. You work for a toy company, right?"

"I guess you could say that this season is pretty much done as far as my part is concerned, has been for a long time. We just watch and see how successful we've been and how accurate we are about forecasting what kids will want. It looks good so far," Livy explained.

Livy liked Bryan but she wasn't sure why. He didn't fit into the Manhattan scene any more than Colin Powell belonged on the Grand Ole' Opry. He was young, too young for her, but quite tall, blonde and very nice looking. He had big blue eyes and they were childlike and bright. He was innocent and trusting but Livy was sure this town would cure him of that really soon. He was like the Christmas decorations only he was real and he always managed to put her in a good mood. He was a nosy little imp, though, and usually she just wanted to just avoid him. He always stopped her wanting to chat and get to know her. He was always cheerful and interested but a bit too talkative. And there was something else Livy couldn't put her finger on. She didn't want to encourage him but he persisted. He seemed like a hick right off the turnip truck, but somehow she could not find it in her heart to dismiss him like she did the Christmas shoppers.

"So why so late? It's nearly ten and if this Christmas is done, then why...?" Bryan began, partly blocking the door.

"Because I'm working hard to come up with some great idea for next year's hit toy or game or collectible... something that will really take hold. These things take months of planning and designing and marketing. So that's my goal...to come up with next year's big product. So Bryan, what are you doing for the holidays? Are you going home to ...Wyoming, was it?"

"It's Idaho, actually. Blackfoot, Idaho, the potato capital of the world!" He said it with such pride.

"Wow!" Livy inadvertently rolled her eyes.

"I don't know if I'll get the chance to go look in on the folks this year. I have so many things that I'm working on. It would be great though, if I could. How about you? Are you going to visit family for Christmas?"

"I don't have... plans. I don't have time for vacation right now. Livy shivered and reached for the door. "But if I did, I think I'd find someone in Florida or Aruba to visit where it's warm!"

"Yeah, Idaho is pretty cold but I sure would like to see my new little sister. She just...Oh duh! It's freezing out here. I'm sorry. You don't want to stand here freezing while I go into my whole family history, do you?"

12

"Sure I do, Bryan," Livy lied. "It's just that tonight I'm so burned out and exhausted that I just want to go upstairs and crash. You know what I mean? Sometime though, I want to see the family photos and everything, all right?"

Inside her though, she hoped that she would never really have to go through the scrapbooks or the family trip to Disneyland, which she was sure, he'd be happy to share. Again, she reached for the door and this time Bryan caught on and opened it for her, as a good doorman should. He even bowed a little.

"Oh! Speaking of photos," he said as he ushered her inside, "you got some mail. It got put in someone else's box by mistake so they asked me to get it to you. Here."

He gave her a holiday postcard with the picture of an attractive young couple in a Christmas setting. The pretty wife was obviously pregnant and from the expressions on their faces, one could see they were very pleased about it. Livy wasn't so pleased.

"Thanks." Livy said, a little annoyed that Bryan was looking over her shoulder trying to read the card.

"Who are they?" he asked.

"It's from Julie, my college roommate, and her husband Kevin. They got married last year and against their better judgment, and mine I might add, they went ahead and got going on a family. They could at least let the dust settle and the wedding cake get stale before they have a baby."

The card read,
There once was a family called Keatings
Who loved sending holiday greetings.
Hope your Christmas is swell...
Ours is, can you tell?
You can tell just how much I've been eating!

Hey Liv!
What are you up to? I haven't heard from you in about a year and I miss you. I want your opinion. Do I have that beautiful motherly glow, or am I just a fat and ugly whale? Kevin gave the right answer when I

asked him, if only to keep his happy home. What do you say? Baby is coming in March and we're so excited! They think it's a boy. What's new with you, Power Lunch woman? Call me, OK?

Love, Julie

"Good ol' Julie. That'll be a lucky kid who gets you for a Mom. Though you are a ditz sometimes."

Bryan cleared his throat. She got his signal.

"Well she is. But I like her and she is probably my best friend. I guess I am happy for her. But what is it with babies?" she asked, shaking her head.

"What do you mean? What about babies?" Bryan asked.

"I mean they poop, they cry, they smell, they soon get into everything, they are very expensive and very time consuming. Who wants to mess with all that? What do the parents get out of the deal? They are so much work and yet some people are crazy about them."

"That's *why* people are crazy about them. You have to invest so much time and love and effort and yes, money into them and you can't expect anything in return."

"Sounds great so far," Livy said.

"But people *want to be needed* for what they have to give and that's what being a parent is about, being needed and being able to give," Bryan said.

He sounded a little canned and probably had no idea what he was talking about. Livy was sure he wasn't speaking from experience as a father. So he obviously came from some pie in the sky, small town family.

"It's like this Christmas nonsense. It seems like the more work and money and time that go into it, the more people like it. I don't get it. It just seems like a lot more stress than fun!" Livy said.

"Christmas is like that to some degree, sure. But sometimes people just get caught up in the wrong things and they stress out. Don't you like Christmas either?"

"It's not that I don't like it. I guess I've never understood what all the fuss was about. I don't have a lot of good Christmassy Santa Claus memories and I'm not religious so—" She shrugged.

"You believe in God, don't you?"

Livy sighed in exasperation and replied, "Sometimes I do, sometimes I don't know. We have this kind of two-way relationship, God and I. He doesn't seem to know that I'm alive and I don't know if He's alive. That's fair, isn't it?"

"He knows."

"Let's not talk about it, OK?" She definitely did not want to be up half the night listening to "the Gospel according to Bryan." "Listen, I really am beat. I need to get to bed so that tomorrow I can come up with that brilliant idea for next Christmas. So...uh...good night, Bryan." She was already at the elevator.

"Okay. Good night, Ms. Thomas." He called out.

"Good night, Bryan, and stop calling me Ms. Thomas. It makes me feel like your old-maid third grade teacher. Call me Livy. We see each other practically every night. Call me Livy, okay?

"Great! Good night, Livy."

"Good night!"

CHAPTER 2

There was no escaping it. Christmas did come a few days later. Livy lay in bed watching the scarlet sun squeeze its way into the sky between the buildings of the Manhattan skyline. She imagined all the kids in those high-rise apartment buildings, waking long before dawn, anxiously coaxing their parents to get up and get the Christmas mayhem started. She remembered mornings like that... sort of. She tried to go back to sleep but couldn't. She was looking at the clock when someone knocked at her door. Who would be knocking on her door at dawn on Christmas morning, for Pete's sake?

She threw on her ratty robe and went to the door. Maybe there was a fire. The knocking was insistent and incessant. She looked through the peephole and saw that it was Bryan. Suddenly his giant eye met hers at the little window.

"I see you in there. Open up! It's Christmas morning! *Jolly old St. Nicolas, lean your ear this way...*" He had started singing loudly and continued the tune with his own words, *"Open up and let me in, don't say go away."*

Livy quickly threw open the door, pulled him inside and slammed it behind him. "Stop that! The neighbors will complain and you'll get fired. Maybe they'll throw me out with you, too."

"They have kids next door; they're up laughing and playing. So, Merry Christmas, Ms. Thomas! Oops! I mean Livy!" He surveyed the room. "I knew you wouldn't have one."

He pulled a tiny 18-inch Christmas tree from behind his back and ran over to set it up in front of the nine-foot tall window overlooking the city.

After plugging it in, he stepped back and admired it. It was totally dwarfed by the majesty of the view but he smiled and said, "Perfect!"

He ran out the door and came back with a loaded black trash bag in his arms.

Livy stood there in holiday shock.

"There are probably 300 apartments in this building. What are you doing at *my* door? Why me? I don't know what to say."

"I'll tell you what to say. You say, 'Merry Christmas, Bryan.' It's just that I'm homesick and I wanted to spend Christmas with someone. And you said you didn't have plans, so...."

"All right, Merry Christmas, Bryan. This is all so sweet, but I don't have anything for you and it's embarrassing." She really felt uncomfortable.

"Yes, you do have something for me. Just let me come and have Christmas morning with you, okay? That's all I need. I don't like the thought of being alone on Christmas, do you?"

"It must be deja vu. I think I spent Christmas morning with Mr. Potato Head when I was about eight."

"Now, no Idaho jokes. Are we going to have Christmas or not?" He whined like a little kid begging for a new toy.

"Bryan, I don't know you that well. I don't know what to say and honestly, I feel a little awkward."

"I'm sorry. I should have warned you. But let's just have Christmas morning...no strings attached. I have gifts and food...please?"

She sighed in defeat. "Okay. Show me how it's done."

And he did. He excitedly opened his Santa sack and laid out four presents around the tree in order of largest to smallest. Then he stood back and waited for her to go for one of them. She reached for the biggest one but he stopped her.

"Nope, not yet. Mom says everybody has to have a cup of cocoa and a cinnamon roll before we open anything. It keeps us from getting lightheaded from all the excitement and not having anything in our stomachs."

With a gleeful grin, Bryan ran out into the hall and produced a cardboard box containing cocoa and cinnamon rolls which he had purchased from a vendor down the block. "Here you are, my dear. It'll warm the cockles of your...wherever your cockles are."

Livy took a sip of the cocoa and a bite of the delicious cinnamon Danish. "Mmm. This is just what I need." She gobbled down several morsels. The treat was a guilty pleasure she had not allowed herself in some time.

"Okay. Now that I have my strength for the day, can I open one?"

Bryan shook his head teasingly. "Nope, not yet. This is when Dad would always stop us and say, 'you can't open anything until I get the video camera set up. Just hold your horses, kids.' And the anticipation was terrible! But it was wonderful, too. It made the moment last a little longer! I don't actually have a video camera with me but I wanted you to feel that heightened anticipation. Did it work? Are you excited yet?"

"Yes, I'm excited. Can I open it now?" Livy laughed.

"Nope, not yet. You have to sit down and I have to play Santa Claus and bring it to you." He sat her down on the couch. "Now which one?"

"The big one, of course."

"Are you sure?"

"Yes," Livy laughed. "I'm sure and if you make me wait again I'm going to throw you out of here!"

She had picked the box that was about one foot by one foot. She was starting to tear away the wrapping when she noticed that he was glaring at her.

"What? What now?"

He shrugged and said, "Oh, nothing. It's just that it's customary to shake it first. And then you have to sort of guess what it is."

She shook it and it rattled and thudded like there were rocks in it, hitting something.

"It's a box of rocks. No...I know; it's lumps of coal because I have been very naughty. I know about these things. I'm practically an elf in Santa's workshop, you know."

She had to admit to herself she was enjoying this. She looked at him as if to say "Now?" and he nodded.

She opened it to find a worn box that said, *Deluxe Deep Fryer.* She assumed that it had to be just a box he found to put something else in but upon further investigation she found that it really was a used deep-fryer. Surrounding it in the box were about six large potatoes. Livy was sort of becoming a health nut and rarely ate anything fried, let alone deep-fried and she didn't quite know what to say.

"Hey, a deep fryer and some potatoes! Great!"

She was thinking that she must have been *really* naughty.

But Bryan was thrilled and exclaimed, "We can make hash browns! Mom always makes deep fried hash browns on Christmas. Those are real Idaho potatoes; I'll have you know. This is just like home! Thanks, Livy."

"What for?"

"For letting me come and do this with you, of course."

"Well, thank *you*, Bryan. Where did you find this?"

"At the Salvation Army Thrift Store. I hope you don't mind that it's used. But that's what us kids usually do for our Christmas shopping. Only in Blackfoot we have the D.I. and the Idaho Youth Ranch Store. You can always find something for not too much money there and well, New York is pretty expensive and..."

"No, this is great, really. That's very resourceful of you. You'll have to give me your mom's recipe for hash browns. Thank you, so much. Do I have to do something now, jump through any hoops or anything before I open another one? Do we need to make the hash browns first?"

"Nope. Just go for it." He was tapping his feet in eagerness.

She started to go for the second gift and then remembered the protocol. After letting him hand it to her very ceremoniously, she shook it and something shifted quietly inside. It wasn't heavy and it wasn't too big.

"It's a stuffed animal?"

"Nope."

She pulled off the paper and inside the box were a multi-colored, but mostly blue, knitted hat, a scarf, and matching mittens. At first she thought maybe his mother had made them. But they were new and store-bought. They had tags on them.

"Thank you, Bryan. I can really use these. You know how cold it can get around here. But I feel so bad about not having anything for you. These are kind of unisex, maybe you should have these for yourself."

"No, I have some that my mom made and they always do the job. I just haven't noticed you wearing a hat or mittens and I thought that you needed them. They're still from the thrift store but they aren't used...unless someone used them with the tags on them. You'll need them today. It's really cold."

Great. He's watching what I'm wearing and whether I'm cold or not, Livy thought.

"Well, I will use them and will always think of you when I do. Thank you again."

He brought her the third gift and she could tell by the size and shape that it was obviously a book.

"I don't have to shake this one. I know it's a book."

"Nope."

She tore away the paper and found not one but two books. One was a copy of the New Testament and the other was *The Best Christmas Pageant Ever.* They were definitely thrift store merchandise.

"I saw this," he said holding up the New Testament, "and thought it would be perfect for working on that two-way relationship of yours. And the other was just me being sentimental again."

He got lost in a silent smile for a moment as if savoring a memory. "We always do a Christmas pageant at home and sometimes the church or even the whole town does one. I missed that this year."

"I believe I was in one once, when I was really little. I played some kind of stable animal, I think," Livy recalled.

He picked up the little paperback. "You'll love this story. It's a hoot. But it has a message, too."

"It's a hoot, huh?" she asked with a slightly mocking tone. "I'll read it next Christmas and try to get more in the mood than I was this year."

"And the other book, will you read that too?"

"I'll think about it." Livy took a long sip of her cocoa as if to change the subject.

When she was done, Bryan took the cup and carried it to the kitchen counter and instructed, "Okay, there's only one gift left but we have to save it for later. That makes the fun last longer. So, is it all right if I make hash browns and you can make something like eggs to go with them?"

It had been quite a while since Livy had cooked for anyone but herself and she thought it might be fun. He seemed safe enough for her to let him stay for breakfast.

"Sure, I can make a mean ham, cheese and onion omelet. How does that sound?"

"It sounds delicious."

Bryan set about grating potatoes and heating up the oil in the deep fryer.

"Here's the super secret recipe: potatoes, oil, salt and pepper. And then of course, fry sauce."

He sang Christmas songs as he worked.

His voice isn't half bad, Livy thought.

She didn't inquire about the fry sauce, as she was sure she'd find out soon enough. For now, she would just go with the flow. The omelet turned out beautifully and she was even able to flip it over without breaking it, a feat she seldom accomplished. Strawberry banana yogurt and orange juice were added to the menu and breakfast was ready... just as Bryan finished a chorus of *Joy to the World*. He had set the table nicely and he walked her around to the far side and pulled out her chair.

Sitting down at his own place, Bryan reached for Livy's hand and said, "Do you mind if I say grace?"

She gave him her hand. What was going on here? Was this guy trying to preach to her or flirt with her or what? He was nice but...

"Dear precious Father," Bryan began. "We come before you on this Christmas morning and thank you for all your blessings and wonders. Especially, we thank you for the birth of your Son that we celebrate today. I thank you that Livy and I could spend this Christmas morning together. Please bless her, Lord, with all the good desires of her heart. Thank you for this food and bless it to our good. In Jesus' name we pray, amen."

"Does that mean that those boiled-in-oil potatoes are good for me now?"

"Better than protein shakes and wheat germ," he said taking the catsup bottle and emptying a good portion of it onto a saucer. Bryan then stirred in a tablespoon or two of mayonnaise. "Hark! We have fry sauce."

He smeared it all over his potatoes and on her precious omelet and looked up just in time to see her wince. "It's a western thing, I guess."

After finishing breakfast, Bryan went over to the little pile of presents, picked up the small remaining box and put it in his pocket. He got the scarf set and brought it to Livy.

"You're going to need these. Where's your coat?"

For this first time since she opened the door, Livy realized that she hadn't even dressed or combed her hair. *I must look like the bride of Frankenstein.*

"I think I need a lot more than my coat. Give me twenty minutes to shower and get presentable before we talk about going out."

She caught a glimpse of herself in the chrome toaster. Her hair was standing out like a true 70's Afro. She was suddenly filled with tremendous gratitude that Bryan had not brought his video camera.

"Why didn't you tell me that I looked like something off a landscape truck? You could have put lights and ornaments on my head!"

Livy quickly started working on a French braid.

"You know, I hardly noticed," Bryan said, laughing. "But that's not a bad idea...a little tinsel here, some spray-on snow there.... But you can't get dressed. You have to come in your PJ's and your robe... and a coat. It's way cold out there."

"No way! Besides, you got dressed. That's not fair."

"Yeah, but I'm the dad here. Mom and Dad go fully dressed but the kids wear their jammies."

"You're my Dad? I'm almost 30...and you're what, 14?"

"Ha ha. It's a Christmas miracle, don't ask questions."

"And where are we going? Does Christmas morning last all day?"

Bryan's countenance fell and his blue eyes lost their sparkle.

"Do you want me to just go and leave you alone? Aren't you having a good time?"

She considered it for just an instant like a little epiphany.

"I'm having a wonderful time. This is the best Christmas I've had...in years. Of course that's not saying much. I didn't mean I wanted to get rid of you. But what about calling home or other plans you might have? I don't want to keep you. You know what I mean."

"Don't worry, I'll check up on the folks a little later. It just isn't Christmas if we don't do the *widow run.*"

Excitement oozed from him again and he seemed like a four-year-old trying to say *little one.*

"If we don't do the what?"

"The widow run." Bryan said, pronouncing it slowly and clearly.

Livy was imagining a relay you do with elderly people and their walkers

22

or something.

Excitement danced in Bryan's eyes as he explained, "We have several widows near us back home and on Christmas, after the presents of course, we take out Great-Grandpa's big old horse-drawn sleigh and go get Mrs. Johnson and Mrs. Webb and Mrs. Bennion, and some others if they aren't with their children, and give them sleigh rides all over the snow covered hills between our farm and the Indian Reservation. It's just about the best part of the day. Dad lets them drive the horses sometimes. That Mrs. Johnson is a corker! You should hear her singing carols at the bonfire at Jensen Grove."

The next thing Livy knew, she was stepping out of a cab at Central Park. She wore a parka over her bathrobe as Bryan had insisted. Her quick attempt at a braid had long since fallen out and she felt ridiculous... but resigned. Taking her by the elbow, Bryan led her over to a path under a little brick bridge. Underneath was a ragged little bag-lady, a tiny, elderly woman covered in layers of tattered clothes, happily feeding pigeons. She was cooing at them cheerfully.

"Merry Christmas, Martha!" Bryan said.

"Merry Christmas, Bryan!" She seemed happy and not at all surprised to see him.

"Did you get to that shelter last night like I told you to?" Bryan asked.

"I did. I'm not stupid, you know. But I'm back here to spend Christmas with my little friends." She gestured at the birds all around her fighting for the crumbs she threw them. Then she nodded at a woman sitting at her right. "And this is Lucille. I've met her at the shelter a few times. Can she come too?"

"Certainly she can come. How do you do, Lucille? I'm Bryan and this is Olivia." Bryan said, extending his hand to the hefty redheaded woman.

She gave Livy the once-over. "Which shelter did you stay at last night, young woman? I hope you had the sense God gave a sandwich and stayed out of the weather! You haven't got enough meat on yer' bones to keep a cricket warm."

"Oh, I did. Uh...thank you."

Livy turned and gave Bryan a look that could maim him for life. He didn't even crack a smile.

"Well ladies, let's go. Are you ready? Oh yeah. I brought you something. Do you like cinnamon rolls?"

"Howard loves them."

"Howard? Is he coming too?"

Martha grabbed a roll and broke it into lots of little pieces and threw them around for the pigeons.

"Howard's the big bluish one over there. See how he dove for it?"

Soon they were climbing into one of the horse-drawn carriages that paraded around the park. Livy was afraid the driver might complain but she found out later that Bryan had paid him extra to be accommodating. It took both men (holding their breath) to get Lucille up in the cab.

Martha bounded right up with vigor and ease and shouted a hearty "Well, gitty-up!" when she saw everyone was situated.

The driver repeated the command and off they trotted. They sang *Jingle Bells* at the top of their lungs and Martha knew all the words to *Sleigh Ride* and *Winter Wonderland*. The rest of them faked their way through, following her lead. Martha told stories about growing up in a flat above a bakery in New Jersey and how her father's Christmas Stolen Bread was the best in the world. Lucile reminisced about her days as a department store model. She would strut around the store in the outfits for sale in the Ladies Better Dresses section.

"I was quite the looker in my day! And in those fancy Christmas gowns? I was a knock out. I had meat on my bones and in all the right places, too," she assured them as she winked at Livy.

Bryan told stories of his childhood exploits with his brothers, how he and Jackson were supposed to hunt down a wild turkey for Christmas dinner. But when came down to the kill, Bryan ran home with Jackson's pellet gun and wouldn't let him shoot the thing. Jackson caught the poor fowl, knocked him out with a rock and then cut the head off. Bryan refused to eat dinner that day. Naming the bird Ralphie was a big mistake; you simply can't kill something that you've named. After that, whenever Jackson wanted more than his share of some meat, he always gave it a name and sure enough, Bryan wouldn't touch it.

"Howard would like you," Martha observed.

The ride lasted about thirty minutes and Livy was surprised when she found she was sad it was over. Bryan kissed each of the women on the cheek as he said good-bye and Lucile pulled close to his ear and whispered something. He nodded and replied, "Thank you, Lucille. I sure will do that. Bye now."

On the cab ride home Livy asked Bryan, "What was that about? What did Lucille say?"

"She was worried about you. She said, 'Tell her to come find me in the park anytime, I'll make sure she gets plenty to eat and some better clothes. I bet she'd clean up real good looking.'"

"She obviously knows where all the best dumpsters are," Livy mumbled under her breath. "Well Bryan, you've taken me from riches to rags today and I hope you're happy. Actually, that was fun. How do you know Martha, anyway?"

By now, Livy was rushing up the stairs to the door of the apartment building, trying to hide her face from anyone passing by. Bryan had to skip steps to keep up with her.

"I met her at the park one day last week and we got to talking. She's been a widow since she was thirty-six. She had one child, a son, and they've lost track of each other. I just thought she was a perfect candidate for the widow run and she was open to the idea so there you are. I don't know Lucille's story. But when you get down to it, they're just people like everyone else." Bryan reached for Livy's hand. "Well, what's your story, Livy?"

She awkwardly dropped his hand and began twisting a lock of her hair. "I told you, I don't have any good Christmas memories to tell. But maybe I do now; I have today. Thank you, Bryan. It's been a wonderful morning. But I still feel bad that I don't have anything for you. It's all been about me. What can I do for you? Is there something that you need that I could buy you?"

"I got more than I bargained for already. I told you I just wanted to spend Christmas morning with you and that has meant more to me than you can imagine. I wanted to taste a little bit of home. It's like that baby thing again, I guess. I just wanted to be able to give..."

"What about Martha and her son? She probably gave and gave and where is he now? Or maybe she threw him out and he never came back."

"I don't know, but I do know one thing. She still loves him. She was positively radiant when she talked about him as a baby—how smart he was, how cute he was and how she liked to dress him like the little Dutch Boy. The more she did for him, the more I'm sure she loved him. That's the way it works and your friend, Julie, will find that out. The more you love and sacrifice, the more you want to give and the more you give the more you love."

"Oh Bryan, what do *you* know? I think maybe I could love a cat. But a baby? I have plans for my life and kids aren't in it. Wait a minute.... wait a minute. You've just given me an idea. That's it! Bryan, you are brilliant."

"I am? What did I say? How was I so smart?" He replied, genuinely flattered.

He pretended to spit on his fingers and proudly brushed back each side of his blonde wavy hair. She grabbed his arm and squeezed it.

"You've given me an idea. A toy that needs you! A toy that demands some work—just like you said. The more they have to do with it and for it, the more they love it. Thank you, Bryan!"

She nearly ran to the elevator to get up to her apartment to work on her idea. Then she stopped and turned back to Bryan who had stayed at the door.

"I'm sorry; I should go while the idea is in my head."

"I really should get going, too. I'm supposed to spend the afternoon working with some troubled kids. You know, my internship and all. This is a hard day for them and that's why I'm here, so ... thanks again for this morning, Livy. Oh! I almost forgot. I still have your last present." He pulled the small square box from his pocket.

She reluctantly walked back to where he stood. "You've already given me so much. I'm still trying to figure out why you singled me out. You really are too young for me and we're not dating. And we don't have much in common. You realize that, don't you? That's not what this is about, right?"

"No, it's you that's way too old for me. But then you saw how I have this thing for old ladies and all..."

She was about to smack him when he handed her the box. Inside, she found a delicate little Nativity set. It was beautiful in its fine detail and craftsmanship. Livy studied each piece. Mary's face was especially lovely though to appreciate it fully she knew she would need a magnifying glass. A beautiful Baby Jesus was cradled in Mary's arms instead of sleeping in the manger as Livy usually had seen him.

"I've never seen one like it before. It really is beautiful, Bryan. Thank you."

"Will you display it?" He asked hopefully.

"I'm not sure what it will mean, but I'll put it out."

She replaced it in the box, smiled at him and moved toward the elevator. He stopped her and tried to give her a hug. She pulled away slightly and so instead he took her hand.

"Merry Christmas, Livy."

"Merry Christmas. Thank you, for everything. That was one of the nicest Christmas mornings I ever had. See you later, Bryan."

As the elevator doors closed on his still smiling face, she again felt just the slightest tingle of goose bumps. She also felt a twinge of guilt. *Maybe I should at least invite him up to brainstorm with me or for lunch....* She hit the open button but when the doors parted he was gone.

CHAPTER 3

The weeks went by and Livy worked tirelessly on her new idea, gathering little bits of unsolicited inspiration from Bryan along the way. The more she worked on the project, the more she liked it. It was her baby and what Bryan said was true. The more she gave it her all, the more she was hooked. It was a very special doll she had christened *Hold-Me-Hannah*, and it would have that same effect on the children who would receive one. Hannah would need them and they would give her all they had. They (or their parents) would buy all the gear, the outfits, strollers, bottles, blankets, and any number of Hannah accessories. It was marketing genius. It would be a gold mine.

By late January she had presented the idea to Mel Jameson, the CEO of JTC. More than a little intrigued, he immediately could see the potential there, but worried about the technology necessary to bring about the prototype. A doll that could actually make facial expressions would indeed be a coup, if it could be done and Mel pledged his support to get it moving. Existing technologies needed only to be modified slightly to fit this concept. As he promised, he personally took the idea to the engineers in the technology department to see if the thing was possible and used his clout as CEO to give them incentive to make it possible.

Livy enjoyed the company of Mr. Jameson. He was impressive man. He stood about six-feet-four inches, had gracefully graying dark hair, a strong handsome face, and wore his authority well. And he, in turn, was impressed with Livy and he seemed approachable to her. She could tell he liked her drive and her no nonsense approach to business. Plus, she was attractive and confident which made a good impression for the company when he sent her on various marketing assignments and conferences. No question, she was valuable to him.

The fact that she was of mixed race, showed the company was fair and progressive. Sometimes, she wondered if race might have been a factor in her obtaining promotions faster. Some of the others in her department seemed to resent her, but so what? She knew she worked hard and deserved everything she got.

There was a vice president position opening up that Livy and several of her co-workers had their eyes on. She felt she was one success away from having that prize within her grasp. In the end, business was politics and as much about appearance as about competence and Livy knew she scored well in both. In the three years she had been with Joys Toys, Mel Jameson had mentored her and schooled her in the ways of the company and the business world. He was the key to her overall plan, and with his help, she would go far. With Livy's contributions, Jameson's company would do well too.

Mrs. Joy Jameson was another matter; Joy belied her name. A generally unhappy person, the Missus was a bit too thin, in her mid-fifties but looking a bit older, and she dressed in styles more appropriate for women half her age. She was fastidious to the point of obsessive about her spiky red hair, her make-up, and nails. Livy knew that Joy felt threatened by her. In spite of being the namesake of the company, she had earned a college degree in English Literature and wanted nothing to do with the family business that carried her name. It wasn't until she married Mel, the company's rising star and her father's protégé, that Joy took an interest in the company at all. She had insisted on taking a major part in things ever since and her father practically left her the position of chairman of the board in his will. Making arbitrary decisions based on emotion and not on business savvy, Joy was out to prove to Mel and to the rest of the employees that she was indeed in charge.

Perhaps she felt that Livy was second-guessing some of those decisions, and if the truth were known, she was. Livy knew Joy terminated some of her projects that had great potential simply out of spite or a need to feel superior and Livy felt angry resentment because of it. Other times, Joy seemed to push some idea that nearly all the executives dismissed as doomed to fail. Last year, it was *Nail Biters - edible fingernails for those who chew*. Joy thought they would really take off with kids. She reasoned that if they bit their nails anyway they could at least buy some press on candy nails that tasted good. Joy pushed the idea as inspiration, while everyone else, including the buying public, thought it was gross. Why didn't she just stay home, read stuffy literature and her *Cosmo*, and just stay out of the way?

Livy looked around her office. There were a few posters with motivational sayings over beautiful photographs and a framed blow-up photo of Livy shaking hands with Martha Harrington, senator from New York, and one day, everyone thought, a serious contender for either slot on a national ticket. On display were Livy's diplomas, including a BS in marketing from the University of South Florida and an MBA from Wharton School of Business. She leaned back in her large custom-made ergonomically designed chair and imagined herself someday as Chair of the Board or perhaps, founder of her own international company or, she chuckled at her thought, even part of a national ticket herself. She only halfway laughed at her delusions of grandeur because her other half was very serious about her ambition. She studied the framed photo of herself receiving the 'Rookie of the Year' award from Mel, a few years back.

I've done everything I've done on my own. And with the help and support of someone like Melvin Jameson, there isn't anything that I can't do.

****

Now mid-February, it was time to present *Hold-Me-Hannah* to the rest of the executives. Mel promised to be there to support her and cheer on her project.

"Well, Ms. Olivia, are you ready?" Mel asked as he entered her office just before the presentation. He looked especially excited for the occasion —his hair perfectly in place, his shirt extra crisp and his smile eager. She was honored that he was so enthusiastic about her project.

"I think so... I hope so." Livy replied with a deep breath.

"I've lined up all the gizmo nerds and they have the technical workups ready and say the thing is definitely do-able...and they'll be there to back you up at the meeting," Mel assured her. "But now the question is, can you sell it? There are some pretty hard cases in there."

"You're the one making me nervous. You are on board with it, aren't you?" Livy asked.

"Absolutely, you know that." Mel smiled and put his arm around her. " I saw genius in you from the start."

Livy gave a nervous stare at the arm on her shoulder and he removed it casually. "Were they able to work up an approximate price?" she asked.

That was always a sticking point with the profit-margin-minded accountants.

"That is the one thing that concerns me just a little. Without knowing all the details, and I don't even know if they're close, but their rough estimates put it at $250 to $300. Do you think that's a bit pricey for a toy?" Mel asked.

Livy gathered her large portfolio under her arm and Mel picked up the rest of her presentation materials. They continued their conversation as they headed for the conference room.

"Well, those video systems are more than that, and do they sell? They do indeed. And what about the motorized Barbie car? That's in about the same range, I think, and it certainly sells. But that's what we've got these great minds gathered here for. They will work out all the bugs and make it happen for the right price and the right profit. Right?"

They were at the door and Livy was suddenly uncharacteristically anxious. She felt as if she was on trial.

"Take a another deep breath. It'll be fine. You'll do great," Mel reassured her.

Most of the executives were already seated and a few more were still arriving. Marcie Jones was wrapping up a conversation on her cell phone, saving the chair next to her for Bob Farrell and slyly pulling her neckline lower for his benefit. Bob was the top dog in his division and Marcie, here just longer than Livy, had hitched her wagon to Bob's accelerating success train. Now both of them felt the pressure of Livy's growing momentum. The two of them worked with Livy in the new products marketing division but usually on different projects.

Bob moved his large frame around the table and sat down in his reserved spot. Marcie filled his ear with some tidbit or other as she was pointed at Livy and Mel entering the room together. Joy was just behind Livy and Mel. Mel let Livy pass through the doorway and waited for his wife. He leaned over to whisper something as she passed but she avoided it and kept her stare on Livy.

"This had better be good, Mel." Joy was warning him.

"It is. You'll see."

Joy walked to her seat at the end of the table, sat down and folded her arms.

Mel placed the materials if front of the screen and walked up the small podium. He instructed everyone to take his seat and began the meeting.

"This past Christmas season was one of our best in recent years and you are all to be congratulated—especially you, Farrell, with the *Beat Box Boogie* project. The success of that product took us all by surprise. Thank you for all your hard work on that. And to all of you, thank you. The fourth quarter reports have come in and our shareholders are very happy and so are we, right Joy? I know this is corny, but give yourselves a hand."

Marcie commented to Bob, "I'd rather just have the bonus."

"Well," Mel responded as he cleared his throat, "the proverbial check is in the mail. Honest, it is."

Then they did break out in applause.

"Everyone's except Jones's that is…. Just kidding. I think you will all be pleased," Mel laughed.

There was a lot of chatter around the room and Mel looked at Livy as if to say, *here we go!* He held his hands up to signal that he again needed their attention and began his introduction.

"Well, maybe next year your bonus will be even bigger if your departments can help us make the magic happen again. As you all know, we are in production for the new action figures for the children's summer blockbuster coming out near Memorial Day weekend. What's it called again?"

"It's *Peter Powerful and the Forces of Oberon*," Matheson offered.

He had been heavily involved in landing the movie tie-in. Bob and Marcie would be heading up the project.

The company CFO, Kyle Fitzgerald, who looked more like a balding, freckled Irish leprechaun than an accountant, piped in, "It's a slam dunk winner. All the kids are reading the book; I know mine are and I liked it, too. Anything derived from it will do very, very well."

"We can always trust Kyle to give us the inside scoop on the childlike mind." Said Bob, keeping his voice low. Marcie smiled in derisive agreement.

"These action figures will be the most animatronic released so far by us or anyone else. It's a bit of a risk but we want to be the company that's cutting edge...leading the industry in the technological arena. And, continuing along those lines and coming in on the heels of that success will be something we think will be our secret weapon in the toy wars next Christmas season. This little number just might give us our biggest holiday numbers ever. Move over Hasbro and Mattel! This idea is really the "brainchild", (he made quotation marks in the air), of Olivia Thomas from the new products marketing division. I'll let her introduce Hannah to you."

Marcie slipped a note to Bob. It said, "Teacher's pet."

Livy stood up and placed her closed portfolio on the easel positioned next to the podium. She smiled and confidently began the most important pitch of her career.

"Thank you, Mr. Jameson. And also, thank you to all the members of the techno team who have joined us today. They have really knocked themselves out to assure us that this little "baby" is possible.

"You know, just before Christmas I got the news from a friend that she was expecting. She was so excited and you know me, I just kind of wondered, *what's the big deal?* Really, I mean babies require so much of their mothers and others, they exhaust me just thinking about it. But then I thought, maybe that's it! That's why people love them. They ask something from them, they make them give, they make the parent indispensable and everyone needs to feel that way to one degree or another...even little kids. I've also heard it said on occasion that babies are cute. Hence...

"Ladies and Gentlemen, I give you *Hold-Me-Hannah.*"

The lights went down and the PowerPoint presentation began. A picture of a faceless baby doll appeared on the screen and a few of those present gasped and some even laughed.

"Hold on, people, don't despair. We will not introduce Hannah to the public quite like this. We'll discuss that little detail of a face later in the presentation. It will be an exciting component, I assure you. But for now, let's talk about what makes Hannah the next *Furbee, Tickle-me-Elmo, Playstation 2* or other such Christmas must-have bank busters.

"She is not like any baby doll we've seen before, although she may incorporate many features seen in various places and products. She may be described as a composite of Betsy Wetsy of a few decades past, the Disney animatronic presidents, and the virtual pets that were so popular in the late nineties." Slides of these items appeared on the screen.

"She is irresistible precisely because she is interactive and requires attention from the child. She pays back big time, too. Her facial expressions will actually change eliciting certain actions from the child and the doll will react in turn with more expressions and actions of her own. The expressions will change according to a pre-programmed cycle but will seem random to the child. This virtual baby will have several modes such as babble-mode, hungry and feed-me-mode, the tired and fussy-mode, and sleeping mode. For example, she would be in fussy-mode and cry some real tears but when the child rocks and comforts her with a lullaby, the doll falls into sleep mode triggered by sensors to either motion and/or sound. The baby can be awakened or would eventually wake on her own cycle, sometimes cheerful and babbling and at other times cranky and hungry. The little mother, or little dad, only has to do what comes naturally to be the perfect parent.

Livy opened her portfolio and displayed some artist conceptions of the different moods and modes of Hannah.

"The feature that I think will be, I don't know, let's say the most popular, will be the pick-me-up feature. Hannah will be in her glory! She'll respond to mommy by raising her arms, kicking her feet and giving an expression of anxious expectation. When the child picks her up, she breaks forth in giggles of pure delight. In this mode, when little mommy squeezes her, Hannah's arms squeeze back in a hug and with more leg kicking. I see her represented as barely pre-walking age where babies still want to be picked up. She may say a few words and can be taught to say some more perhaps, something along the lines of the *Furbee.*

"...And Hannah will have a feature that most parents will wish their real child had...*an off-switch* so baby won't bother everyone at the dinner party or in the middle of the night."

Some executives nodded and smiled in agreement.

"So now, we get to the face. As you have seen, the facial expressions of this doll are key and so it has to be just the *right* face, one that with just small adjustments can be *an everychild*, as it were. It can be changed slightly to be Asian, Black, Hispanic, or White and yes of course, a male version of any of the above. So we need the right face and where will we find that perfect face?"

Fitzgerald immediately jumped up, pulled out his wallet and let the whole photo album unfold showing his wife and seven children.

"Here," he said. "Take your pick. I have all the fabulous and irresistible faces you'll ever need to choose from."

Livy laughed. "You have stepped right into my trap, Kyle. You exemplify exactly what I have in mind. Most every parent thinks they have the most beautiful kid in the world, am I right?"

Fitzgerald remained standing, smiling and still exhibiting the photos. "Yes, but the rest of the world is wrong!"

"So, we have a contest. I'm sorry Fitz, you cannot enter your kids; you are an employee. You may want to sit down now."

Fitz sat back down looking disappointed.

"We will ask families all over America and everywhere else for that matter, to send in their child's photo to be considered for the face of Hannah and/or the boy counterpart. This will pique their interest in the doll long before it is released and give them a reason to stay tuned for that big day when Hannah takes the stage. The winning family will get some great prizes and we will take computer images of the child in various expressions to use as models for the doll. All the entries will receive some kind of coupon for a discount on the doll or for a free accessory so their interest remains high.

"We'll hype it up big and before Hannah is even unveiled, she will be a household name and a given as far as purchasing is concerned. We will also get a nice big list of families with children to work with in future marketing efforts. Even though we are in February now, all of this needs to happen immediately so everything can be ready for an October or maybe even September release. I want my girls sold out by Thanksgiving!" And then we unveil the boy..."

Bob's hand wafted up in a sarcastic gesture. "Hold-me-Hannah! What about the boys? What are you going to call the little wonder boy, Beam-me-up Scotty?"

Some in the group chuckled.

Marcie said, "Not bad!" and gave Farrell a high five. Then she added, "We could always name it in honor of you and your kid, Bob. How 'bout *sit-down-and-shut-up-Sammy?*" She looked around at the others staring at her. "I'm sorry, I couldn't resist."

"How 'bout we name it in honor of your kid and just call it *Chucky!*" Bob answered back.

At company get-togethers, Bob's boy had distinguished himself as the hyper nuisance while Marcie's son was obviously spoiled beyond belief.

"See? I told you," Livy said. "Somebody needs that off-switch. But this is no Chucky, I assure you. She's just a sweet, needy baby."

"Needy? Is that what we want?" Jameson asked.

"Oh yes, definitely. She needs a new outfit, she needs a stroller; she needs lots of things. See what I—?"

Bob cut her off, loosening his tie and releasing the top button that struggled to contain his sizable neck. "Now I know why you were saying that we have to make the 'magic' happen. This is fantasyland. First of all, can we really do this? *And* can we do it in the time that we have?"

Matheson from procurement jumped in with, "I agree with Mr. Jameson. If this is done well and with the contest and everything, we could have a real winner on our hands. But Farrell does have a point. Is this too complicated, too technical and too expensive? I want it to work and be ready by the Christmas buying season with no delays. We'll have to keep the momentum we build with the contest."

"The gizmo-nerds," Livy started to say and then cleared her throat, "excuse me, our techno-geniuses say they can do it and they have a few pro-totypes to show you in just a few moments. Patents are being applied for as we speak and as you can see, we've already invested some in R&D. It's coming along but before we go any further, we want to know that all of you, the backbone of this company, are behind the project 100%. After you see what they have to show you, then I will need to know we have the full go ahead and what your different divisions will need to make this happen. Thank you and I'll give the floor to technology. Mr. Howard?"

Before Livy could sit down and Mr. Howard could begin speaking, Mr. Jameson stood up and said, "I think when you have heard what Jeff Howard has to say you will become believers like I have become. I hope you will get on board and support this whole-heartedly. Let's have a round of applause for all the hard work that Thomas has put into this presentation."

The room broke into applause except for Bob, Marcie and Joy who all sat with their arms folded.

Mr. Howard began his impressive demonstration of Hannah in action and why he thought she would be a major step forward for Joy's Toys.

If Livy read things right, she and Hannah were both on their way.

CHAPTER 4

Mr. Jameson and Livy waited in his office until after quitting time on the day that each department was supposed to give its verdict, yea or nay, on the Hold-Me-Hannah project. By about 5:40, the results started coming in. By 6:30, it was a done deal. Most of the emails were overwhelmingly positive and there were just a couple who weren't enthusiastic but wouldn't stand in the way. Joy didn't weigh in. She and her husband had their debate at home and he had won, at least *this* round.

After they had read all the emails from the different departments Mel exclaimed, "Congratulations, Livy! You did it!"

"Yes!" Livy threw both fists into the air in a gesture of victory. "Yes! Yes! Oh Yes! Houston, we have ignition!"

"This is going to be great! But don't use that space analogy; it makes me nervous. This better not crash and burn on lift off. It's a lot of responsibility on your shoulders, you know. But whatever you need to make it happen, you just let me know."

"This will make it and make it big! Thank you, Mr. Jameson. Thank you for everything!"

She almost lost it. She wanted so badly to just hug him! But he was the boss, so she restrained herself.

"Please call me Mel! And thank you! You did it and deserve the credit. Go home and celebrate with your boyfriend. Open some champagne! Tomorrow's Valentine's Day, you know. Make it special."

She wondered if he was floating a trial balloon to get her to confirm or deny that she had a boyfriend. She wasn't biting.

"Thanks Mel, that's good advice. I hope your Valentine is okay with all this."

"Don't worry about Joy. She'll be on board as soon as the money starts rolling in. I've assured her that it will."

"All right, the Hannah train has left the station and I am outta here!"

Livy gathered her purse, her coat and her briefcase and fairly floated to the elevator. She didn't know she could feel so good.

She got on the subway at her usual station but after only two stops she decided to get off. *I feel like walking. I feel like queen of the city and I want to be out about among my subjects!*

She laughed at her ridiculous thought. *I am really getting full of myself, aren't I?*

She got off at a stop that left her about 20 blocks of walking. She wondered how many miles that was. And it was still winter. However, she was feeling warm from the inside out. She walked through the park; it was well lit and there were lots of people around. Nothing could touch her tonight. It was her night. She was certainly caught up in her own euphoric feelings but for some reason, she was more aware of the people around her than she usually was.

She noticed the lovers snuggling in the cold. She observed the families with children returning from some outing or another. One father carried a sleeping little toddler in his arms and he kept looking at his daughter like she was the most beautiful and wonderful thing the world had ever known.

She heard that voice again, echoing from distant memory, spitting out the words, *"I'm not your Dad; not anymore. You have no home here!"*

She shook it off and reminded herself that tonight she would celebrate; tonight she was the queen.

It was after nine when she finally reached the 83rd block and was near her apartment. Bryan would be on duty again. He was always the one there after 8:00 p.m. Did she feel like dealing with him right now? He'd want to know all the details and would keep her talking. She just wanted to go take a victory bubble bath. Maybe he'd trap someone else into a conversation tonight and she could sneak upstairs unnoticed, but not likely. She still thought maybe he had a crush on her. Maybe he was lonely and sensed she was kind of a loner too, and thought she wanted the company.

He's just too much of a goody-two-shoes country boy for me.

His radar was on tonight. He spotted her way down the block and he lit up like a Christmas tree. When she got a little closer, he bounded to the bottom of the stairs and took off his hat. He waved it across his middle as he bowed and said, "Good evening, Ms. Thomas!"

"Hello, Bryan. You haven't called me Ms. Thomas since Christmas, remember?"

"Oh yeah, third grade teacher and all that. I was just trying to be very official. You don't look like my scary old schoolteacher at all so don't you worry about that. Old maids are more than just single. They are no fun and not too attractive because they don't care to be. That's not you at all."

"Thank you, I think; although I'm often mistaken for a homeless person."

"You are beautiful and you don't even have to try. And I think that you work too much. Here it is after 9:00 p.m. and you are just coming home from the office? Again?"

"Yeah, but tonight I don't mind so much."

"Why is that? You do seem like the cougar that ate the cat that ate the canary."

"Well, my Christmas roll-out idea was accepted and is on the fast track for the coming season. It's kind of exciting." She was trying to keep her exhilaration inside but despite her efforts, it was leaking out.

"Kind of? It's really exciting! What are you going to do to celebrate? Party time? Go out on the town?" Bryan said, dancing around caught up in her exciting news while she only shook her head. "Hey! So this has to do with when I was brilliant? The baby-doll idea?" He asked.

"That's the one. It was approved!"

"So I'll celebrate with you! I get off in 20 minutes. What do you say?"

Oh boy! Here he goes. "Hey! You're not supposed to hit on the residents. And besides, you are way too young for me," Livy said chidingly.

Actually, she could have entertained the idea of a good-looking younger guy but she hoped he'd be a little more sophisticated than Bryan.

"I'm not hitting on you… just thought that you might like some of my brilliant company."

"Don't think there's anywhere to go cow tipping around here, do ya' think?"

"I'll ignore that. You have to celebrate something this good and I happen to be the only one standing here, so let's go do something."

"You're right. I should do something. But I don't know...now don't go getting ideas about you and me. But oh hell, why not? You did help inspire the idea. Want to go get a burger or something?"

"Burgers? You call that celebrating?

"You're right again. How about steak? And yes, I'm buying. What do you say?" She knew he would agree so she opened the door and entered the building. She turned and said, "I'll change and be back here in twenty minutes."

He was beaming and called after her, "You're buying? Then I know just the place...now you just remember that you're too old for me."

Livy laughed in spite of herself and called back, "We've established that, now don't push it!"

In twenty-five minutes she was back. She was wearing jeans and a big oversized sweater and the hat he had given her. He had changed as well. He was in jeans and a sweater and a large-plaid wool coat and Livy almost snickered when she saw it. They began walking up 83rd Street.

"So...where are we going?" Livy asked.

"It's called *Phantasm* and it's considered very cool."

"And so why would *you* know about it?" she teased.

"I've heard some of the residents talk about it and they all really liked the food and it's got a fun atmosphere. You don't think I can be cool, do you?"

"Not really, no. And, if anyone asks, I'm your old maiden aunt, okay?"

"You've got no coat, Livy."

"Strike that. If anyone asks, *you* are *my* mother." Livy jabbed at him.

"Please. Let's just say I'm your little brother who doesn't want you to catch pneumonia. Do you want to wear my coat?"

"Not unless you have a gun to my head. Fine, I'm your big sister, huh? So tell me about our family, bro."

"Well, there's you and me and Mom and Dad, and our 15 brothers and sisters."

Livy nearly choked. "What? You're BS'n me, right?"

"No, I'm not." Bryan laughed and raised an eyebrow in a mock-sexy way and said, "Well, you know, there's not much to do in Idaho and it's cold and one can always use more help on the farm. I told you that I

41

recently got a new little sister."

"You are how old?" Livy asked, still in shock.

"Let's see...I'm 22 in April."

"And your Mom, excuse me, *our* Mom is still poppin' out kids?"

"More like pickin' up kids. Eight are their natural children and the rest are adopted or fostered. My new little sister is seven and she is from Ethiopia."

"Wow! How big is your house?" Livy was astonished.

She knew he was a farm boy but didn't know they raised kids like cattle. *Maybe they'll get 30 head 'afore they're done.*

"Not that big, really," he explained. "The four older boys, we had a heated room over the barn and Mom and Dad made a bedroom for themselves out of the garage. You could say it's a bit too cozy, I guess, but it works. Oh...and one brother and one sister are married now, so there's plenty of room for you."

"Oh good. I don't want to put anyone out or anything. How was it growing up like that? Were you starving for attention?"

"No, I was just starving. You really had to jump for the food because if you hesitated, it was all gone. But really, it was a great way to grow up. We had our huge farm to romp around on and animals and there was always someone to play with. And, oh yeah, lots of work to keep us busy." He made a nerdy face and said, "You see? I'm very well adjusted!"

"I'm glad to hear it because I just now realize that outside of your yuletide traditions I really don't know anything about you. For all I know, you could be a serial killer."

Bryan took on an ominous expression and tone. "I am. It's true. I kill cereal. I finished off Tony the Tiger and the frosted flakes this morning, and tomorrow? Little Miss Fruity Pebbles is history. So now that you know, do you still want to be part of the family?"

"I'll have to give it some serious thought."

"So, tell me about your side of the family, sis."

"My family? Well, like I told you, that isn't a subject that I like to discuss much."

"Can I ask why?" Bryan queried.

"There's nothing to tell. It's not much of a family story. It certainly isn't interesting like yours must be."

"Your family must be proud of all your accomplishments... you know, your degrees and your executive job and all that. And when they hear about this—wow! They must think that you're pretty great. I'm sure they are very pleased that you are doing so well."

"Let's just say that I don't know what they think and I don't care. We're not in touch."

The tone of her voice pretty much said, *drop it!* Bryan got the message.

"I'm sorry. Well, you are part of our family now and WE think you are AWESOME!"

"Thank you. You are pretty...well, you are really something...yourself."

It didn't take long to reach the *Phantasm Café*. It was now after 10:00 pm and there were still lots of people waiting for tables. It was lively and raucous; all around were the sounds of people having a good time. Bryan put the name Kimball on the waiting list and told Livy that the wait was likely more than half an hour.

There was a group of people at a nearby table who had just received their entrees and oohs and aahs were heard as each plate was delivered. Bryan and Livy looked on hungrily and then one attractive young black man in the group glanced up and made eye contact with Livy. A look of total surprise and recognition lit up his face. He got up, excused himself from the group and made his way through the crowd to where Livy and Bryan were standing. Bryan saw him coming and decided it was a good time to hang up his coat. He tried to blend into the crowd as he wandered back.

"Livy? Is that you?" The big handsome man opened his arms.

"Garrett!" She gave him a somewhat uncomfortable embrace. He had another five or six inches over her six-foot frame. "What are you doing in the Big Apple?"

"Being a worm and eating my way out. I just got the most enormous meal served to me. Sooner or later everyone ends up here in New York, don't they? It's like an American pilgrimage. Do you want to come join us?"

Livy nonchalantly reached over and grabbed Bryan's arm and pulled him closer.

Garrett took the hint. "Oh, I'm sorry. I'm interrupting."

Bryan smiled and said, "No, no you're not. I'm like her squirrelly little brother and it's probably well past my bedtime, so why don't you two just visit?"

"Bryan! We're supposed to be celebrating! Garrett Garner, I'd like you to meet my friend Bryan Kimball. Bryan, this is Garrett. He's an old friend from college."

Garrett extended his hand to shake Bryan's. "It's nice to meet you. I'm sorry. You two go ahead and celebrate. It is so good to see you again. Can we talk while I'm here? How can I reach you? Then you can tell me all about what you are celebrating. We can catch up."

He was obviously sincerely happy to run into her.

"Okay, I might as well tell you," Livy said as she wrapped her arm around Bryan's. "Bryan and I are having a baby."

Bryan and Garrett looked at each other with equal shock. Bryan was beet red and shaking his head.

Livy continued, "I will have to tell you all about it. Here's a napkin and I'll put my cell on it. I'd love to hear how you and Shelly are doing. Really Garrett, call me, okay?"

"I will. I'll call you tomorrow sometime, is that all right?"

He still looked somewhat stunned.

"That will be great. Call me around lunch time."

"I'll plan on it. –Great seeing you. I'll talk to you tomorrow," Livy said as Garrett made his way back to his table and waved good-bye.

"Why did you say that?" Bryan asked, still shocked and embarrassed.

"I said it because it's true. Because of your inspiration, at least partly, my new baby-doll will be the next toy sensation. That's what we're celebrating. I wasn't going to leave our party and go join his. That would be rude."

"But what must he think? First I say I'm a little brother to you and then you say we're having a baby. Sheesh! Who is he anyway? Were you glad to see him or trying to scare him away?"

Livy thought for a second.

"That seems to be one of the major questions hanging over my life," she said, finally. "The answer is both, I guess. At one time we were thinking of getting married."

"And?"

"And we didn't."

"Because…?"

Livy heaved an exasperated sigh and answered, "Because I wasn't ready, I suppose. And he was ready. And so rather than wait forever for me to get ready, he married someone else."

"I'm sorry. How did you feel about that?"

"What was I supposed to feel? I was the one who broke it off. I told him he was free to move on with his life."

"But did you love him?"

"*I think* I did. Especially now looking back at it." Livy sighed again.

"You think you did? Why couldn't you marry him?"

"I just couldn't believe that if he really knew me he would love me or even if he did that he would keep loving me... just like... I couldn't trust the idea of commitment."

She abruptly stopped talking and asked, "Why am I telling you all this? I don't do this. I don't air this stuff to anyone." She was sounding almost angry. "Um...Suddenly, I'm not hungry and I don't feel like celebrating anymore. Do you mind if we just go home?"

"Maybe it's time you did air it to someone. We don't have to stay if you don't want to. I can walk you home and you can just talk. It's okay. I'll be quiet and just let you say whatever you want. Deal?" Bryan suggested gently.

"Oh that's right. You're here doing some kind of social work internship or something. Well, I've had enough of shrinks and I don't want you to practice on me." She could feel her walls coming up, shutting her off from anyone trying to get close.

"I'm going to get my coat." Bryan said.

"Oh must you?"

"Very funny. Livy, I'm just trying to be a friend. And I do think you need one."

"A shrink or a friend?"

"A coat! ...And a friend."

"Well, I don't need anyone. In the end, I take care of myself. It's easier that way. I don't want to talk about it, okay?"

And they didn't. He walked her back to the apartment building in strained silence.

CHAPTER 5

Kyle Fitzgerald, the holiday fanatic, had done it again. His office was decked out in all new Valentine style. There were hearts on the door and candy dishes full of conversation hearts. Cupid was hanging from the ceiling light fixture. When the door opened, a sensor would activate cupid to shoot a plastic arrow at the person entering. There were pictures of Kyle's wife Debbie, and his seven children displayed all around the room. Livy knocked on the door and ducked the arrow when she opened it.

"Kyle, you never cease to amaze me. Every holiday you manage to come up with something new and cute and annoying. I can't believe that someone like you is an accountant."

Kyle didn't bother to take offense. He cheerfully told her, "I'm one of those people whose mother forced them to eat with their right hand and play the right-handed guitar even when she knew I was left handed. It made me both right and left brained, I guess."

"Or maybe just hair-brained," she teased.

He played with the remaining five red hairs on the top of his head. "Is that where my hair went? Is there something I can do for you, Olivia?"

"I'm sorry. Anyway, do you have the estimated numbers on the contest costs?"

"I don't have enough details to go on yet. You have to let me know exactly what it is you want. How much TV do you want? How much print? Which networks? Then I can work it up."

"Marketing hasn't got all that to you yet? I thought that would be done by today."

"Olivia, the project was only officially approved yesterday. Give them a little time."

Kyle always tried to be the peacemaker in the office.

"I still say that you could save money and cut to the chase just by using one of these little darlings. Look at those faces," he said as he gestured at the pictures of his children around the room. "It'd be so easy, you know."

"Call me crazy, but I really do want the whole entire country to choose from—not that your kids aren't spectacular. Let me know when you've got the projections. This has to happen fast. All right?"

She turned to go and bumped into her secretary, Barbara, in the doorway. She got hit with another arrow. Barbara retrieved it and playfully chucked it back at Kyle. She was one who appreciated his festive spirit.

"Excuse me, Olivia. You have a phone call on your cell in your office. I answered it for you," Barbara said.

"So what else is new? Who is it?"

"He said his name is Garrett something…He didn't say what company he was with."

Livy tried to show no reaction to Barbara but she had been kicking herself all night that she had made that silly remark to Garrett about having a baby. What did it matter what he thought now, anyway? He was a part of her past and what was done was done.

"Tell him to hold, please. I'll be right there." She turned to Kyle. "How do you do it, Kyle?"

"Do what? The decorations? The projections?"

"No, the family. That's a whole lot of responsibility, isn't it? But do you know what? I found someone who's got you beat. They have 15 or 16 kids."

"16? That's why it's good that I'm an accountant. I can add and I can stop adding at seven."

"Anyway, see you later, Kyle."

****

Garrett had picked up from her asking him to call around lunchtime that she might be free for lunch and asked her to join him in the park near her office. She was to meet him at the hot dog vendor just inside. For

February, it was a beautiful day—bright and sunny and not too cold. She caught sight of him from the street and felt that familiar tingle go through her that she had always felt when she was with him. It was a wonderful and yet annoying tingle. It made her do and say stupid things and feel extra self-conscious.

He's a married man now, why can't I just relax?

He spotted her and walked toward her, smiling that devastating dimpled smile of his. He was decked out in an expensive gray suit and burgundy tie and was still gorgeous, maybe even more gorgeous than when they parted six and a half years ago. Marriage agreed with him.

"Livy! You came!" He gave her another hug.

"Of course I did. How are you, Garrett? Are you enjoying your visit to New York?"

"I'm okay, I guess. And yes, I'm enjoying New York. I haven't had time to see much of it though. I'm in seminars and meetings most of the time. They want all of us to get ready to take the New York Bar. And I leave tomorrow. I'm glad that I could get the chance to see you today. It's amazing that I ran into you like that. Can I buy you a Polish dog?"

"By all means, thank you."

"Where did you go last night? I looked for you to say good-bye but you had disappeared."

"We decided it was too late to wait a half hour for a table so we just went somewhere else."

"You weren't trying to avoid me, were you?"

"No, of course not," Livy lied. "I'm sorry if I was weird last night. It was just such a surprise to see you."

"And you're not really having a baby with him are you?"

"Who me? You know me better than that. I'm not sure that I ever want to do that." *I might have felt differently if I'd married you, Garrett,* she thought.

"And Brandon, was that his name? He's not your brother either, is he? You never told me anything about having a brother."

"Yeah, sure he is. I just came out all dark meat and he came out all white," Livy teased.

"Are you seeing him?" Garrett asked as he paid the vendor and took the hot dogs. He gave one to Livy.

"His name is Bryan and he's not my brother or my boyfriend. He's just a nice, young—"

"Safe!" Garrett supplied.

"He's just a guy. I have a baby-doll project at work and it...he sort of inspired the idea...and we were celebrating that. Anyway, he's like a little brother to me in a way."

"So...where do you work?"

"I'm at Joy's Toys. I'm in the new products marketing division."

"That's great but it's kind of ironic. Someone who doesn't think she wants kids is coming up with the latest and greatest toys. So what's with this doll? What makes it special?"

"It's going to be very interactive. The child does something and the doll will react and do something. It's kind of along the virtual pet lines except in human form. It's complicated. But the kicker is, and you might be interested in this, we are having a contest to find the best baby face in all of America. You must have some kids by now. Am I right? Don't tell me. You have... uh...four."

"What? I only got married five years ago; I have two. I have a boy, Mark, who is four and a girl, Stacey, who is two and a half and looks just like her mother." Garrett's eyes conveyed affection and something else, something deeper.

"So you are a proud papa."

"They are my life." Garrett brightened just talking about them.

"*Two* kids, huh? Well good. Everyone I meet lately seems to be over-populating. So how are you doing? Are you still with the big old law firm in Pennsylvania?"

"Still there. Shelly's parents are there and they want to be very involved with the kids. So it's a good place to be for now. Is this a good place for you? Are you happy here, Livy?"

"Where better to challenge myself than here in the hub of everything? I've always had to prove myself. These are the big leagues. There's energy and an excitement in this town. I'm good. I'm moving up the ladder in the company and my boss seems to appreciate me."

Garrett got a suspicious look on his face. "I'm sure he does."

"No, not that. At least I don't think so. I sure hope not. He's just mentoring me and grooming me for bigger things."

"Uh huh. What kind of things?"

"Really, he is not like that. Besides, his wife is his boss."

It was flattering that Garrett was concerned about her honor. He looked down at his food and seemed to gather his courage.

He finally asked, "But are you happy, Livy? Are there some real live people in your life? Not just co-workers or the latest toy or promotion or whatever?"

"Of course there are."

"Like Brandon—Bryan I mean? Someone safe you don't have to worry about getting hurt by? He's not going to demand anything from you, no commitment, and no ties. You're older and you have all the control and none of the risks."

"Garrett, you are making something out of nothing. I was taking him out to dinner. Big whopping deal. Why do you care who I have dinner with?"

She was doing it again. She knew she was going to do or say something stupid.

"Liv, you're right. This is none of my business. I just want you to be happy. I just want you to belong to someone."

"Oh, so like now I'm a lost dog?"

"Being married and having kids has just opened my eyes to so much and I want you to...it's just that I still care about you."

"Thank you; I care about you too but why are we having this discussion after all these years? You have moved on and are living happily ever after with Shelly and kids and that's your life. This is mine and I like it this way. I'm okay with it. You can be too."

"Have you *ever* needed someone? Have you ever let someone really need you? Do you want to go through life alone with no one to witness how wonderful you are?"

"What's so *wonderful*? Why are you doing this?"

Is he just trying to make me miserable about all the decisions I've made in my life? What's this all about?

Garrett shook his head and asked, "You haven't changed at all, have you? You've got to look for some dark, secret motive, some reason not to trust that someone just plain cares about you. You have to shut everyone out."

"Do you want to start something up again? Is that why you seem to object to Bryan or my boss? You want to start some kind of fling while you're away from the wife and kids?"

Garrett's face froze in a mask of pain.

"Shelly's gone, Livy," he said quietly.

For the first time Livy glanced at his left hand. "You're not even wearing your wedding ring...and you're lecturing me about belonging and commitment? You're not even married anymore?"

Garrett looked fiercely into her eyes and in a flash of anger barked, "Nope, I'm not. That's right, she had no staying power. She just up and left me with two kids! Is that what you want to hear? Do you want to say 'see I told you so'?"

"So you're divorced? So who are you to tell me about...? You're nothing but a hypocrite!"

"She died, Livy. Shelly died last fall."

He threw the rest of his food in a nearby trash barrel and stormed away.

Livy felt like she had been slapped.

"What?" She asked as she trailed after him. "Oh Garrett. I'm so sorry. I feel terrible. Why didn't you tell me? Why did you let me make such a fool of myself?"

She put her hand on his arm and tried to make peace. "How did she die?"

Garrett kept walking but slowed down. After a moment he turned to her and spoke slowly and painfully. "It was a brain tumor, a damn vicious one. It tore her apart in a matter of months. There was nothing they could do; it was inoperable. There was nothing that *I* could do except to stay at her side and helplessly watch her be eaten away by it. Week after week, she was just eaten away. They found it in August and by November she was gone." Tears were gliding down his cheeks and he sat down on a bench, emotionally spent.

"How do you handle it?"

He licked a tear from the corner of his mouth and said, "Obviously, sometimes I don't. But mostly, I have to. I have to keep going for the kids.

I have to be there for them. I'm so afraid that they will forget their mommy and I just can't let that happen. She hated leaving them so much...and just one month before Christmas."

Livy sat down on the bench next to him. She stared at her feet as she kicked a rock across the cement.

She was mostly talking to herself when she said, "But everyone does. Everyone leaves. They die or maybe they walk away, they grow apart, they move on. Or they don't want you anymore. Garrett, you bought into forever, but it never works out that way, does it?"

"I didn't leave you, Livy. You sent me away. You pushed me away," he said gently.

"I know I did. I was afraid."

"Maybe I should have been afraid that something like this tragedy would happen, but you know what? I thank God for those five years with Shelly even as I curse the next 50 years without her. I'll miss her terribly but there's something much sadder, Livy, and that's having no one to miss. I'm grateful that I got to be there at her bedside and hold her hand and tell her how happy she had made me. I got to thank her for giving me those sweet, wonderful kids and for loving me and letting me love her so completely that it would hurt this much to lose her. It was a privilege, Livy, a privilege to be there when she walked into eternity. And I knew that I *knew* what love really, really was and that I had walked in its sunshine— and in its shadow. We had five good years, wonderful years that I will treasure forever. You see?"

He lifted Livy's chin and looked her right in the eye.

"In a way, I do get forever after all. And I have Mark and Stacey and—"

"I'm so glad that you have them. I'm sorry that I was such a jerk. I wish you had told me before I made an idiot of myself."

An awkward silence hung in the air for a moment.

"I need to be getting back to the office," she said. "Walk with me and tell me about those kids on the way, would you?"

Garrett was happy to oblige. He described how beautiful they were and the funny things they said and how he loved to peek in and watch them sleep. He said sometimes he would carefully pick them up and just hold them as they dreamed. He made it sound wonderful, bittersweet and fulfilling. Maybe it was.

All too soon they had walked the seven blocks to her office.

Livy said, "This is my building. You are leaving tomorrow then?"

"Yeah, 8:00 a.m. flight. So...uh, take care of yourself, Liv."

"I always do. Take care, Garrett. I'm so glad that we got to see each other. I don't know what to say except I hope that you will forgive me. Keep my number. Maybe give me a call and let me know how you are doing and all about the kids. And don't forget to enter our contest." She took his hand. "I'm sure they are beautiful children. Shelly was, wasn't she?"

"Yes, she *was* beautiful...inside and out. Well, good-bye Livy."

He dropped her hand and gave her a nice warm hug. She kissed him lightly on the cheek.

"Bye Garrett."

She opened the door and walked inside. He turned and started down the street. She opened the door and watched him walk away... probably for the last time.

CHAPTER 6

After the encounter at lunch, Livy had a hard time getting herself back into working mode. There wasn't a lot she could do about her project while she waited for initial department reports so she decided for once, she'd go home early—five o'clock—like a normal person.

She had just come out of the building when she met Bryan coming towards her. He was carrying the telltale white bags of take-out.

"Since you deprived me of my celebration dinner last night, I brought one for tonight, thoughtfully delivering it in person to your office. Instinctively I knew there's nowhere else you'd rather spend Valentine's evening than behind your desk.

He looked very proud of himself until he noticed Livy's coat and brief-case.

"I guess I was wrong. Hot date?"

"No hot date. Just don't feel like working."

"Great!" Bryan grinned and said, "You get me, dinner AND the dining location of your choice! But it better be close because dinner will be getting cold in a second."

Livy paused, considering whether she wanted to hurt Bryan's feelings and just make a beeline for home, or to eat in the park for the second time in one day. Looking into Bryan's cheerful, affectionate face, she realized she had no choice.

"Follow me, Boy Scout. I have the perfect spot." She said, and steered Bryan to the same park and the same bench she had recently shared with Garrett.

"So, did he call you?" Bryan asked, uncannily seeming to read her thoughts.

"Who?"

"Don't act dumb. Him...what's his name...Garrett?"

"Yes he did and we had lunch today."

"Well, how was it? I mean I know you said he's married and everything but ..."

"Oh, I don't know. I just made a total ass of myself."

"You did not. Look, I see no ears, no tail, ... no evidence of jackass whatsoever. What happened? Here, eat your double cheeseburger and tell me what happened."

"Cheeseburger? What happened to steak?"

"You weren't buying so...."

"Give me that. It'll probably kill me and right now I hope it does."

Livy took a big, fat, angry bite and said while still chewing, "He was giving me this big spiel about commitment and belonging and I flat-out called him a hypocrite."

"What?" Where did that come from? You must have had a reason."

"Well, when I looked at his hand and didn't see a wedding ring, I thought he was talking about commitment while dumping his wife and hitting on me or something. So, I'm in the middle of yelling at him and he just mentions that, oh, by the way, she died. He's still mourning her and I'm screaming at him. I'm such a creep."

Bryan made a face.

"Eeeeoooh, that was awkward."

He put down his burger, dug out a napkin and wiped a smear of mustard from her cheek. "So what happened? So, did you leave it like that? Did he stomp away all mad and insulted and everything?"

"He started to, but I sort of smoothed things over... I hope. I'm not sure, but I'll bet he thinks I'm the biggest jerk. I hope he...well, I think he was hoping we could be friends again. But I sufficiently erased that idea from his mind, didn't I?"

"Did you clear up the you-and-I-having-a-baby thing?" Bryan mumbled while his mouth was working on his second burger.

"Oh yeah. I blew that part too. I pretty much convinced him that I don't ever want kids and then he tells me that he has two."

"Hmm...Well, Livy, he's not ready for anything yet if his wife just died. He was unavailable before and nothing's really changed. Just give him a few months and then call him, you know, just to see how he is doing. Show him that you care, that's all."

"Thank you, Dr. Laura. Any other advice you'd like to pass along from your vast experience as an Idaho tractor jockey? What do you know about *love*? Do you even have a girlfriend?"

"Not right now. I have someone in mind but I have to give her some more time. Timing is everything, you know."

"Yeah, like today, my timing was fabulous. What's her name?"

"Uh uh." Bryan shook his head. "You'd go look her up and tell her I'm a loser and that I dress funny. Uh uh, not gonna tell ya."

Livy grimaced and was starting to think to herself, *yeah, because it's me,* when he said, "And no, it isn't you. Her first name is Lou Ann and that's all I'm going to say."

"I never said you were a loser, but..." Livy said, staring at his used bowling shoes.

She wadded up the trash and stuffed it back in the bag.

He took the bag from her and shot it like a basketball into a nearby trashcan. "Yeah, but you thought it. And what's wrong with my shoes? They were 50 cents. And now for the second part of our activity," he said.

"What? What now?"

"If you are going to go around creating toys then you have to remember what it was like to be a kid." He stood up, walked forward with his back to her and squatted down. "Get on."

"What are you doing?"

"I'm giving you a piggy-back ride."

"No, you're not. I'll break your back."

She kept licking the catsup from French fries she was eating.

"You won't break my back," he said as she shook her head. "I'm superman. I double-dog dare you. Just get on."

She put her food on the bench and looked around. There were a few little children on playground equipment across the park, but other than the kids and their mothers, there was no one else around. So Livy climbed on Bryan's back, all six feet of her. She couldn't remember ever having a piggy-back ride before. He trotted around the park to the laughter and amazement of the children playing on the bars and swings.

"Is this what they do in Idaho for excitement?" Livy gasped in a bouncing voice.

"Oh yes. We've elevated it to an art form in my—*our* family. The bottom guy is the horse and the top one is the knight. We get those long foam pool poles and we joust. It's a blast."

"You sound like you still do it, not like it was years ago when you were little."

"We *do* still do it and even my Dad does and sometimes Mom joins in. We all speak in these really bad British accents and chase each other all over the potato fields. The last knight standing wins," Bryan said in just such an accent. "Grab that broken branch up there in that tree; there's your lance, Sir Livilot."

"You're crazy and this is embarrassing!"

She was laughing almost uncontrollably.

He made a loop and ended up once again approaching the tree.

"Come on. Just try it! You'll get this amazing sense of power!"

Bryan wrapped his hands around Livy's feet and she was now standing on his forearms. He didn't slow down as she made a desperate grab for the branch. She missed it and ended up swinging wildly from a lower attached limb as Bryan kept on trotting with only her shoes in hand, pretending that he still carried Livy. By now he had the attention of the kids and they were delighted, chasing him and laughing at his ruse.

"Well, m'lady. How light you are! You're like a feather."

"Bryan! You come back here! It's too far to drop! Come get me down!"

"You lost your lady! She's yelling for help," the children giggled. "She's over there hanging from the tree."

Bryan looked in the wrong direction.

"Where? I don't see her."

"BRYAN!" Livy called, no longer amused. "Get me down from here! And I need my shoes!"

"What's that I hear? My lady is in trouble. I must save her at once!" He and his little army hustled to the rescue and assembled under the tree.

"This is an expensive Bill Blass pants suit and if you make me ruin— "

"No need to fear, oh beautiful damsel. We've got it under control, right guys?" He raised his arms up and instructed his little friends to hold him up from the sides. "I am ready, fair maid. Release the branch. I'll catch you."

"Are you sure?"

"Trust me. Let go."

She did and he caught her safely but making staggering steps as if losing his balance and then falling backwards with Livy on top of him.

Bryan said, "Dogpile!" and suddenly there were kids crawling all over them both.

Livy jumped up like she had discovered she'd sat in a nest of spiders. She dusted herself off, quickly slipped on her shoes and explained, "It's February, for Pete's sake. The ground is all wet and muddy."

But Bryan sensed it was the kids more than the fairly dry ground that made her uncomfortable.

The mothers had gradually wandered over to watch their children in this momentary drama and now gathered them up and led them away. As Livy watched, one curly-headed little boy of about four suddenly stopped, bent down to the ground and then ran back to Livy and held out a little purple crocus.

"This is for you, my lady. It's the first flower," he said.

She bent down to take it and the little fellow rose up on his toes and kissed her cheek. Livy started to thank him, but he had already run back to take his mother's hand.

CHAPTER 7

Linda's Story part 2

Who is it this time? Sister Bernadette wondered when she heard the completely out of pitch wail during the singing. *Someone should make decent singing a prerequisite for becoming a nun. No monotones allowed.*

The elderly woman's hearing wasn't the best but even she knew something was out of kilter in the sound. After a moment she realized it wasn't an errant soprano; it was a baby's cry.

She grabbed the sleeve of the also-elderly Reverend Mother sitting beside her and whispered, "Do you hear that?"

"Hear what, the singing? I'm not deaf yet, sister."

"Listen, I think I hear a baby crying."

"A baby?" She listened intently, smiled and said, "I think you're right. We must have company!"

"Another poor unfortunate girl!" Sister Bernadette cried.

"We can't feed the children we have now over at St. Anthony's. We fast and pray for funding and we get another mouth to feed," the Reverend Mother said.

Searching the hallway for the baby or the poor girl who must have brought it, the sisters found no one. The sound was coming from the vestibule. There, just inside the door and bathed in colorful light from the setting sun shining through the stained glass window, was a beautiful but very unhappy baby. Finding no mother, and hoping to find a note, Sister Bernadette searched the diaper bag and nearly fainted when she found $10,000 in crisp one hundred dollar bills.

As fate would have it, this convent was affiliated with one of the last religious orphanages on the East Coast. State funding was drying up fast and this little godsend of cash would see them through the present crisis. The nuns had just finished a three-day period of fasting and prayer.

Linda would be assigned to the care of Sister Marian Margaret, a loving nun and teacher, in her mid-forties. It was love at first sight, for both of them.

The two became quite a pair of M & M's—Marian Margaret and Little miss Minnie Mouse. According to information, also gleaned from the bag left with the little one, her name *might* be Linda. Someone, probably her mother, had written *Angelita Linda* on a photo. It could mean pretty little angel or little angel Linda. They went with the name but the nun always called her Mini-Linda. When Linda learned to talk, she called her nun, Sister M & M and eventually just Sister M.

She got along well with the other children there and was quick to learn. She learned to read, to run, dance, and to sing. All in all, she was a happy child. Now and again, a child would be adopted from the orphanage. She began to wonder when her new mom and dad would come and take her home. She wasn't anxious about it because she was happy with Sister M and the world she had come to know. She just wondered.

"Sister M, what does eligible mean?"

****

It was just after Christmas of her sixth year when Linda's life would abruptly change again. Her deeply loving bond with Sister Marian Margaret was about to be broken.

A judge, somewhere, who had never met Linda, decided that although she had been abandoned at a religious institution, there was no proof that a parent was voicing a desire for her to be raised in any particular religious setting. She was now to be taken into the state system and go to state run foster care. The same applied to several other children at St. Anthony's Boarding School for Needy Children. The change would soon bring about the end of St. Anthony's.

There was also that matter of a father's rights. It had been assumed when she was abandoned, that since the child had a picture of someone who was most likely her mother, then the mother had given up all rights. There was no indication of the father's wishes or whereabouts and therefore, the child was determined not to be free for adoption until at least a token search for the identity of the father had been conducted. After six years, that detail still had not been completely settled.

Sister M&M tried to remain cheerful as she helped little Linda pack her Minnie Mouse bag. She checked her neck. "Do you still have your little daisy-cross on? Okay, don't ever lose that." She took an undershirt and gently wrapped Linda's now framed picture of Mommy in it and tucked it inside the bag. "Don't worry. It will be like having a real family, my little darling. You'll have a mommy and a daddy and maybe brothers and sisters, too."

"But I won't have you. I want to be with you. I don't want somebody else's mommy and daddy. I want you."

Linda buried herself into the folds of the Sister's habit.

"I know, Sweetheart. I know. I want to be with you, too, Mini Linda."

She held her close and then gently pushed away to see her face.

The nun smoothed her hair from her forehead and said, "There are just some things that happen that we can't help. You can send me pictures that you draw and write me letters. Will you do that?"

Sister M&M could hardly finish the question for the lump in her throat. She couldn't love Linda more if she were her own.

A stern looking woman in gray hair and a gray suit had appeared in the dormitory doorway watching the farewell scene unfold.

"We don't encourage that type of thing, Sister. It just hampers the child's ability to make new connections. It's better if she just makes a clean break. What's the child's name? This is Linda, am I right?"

The child answered, "I am Linda and I don't want to go." She turned back to Sister M. "Why do I have to go?"

"Promise me you'll try your best to be happy," Sister M said, blowing a kiss.

She gulped down the knot in her throat and nodded. Her eyes were wet and solemn.

The woman took Linda's bag and her hand and without another word to the nun, she marched Linda down the hall. Linda turned to see Sister

Marian crying and waving good-bye.

"We have a great big van downstairs. It will take you and the other children to the big city. Have you been to the city before?" The woman asked her.

Remembering her promise, Linda took a deep breath and tried to answer cheerfully," Once I went to the zoo. Is that the city? It didn't smell so good in the zoo."

"I promise the whole city does not smell like the zoo. You will get to meet your new family this afternoon. How does that sound?"

Her first family was really just a temporary weigh station while the children's welfare people looked for a more permanent placement. She went to three such families, for just days at a time, and spent two nights in a respite care facility.

She went to the Sheila and Eric Jones household in Raleigh for about six months. Mrs. Jones was nice and Mr. Jones was almost never home. When Mrs. Jones found out that she was pregnant she decided that she had better put her time and attention toward preparing for the birth of her own child.

Tina Winston took her in for about six weeks. Ms. Winston was a single mother of five children and shortly found out that six was indeed beyond her limit, emotionally and financially. She called the children's services department to come and pick Linda up... two days before Christmas. Even though she kept Linda's state money, she said there was not enough to go around.

"I'm sure you can find some nice place for her for the holidays," the woman said.

The stay in the interim home did little in the way of celebration and nothing for Linda's lonely little heart.

After the New Year, Linda was assigned a new caseworker, Stephanie Clancy. New to the system, Mrs. Clancy took Linda's case to heart and found her a home that looked very promising. She said that she was going to a couple's home where she might very likely be adopted, when the state was able to make her eligible. The young foster-mom had found out from her doctor that she wouldn't be able to have children of her own and she was interested in adoption. They were a mixed race couple and it would seem natural for them to have a brown child like Linda. Already, Linda was learning to be careful about trusting people, especially those who seemed overly kind to begin with, and she held back quite a while before letting herself hope that she had found a real home with these people—Karena and Rick Marshall.

Over time, Linda couldn't help herself. She was bonding with Karena in ways that she hadn't with the other short-term "moms". Karena and Linda seemed to have similar senses of humor and laughed at things that Rick just didn't find amusing at all. Because Rick was a marine and had that "inspection mentality", Karena kept a house that was immaculate. Linda learned that she, herself, was tending to be somewhat of a neat-nik and she felt at home in the orderly environment. Some of her previous domiciles were less than tidy and that added to her discomfort in those situations. When she and Karena went in to town to go shopping, sometimes Linda felt like she was Karena's doll and that Karena was playing dress-up with her. When Rick was away they'd indulge themselves in girl's night out, going shopping, or to a chick-flick, followed by doing each other's hair and nails.

Karena watched, as Linda grew more confident and more comfortable. Looking better made her feel better and she grew more outgoing socially. A girl from her second-grade music class, Daphne, was becoming what Linda imagined a best friend must be. She had never had one before. They shared whispered secrets and laughed at all the boys in class. The girls were inseparable at school. At the Marshall home, they made up dances and sang into hairbrushes and made their own music video with Daddy Rick acting as cameraman. For her three-month anniversary of being in this home, Linda had a sleepover with Daphne. They ate pizza and watched a scary movie on TV and then could hardly go to sleep because of it.

Karena had read the file and knew that Linda had had a difficult time adjusting at her last two temporary homes and was pleased that Linda seemed to be becoming a real kid, a normal kid. Most everything seemed to be going so well. But lately, she had begun to withdraw from Rick and Karena just a little and Karena wondered if it was because she was thinking that at any time she might be sent away. That was the last thing that Karena wanted. She had found a match: a little girl made just for them. She called

Ms. Clancy, the social worker, to come over and discuss the future of their arrangement.

Karena was told that Linda was now free to be adopted and that only some last legal hurdles needed to be cleared and of course a final home inspection would have to take place in order to make them a *real* family.

Gleaming and inviting, like something out of *Better Homes and Gardens,* the house awaited final approval. Karena and Linda had scrubbed and straightened, polished and primped. Ready or not, the appointed time was here and Linda was sure that at last she had found a place to belong...finally a real home.

Sending Linda upstairs to dress in her new outfit, bought especially for this occasion, Karena thought of one more detail that she had better see to. Mr. Marine was a gun buff and had a chest where he kept some of his prized weapons. If the social workers were to find those weapons unsecured it would probably ruin any chances for approval. She better make sure the chest was safely locked.

It must have been inspiration. As she was digging in the back of the closet of Rick's den, she found the chest open, with the lock lying on the floor beside it. She was so glad she had thought to check it... so glad until she looked inside it. She didn't just find three German pistols and a semi-automatic rifle; she found stacks and stacks of pornography.

She tried to put her best spin on the situation by rationalizing, *well, he's a marine, and a macho kind of guy and you have to expect a certain amount of—*

Then her world and her dreams of a family with wonderful little Linda came to a screeching halt. It was child porn. She rummaged through piles of horrific pictures. There were movies, magazines and loose photos. Under several magazines lay the most damning evidence of all. Some of the pictures were of neighborhood children that she recognized as shot literally in her own backyard. Obviously, Rick had to have taken the pictures; who knew what else he had planned or what else he had done. She could only pray that Linda had not been part of this. *Not my Linda! Not my Rick! This cannot be happening!*

For a moment, Karena couldn't breathe. She couldn't think. How does one breathe or think or go on when her heart has been so thoroughly broken? Suddenly the doorbell was ringing and she heard Linda's happy greeting.

"Mrs. Clancy, we're all ready! Do you like my new Capri's? Mommy Karena bought them for me."

Karena knew she couldn't let her stay and be part of this hideousness. But she had not yet come to the point where she was ready to turn Rick over to authorities, either. He would go to jail. If she confronted him, perhaps she could help him turn away from this evil addiction. Losing them both would be more than she could handle. But one thing was sure; Linda, darling Linda, could not stay in that house. The worst of it was that Karena couldn't tell her why. Naturally, Linda would tell one of the counselors and they would come and take not just Linda away, but Rick too. Linda would never understand that this heartbreaking disappointment was for her own good.

Despite her weak knees and brimming eyes, Karena made it down the stairs and into the living room. "Linda honey, run to the kitchen and get the pitcher of lemonade I made and a glass for Mrs. Clancy."

She skipped cheerfully to the kitchen. Karena sent her out of the room because she couldn't bear to see the hurt in Linda's face when she told the social worker they couldn't adopt Linda.

"What's wrong, Mrs. Marshall? Are you quite well?" Mrs. Clancy asked noticing her troubled state.

Karena's voice shook with emotion. "You know, Mrs. Clancy, I'm so sorry to tell you that I don't think we are ready to go ahead with the adoption after all."

She was twisting her skirt into a knot.

"What? After everything we did to expedite it? I thought it was all settled." Mrs. Clancy was clearly dismayed and baffled by this turn of events.

"As you can probably tell, I'm very upset about coming to this realization right now, of all times, but Linda needs to find another family to adopt her. It's just not the right move for us at this point."

She heard a crash and turned to find Linda standing in the doorway over the broken pitcher she had just dropped. She had heard.

She ran over and fell at Karena's feet. "Why, Mommy Karena? Why? I want to stay with you!" Karena just stared painfully at the ceiling, the tears now flowing down her face.

Karena did all she could to avoid looking at Linda's face; she couldn't bear to see the hurt she was causing.

"Has she done something to make you abruptly change your mind like this?" Mrs. Clancy asked.

"No, no. It isn't her. She's been an angel and I would love to keep her, but I realize that Rick is not ready and our marriage is in serious trouble. I can't force this on him if he's not ready."

She finally turned to face her would-be daughter.

"Linda, please understand that I wanted more than anything to be your mommy, but I just can't. We just can't."

"Why, Mommy Karena? Why? Did I do something bad? Please tell me and I won't do it ever again. Please tell me, what did I do?" Linda pleaded at Karena's knee.

She dropped down to Linda's level and embraced her fiercely. "You didn't do anything wrong, I want you to know that. I love you and want to have you here with us, but I can't, my sweet Linda, I just can't."

Once again, Linda packed up her Minnie Mouse bag, her doll, her picture and necklace, and set out to face the world alone. Quietly sitting in the backseat of Mrs. Clancy's car, she felt a jumble of emotions: overwhelming sadness, confusion and fear of what would happen to her next.

She made me go away. I must be very, very bad.

CHAPTER 8

Out of necessity, the marketing team worked up the contest campaign in record time. After consulting the legal department, a double blind receiving system was created to insure impartiality. Each entry form was dated and filed in a cryptographically monitored database, leaving each picture identified only by number. The family of the winning photo would receive $50,000 cash and a Fantasy Line Cruise for up to eight family and friends. The child would be photographed by world famous photographer Lee Rockwell, and given the option of a modeling contract with the prestigious New York-based Kate Kline Agency. Ten finalists would also win a cruise for eight, and receive a limited edition Hannah doll of their choice; sure to be valuable collectibles in the future. Entries were available at Wendy's Restaurants nationwide, or online at the "Hold-Me- Hannah" website sponsored by Joy's Toys. Applications were to be submitted online and all photos electronically scanned. Entries needed to be received by midnight April 1st; Joy's Toys employees and their families were not eligible. The winner would be announced April 30th on live national television.

The country was bombarded with ads in print, television, and radio and Wendy's Restaurants everywhere sported huge displays with application instructions. The advertising department invested in pop-ups on every imaginable website regarding parents and children. Everywhere in the country, ads reached out and tapped limitless proud parents. Ads like:

Announcer Voice Over:

It happens all the time, doesn't it? People constantly telling you that your child is "just a doll!" C'mon, admit it. They're right! And now you can prove it! Mom! Take that picture off the wall! Grandparents!

Get out that brag book and show us that special face—the one no one can resist, the face that melts every heart."

Livy's instincts had been right. The hype worked even better than predicted. Grandparents raided stacks of photo albums and scanned in shots of 20 grandchildren. Parents of every race sent in baby pictures and school photos. Glamour and kiddie photography shops were booked solid for weeks in advance. People everywhere were sure their child was the best, the brightest and, of course, the most beautiful. Entries poured in by the thousands. Even some vain adults sent in their own baby pictures. What the heck? Why not? Soon the computer techs couldn't keep up with the submissions. 50 temps were hired to organize the vast quantities of data and help the judges to select the finalists.

Although she would never have admitted it, even Livy was amazed at the response, as former skeptics like Bob Farrell and Marcie Jones congratulated her on her success. After his initial disappointment, Kyle had become a genuine supporter of the company choosing a wonderful mystery child instead of one of his own, and Mel was thrilled to refute his wife's prediction that the whole idea would bomb. Hannah was becoming, even more than Livy predicted, a household name.

****

Several states to the South, Carlos Sotomayor couldn't believe his eyes. He had spent most of the last few years in the Florida State Penitentiary and had been released only days before he saw the commercial announcing the Joy's Toys baby contest.

How fabulous! How convenient! —Just when I need a little funding. This is just too easy! I am back, ladies and gentlemen—back in business.

Pulling out the wallet graciously stored at government expense for such a long time, he let out a wicked chortle. Yes, the picture was still there.

Oh Patti, my dear, I know you gave me this photo to make me feel ashamed but once again, I have no shame. Sin verguenza! My little gold mine just might pan out after all.

He knew she was exactly what they were looking for. She was perfect–her little arms reaching up, her lovely longing little face—just epitomizing the name of the doll: *Hold-Me-Hannah*. He knew that entering the photo would shake things up a bit for that New York witch, as Patti had dubbed her.

But oh, Patti, you must admit, she deserves it!

How he would take pleasure in squeezing every possible dime out of her!

She's practically leaving the door to the chicken coop wide open for the wolf. Hmm...Let's see, where will I find the offices of Joy's Toys Corporation? It's so simple. Our little darling wins the contest and the witch pays through the nose. It's as easy as child's play!

CHAPTER 9

It was a spring Saturday, about 7:00 a.m. and Livy was in the midst of a delicious dream about the beautiful horse property she was hoping to buy in upstate New York. If the doll were the kind of success she hoped it would be, then the beautiful rural estate near the Finger Lakes would be well within her financial reach. The listing photos on the Internet displayed rolling green pastures lined with beautiful trees captured in a time of autumn splendor. In the dream she now wandered happily along a leafy trail leading to a large barn. As things in dreams often do, the scene morphed from colorful fall glory to winter fairyland in an instant. Suddenly the lovely grounds were covered in new fallen snow sparkling like diamond dust under a December moon. The path was now marked with glowing lanterns and Livy felt drawn toward the barn as if something wonderful awaited her inside. Abruptly, the peaceful setting was shattered by the sound of her dream horses kicking at their stalls. She was startled but pushed on. The pounding continued and she then reluctantly realized it wasn't the horses. Someone was banging on her own apartment door.

Oh, who is knocking on my door at this hour on a Saturday morning? Why don't they go bother someone else?

When the knocking didn't stop, she finally donned a robe and pulled her voluminous hair up in a twist and answered the door. It was Bryan in sweats. In the past few months Livy and Bryan had truly become the brother and sister team that they had originally only joked about. It was kind of frightening. They spent much of their free time together and Livy had to admit that she was becoming as close to Bryan as to anyone she could remember throughout her life. What was even scarier was how much she had come to care for him despite her original resistance. This morning he was bright-eyed and about as bushy-tailed as any rabbit she'd ever seen.

"Hey! Did I wake you?" He asked with a laugh. "Nah, couldn't have, you're a workaholic and you don't know how to sleep in."

"Wrong! I was just having the most delicious dream and you were not in it. No, on second thought, you were in it at the end. You were the back-end of a horse. What are you doing here?"

"I'm taking you on an outing, dear sister."

"What if I told you that I have plans, pesky brother?" Livy asked, not really annoyed.

"What plans?"

"I was going to the gym and then I thought I would rent a car and go for a ride out in the country."

She thought she might just go looking for that lovely country estate.

"Well, this outing will accomplish the same ends, so get dressed in your gym clothes and let's go."

He was jumping around the apartment like a kitten on catnip.

"Go where? What are you so excited about?"

"You'll see. You've wanted to know a little about what I'm doing, so I'm taking you along on some fieldwork. You'll like it; don't worry. Get yourself some good sports shoes on."

"Does this mean I'm supposed to roll in the mud with some kid again or something? Thanks anyway, I'm not in the mood."

"No mud, I promise. But I really want you to come."

She looked at those big blue pleading eyes of his and relented with a sigh. "You know you really are a little on the pushy side." Livy managed to round up some gym clothes and shoes and when she was all ready she asked, "Do I need a jacket?"

"Nah, it's an absolutely gorgeous spring day."

Fifteen minutes later, they were on the subway platform waiting for the train. Forty-five minutes later, they were in the South Bronx approaching a public housing neighborhood. Many of the windows in the dilapidated buildings were shattered and some were boarded up. Poverty and hope-lessness seemed to hang over the apartments like a brooding cloud. Most of the walls sported graffiti in vivid color and artistic style. Only trash wandered through the streets on the April morning breeze; people were strangely absent. There were no trees in blossom and no grass was visible anywhere. It was a typical Saturday in "the projects."

"What are you up to, Bryan? Why are we here? Is it safe?" Livy asked, sizing up her surroundings.

"Just thought you needed a little exercise and I want you to meet some friends of mine. We've been hangin' out for a while."

"You're hanging out here? I don't think that's too wise. You tend to stand out with your blonde hair and skin that's roughly the color of a vanilla shake."

She was half teasing and half seriously concerned.

"That's why I brought you—protection."

"What? You're using me for cover? I have a bad feeling about this place, Bryan. Let's go back."

"It's okay, Livy. Trust me. I've been over here lots of times and they don't seem to mind so far."

"Who are *they*, exactly?"

"My young basketball buddies. They wanted nothing to do with me at first but I warmed them up a bit."

"How did you do that? What could you possibly have that they'd want?"

"Thanks a lot, Livy. I thought you liked me now," Bryan said sounding just a little offended.

"I'm sorry. You know I like you, it's just that...well..."

"You're right, I can't be cool even if I try. But if you must know, I told them I was going to write about them and they liked the idea. Doesn't everyone want to be noticed...have his or her life witnessed and valued?"

"So now they are part of your case studies?"

"Yup. Here they are, my loyal 'subjects' so to speak."

He guided her towards the public housing playground.

Six boys between the ages of 11 and 13 were playing basketball on the fenced-in court. The painted lines on the pavement were nearly all worn away and the basket was merely a bent piece of metal. Any semblance of net was gone ages ago. The boys didn't care. They were having a marvelous time and were really quite skilled. On a makeshift bench, fashioned out of two two-by-fours suspended between two large paint buckets, sat a little girl who appeared to be about five years old. She was intensely studying a bug on the pavement under her swinging feet.

Ricardo, a shirtless, muscular Hispanic kid of about 12, was the first to notice Bryan and Livy approaching. He grabbed the ball from Leroy and tossed it out the gate at Bryan.

Leroy protested, "What you doin', Bozo?"

"It's Bryan! I just thought I'd wake him up, see if he payin' attention," Ricardo replied.

"Hey, white boy! You ready for your lesson?" asked Jamal, a tall, older black boy. "You gon' get schooled today!"

"How do you know that I'm not just holding out on ya'? How do you know that I'm not a Larry Bird kinda white boy just waiting for the right moment to go in for the kill?" Bryan sauntered around the court, dribbling now and then.

"Who's Larry Bird?" Jamal's little brother Terrence asked.

"Nobody!" The other boys replied in unison.

At that, Bryan made a power run at the hoop and leapt up for a dunk. The power behind his vertical jump was impressive but the aim was lacking. The ball slipped from his hands, hit the rim and sailed across the court to near where the little girl was sitting. She jumped up and ran after it, as if it were always her assigned duty. She held it up, ready to toss it back to them, but then she changed her mind. Instead, she threw it to Livy.

Taken a little off guard, Livy didn't quite react fast enough to snare it. It bounced off her hands and she made a few sad attempts to capture it, finally rolling back on to the court.

"Who da sister?" Jamal asked.

"She's my sister," Bryan answered with a totally straight face.

Jimmy laughed and slapped Bryan on the back. "Your sister is a *sister*?"

"Yeah, so how cool is that?" Bryan stepped over to Livy's side to introduce her.

"It's cool for you, but I feel sorry for her, having you for a sorry a..." Bryan glared at him and he didn't finish the word, and added only, "brother."

"Don't mind Jimmy, Olivia. He loves me, he really does. Boys, I'd like you to meet my sister, Livy Thomas. I thought maybe she could show us a few moves but after that sad display we just witnessed, maybe not."

She took the bait. "Excuuuuse me! You big...." She couldn't think of the appropriate word so she grabbed the ball away and dashed in for an impressive lay up of her own. She easily made it and came back and handed the ball to Bryan. She faced the boys and said, "University of South Florida Women's Basketball team. Full scholarship. Now, can I have a little respect?" She turned back to Bryan. "Please?"

The boys were laughing their heads off. "She nailed you, brother white boy!" said Frankie, the smallest and youngest of the group. He was probably 11 or maybe younger.

"And she's older than you, too. She yo' old lady?"

They laughed louder.

"Well, so much for respect!" Livy said in mock sadness. "Who is our little friend over there?"

"That's Josie, short for Josette," Frankie replied. "She's *my* sister. I'm always stuck with her on Saturdays 'cause our mom's gotta work."

"And he's Frankie, short for *Francois*," Jimmy said with a very exaggerated French accent. "Their mother's from Haiti."

"You got a problem wid 'at?" Frankie said in a mock accent of his own. "Yo mutha's from Hades," he retorted.

Bryan stepped between them. "Boys! Let's play some hoops, okay? My Dad's from Paris...Idaho, so who cares? Why don't you show me that pick and roll you've been working on?" Livy was amazed at how Bryan got them back into friendly game-mode. They happily got to work on the fundamentals of basketball. Bryan motioned to Livy to join and she reluctantly did and demonstrated some defense strategies. She was able to coach much-needed follow-through into Jamal's suffering foul shots, and strutted her stuff over and over at the hoop. The boys were impressed but she sensed they were a little deflated by her prowess.

Fine. I don't really want to be here anyway.

Faking an ankle twist, she limped over to sit with Josette.

How did I let Bryan drag me into this?

"Hi, Josie. I'm Livy. Do you want to take that jacket off? It's getting kind of warm." She put her arms out towards the child to help her remove the little hoodie.

Pulling away, she looked at Livy with suspicious eyes. "Mommy says I can't take it off and 'sides, I don't have no shirt." She pulled her ragged little warm up jacket around her protectively.

"Okay. Do the boys ever let you play?"

"No, 'dey say my job in the game be to chase da' ball."

"I noticed that. You throw it really well though. Have you ever tried to make a basket?"

"I'm too little. I can't throw it dat high."

After a few uncomfortably quiet moments, Livy finally asked, "How old are you, Josie?"

"I'm seven but I's little for my age, my mama says. Dat's why the boys never let me play...and 'cuz I'm a girl." She returned her gaze to the bug on the asphalt.

"Yeah, they don't get it," Livy added in commiseration. "Boys da fool and girls RULE!" That made Josie look up and beam a smile.

Something inside of Livy was touched by this little waif. She squatted down in front of her and whispered conspiratorially, "When I was a kid I was always taller than everyone else and wanted to try being little for awhile. Why don't you get on my shoulders and try out what it's like to be big, okay?"

Josie studied her for a moment as if trying to decide if she could trust this tall stranger to not only touch her, but to pick her up. She evidently chose to risk it and she put her arms up toward Livy and climbed aboard. She seemed almost weightless on Livy's shoulders as she gripped Livy's ponytail for dear life.

"Josie, wrap your feet under my arms and around the back, so you can use your hands too." Livy instructed as she ran onto the court. "Hey watch out, guys! Here we come!" she taunted. "Together we make a center that can look Shaquille in the eye and he'd feel the heat!"

Livy motioned to Bryan to pass the ball. She caught it and drove in toward the basket. She handed it up to Josie as she reached the bottom of the key. Josie shot with ease and the ball swished perfectly through the invisible net as Josie giggled with delight.

CHAPTER 10

Everything about him unnerved the secretary. Carlos, alias Charlie Majors, sat waiting in the office. The prison-gifted suit gave the appropriate impression and so did the scar on his dark cheek... also acquired in prison. He had assured the secretary that he indeed had an appointment and that his business with her boss was urgent for both. She probably had just been detained.

Her hand shook slightly as she handed him the cup of coffee he had demanded with off-hand assurance. "Cream," he'd suggested. "And three sugars...and a donut or something if you've got it."

She thought it unlikely that her boss would have forgotten an appointment with such a man but she didn't dare cross him. He looked like the kind of character who could make trouble.

"There are some muffins and Danish on the credenza," she said, deftly setting the phone to intercom while pretending to straighten articles on the desk. She wanted to hear if he started rummaging around the desk or opening files.

"Thank you," he said getting up to check out the choices. "I left my hotel without breakfast and—"

"Sure, help yourself," she replied.

She was getting bad vibes and definitely did not trust this guy. Once before, she had been taken in by a competitor's corporate spy and had nearly lost her job over it. It wouldn't happen again, not if she could help it. It was too bad that she couldn't throw him out. She could call security but if he was the important big shot he claimed to be, she could be fired for that too. What to do.... what to do... Reluctantly, she left him alone in the office.

When the "New York witch", as Patti had called her, appeared moments later; Carlos went for her like the easy mark she had been before.

When she extended her hand to him, he took it and held on to it menacingly.

"I'm sorry," she said, trying to appear calm, "but I'm quite sure there's been a miscommunication here. You say we had an appointment and yet I don't have anything written here in my planner..." She pulled her hand away to open the Franklin that she carried in her other hand. "Charlie Majors, is it?" She finally looked him squarely in the face. " I'm...uh...have we met?"

"Oh yes. We've had a pending appointment to clear up some unfinished business for a long time now. It's about time we kept it," Carlos said with a wicked smile and then waited patiently for recognition.

The touch of Spanish accent, his eerily familiar face, his manner, they all chilled her blood. Then suddenly her heart stopped and she knew him. It all came back, that Christmas Eve she had tried so hard to erase from her mind.

"I see that you remember me now. I'd be so hurt if you didn't. We meant so much to each other. How could you forget that one night we shared together?"

"What do you want?" She tried to sound firm but he could feel that she was terrified. He liked that.

"Before we talk business, I think maybe you should turn off the intercom." He watched her hastily do it and added, "Good. I think your secretary thinks I'm a little bit dangerous. And our business is very personal; I'm sure you agree. No need to concern anyone else...yet. It seems we have some new business to discuss."

"What business? I gave you everything you asked for. That was supposed to be the end of it."

"Of course, I wouldn't hold our...previous arrangement...over your head. It's just that your little contest reminded me of something. Or should I say someone? ...And naturally I thought of you and how much I've missed you."

"Why didn't they put you away for good?"

"They tried." He moved around the desk toward her and produced his copy of the photo from his pocket. "Let me refresh your memory. Isn't she sweet? Isn't she just a beautiful child? What a shame you didn't keep her."

She stared at it in disbelief. He waved it close enough for her to get a good look and pulled it quickly away when she tried to grab it. He made a clicking sound with his tongue and said, "No, no, no. We mustn't touch."

"What do you want?"

"I'm sure that you're starting to understand that it is very important that our little beauty wins the contest. You just make sure that the winner is kept anonymous and the prize money goes to charity when she wins…very specific charities that will be eternally grateful for your kind donations. Here are the names and accounts. You'll all look so generous and socially responsible. Everybody wins."

"You can't get away with this. Don't you see how much attention this contest is drawing? Someone is bound to scrutinize everything we do and then you will go to jail."

"Been there already—the food's not bad—no good lookin' woman like you around to keep me warm at night but…" He was running his hand up her arm.

She shook herself free of him. "Stop it! Shut up! Just shut up, you are making me sick!"

He cackled at her fear and repulsion. "Now, I may go to jail, but let's look at what happens to you if something goes wrong and all this gets out. You may also go to jail, maybe not. But even more interesting, is all you have to lose. It must be so nice to have the kind of life you live, the money you make, the nice place you live in, the clothes …all yours because of children. You just *love* those little children. Ha! They would be so crushed to find out the history behind this little one, don't you think?"

He reached out and grabbed her again. "And, you've got even more to lose now than just the man you loved. There's so much more riding on this little girl now. You don't want to lose it all now, do you? Not to mention the company. You'd take *it* down with you. Like you said, this contest is drawing a lot of attention. A little DNA is all I need to prove everything."

"Where is she? What did you do with her?" There was panic in her voice.

"You didn't care what happened to her then, so why now? You said to get rid of her and we did. It wasn't pretty but that didn't matter, did it? Not to you. All it would take would be one phone call to tell her and the world the whole disgusting story. She'll be so touched to know that you've changed your mind...to know you're looking forward to a nice family reunion," he said. "But let's not talk about that for now. I happen to have a lock of her hair that Patti saved. She was so sentimental that way. You remember Patti, don't you? That's all I need. Science is so amazing! The things we can do with just a piece of hair!"

"So now what? You seem to have thought of everything."

He produced a sweat soaked piece of paper from his pocket. "Here is the information about the charities. If you stick to the script, then we'll be just fine. You'll be fine. I'll be finer," he laughed.

"But I have other people involved in this project, you know. I don't have total control."

"No, *I* do. Just make it happen...or it will not be a pretty day for you and that baby doll. I'm sure the company has sunk millions into it already. There's no going back now." He gave her a pre-paid cell phone with a direct connection feature and instructed her to only contact him through the phone. "You can be sure that I will be watching your every move. I'll be in *"touch,"* he said as he ran his hand slowly and sinisterly across her buttocks.

She was shaking and backed herself into the bookcase. He pinned her there and whispered, breathing his cigar stench into her face.

"Now, if *you* can't handle it, there's someone else I can think of who might just love to help. You know who I mean. Should we ask for some help?" he asked in his raspy growl.

"No, please! I'll do what you ask."

"Good girl! Here's a chance for you to show just how capable and strong you really are." He gestured at a diploma on the wall. "All that college education made you so smart. You can do it. And if you don't...well, that's not an option."

He was having more fun than he'd had in years. As he left the office he spied the Danish and muffins remaining on the credenza. He took them all. "Don't mind if I do."

On the way down the hall to the elevator, he bit ferociously into a cheese Danish as he realized that he would have to find and silence Patti once and for all. Things were going so well. The last thing he needed was for her to show herself and mess things up. *I tried to kill you once, baby; don't make me have to try again. This time I won't fail.*

CHAPTER 11

The very next Saturday would be the day before Easter and once again Livy had to learn the appropriate Kimball family customs. Soon, she would be an expert on what it was like to be a child in any season in Idaho on the Kimball family farm. She could name all the Kimball siblings and all their ages. She learned about the hunt at Jensen's Grove for the notorious missing basket, the bunny they dyed green, and all about the store bought eggs that eight-year-old Bryan had tried to incubate in his closet with the use of the string of blue Christmas lights (and the horrible smell that ensued). And, she learned all about sunrise services on Easter morn, the private Kimball ones. Easter was a very special holiday for the Kimball family; they seemed to embody the very meaning of Easter. When each new child came into the Kimball home, his life began anew, just like it had for Jesus on that glorious resurrection morning. This year, a new life had begun for Sarah, Bryan's recently adopted little sister from Ethiopia.

Naturally, Easter meant that an Easter egg hunt would be involved. Bryan roped Livy into helping him put together such an event for the kids he was working with from the *Projects*. City Square Park would be the site and he figured they could get away with a mere one hundred and fifty colored eggs.

"150? I'm supposed to boil or blow 150 eggs?"

"Nah. You're not supposed to use real eggs anymore. They're afraid they'll go bad and all the kids will get bird flu or 'Sal Minelli' or something. We have to stuff plastic eggs with candy and hide them around the park at about dawn. If we do it the night before, animals or homeless guys might find them first and then we'll have a bunch of unhappy kids. You don't want to be around a horde of angry kids, believe me." Bryan sounded like he'd had some true kid-combat experience.

"I'm not thrilled to be around any unhappy kids. One's more than enough if he's like the one I sat next to on the plane to Toronto last month. Drove me nuts! Bryan, why do I let you talk me into this stuff? People at the office would freak if they knew half the things you dragged me into. And why an Easter egg hunt? With the possible exception of Josie, these kids are too old for that, aren't they? They're not little tiny children, you know."

"That's just it. For the most part, they never got to be little kids. They were practically born with adult-sized problems. I'd like them to have a day away from all that...away from the concrete and broken glass and the discarded needles... a day just to be children...out in the fresh air, rolling in the grass, having fun. I really want them away from there, just for the day. I don't have anyone else to help me, so are you in?"

She failed to come up with a good excuse. She scowled at him and said, "You are not getting me into a bunny suit and that is non-negotiable."

"How else are we going to manage to hide your identity? Those people at the office are sure to find out all your dirty secrets if we aren't careful," Bryan laughed but she took him seriously.

She teasingly grabbed him by the shirt collar and made herself clear. "I'm not kidding...non-negotiable!"

And sure as the sun rose, Livy was out hiding eggs in the park on that Saturday morning. By 10:00 a.m. she was deep in the hunt, pointing their young friends in all the right directions. This time there were no pictures to prove it, no Joy's Toys PR paparazzi, but Livy *was* starting to enjoy the company of these kids and was amused to see how much they seemed to like her. Livy and Josie grew closer that day. At first, Livy kept her distance and almost resented Bryan for having involved her with the kids. Josie sensed it and was a little slow to warm up to Livy, too. Gradually though, despite their initial reluctance, true and sweet affection grew between them.

At one point, Livy spied Josie sitting dejected in the grass. "Aren't you finding the candy, Josie?"

"I just see one and then da boys come and steal it," she said almost in tears.

"Come with me. I know where all the best stuff is hidden!" She would piggy-back Josie to the best remaining spots but leave the actual discovery of the candy for her to make. The child's infectious laugh and huge smile was a wonderful reward as she grabbed up her basketful of goodies.

After the hunt, Bryan taught them all his favorite Easter game, *Colored Eggs*. Each child had to pick a color. Bryan would be the wicked wolf who would come knocking at the door asking for colored eggs. They would ask, "What color?" and he would reply, "Blue" or whatever color came to mind and the kid with that color had to run around a mini-obstacle course with the wolf chasing them and then back to home base. If one was caught, he had to join the band of the wicked wolf until they had caught all but one. That one was declared winner and became the head wolf for the next round. And on and on it went. They had a blast acting like a bunch of six-year-olds.

Interestingly, it was Jimmy who got into the action the most enthusiastically. He was the oldest and tallest and could outrun them all but he liked to draw it out and tease and trap, making the fun last longer for the smaller kids.

Livy became the arbiter of rules.

"Nobody ever call out my color!" Terrence complained. "I don' never get to run!"

"What's yo color, dumb ass?" Jamal asked.

"Magenta. You know dat my favorite color!"

"Terrence," Livy explained, "sometimes you want to just be plain purple and not get so creative, unless you don't want to run."

Bryan added, "Yeah, when I was little, I always picked *metallic gold* and wondered why I never got a turn. I finally figured it out...last week."

The boys were bonding with Bryan in a way that no one would have expected. There was always plenty of teasing and pretended hostility but nothing of substance. Behind all the 'white boy' talk was a genuine respect and gratitude for someone who had taken an interest in them and genuinely cared. Bryan knew that when they got back to the neighborhood the boys would never brag to their friends that they had spent the morning with a white nerd and the wicked wolf. But he also knew that they'd never forget that day...for many reasons.

Bryan was learning a great deal about the lives of these boys by now. Some opened up more than others. They had experienced more horror and disappointment in their few years than he would ever have experienced in Idaho in a lifetime. Between the six of them, they had three family members serving time, two siblings who had dropped out of school, five running and using drugs and Jamal's sister had been raped. Jimmy's older brother, Aaron, was a leading member of the *Jex Jax*, a local gang. Only one of the kids—Leroy—had a relationship with his father.

Josie looked so frail and undernourished and it bothered Livy. She was glad when Bryan suggested they hit Burger King before accompanying them home.

Knowing Bryan's part-time job as doorman wouldn't pay much and wanting to avoid the discussion, Livy walked up to the restaurant counter and announced, "I'm buying! Get whatever you want but please try to find a food group in their somewhere!"

One would think they hadn't eaten in weeks. They ordered Double Whoppers, super-sized fries, desserts and gallons of sodas.

Frankie and Josie hung back from the group. Frankie shook his head at Livy. "I got it," he said determinedly.

"It's my treat, okay Frankie?" Livy insisted.

"I take care of Josie and I take care of me. I got it." He pulled a fifty-dollar bill out of his pants pocket.

She couldn't help herself. "Where did you get that?"

"My mom gave it to me. She said not to owe nobody nothin'. They be your boss forever that way." He pushed his way to the next cashier and ordered kids meals.

Bryan, who had been watching, just shrugged his shoulders and changed the subject. "Let's take that corner over there by the jungle gym. You can play while we wait. I know, you're too big and too old. But not today, guys, not today. Just play."

They ate like NFL jocks; they played like toddlers. After a while Livy was ready to call it a day.

"Bryan, let's pack it in. I've got other things on my agenda today that I'd like to get to. Let's get these kids back home."

Bryan glanced at his watch. "Just ten more minutes...then we can go."

"Why ten more...?" Livy began.

Bryan cut her off. "Just a few more minutes. Let 'em play."

Soon enough, they put their shoes back on and headed for the subway to go home.

When the little crowd of friends got off the train near their neighborhood, they laughed and reminisced about the day they had enjoyed.

Over the scream of sirens, Leroy elbowed Jimmy and taunted, "Dog, Jimmy, you run like a girl! You couldn't catch me no way."

"Oh yeah? I'll catch you now!" Jimmy barked back and chased after his teasing friend.

The boys rounded the corner at Rhoades and Walker Street and stopped cold. Up ahead was the playground where they usually spent their Saturdays with Bryan. Cop cars surrounded it with lights flashing. EMT's loaded injured teens into ambulances and a few frightened neighborhood residents began to emerge from the nearby apartments to comfort each other and to see what had happened. One tattoo-covered gangbanger, knife still in hand, lay in a pool of red up against the chain link fence. A rival gang had challenged the Jex Jax for the playground turf. The Jax retained control but had lost Jimmy's brother Aaron in the process. The whole event had lasted no more than a few minutes.

Terrified, little Josie climbed Livy like a tree and clung to her desperately, burying her face in her protector's shoulder. Livy held her tight and stroked her back but she just wanted to be out of there. She carried Josie to Frankie and left her in his care. "Take her home, Frankie. Just go home and lock the door and..." She wasn't sure there was any safety there either. "Just take her home, okay Frankie?" She brushed a tear from Josie's cheek and sent her with Frankie.

Livy was suddenly hit with a startling realization: If the kids had stayed and played basketball at their usual time, they would have been caught in the crossfire. Or perhaps, if they hadn't stayed to play on the jungle gym for just those extra few minutes ...God only knew what might have happened.

She wanted all of them to be away from there. She turned to talk to Bryan but he had gone over to comfort Jimmy who was kneeling at the lifeless body of his brother.

The boy wasn't crying; he was just rocking back and forth repeating, "Aaron? Not Aaron, man." He sensed Bryan's presence and said without turning, "You gotta write about Aaron. Please, Bryan. You gotta tell about my brother."

Bryan knelt beside him and laid his arm around his shoulder. "I will Jimmy, I will. I'm so sorry, friend." Bryan glanced up. "Look, your mother's coming. You'd better go help her. She looks like she can barely stand up."

Jimmy got to his mother just in time for her to melt into a sobbing rag doll in his arms.

Feeling this was a private moment, Bryan shuffled slowly and sadly back to where the other boys and Livy stood watching. Livy pulled Bryan aside. "We are getting out of here. Maybe you can't see it right now, but the tensions have to be rising and I don't think we should hang around waiting for more trouble. Let's go."

"You don't have to get mad. It's okay." Bryan said.

Now she was angry. "Do realize that if we had come back here just a little earlier... or if you and the kids had been on that playground, what would have happened?"

"But it didn't...not to us." He looked back at Jimmy and his mom. "We're alright. I wish I could say as much for Jimmy's brother. I'm just going to say goodbye to the guys and then we can go."

Their goodbyes consisted of silent expressions, waves and touches. Livy stood apart, lost in her own thoughts and fears.

CHAPTER 12

The time for the judging had arrived and it had become quite the anticipated event. Livy was in a panic. What if something went wrong and the whole thing blew up in her face? She was a professional, possibly the next executive VP of New Products Marketing, and she could handle it. She had to handle it. All eyes were upon her and upon Hannah. Joy's Toys had extended the invitation to all to send in their best and most beautiful children's faces and the nation had responded in record fashion. "America's baby icon" was the vernacular for the Hannah phenomenon. Preorders for the doll and her gear were already pouring in. She, Hannah that is, had not recouped her investment money yet but that would only be a matter of a few weeks and it was only the end of April. Livy wondered what kind of money they were likely to see come October and November.

Inside the office, there was a lot of jealousy and she knew that behind her back Marcie and Bob were still calling her "teacher's kiss-up pet." Mel's attention was focused almost completely on Livy and her project. The rumor they sparked was that there was more going on there than just "toy maker and his apprentice." The movie tie-in figures they had stressed over so, were getting totally lost in the Hannah hype and Farrell's last Christmas's star toy was practically forgotten. Everyone knew that Bob Farrell had decided long ago that the VP job was his. He had been with the company longer and he was older and more experienced. Joy was definitely in his pocket. But now, with Livy on the march, *his* promotion was very much in doubt. Things couldn't fall apart for Livy now or could they? She was becoming a bit of a celebrity herself, along with her doll, and she knew that one extra-nosy reporter could cause her a world of hurt. What would happen if they discovered the real reason she came to JTC and everything else she had carefully tried to hide?

Having found the epitome of the "heartland of America" in Black Rock, Tennessee, JTC was ready for the big announcement extravaganza. The press, the cameras, the spectators on hand, and all of the country by TV, swarmed around the *Wendy's* restaurant in the tiny Tennessee town. *Wendy's*, well known for their child friendly atmosphere and advocacy for kids, was a natural fit.

Today, the winner would be chosen and Hannah's face would be revealed. Livy was not the only one with nerves on edge. The families of the finalists were undoubtedly glued to the proceedings with fingernails poised, ready to be chewed. The Hannah event staff was on pins and needles as they readied the voting machines, went over the latest rewrites of the script with the announcer, checked mikes and cameras and tried to please the celebrity judges, some of whom demanded royal treatment at inopportune times. The company bigwigs, headquartered in a tent out in the parking lot, seemed to be the most frantic of all. One would've thought that the future of JTC itself was on the line. Just possibly it was.

Livy was outside in the tent, nervously doing laps around the small enclosure.

"Calm down, Livy. You're pacing like a cat with one paw nailed to the floor. It's going well. Just relax," Mel advised. "This is just what you wanted. It's all going according to plan."

If you only knew my plan, she thought. "Well, so far so good. The response has been unbelievable, don't you think?" Livy said.

Joy put in, "We should have taken more time. Everything's so rushed. Is it going to make it to market in time for the big push? What happens if the entire country is ordering dolls and it turns out that we can't make them or that they won't be ready by Christmas? That could ruin us."

"Oh Joy! The engineers assure me that Hannah will be right on schedule. The prototypes are just about there. Why are you always looking for a reason to panic?" Mel asked.

"Because this is my company and I have the most at stake. I think if it all went up in smoke tomorrow, you might not even care."

"Of course I care! I just don't stress out in front of everyone like you do. The captain of the ship has to keep his cool or everyone else will assume the worst and head for the lifeboats. You should try being a little more upbeat if you want this company to succeed, and most importantly right now, this project to succeed."

Interrupting their conversation, Livy announced, "We're live in five so all eyes on the monitor."

An overhead helicopter shot circled around the *Wendy's* and the exuberant crowd that had gathered outside. As the shot zoomed in on the multitude, they were given the cue to release the thousands of JTC balloons they had been given as their part in the festivities. The announcer stood at the door, poised and smiling, ready to lead the viewer inside to where an enthusiastic live audience waited for the fun to begin.

Mike in hand, the announcer began, "Good evening Ladies and Gentlemen and children across the U.S. and Canada! I'm your host, Randy Carlson, and we are gathered here at the Wendy's in Black Rock, Tennessee to select the winner of the Joy's Toys *Your Baby is a Doll Contest!* We have our distinguished panel of judges assembled here and some of these people you will recognize, I'm sure. You remember *Joey* from *Palmer Family Chronicles*, also known as Parker Hemingway."

Parker stood and waved enthusiastically to the crowd and some girls did as they were instructed and let out an appropriate swooning scream.

"Next, we have Jessica White who is starring in the upcoming summer blockbuster, *Peter Powerful and the Forces of Oberon,* due to be released on Memorial Day weekend. And by the way, we at Joy's Toys have an action figure of Jessica that all of you will want to get 'hot' off the assembly line, if you know what I mean. She's almost as gorgeous as the real thing!"

Randy took her hand and she stood and waved to thunderous applause. He went on to announce the other celebrity judges: Jerry Stradling, a producer of many family-friendly hits, and Dan and April Mendez, a chart-climbing brother and sister singing duo. "These judges," Randy went on, motioning to three more seated at the long baby-bunting draped table, "are representing JTC and their affiliates. They are: Bob Farrell, Joyce Barker and Joel Cartwright. They aren't famous, but give them a hand anyway, won't you? This is a tough job picking America's most appealing baby face."

The excited crowd obliged and gave them a healthy round of applause.

"We have had these and a panel of 100 expert judges, from photographers, to modeling agents, to stay-at-home moms, to help us pick the adorable ten finalists you see before you. Thank you to all of the folks out there who sent us the pictures of your charming and endearing children. The response was overwhelming and we wish we could make a doll with the face of every one because they truly are beautiful. We have one more judge as well, and that is you, out there. You can vote online at JTCbabycontest.com/winner or text message us at 800-555-5432. You can only vote for 30 minutes after the lines open up, so if you are unable to get through, please keep trying."

"Will our winner be baby A?"

And on down the line of finalists he went until the camera had focused on each one and the variation on the phone number or web address that would register a vote for that child.

"And there you have them, the cutest little girls and only one can be our Hannah. We will be selecting our boy winner in a matter of a few months so be sure to watch for that. All right, North America, the lines are open NOW! Make your choice! We will be back here in 60 minutes to announce the winner. Don't miss it! Right now, let's take a sneak peak at just how wonderful Hannah will be and why we wanted to find just the right face for her... and soon, for him." Then a commercial for *Hold-Me-Hannah* using a computer-generated face was broadcast expounding on all her glories.

****

Somewhere back in New York, an expert hacker was insuring that the results came out exactly as planned. Baby F must win the day. Carlos would have his way.

****

Outside in the tent, Livy and the rest of the executives present exhaled... so far, so good. Still pacing, Livy asked Mel, "It's going well, don't you think? The celebrities worked out well, I believe. They probably brought us more viewers and more interest."

"It will be fascinating to see what our TV market share was for that five-minute slot." Mel wondered aloud. "Can you really believe that millions of people out there actually care what our doll looks like? It's amazing what a little hype can do."

"I just can't help thinking about all that you have risked with this undertaking. My father built this company starting with next to nothing and gave his whole life to it. I'd hate to see it all crash and burn if this doesn't work," Joy moaned.

Livy tried to assure her with, "We're going to only add on to the foundation he built, Joy. This is going to be something he would be very proud of if he were here. Don't you think he would want to be the company out there taking leaps like this and pushing the industry forward?"

"Maybe you're right. But he was always very careful, very sure that everything that went out there with *my* name on it was a good product."

"And this is good stuff, my dear." Mel put his arm around his wife. "It's true that he built this company as a monument to you, his only daughter, and he wanted it to be something that would last for generations. I'm sure, though, he wouldn't want us to just play it safe and stick with mediocrity."

"I know you wish we had a next generation to pass it on to. I failed you in that regard, didn't I? You always wanted children and we couldn't have any. I'm sorry, Mel, that I couldn't give you someone to build your monument to. So, this company is our baby; that's how I think of it. That's why I'm so protective of it. Sorry if I'm a downer."

This was getting much too personal for Livy's ears and she suspected that Joy had had a couple of drinks to settle her nerves and that she would be sorry later for her candor.

Livy was about to exit the tent for some air when Joy called after her. "That's why I'm nervous, Olivia. That's why I give you such a hard time about this venture. This is my baby; it's all I have—the company, and this man that my father handpicked to run it and to take care of me. Only the best would do for Joy. Only the Harvard MBA with the proper pedigree would pass the test...and oh yes, his family's money to shore up the bottom line." She turned to Mel. "Tell me, was I a credit or debit on your balance sheet? Was I a liability or a company perk?"

She looked like at any moment she might erupt into tears. Livy had never seen this side of Joy before. This was a woman who never let down her guard. Mel looked embarrassed and confused.

Kyle, who was there watching the numbers roll in on the computer, hadn't seen Joy this way either. Sensing the tension, he put on his bunny ears, grabbed a festive Easter Basket and began passing out goodies.

"I sort of went overboard with the kids' Easter candy this year so I'm thinking we could all do with a little chocolate overdose. What d'ya say? I have bunnies and chicks and these peanut egg things...."

Livy tried to lighten the mood as well. "It's almost May and Easter was a couple of weeks ago, Kyle. You're slipping. I am definitely due for some chocolate. It's been at least an hour." She caught Mel's eye and gave him a look that asked, "What's with her?"

He seemed bewildered too. They had enough to worry about without Joy having a meltdown...especially since inside, Livy was having one of her own.

****

When an hour had nearly passed, Kyle totaled up the numbers, double checked with the others at their stations, and put the results in an envelope. He was about to seal it when Joy asked, "Well, aren't you going to let us see the tabulations? We want to be the first to know who America's Sweetheart is, right everyone?" Her words were appropriate but her tone was cheerless. Livy couldn't help thinking that Joy didn't need chocolate; she needed some strong black coffee. Livy could use some herself. Kyle handed over the envelope.

Joy peeked inside and said, "Fine, now I know." She closed up the envelope and gave it back to Kyle to take into the restaurant for the announcement segment. She motioned for him to get going.

"Well?" Livy asked. "Who is it?" She had to know. Everything she'd worked for was riding on this little girl. Everything she'd pinned her hopes on was on the line.

"You'll find out with everyone else."

Once again Joy had to be in charge. She had to prove she was one up on everybody.

The music cue brought up loud strains of *"I Found a Million Dollar Baby in a Five and Ten Cent Store."*

The camera once again zoomed into the restaurant and then to Randy Carlson who began in singsong, "We're ba-ack. Hello again. I'm your host, Randy Carlson and we're here at Wendy's and just about to find out the results we've all been waiting for. Who is that lucky child whose face will become part of the fabric of American childhood? Who is that fortunate family who will enjoy the $50,000 prize and the cruise? They haven't given me the envelope yet; so let's do a little exit polling, shall we? Let's ask April and Dan who their favorites were and why. April, how did you vote?"

April explained that she had voted for Baby F. She knew she'd be in trouble at home because her niece looked just like Baby A but she just had to go with that darling Baby F. "She makes me just want to pick her up and squeeze her!"

Dan, April's singing brother, also had the dilemma about the niece and went the other way and voted for Baby A. After polling a couple more celebrities, Randy received the envelope from a staffer who was visibly trying to position himself to be seen on camera.

Before he made the announcement the camera took one more sweeping pan of the giant photos hanging in front. "Which one is our winning girl? Don't forget, in a matter of a couple of months we will choose our boy as well! Drum roll, please." He opened the envelope and announced, "Well April, a lot of people must have felt like you did, that she just needs to be picked up and loved. Our winner is... Baby F!"

The audience clapped and cheered the winner with some few moans of disappointment. He took the paper that had just been handed him and quickly announced the names of all the finalists who would win cruises and dolls.

"Now let's find out who this little winning stranger is and who her parents are." The staffer again appeared with another envelope and then whispered something in Randy's ear. He looked confused as he again lifted the mike to his lips. "Now this is a shocker. As for our little Hannah...we don't know who she is. I have just been informed that her entry blank specifically stated that she was to remain anonymous and that if she won, her prize money would go to charity. Now this is a surprise for everyone at JTC, I think. They seem to be at a loss as to what to say about this...Oh, maybe not. Here comes the CEO of Joy's Toys. I'll let him take it from here."

Melvin bounded onto the stage with an energy that seemed to belong to someone half his age. He was actually excited about this turn of events.

"Hello everyone. My name is Melvin Jameson and I am CEO of Joy's Toys. As you know, we kept the applications blind until this very moment and we are just as surprised as you are to learn of *Hannah's*, for lack of a real name, ...to learn of her family's wishes to remain out of the spotlight. I think it is a fabulous opportunity for Joy's Toys to be able to give back something in return for all that we have been given. I'm announcing right now that we will double the prize money that would have gone to the winner and we will give that to worthy children's charities."

The press in the front row looked dubious.

One reporter shouted out, "Are we to believe that this was not planned all along? It so conveniently adds to the suspense and mystique of the product. How could you not know that this entry was anonymous?"

"We kept all the personal information in separate files from the pictures. Only a number identified them until the computer spit out the personal information just minutes ago. We learned about it at the same time, almost, that you did. We had planned to go to the family home with Randy here, balloons and the giant check and the whole nine yards. But I do think that it is a wonderful thing that Hannah can share her winnings with other children."

"What charities will you be donating to?" The reporter persisted.

"We just learned about this so that decision has not been made at this time. We'll do a press release later and let you know. For now, I'd just like to say, Congratulations to all the finalists! You are all winners and you are all beautiful. We will be contacting you, the families of the finalists, very soon so you can claim your prizes. Enjoy your cruises! And all of you out there will love that little Hannah...whoever she is. Thanks again for being here. Good evening to you all."

Mel waved at the audience and to the camera. Then he turned and silently addressed the giant photo of the winner projected behind him. "Who are you, little one? You have just the expression we all wanted. –The longing for love, the anticipation of receiving it. It's all there in that little face. Well, sweetheart, here we go on a wild adventure together. I hope you are ready for the ride!"

Livy was making her way over to the tent. *Are they going to buy this? Will they think we set this up as a stunt? I thought I'd feel better when we got this far but—*

****

Carlos pressed the speed dial button on his phone. "Can you talk...then just listen. Great job! Now that wasn't so hard, was it? You just stay on course and we'll have no trouble. No...obviously nobody suspects anything...keep it that way! I'll be in touch."

CHAPTER 13

Linda's Story Part 3

Linda's next placement was in the home of Bill and Arlene Harris. When Mrs. Clancy drove up to the house, Linda was somewhat encouraged. It was a nice sized blue house with an attractive porch and it was clean and neat. Walking up the path to the front door, Linda was greeted by a yellow-striped cat staring at her from inside the living room window.

"Hello, kittycat," she said aloud. It might be fun to have a pet, Linda thought.

Mrs. Clancy rang the doorbell and gave Linda last minute instructions. "Okay, sweetheart. Stand up straight and tall and shake hands with Mr. Harris. Show him what a bright and good girl you are." They both were holding their breath.

Arlene Harris answered the door with an inviting smile. She bent down to Linda's eye level and in her charming Carolina drawl said, "Come in! This must be our little Linda. I'm Arlene."

She was a petite, attractive woman with friendly eyes and Linda felt things might work out here after all.

Mr. Harris stayed on the couch as Mrs. Harris led Linda to him by guiding her gently from the shoulders. "Linda, this is Bill. We've been looking forward to having Linda come to stay with us, haven't we Bill?"

Linda offered her hand to him as Mrs. Clancy had instructed.

He shook her hand while his eyes sized her up. He grunted a some-what forced hello. Instinctively, Linda backed towards Mrs. Clancy.

"Bill!" Arlene noticed his less than enthusiastic greeting as well. She let out a nervous laugh. "Don't mind him, Linda. He's just tired because I made him clean out the garage before you came." She turned and called up the stairs, "Jody! Billy! Come and meet our guest. Linda's here."

As if on cue, Jody and Billy marched down the stairs and into the room, dressed in their Sunday best. Billy, 14, looked like he was uncomfortable with the "show" and just wanted to be out playing somewhere in his cutoff jeans. Jody, on the other hand, fairly pranced around showing off her fancy dress.

Linda looked down at her own simple plaid jumper and white blouse that had been her recent school's uniform.

Jody looked down at it too and said, "I'm Jody and we're the same age. Will she be in my class, Mama? Oh, I forgot; I skipped a grade."

She was letting Linda know just how superior she felt.

"Let's ask if we can get you into Mrs. Bartlett's class ...Jody's teacher last year, she's fabulous... when we register you tomorrow, all right, Linda? She'll be sure to give you any extra help you may need," Arlene assured her while taking her Minnie Mouse bag from her and the small plastic bag of belongings from Mrs. Clancy. She handed them to Jody. "Why don't you take Linda upstairs and show her where to put her things."

Mrs. Clancy went over the paperwork with Mr. and Mrs. Harris and pleaded with them to give Linda a chance. "She's had some disappointments so we hope that this will be a good long-term arrangement for her. That is what you have in mind?"

"Yes, of course. She seems like a very nice little girl." Arlene said.

"Give her and your children some time to adjust and she'll be fine. I think she would really like to have sibling...well...you know...like a brother/sister relationship. It could mean so much to her." Stephanie Clancy studied their faces. She was getting very good at reading people.

"But this is not leading to an adoption, you understand... just a temporary home, right?" He turned to his wife but continued to speak to the caseworker. "We are not interested in that kind of long term," Bill stated firmly, his eyes returning to Mrs. Clancy.

As Mrs. Clancy walked to her car, she felt that familiar ache in the pit of her stomach... so many children, so many cases and yet so few happy endings. She could see it plainly; the Mrs. was idealistic and looking to feel good about herself; he was looking for a check. And for some reason, Jody was looking for trouble; Mrs. Clancy could feel it.

It was always easy for Linda to make friends at the St. Anthony's home. There were kids of every color and age and each had a different story to tell as to how they came to be part of the St. Anthony family. Linda's story was that she didn't know her story. Sister Marian had said that Linda could make up her own. Maybe she was a princess or a magic fairy, who knew? At the new school, when Jody announced that she had a foster sister, everyone had questions and Linda didn't think they would like her fairy-tale answers. They wanted to make up the story and the ones they created weren't nice.

One third-grade boy, Joey, mocked, "I know where you are from— another planet."

Anika, a former friend and now enemy of Jody's, put her hands on her hips and said, "Maybe your daddy took one look at you and threw you in the garbage can. So then, they heard you crying and had to find you someone to live with. Too bad it had to be with Jody." Anika laughed and laughed and others joined in.

Jody told them to be quiet and to leave Linda alone. Jody liked assuming the role of the older or at least wiser one. She was the 'big sister' for a change and not just the little sister who was picked on by the big brother. She was in charge.

Jody showed Linda the ropes at school and at home. She showed her how to do her chores, where things went and unfortunately, she also showed her things she should be sure to do that Jody knew would get her in trouble with Bill and Arlene. She showed her things to get into that were forbidden, such as how to eat the ice cream that Jody knew was specifically saved for the Ladies luncheon Arlene was in charge of, or how to find where Bill kept his wallet and to "borrow" a few dollars. He wouldn't miss one or two and she said that he had told Jody it was all right to have a little allowance.

When a 20 bill was missing on one occasion, Jody had of course helped herself to a 'little extra allowance' but assured her parents that it was Linda. "That's what you get when you let someone in your house who hasn't been taught not to steal," she counseled them.

The worst thing Jody taught her was to regularly let the cat out to get "some exercise." This time, when Linda let the cat out, disaster struck, as Jody knew it eventually would.

When Linda came down the stairs that morning on her way to get her coat for school, the cat sat waiting by the front door, waiting to go out, she assumed. She obliged. When she and Jody returned that afternoon, the mangled cat lay dead on the porch.

"Oh no! What happened? The poor kitty!" Linda cried and turned her eyes away.

"I told you never to let the cat out! You did it, didn't you?" Jody pushed the door open. "Mom! Linda let the cat out again and now he's dead! Mom, come see."

Her voice was frantic but her face suppressed a grin.

The neighbor down the street had shot it, just as he had vowed to do if it ever trespassed on his property. Now he had deposited the remains as verification of making good on his promise. Jody had always hated the cat and the trashy violent neighbor as well; this was her way of making trouble for both.

It was big trouble for Linda, as well.

Arlene came running and dissolved into a puddle of grief when she saw the cat.

"Tiger baby!" She lifted the lifeless head and let out a wail as she turned to Linda. "That Delbert McCoy's gone and killed my cat! What have you done? This was my baby!" She grabbed her by the arm and shoved her toward the stairs. "You go to your room! I can't even look at you right now!"

"But... Jody said..." Linda stammered, trying to hold her ground.

Jody jumped in. "I told her, Mama. Never let Tiger out. I told her lots of times."

"No, you said to let him out to exercise," Linda protested.

"Jody, is that true? I know you don't like..." Arlene began.

"See, I told you Mama. She lies. She lied about the ice cream and the money and now this. I've tried to be nice to her but she just keeps doing stuff...like this. It's 'cuz she never had a mama to teach her any better." Jody caressed her mother's arm and half whispered in her ear, "She even runs around naked in front of Billy after her shower!"

Linda heard and shouted back, "You did that, not me! And it's not my fault I never had a mama!" She glanced pointedly at Arlene for a moment and then turned back to Jody. "And if I did, my mama would never teach me to be a mean liar like you!"

Arlene raised her hand preparing to slap Linda's face but stopped herself.

"Go ahead and hit me. Everyone else does!" In tears, Linda ran up the stairs and slammed the bedroom door.

Later, when Linda's sobs quieted and she sat in silent lonely tears, she overheard Arlene filling Bill in on the events of the afternoon.

"I tried to warn you, Arlene," Bill said with an I-told-you-so air. "You just never know what you're getting into when you take these kids in. I don't know why you wanted to mess with her in the first place. That measly check is not worth the tension she's brought into our family."

"I know honey, but I was just trying to be kind to someone in need. This is the thanks I get. My poor Tiger, dead."

A moment later she heard Bill asking for Mrs. Clancy on the phone.

"Yes, Mrs. Clancy, I know I said we would try to give her a long-term place, but it's just not working out. She's disrespectful and she won't try to get along with my daughter and it's damaging our family. My wife has bent over backwards for that child and she pays us back with lying and stealing. You must find another place for her, right away. I understand your concern for the kid, but just talk to my wife."

The conversation was muffled for a moment and then she heard Arlene tearfully say, "No, we have thought about it. We have been living with this chaos for about six weeks now. I tried to be openhearted and treat her like one of the family, but it's just not going to work any longer. Do you know that today she was responsible for the death of my sweet cat? When can you pick her up?"

Linda didn't know whether to be relieved or sad at this point. She definitely did not want to stay but she felt so lost, so afraid of what might happen next. She began to pack her bag and cried aloud, "Oh Sister M! I want Sister M!" Her tears spilled onto Minnie Mouse.

Outside the door, Jody mocked in high-pitched Wicked Witch of Oz style, "Sister M! Sister M!" She broke out in giggles.

Within the hour, Mrs. Clancy arrived to take Linda away. She tried to take Linda's hand as they walked to the car but the child shook it away.

"I didn't do anything! I didn't do anything!" She turned and faced the house. "I HATE YOU! I HATE YOU ALL!"

"Do you want to talk about it?" the caseworker asked gently as she helped Linda into the backseat.

"No!"

Another door was slammed.

****

While driving in the uncomfortable silence, Mrs. Clancy was formulating plans to get another job. This one was just too painful. How she wanted to go home, hug her own children tightly and block out all this misery. *I can't be part of this anymore.*

There were few homes available and the wait for another home turned into months and months in a group home that felt like children's prison. It was not at all like the home where Linda had been with Sister Marian. The hard-core girls organized teams, which were more like gangs, and preyed on the younger girls to serve them (do their work details) and to give them part of their food as protection payment. Most of them had learned to swear like longshoremen and could be very intimidating. If they caught a little one crying they taught her how to be tough by unrelenting, brutal name-calling. The older predators had learned to use the proverbial phrase, "We'll give ya' something to bawl about, you baby!" If the desired toughness had not been achieved in one or two sessions of verbal whippings, then the abuse became physical. Linda only let herself cry when she was trying to go to sleep at night, when it was dark and the scary girls were in another room. She held onto her little cross and to her mother's picture, but it was Sister Marian she cried for... and for Jesus. Sister Marian told her to call on Jesus to watch over her and she knew she needed Him now. If only they could find her Daddy. Somewhere she had to have a Daddy.

By the time Linda was ten, she had had four more family placements, five more schools and two long stints at two different group interim homes. Both of them had lasted over Christmas Holidays. There she had experienced two incidents of sexual abuse, and some physical abuse as well. She had stopped trying to make friends and didn't care about her school performance although her tests all showed her to have higher than average intelligence. She had just about given up on having a home where she really belonged.

By age 12, Linda no longer cried herself to sleep at night. Some girls had stolen her Minnie Mouse bag, written profanities all over it and left it in a toilet. She was too old for that now anyway. She now moved her few personal belongings in a pillowcase. She still carried her photo and cross with her whenever she was moved but they had lost some of their meaning. Instead of feeling good that there must have been someone out there, who at least at one time, loved her, Linda was beginning to feel anger and resentment at her mother for abandoning her. While it was true that she may very well be dead, even that made her furious.

Why would my mother have to die? Other kids have real moms who keep them and love them, no matter what they do. With these fake moms, the least little thing happens and they throw me back into the loser's den.

If the scenario was that her mother hadn't died, but had abandoned her as a baby, then her feelings were even more intense.

Why couldn't you love me, mother? I was only a baby, your baby. Everybody loves babies, don't they? Why can't anyone love me? White families don't want me and brown and black families don't either because I'm somewhere in between.

When she held her cross with the daisy, she got angry with Jesus and Sister M., too. Sister M. had told her that the daisy in the center seemed to represent how new life, fresh and beautiful, can spring forth miraculously out of suffering and pain and even death. Linda was ready for that new life to begin, a new kind of life for her. When would Jesus realize that she was in pain and waiting for that new and better life?

CHAPTER 14

The spring blossomed and the summer sweltered and Livy barely noticed. She was always flying here and there around the country and the world at large signing contracts with manufacturers and distributors and was busy with her team working on marketing campaigns.

Bryan was always there at the door to greet Livy and help her keep her head about her. After the *Japanese Hannah* deal was negotiated, she and Bryan finally went to *Ruth's Chris Steak House* for their celebration steak dinner.

"Wow!" Bryan said as he pulled Livy's chair out for her, glancing around the establishment. The atmosphere was elegant and the smell was heavenly. "This has to be the nicest restaurant I've ever been to. That steak smells so good!"

Livy laughed as Bryan moved to the other side of the table. "It's no one you know, I'm sure..." She saw that Bryan looked around, baffled. "I mean the cow...the steak...it's no one you know."

"Good!"

The waiter appeared and brought water. "I'm Travis, your server today, and could I bring you something to drink this evening? Would you like a moment to look at the wine list?"

"Give us a minute, okay?" Livy answered him. "Hey, Bryan, you're always trying to get me to be a kid again. How about I help you act like a grownup?"

"What do you mean? Aren't I acting like a grownup? Did I wear something stupid again? Am I undone?" Bryan asked, checking his fly.

"No silly boy. We're celebrating, right? How about I get you some wine and for once in your life...get you nice and drunk?"

"You're kidding, right? You know I don't drink."

"I know but it's time to be a man, Bryan."

"And to be a real man I have to get drunk? Is that what you look for in a guy?"

"Just try some. They have a good selection here. I'm not trying to corrupt you for life or anything. Let's just celebrate with some champagne."

"You go ahead. I'll toast with my water glass."

"Well, I'm not spending big bucks on champagne just for me."

"I'm not all that smart and I'm a total klutz without alcohol; with it I'd be in real trouble!"

"Why do you always say things like that?" Livy asked.

"Like what?"

"Oh I don't know. You always try to make it sound like you were the dumb kid; the poor kid who didn't catch on, the one who never got picked for the teams or anything. Just looking at you, I know that isn't true. Don't get all full of yourself when I say this, but you are very good looking and you seem confident and you're not a klutz, so why do you act like you were?"

"Some of us just take a little more time to 'come into our own', so to speak. I *was* really like that. The kids made fun of me all the time. Once, after gym, the other boys 'pantsed' me and ran my underwear up the flag pole while I stood naked, crying at the bottom trying to pull it back down."

Livy could relate more than he knew. "That must have been awful. I just can't imagine it happening to *you*."

"But the kids in our family always stuck up for me. They were my team and didn't let anyone mess with me... not if they could help it. Have I told you about my big brother David? He was my hero, just like David in the Bible. He'd stand up to any old giant for me."

"It must have been great to have that kind of support system," Livy sighed.

"The only exception was Becky, my foster sister."

"Why? What did Becky do?"

"She's the gorgeous one who got herself in some boy-trouble and got thrown out of her house. So I kind of took it upon myself to keep other boys away from her. She didn't like that too much. She called me every name in the book and loved to embarrass me in front of the other kids. It hurt a lot sometimes. I just thought I was just trying to help. She mellowed over time, though. I guess she was hurting too."

"I thought all the Kimball kids were perfect like you."

Bryan rolled his eyes. "Not exactly. We have all kinds of kids with all kinds of things to work out. So we're about as human as you can get." A mischievous smile crossed Bryan's face. "Did I ever tell you about the doorbell?"

"What doorbell?"

"Clayt—he's the practical joker in the family, always in trouble before he came to us—well, he and I were down in Grandpa's basement and we were digging around and found the wires to the doorbell. Clayt discovered that if he stuck a pin in the wire, it would make the bell ring. He could hear Grandpa get up out of his chair and head for the door to find no one there.

"So Grandpa's yelling, 'Darn fool kids!' He was so mad to think some-one had doorbell-ditched him.

"So Clayt kept it up. As soon as we heard the chair squeak and figured he was comfortable, we'd ring it again, and again and again. Pretty soon he was out the front door and out on the front lawn, yelling and screaming and swearing. "You little sons of...&*%$(#! I'll catch you little $%&* and I'll tell your parents and %&*^*$#^! I never ever heard him swear before or since. I have to admit, it was hysterical. Then he'd come back and find some kid had taken over his chair and he'd yell at 'em and chase 'em off. Just when we figured he was comfortable, we'd ring it again. He'd get up again and out the door he'd go, waving his cane into the bushes and screaming. The neighbors thought he was having a stroke or something. Then he'd come back to find some other poor kid in his recliner who did-n't hear the first one get bawled out. Probably nearly did have a stroke! Then finally, Jackson told on us and we got in big trouble." Bryan was laughing at the memory and Livy was too as she imagined the poor elderly gentleman out there shaking his cane and swearing into thin air. "Yeah, we're about as human as any other family, probably more so."

"Human, but fun. How does your mother keep her sanity with all of you?"

"She is amazing. She's gotten very good at keeping us all very busy.

There's always work to do with a farm and with that many kids, folding laundry alone can keep you occupied for hours."

"I can imagine. Does she ever get some time to herself?"

"Now that the twins, the youngest, are in school, she has a little more time. But even her spare time she spends on us. She loves scrapbooking. Looking at those, you'd think every one of us kids was someone really special and important."

"So that's kind of what you are doing for those kids in the projects... keeping a record, a little story of each of their lives." Livy was sadly quiet for a moment. She remembered what Garrett had said about there being no one to witness how "wonderful" she was. She tried to imagine someone, anyone, having pictures of her in his or her scrapbook. She was sure no one would.

"Livy? Livy?" Bryan asked for the second or third time. She finally looked at him. He continued, "I'm sorry. Did I say something wrong?"

"No, it's just that.... never mind. It's okay." She played with the napkin in her lap.

"Are you thinking about your family? Are you ever going to open up and tell me what happened with them?" Bryan asked gently.

Livy swallowed and began, slowly, "I had a family...thought I did, anyway. But I screwed up. I screwed up so badly that they didn't ever want to hear from me again. I tried lots of times... but they made themselves pretty clear."

"Do you want to talk about it?" Bryan asked and Livy shook her head. "And here I am. I just keep going on and on about my family. I'm sorry. My family is just my whole lifeline, my frame of reference. Do you want me to stop mentioning them?"

"No. Don't stop. I love hearing about them and even imagining that I'm one of you... that you're really my brother. I want to meet them someday, I really do."

"Someday you will. I'll make sure of it."

The server returned and Livy ordered huge Porter House steaks for both of them but didn't order any wine or champagne.

It was a good thing, too, as she had had to fly to Houston the next morning and she got sick enough on flights without having a hangover.

What would she do without Bryan? Probably have a good time. Sometimes he was more father than brother, watching over her like a mother hen, giving her advice and at times making her feel guilty about silly little things, like the $400 shoes.

He was constantly bugging her, saying things like, "Do you actually have that promotion yet?" No, she didn't. "Did you get that bonus yet?" No she hadn't. "So stop spending money you don't have."

She didn't mind actually. He kept her grounded in reality and it was great to have someone outside the office to share this triumph with, even if cautiously.

Early in July, on the way into the apartment building, she let it slip that she was finally going to have some time to herself and Bryan seized the opportunity. He sat her down on the apartment entrance stairs.

"Hey, then you can come over to the neighborhood with me! Josie has been asking for you."

"It's not safe over there, Bryan… especially for you."

"That's why I need you, Wonder Woman."

"No, seriously, you've got enough to write about by now and you should tell them it was great but now you gotta get out of there."

"I'm not worried. It's like they don't even see me. Nobody bothers me and things have calmed way down. Just come and see Josie and Frankie. It would mean a lot to them. Come on Livy."

"How's Jimmy doing after what happened?"

"He's okay I think. He talks about Aaron but not really about what happened to him. He says things like, *'If I grow up,* I'm gonna travel. Aaron wanted to travel.' or *'If I grow up,* I'm gonna buy me and Mama a house and get outta this place. Aaron shoulda got outta here'… stuff like that and it's pretty sad. He seems ready to accept the possibility that he might not get to grow up. But then, he never really got to be a kid and neither did Aaron."

Livy didn't want to think about that fateful day. She hadn't been able to get Josie out of her mind, nor the rest of them either, for that matter. And that was the problem. She didn't want to care. She didn't want to get in over her head.

"Look, I'm not a bleeding heart do-gooder like you, Bryan. I'm a businesswoman who is very busy right now, in case you haven't noticed."

"Uh huh, and guess what? Children *are* your business; have *you* noticed? And you need a life outside the office."

"And you're in charge of that? So who made you my fairy godmother and social chairman?"

"Speaking of which, have you called Garrett?"

"Not that it's any of your concern, but no, I haven't. Why do you keep bugging me about it?" Feeling a bit perturbed, she was getting up to go inside. "And, by the way, he hasn't called me either."

He grabbed her hand. "I'm sorry, but you were the one who felt terrible because you thought you offended him and then you don't call to apologize or tell him you hope he and his kids are doing well...nothing. You're the one that has to call and open the door. I know you care, so...?"

Changing the subject, Bryan suggested, "Why don't we do something with the kids for the 4th of July?"

"Okay, I'll bite. What do you do in Blackfoot on the 4th of July?"

"We race snowmobiles into the lake at Jensen Grove."

She looked at him like he was crazy. "I'm not even going to ask. But I know!

Hey! Why don't I take you and the kids to that new movie, that *Peter Powerful* thing? We have lots of passes at work and maybe then you'll stop badgering me. We could go pick up the kids and get them out of the neighborhood for a while. The flick is supposed to be pretty good for all ages. Happy now?"

"Ecstatic! I'll arrange it!"

****

The next afternoon, Josie was ecstatic too when she looked out the window to see Livy and Bryan approaching on the courtyard between buildings. She had been anxiously watching for about half an hour.

"Livy! Livy!" She called and waved from the window and then scrambled down the stairs along with Frankie. She raced straight to Livy's legs and embraced them because Livy's arms were full. "I missed you so much," she squealed.

Livy put down her shopping bags and hugged her. "I missed you too, baby. Look what I brought for you!"

Frankie looked at her suspiciously.

"It's all right, Frankie," Bryan said as he set off to round up the other boys.

"Yeah," Livy said. "It's just some apples and oranges, some veggies and some books and things from the warehouse at my work. They're promo gifts. It's just free stuff. You don't *owe* me anything, okay? Let's go upstairs and put this food away in your fridge."

She gathered the bags again and started toward their building.

Frankie stopped her. "I got it. You can't come up; my mama's busy."

"I'd like to meet your mama," Livy suggested.

"I tol' y'all, she busy," he said, gathering up the bags from her and walking toward the building.

"Wait, Frankie."

Livy caught up with him, reached inside one of the large bags and pulled out a smaller one and then let him take the rest. He gave her a wary look and then headed for the stairs. She turned to Josie and gave her the bag to open.

A beautiful grin lit up Josie's face as she peeked and then reached inside. She held the little pink-flowered up against her body in obvious delight. Then her smile faded away, replaced by a furrowed brow.

"Let's go try it on you," Livy said but Josie just clenched her jacket tighter. "Honey, it's too hot to wear that hoodie today. It's going to be 95 degrees out here."

"I can't take it off; Mommy said."

"Why, sweetheart?"

"She say if I take it off, she don't be my mama no more."

Just then, Bryan arrived with the boys and they set off for the nearest theatre complex. Jimmy declined the invitation on the grounds that it was for little kids; he was beyond that now.

Josie spent a good portion of the movie in Livy's lap, hiding her eyes when huge fantasy monsters appeared. Soon she found she liked the safe and comforting feeling of Livy's lap and Livy's arms, with or without monsters. Livy liked having her there too, just as she was afraid she would.

CHAPTER 15

At last the time for *Hannah's* debut had come. It was mid-August, and a bit early to push the Holiday buying season, but Livy and her marketing team had decided that they couldn't leave Hannah off the public stage for too long or the momentum that they had built for her would evaporate. They had used the *Wall Drug* technique. There is an Old-West style drug-store somewhere in the Black Hills of South Dakota that alerts travelers for miles ahead about the virtues and the ever-increasing nearness of Wall Drug. "Only 55 miles to Wall Drug!" "Hang in there, only 27 miles to Wall Drug" "Don't turn off now, there's free ice water at Wall Drug!" etc. etc. By the time the traveler actually gets there, he absolutely must see what all the fuss was about.

The *Hannah* commercials had started slowly after the winning face was announced, and built and built, counting down the days to her unveiling. And just like with Wall Drug, it worked. *Hannah* was a big splash indeed! The night of *Hannah's* coming-out-party, as it were, JTC was to host a huge banquet and bash for Toy Retailer Executives from across the country. All the big-box bigwigs were to be there and all of them would have the chance to meet the brain behind the baby-doll.

Bryan wouldn't let up on Livy. Every day he had asked, "Have you called Garrett yet? This is the perfect excuse. You just need a date in a hurry for this gala and you thought of him. You wondered how he's doing, blah, blah, blah. It's a natural. Just do it!"

She resisted and made excuses why she couldn't or wouldn't call him. Finally, to get the big Idaho spud off her back, she made the call.

She heard Garrett answer and that feeling was back, the butterflies and thick-tongued impairment she always felt with him.

"Hi Garrett. Uh...I...Hi, how are you? It's Livy."

"Hi Livy! How are you doing? That's a dumb question, isn't it? You must be flying like a kite. We all knew you'd make it...you'd climb to the top, no matter what!"

"So you noticed, huh? You've seen our contest and everything?" She was flattered that he'd been paying attention.

"How could I miss it? It's everywhere. I knew you'd make a success of it!" "You're nice to say that after I was such a creep the last time we met. I'm sorry."

"You weren't a creep. It was my fault. I should have explained my situation."

She fiddled with the phone cord for a moment and then said, "I'm sorry I didn't call."

"I can imagine you've been really busy." He stammered a little. "I guess that's why I haven't called you. You're probably never home."

She gathered her nerve. "I've thought about you a lot...about some things you said. Are you all right? How are the kids handling things?"

"We're going to be fine. We just take it one day at a time." He paused a moment as if choosing his words carefully. "Livy, I've decided that it's time. For their sake and mine, it's time to move on and let someone into my life again. And I wanted to tell you... Oh, hold on a second."

In the background Livy could hear a female voice asking, "Garrett, honey, Stacey's fallen asleep in her clothes, do you think I should put her pajamas on?"

"Sure," he replied. "She'll be back to sleep in two minutes."

Livy felt an uncomfortable wave of disappointment sweep over her. Of course he would want to go on with his life. He obviously had. He found someone and she was there with him now. Naturally, he wouldn't wait for Livy to learn how to love, to like kids, and to trust. But he didn't know how far she had come on all of that with Bryan's help. But now she was too late.

"I'm sorry, Livy. What were we saying?"

"You were saying you're moving on. I'm glad for you. Shelly would want you to be happy. You deserve some real happiness."

"Was there something you wanted to tell me, some special reason why you called?" Garrett asked hopefully.

"I just wanted to...uh...see how you are and you're good.... so... well, I've got to get my other phone. I have to take this, sorry. I'll talk to you later, okay? Bye."

"Livy wait...I wanted..." Garrett heard the click. *Livy, don't run away from me again.*

What Livy didn't know was that the woman in the background was his mother-in-law, there to help out. Garrett wanted to see Livy again but felt the old familiar hesitation in her tone.

She glared at Bryan as she put down the phone. "Why did you make me do that? I feel like a fool. AGAIN! He's moved on. He's got some woman with him right now. You get me all worked up for nothing!" For punishment she commanded Bryan to go with her to the gala event despite his protestations.

****

Livy rented a tux for Bryan to wear as her escort but at the last minute, he couldn't come. Of course, he had to rush to be with another grief stricken child. She really had wanted him to see her in her element and to be there in her moment of triumph.

Livy dressed in her new red-sequined designer gown that couldn't have been more perfect if it had been designed especially for her. It was long and had a slit in the back, accentuating her long gorgeous legs and model-like height. Her hair was piled high with just the right wisps of curl around her face. The success she had dreamed of was here in her grasp and as she studied herself in the mirror she marveled. It was almost beyond her ability to take it in. She had made it. Despite the panic and the setbacks, and those who would tear her down, it was happening; it was real.

Please let this be real!

She entered the hotel ballroom with confidence and flair despite her inner butterflies. Mel was busy with Joy, schmoozing all the important guests and didn't have a lot of time to spend with Livy right away. After a while, he excused himself and sought her out at the champagne table.

"May I have this dance?" he asked.

"Certainly, sir. But I must tell you I don't dance very well. Remember, you've been warned." She let him lead her to the dance floor.

"You look beautiful tonight, Livy. Your success is very becoming and in that gown, well, let's just say all eyes are on you for lots of reasons."

She was thinking, *you look wonderfully elegant in your tuxedo too, Mel.* But she didn't dare say it. And the look of pride and approval of her in his eyes was the most beautiful and satisfying of all. Maybe she would be able to dance. She already felt like she was floating.

"Where is your date?" He asked after a few moments of the dance.

"At the last minute he couldn't make it. I'm really disappointed that he wasn't here to see this. He's a social worker and was called away."

"So, is this something serious that I should be aware of?" Mel inquired, one eyebrow raised.

"We're just friends, I guess, but really good friends."

She missed Bryan so much right now. She didn't see that he was standing in the back, partially hidden by a column. He had managed to break away to be here for her once in a lifetime moment. He observed the two of them dancing and could see just how much this evening meant to her; he'd never seen her this happy.

When the music stopped, Mel led her by the hand to the podium and turned on the mike.

"Ladies and gentlemen, could I have your attention please? For those of you who don't know me, I'm Melvin Jameson, President and CEO of JTC. My lovely wife Joy is our Chair and she makes me do all the dirty work... like speeches." He held his arm out indicating where she stood. "First of all I want to thank you for joining us on this wonderful occasion...we're celebrating the birth of a very remarkable little girl...our Hannah! We want to thank you all for your efforts in making this project such a fabulous success. We owe so much of that success to you and your partnership with us. I can see that we will all be richly rewarded. In fact, as of five o'clock this afternoon, *Hold-Me-Hannah* broke the record for first day sales, a record that held for about 17 years. We knew she was something special!"

The audience clapped and cheered and Mel held his arm up to continue.

"Right now, I'd like to introduce you to someone very special: the creator and visionary behind this project. She and her team have worked tirelessly to pull off this major coup. I'd like you to meet Ms. Olivia Thomas! Please give her a great big well-deserved round of applause." He held her hand up in a motion of victory and the crowd erupted in thunderous applause. "Olivia, would you like to say a few words?"

She wasn't expecting this and hadn't prepared a speech but she took the mike confidently. "Thank you for your kind ovation. It feels really good to know that you like what we've done here." The crowd started to cheer. "It feels even better that the buying public likes what we've done here." They cheered louder. "I'd like to thank Barbara, my assistant, and my whole team...they are the ones struggling to hold themselves up over there at the open bar. We've been under a little pressure lately as you can imagine. And of course, I thank Mr. Jameson for all his wonderful support from the beginning. *Hannah* would not have been possible without his sustaining and guiding hand. Thank you all for being part of this wonderful night and I hope you're having a great time."

She waved at the crowd and they clapped again. Many of them pushed through the throng to meet Livy and to personally congratulate her. Joy stood with Bob Farrell in the back of the hall during the speeches. They had clapped absently, unenthusiastically. Livy noticed but she didn't care. *They can't argue with millions of dollars, now can they?*

Finally, Mel led her to the side, away from the group. "What can I say, Livy? You have done it! You and your team have pulled this off and I can't express how pleased I am with you. This is your night and just to top it off," he looked around to make sure that no one heard his next words, "I'm going to do everything in my power to make sure that the VP job is yours. No one could be more deserving." He took her hand warmly and leaned in to give her a kiss on the cheek. "The board meets next week."

He left in search of Joy who had started dancing with the head of a new European toy distribution company. Livy watched Mel work the crowd as he crossed the room. He turned back one more time and gave her a nod. When he reached Joy, she glanced over and gave Livy a plastic, insincere smile. Livy mingled smoothly with the crowd and savored every delicious compliment.

Could it get any better? Who'd have ever thought that she, Livy, the lonely lanky loser would literally be Cinderella at the ball? (Complete with wicked-stepmother, Joy). She glanced up at the entrance expecting to see a clock striking twelve but instead saw Bryan crossing the hall and looking absolutely like the most beautiful man she had ever seen; he almost glowed. It must have been because she was so glad to see him. He was just the one she wanted here and was not merely second choice. It *had* gotten better. Bryan was here to share in her glory and by rights he should share in it. He had given her the idea. It was all she could do to keep herself from running to him. Looking like a lost lamb, he scanned the crowd trying to find her and appeared completely out of place. He looked gorgeous in his tuxedo but still, and it might have been the white socks, he had Idaho written all over him somehow. And that was just how she liked him.

She cut to the side of the room, sneaked up behind him and covered his eyes. "Guess who?"

"Lucille? Is that you?"

She playfully slugged him when after a second she remembered the dear homeless woman from Christmas day. "No, silly. It's me, Vice President Olivia Thomas," she whispered enthusiastically in his ear.

He pulled her aside and enveloped her in his arms. He swung her up into the air. "Wow! That's fantastic!" He took her hands and stepped back to admire the view. "Sheesh! You *do* clean up real good lookin'!"

Livy guided him excitedly to where the newly unveiled and celebrated dolls were royally displayed. The different variations of skin color, eye color and other distinctions made each one unique and yet they shared a common expression of hopeful anticipation and echoed back to the original winning Hannah face.

Indicating the one that was created first, the one most similar to the photograph, now widely recognized as *Hannah* herself, Bryan was astonished at how well they had achieved the likeness. "She's amazing, Liv... so remarkably like the picture."

"Of course. We do good work. She had to be perfect and I think, if I do say so myself, that she pretty much is. These are hooked up to the security system for this event so I can't let you play with her but she really is marvelous. Come and see this demo DVD." She loved watching Bryan's

114

face as he studied the video with fascination and delight. He was obviously impressed with his "sister."

"Mom and Dad will be so proud!"

"Oh Bryan, stop. They don't even know that I exist."

"They know and they love you already!"

She led him to the dance floor even though neither of them knew how to dance to the music the band was currently playing. They couldn't get much dancing done anyway because of all the throngs of people that had to stop to congratulate Livy on her achievement. They didn't seem to notice Bryan was even there as they gushed over her achievements. She glanced at Mel who was looking her way. She pointed at Bryan as if to say, "My date made it!" and Mr. Jameson gave her a thumbs up on him. He approved.

Finally, they headed over to the food table and Bryan was in his element now, or so he thought. He didn't drink and obviously didn't dance but he could eat with the best of them. He tried some Sushi and managed to gag it down while Livy laughed at the face he was making. He took one taste of caviar and thought he was going to lose it along with the sushi. He stealthily spit it into a napkin and dropped it at the base of a silk fichus tree.

"That stuff costs $200 an ounce? You gotta be kidding."

Livy surveyed the room and realized that she had met everyone she had wanted and needed (for business purposes) to meet and she just wanted to spend the rest of the evening with Bryan. She just wanted to fly, to laugh out loud and rejoice in her amazing triumph. What a fabulous, exhilarating feeling to have someone so dear to her there to witness how wonderful she really was... to share the most marvelous night of her life!

****

Carlos was beside himself as he watched the news about the success of the doll. *They owe me, big time! Do I know how to pick a winner or what? Their big windfall is going to be my big windfall as well! A lousy $100,000 is not going to cut it.*

He finished his tall beer and wiped his mouth with his forearm. Rubbing his hands together, he was excitedly formulating all new schemes.

It's playtime again.

He couldn't wait to set up another appointment and watch her squirm when he laid his hands on her and demanded more…much more…or else! He relished the possibilities that the words, "or else", opened up. He could ride this wave all the way to Christmas and beyond. Happy Holidays indeed!

He vowed once again to find and silence Patti…if she wasn't already dead. She would be the only one who could poke her nose in and spoil the fun. Nothing else could stand in his way.

CHAPTER 16

"Hey! Let's blow this joint and go cow tipping. What do you think?" Livy suggested.

"I wish we could go to Rupe's Drive-In for super shakes and burgers," Bryan said. "That's what we always did when someone did something worth celebrating. It's right across from the giant potato at the expo. But I guess New York will have to do."

They hit the street and immediately he squatted down like he had that day in the park and this time she knew just what to do. With Bryan in his dapper Tuxedo, and Livy in her fabulous designer gown, she got the piggy-back ride of her life. Bryan kept shouting her success to everyone they passed. "This woman is a genius! This is the queen of Madison Ave!" He'd stop people and ask, "You know that new 'Hold-Me-Hannah' doll?" They all did. "Well, she created it. She made it. Isn't that great?"

Finally she was sufficiently embarrassed and made him stop, but not for a good long time. This moment, with this guy on this magic night, was just too delicious to put an early end to. *He must be exhausted; he's carried me all over Manhattan.* She climbed down from his back and pushed him down to rest on a bus stop bench.

"You know, Bryan, I remember when I first came to this town. I'd never seen it... you know, actually been here, until the day of my interview with JTC. All that time at business school I never made the 'pilgrimage', as Garrett called it. Everybody else came up lots of times, but I never did. So that day when I came in the taxi, I was blown away. We came in from the Lincoln Tunnel and right into the heart of the Theatre district. Broadway. It was fitting. I felt like I was auditioning for the part of 'rising star'. It wouldn't really be me, but perhaps I could pull off the performance of the role. I was excited and confident and terrified all at the same time. Those giant buildings were intimidating and the monsters I imagined inside, even more so. But the confident part of me felt this sense of destiny. 'I can do this. I'm ready!' And I did it, Bryan! You know, vini, vidi, vici! I did it! I came, I saw and I conquered! I created the marketing coup of the year!"

Bryan cleared his throat in mock insulted pout.

"Oh, of course! I'm sorry. WE came up with the must-have toy of the year! I'm sorry, Bryan. Am I sucking all of the life force out of you? Am I a drag or what? It's all about me, me, me. Does the train stop here and you just want to get off? Let's talk about you, and what about your life? What do you want to conquer? What are you going to do when you've got all your case studies and you write up your thesis or whatever? Then what, Bryan? Are you going to go on playing basketball in the projects, counseling endless troubled kids and never ever win? How can you ever win? What can you conquer?"

"I'm not in it to conquer. Just the opposite."

"What? Sure, you're in it to be the loser. What do you get in the end? What do you gain?"

"My mom always said it was like playing chess backwards. That's the game she and Dad live, that I'm living too, I hope. They even made up a story about it and we kids drew the illustrations. They're pretty bad."

"Chess backwards? I'm confused," Livy said.

"In the story, life is like a big chessboard battlefield. There are people out there, those who are like the knights, charged with protecting the helpless, but some are obsessed with their own power and always maneuvering for position. Others are like the royalty, those who are just too important to notice the little pawns they trample along their way. And sometimes even the Bishops, meaning the church in general, fail to teach the little ones the true principles that will bring them freedom, protection and purpose in life. There are so many little souls out there languishing and barely holding on. They're the inconvenient and sometimes invisible victims caught in the middle of someone else's war…. the dispensable and disposable pawns. There they are, left to suffer and struggle on their own, neglected and abused, wounded, forgotten, unwanted and unloved.

"People like my parents, like an ordinary peasant in the story, go out there into the fray to pick up and nurture the wounded little ones from the battlefield. They bring them on their shoulders, carry them in their arms and help the stronger ones to walk and be ready to carry yet others to their castle, a beacon of safety and love. (Not that our house is really much of a castle...but you get the idea.) They feed them and clothe them, care for them and love them. They bind up their wounds with the true King's healing balm and teach them his words. And when they do, that's when the real magic happens and true royalty is revealed. In time, the little pawns can begin to transform into something wonderful, something so beautiful and pure that one might want to kneel before them and weep with awe and joy. How could something so marvelous, so holy, be forgotten and neglected? How could someone, anyone, leave magnificent beings such as these behind?"

"It's easy, I guess," Livy said.

"But then the peasant begins to see that he himself has morphed into a marvelous being too, just by helping the little ones," Bryan continued.

"But there are those who eventually make it off the battlefield on their own and they are not going out there ever again. It's asking too much, it's too painful."

"But that's how they *win*, Livy. The peasants and the little pawns become the queens, kings and the knights and the bishops. Their struggle is not in vain; the pain has purpose when they can turn it around and lift another. That's how I want to win, Livy."

Livy sat quietly for a few moments after Bryan finished. She imagined the storybook with illustrations drawn by children and smiled at the thought. "And *what* do you win? What happens then?"

"I get to take my little friends and family and go live in that wonderful castle forever and ever. I suppose that all the gang shouts, 'We win!' And then we all go in to the palace where the King has this really cool plasma hi-def big screen and they watch the replay and eat nachos and pizza and French fries and stuff. It's kind of like Rupe's Heavenly drive-in. Absolutely no caviar is allowed!"

"Sounds great to me!"

CHAPTER 17

Every Saturday, as the summer went by, Josie perched on her bench anxiously waiting for Livy and Bryan to come. Her face would light up when she spotted them coming up the street. Out the gate she'd skip singing, "Livy! Livy!" Whenever Livy had to be out of town on business trips, Bryan was a poor substitute. Hard as he tried to cheer Josie, her affections were centered on Livy and her disappointment was clear. Livy arrived one afternoon, after having been gone two consecutive weekends, to find Josie in tears.

"Josie, my girl, why are you crying? I'm here and I brought you some-thing. I've missed you."

Before Livy could present her with the box she had brought, Josie wrapped herself around Livy's long leg and sobbed.

"I thought you were never coming back and I think my mommy's gonna die. I'd be all alone...'cept for Frankie."

She gathered her up in her arms. "Honey, why do you think your mommy's going to die?"

"Last night, I was in my bed, in the dark and I heard her crying out. That man was shouting and banging things and I didn't dare move. When I got up this mornin', Mama be on the floor and I couldn't wake her up. Frankie said she was breathing and she be okay but...I thought she was gonna die."

Livy could imagine a scenario where the mother had brought home some man, had a rather indiscreet and rough romantic adventure and ended up drunk on the floor. But how do you explain that to a terrified seven-year-old? Didn't the woman realize her kids were in the house?

Some parents are oblivious to the fact that they even have children. But this was not Livy's problem; she couldn't handle this kind of thing. Part of her just wanted to run from the situation and part of her just wanted to sit down with Josie and cry. What had Bryan gotten her into?

When she had let Josie cry enough to feel some relief, Livy gave her the box. Inside, was a numbered, first edition, dark-skinned, dark-eyed *Hold-Me-Hannah*. It was beautiful and so was Josie's face when she embraced it.

****

On one particularly warm September Saturday, something happened that would change their little gang from then on.

"Hey Jimmy! Where's Frankie?" Bryan asked when he noticed him missing.

Livy looked around to find Josie but she wasn't there either.

"He's probably shoppin' around for my birthday present. I'm 14 today, Bryan. Did ya'll know that? 14! I be gettin' as tall as you, pretty soon," Jimmy replied.

"Happy Birthday, dude. A little older, bigger and wiser, eh? I shoulda' brought a cake." Jimmy looked disappointed. Then Bryan pulled something from behind the back of his shirt and said, "Hope you like 'em." Bryan had brought him some basketball shorts. Jimmy tried not to show that he liked them, but he did. He tried not to show his hurt that no one in his family had said a word about his birthday.

Livy asked Jimmy what she should give him for his birthday and he replied, "You can teach me all about.... you know what, pretty lady. My place or yours?" All the boys howled with laughter and were flabbergasted at his boldness.

"She was thinking more along the lines of a video game, I think. She works for a toy company, you know." Bryan tried to steer the conversation to something a little safer but Livy took Jimmy's bait.

"I can teach you all you need to know right here and right now." Then the boys really howled and cat-called. They sat down on the pavement as if to watch a show. She looked Jimmy right in the eye and said in a somewhat sultry sexy voice, "Sex is like nuclear power."

"Whoa! That's what I'm talkin' about. She's had some serious sugar!" Jimmy waited for the juicy part to follow.

"That's right. Sex is serious stuff. Used wisely, it can give life and light to the whole world. It can give endless power and it can bless and bind an entire society. Or, used unwisely, it can take down everything in its path. It's very serious stuff that can mess you up, Jimmy, and I suggest you stay away from it. You are only fourteen. Be a kid for a while, okay? Just be a kid, Jimmy, please."

The boys were surprised at Livy's intensity. There was a lot more to her story than she was telling.

"Somebody done somethin' to her, man." Ricardo said.

"Maybe somebody knocked her up and didn' leave no forwarding address when he took off," Jamal suggested.

"Happens all the time, so what?" Jimmy said. "I was just askin'; havin' a little fun." With that, he took the ball from Ricardo and started dribbling toward the basket.

"Now *that's fun*, Jimmy. When you want some fun, go shoot hoops or go bowling or hang with your friends. Don't mess around with something as powerful and dangerous as a little 'sugar'," Livy added.

Just then Frankie came running into the playground screaming, "They're gone! My mom and my sister are gone!" He was panting and could barely get the words out.

"What?" Bryan asked. "Slow down and tell me what happened."

"The police came and took my mom away and some white car that said NYCDFS on it took Josette!" He was frantic. "I hid and they didn't get me. They said my mama was workin' her street and one of her Johns was a narc and he found cocaine in her stuff. She goin' to jail! But where'd they take Josette? What do NYCDFS mean?"

"It means Division of Child and Family Services and she's going into foster care. And as soon as they find you, you'll go there, too." Livy said in matter of fact tone. A dull ache manifested itself in the pit of her stomach.

"Don't let 'em take me, Bryan. I don't want to go to foster care. I've heard about that from my friend. They beat you and starve you and stuff like that."

"No, cases like that are rare, Frankie. Most foster parents are very kind people who just want to help kids who need a place to stay. My family takes kids in. You'll see. She'll be okay and so will you. We'll figure this out." Bryan put a comforting arm around his shoulder.

"Yeah, I'm a foster kid and do I look starved to you?" Ricardo revealed. "I've been with these people for two years and they're pretty good to me."

"You're a foster kid? Where's your mama?" Frankie was shocked.

"With her boyfriend, I guess. He made it clear, he didn't want no kids around so she dumped us and took off. I say I'm better off now than with her." His voice caught and betrayed the toughness in the words. "I do miss my lil' man Miguel. He's my little brother...went to some other family."

Now Frankie really looked worried. "Some other family? I just want my mom and Josie back. I can take care of her; I always do."

"I know you do, buddy. You are the best big brother." Bryan agreed.

"Can I stay with you until she comes home? Bryan, please, I can't go with no stranger."

"Maybe. We'll work something out."

"What? What can you work out?" Livy asked. "If you just up and take him home, they'll get you for kidnapping. Not even a do-gooder like you can just pick up a stray kid off the street and just say 'Wow! Finders, keepers.' Even though it seems that that's exactly what *they* do, the agencies, I mean."

"I mean I'll have to talk to my superiors; maybe I've got some resources in this kind of thing. But what do we do in the meantime? That's the question. Frankie, do you have any other family members around here that you could stay with?"

"No, nobody. We only have an uncle in New Jersey and the rest are still back in Haiti. I don't have a dad."

"We'll talk to them. We'll find out what's going on. There may not be anything else we can do right now but we can at least find out what's happening and where Josie went. Maybe it would be better to just face the situation head on and try to work with the system." Bryan advised.

"No. I don't want to go to no home, and besides, who's gonna wanna take me home wid them? They probably just throw me in juvie with the real criminals and gangsters."

"The system stinks. I'm sorry, Frankie. I wish I could say something or do something that would help." Livy said as she turned and walked toward the entrance of the playground.

"Jamal? Can I stay with you for now? Just ask your mom if it's okay if you and me have a 'sleepover' for a day or two."

"I think that would be okay. My mom's pretty cool. I'll just tell her that your mom is sick or something."

Frankie was just starting to calm down when the white Buick sedan pulled up to the playground court. Sure enough, it said NYCDFS on the doors. Two men in suits and a tall heavy-set woman got out. Josie was not with them.

One of the men spoke to Livy at the gate. "We're looking for Francois Martine."

Before he could say another word, Frankie dashed out the gate and raced down the street. One of the men got in the car and gave chase and the other took off after him on foot. Frankie was fast and was able to get about three blocks away before they caught up with him. The woman and the group at the playground watched the chase unfold.

"I take it that was Francois?" The woman asked.

Livy nodded and added, "He likes to be called Frankie. And please don't treat him like a criminal; he's done nothing wrong. He's a good kid."

"It's our job to do what's best and to protect society, no more, no less." The woman was emotionless.

"Yes Ma'am. You be sure and protect society from kids, now." Livy said caustically. She turned and walked a few steps away, staring blankly into space. She didn't want to hear or see any more.

The woman merely huffed.

Bryan tried to make peace. "Can he go home and get some things of his own and his sister's to take with him?" Bryan asked. "And can we find out where the little sister went? They need to stay together. They need each other."

"Since he's obviously not coming willingly, I don't know if we can stop at the apartment at this point. He may want to try to get away again. And as for where they are going, it's confidential. You can talk to the family

124

court judge if you want the okay to get information. That's about all I can tell you." When the men had come back with Frankie she told them to "secure him" in the back seat.

Did she mean they were going to cuff him? Livy wondered.

The warm wind kicked up and seemed to push the sedan away from the solemn crowd of friends. Bryan walked the boys back to their respective buildings in silent procession. Livy lagged several paces behind. It felt like someone had died or something terrible was going to happen. But then bad things had been happening for a long, long time. Jamal filled in some of the details that Frankie had shared. Many different men had been coming in and out of the apartment for years. Some seemed almost nice to the children. Some were dirty and violent. One particular man seemed to think he owned Madeline and Josie, too. He'd always leave his calling card in the way of beatings and bruises and fifty bucks on the dresser. Some of the men passed out on the floor from drug use, as did Madeline, the mother. Frankie not only tried to protect and take care of his little sister, but he took care of his mother, too, who was usually high or on a very dangerous low. He had kept their little world together. Had things gone from bad to better or from bad to worse?

****

The subway ride home seemed to take forever. Livy and Bryan still hadn't said much to each other and there were only two stops remaining until they reached her station.

Finally, Livy said, "Bryan, why did you take me there and get me in the middle of this?"

"You're not in the middle of anything. I wanted you to go with me and give me some credibility. And don't tell me you don't care about them. You really are good with them," Bryan told her.

"Did you know what was going on with that mother?"

"I had a some idea. But he's just such a good kid. He's smart and tough and amazingly responsible."

"Josie's so sweet and seems untouched by all that ugliness around her, at least so far."

"This could be a turning point for them both."

"Yes, but which way will they turn?" Livy asked rhetorically.

"Can they turn to you?" Bryan asked pointedly.

"Me? You think I should be their foster parent? Why not you? They all love you."

"Single guys my age who are on temporary assignments are not considered good candidates for this kind of thing."

"Single women who work until nine or ten at night aren't exactly ideal either, are they?"

"You don't *have* to always work late. You choose to. The office is your life. You could diversify your life portfolio a little."

"No. I can't do it. I care about those kids but it would be temporary and it would hurt too much when they took them away."

"It's all about you, is it? What about the hurt they feel?"

"That's the hurt I'm talking about, their hurt. The system will keep trying to give them back to their mother until she has either killed them, or killed herself or gets 25 years in jail and then they will finally think about terminating her parental rights. By then the kids will have been yanked in and out of care situations eight or 80 times. I can't stand by and watch that—watch them get tossed around and have their lives ruined. I certainly don't want to be part of their pain."

"Then don't stand by. Do something; fight for them. They need someone on their side."

"*You* do something. You're the one with the connections. You must know someone who could help. I can't do it, Bryan. I know I can't."

"Why not?"

"Because you can't give what you never had."

Bryan jumped in right on top of her words. "And you can't have what you won't receive."

After another long stretch of silence Bryan asked, "Have you ever tried to call Garrett again?"

"No and he hasn't called me either."

"Take a risk, Livy. Just show him that you care. He's hurting and you care, that's all. There's love all over the place if you'll just grab some of it. Stop being afraid."

126

"I love you, don't I? Why *do* I love you, anyway?" The words had just tumbled out of her mouth on their own volition.

"Because I loved you first." He said it like a kid taunting, and then sang, "Nanner, nanner, nanner."

"I think it must be that you're low risk." She said it half-teasingly.

"Yeah, I guess I'm not much to lose."

"You know that's not what I meant." She wanted to say that he was one person that she did trust to love her, no matter what. He would never turn against her and never abandon her. She wanted to say that he was as close to family as she had and that he was her refuge, her sanctuary. She had said that she loved him and that realization itself was an epiphany. Being able to say it right out loud was a major breakthrough. Garrett was right. Bryan was "safe." She didn't actually say anything more but put her head on his shoulder for the rest of the subway ride.

She watched out the subway windows and noticed the graffiti flying by. It reminded her of some 'tenement art' she had studied near the playground that had struck some deeply buried chord within her. A young artist was screaming to the world, "I'm here. I'm not invisible. I want to be seen. Hear my voice. I have value." Suddenly Livy could hear, ever so clearly, Josie's frightened plea. "I'll be all alone..."

CHAPTER 18

"I want my girls sold out by Thanksgiving!" Olivia had made that bold statement at the meeting where she had first introduced the Hannah idea and didn't really dare believe that it would come true. The prophecy was fulfilled more completely every day. It was mid-November and dolls were getting as scarce as '65 Mustangs and were practically worth as much. The company hadn't over produced the dolls, like they had with products past. Stores everywhere were running out and ordering more. They'd receive a few more and a few more; the plan was carefully devised to keep the scarcity mentality. Sales on E-bay were skyrocketing along with the highest bid.

The media picked up on the already well-known doll and her popularity. Local talk shows across the country gave Hannah sighting alerts for listeners still desperate to find a store that might have one left for a hopeful little girl to open on Christmas morning. Livy was featured in an article entitled, *"Olivia Thomas: The Woman Behind JTC's Baby Boom."* in one of the most prestigious business insider magazines. The inquisitive writer, Kent Duckworth, was frustrated to find Livy unwilling to expose any life details prior to her college days. He played up the sports angle. "Ms. Thomas credits her drive and will to succeed to her competitive days as a forward on the University of South Florida Women's Basketball Team. 'She had a passion about the game,' said one of her former teammates, Julie Keating. 'She had something to prove and wasn't going to let anyone or anything stand in her way.'"

Curious Kent just ached to know what it was she had to prove. He would start once again with Mrs. Keating and dig a little deeper. The real story to be told had little to do with a doll; he'd bet the farm on it.

****

The woman at the child services agency was just thrilled to meet the creator of the famous toy. "I saw you on 'Good Morning, America' last week! I'm Sylvia Barrett, by the way," she reached out excitedly to shake Livy's hand.

She was not as thrilled to share with Livy the current status and location of Francois and Josette Martine.

"We have to be very careful in these cases. There is always the chance that someone might not have their best interests at heart and heaven knows what might happen if we tell just anyone what's going on with them and where they are placed," Sylvia explained. "Sometimes people just want to use them to get money or some relative wants to use them to get back at someone. You have no idea of the kinds of things we've seen."

"I wouldn't be surprised. But I'm not just anyone. I have no ulterior motive. I don't really need the money and I know these kids personally and I want to help them out. Does that count for anything? Can I just fill out an application to be a foster parent? Then if you approve it, you can help me find Josie and Frankie and ..."

Livy could not believe that she had just uttered those words. *Me? A foster parent? Not even in a parallel universe. What has Bryan done to me?*

"Oh, but there's a 30 day training and a background check and by then," Sylvia leaned over the counter to speak more privately, "I'd be willing to bet the state will have sent them back to their mother. Happens every time. You just get someone picked out and ready to take some kid in and the parent gets clearance to take 'em home."

"And everyone lives *happily ever after*, right?" Livy asked sarcastically.

"Ha! I'd say eight out of ten times the kid is taken out of the home again, and again and again. This place needs one of those revolving doors."

"Can you at least tell me if they are together? They really depend on each other. Don't take away the one family relationship they have that is working!"

"Unfortunately, I can tell you nothing. I'd lose my job. You're not related to them and have no guardianship paperwork. You have no standing. I'm sorry."

"I'll fill out the application and do the training and hope for the best. Is that all right? Is that a start?"

The woman merely shrugged.

****

Bryan had no standing either. He was a student doing case studies, period. He was not officially anybody. The kids he actually worked with were ones assigned as a case study from outside sources. The kids in the projects were just that, his private projects, fieldwork, support subjects for his findings.

"I say we start with their schools," Bryan suggested. "Maybe they are back home and back in school and we can go from there. Or, maybe they were placed somewhere in the same school boundaries."

"But who are we to poke around at their school? Nobody. The administrators won't tell us anything, either," Livy pointed out.

Bryan thought a moment and then brightened. "What if you come at it from where you *are* somebody? What if we contact the school and say that a representative from JTC, that famous fabulous toy maker, Olivia Thomas, would like to come and have a special day with second-graders? You could bring a doll and show them how it works, how it was made and blah blah blah. You could tell them all that they should study hard and grow up to become beautiful executives like you. It would be very educational and they'd love it. Then you could just say to the teachers, 'By the way, I know a second grader from this school...' and maybe we could find out something. Worth a try?"

It was remarkably easy. They took a little field trip to the Bronx school and arranged the second-grade event. The administrators were impressed that someone of Livy's growing stature in the business realm would come and generously offer her time to an inner-city elementary school. They couldn't have been more hospitable. JTC, naturally, was pleased and wanted to send the photographers and the PR team. But this year, Livy had enough clout to call the shots and say that she'd rather handle it on her own with assistance only from some technicians and from Bryan, of course. This was business, personal business.

The event unfolded flawlessly. The kids were fascinated and thoroughly entertained. The company had sent over some small give-away toys and the children all got something. Livy wrapped up her presentation by challenging each of the kids to dream big and to believe that they could be part of something exciting and wildly successful. "I thought up something and it turned out to be pretty good. Why not you? My young friends, when I was a second grader, I had no idea that I could grow up to do wonderful things. People pretty much told me I wasn't worth a dime. I wonder what they would say now. There is a little voice inside you that says, 'You can do it. You can make it through. Keep plugging along. You can succeed.' Listen to that voice. It knows what it's talking about. I know because I heard it too. No matter what the other voices are saying, you listen to that voice! You can do wonderful things!"

Afterwards, the kids, the teachers and administrators all rushed to thank Livy for coming and to applaud her message. Some of the little girls even gave her hugs. As the kids and some teacher aides ran out to the playground, one teacher stopped by to caution her with, "Don't you go putting too many dreams in those little heads. They'll just find out its a white man's world and there isn't anything they can do about that."

Livy couldn't help herself and answered tersely, "In case you haven't noticed, I'm not a man and I'm not white. I refuse to be a victim, that's all."

"That's all it takes? Wow. Like clapping your hands and saying, 'I do believe in fairies, I do, I do.' *White* is a learned behavior, I guess." He turned to leave.

"No, but tenacity is. When you've had to fight for absolutely everything you've gotten in life, then you learn that sitting and crying about it never got you anywhere. Getting off your butt and doing something did. Teach them that." Thankfully, the other teachers crowded in and mostly sided with Livy. They asked questions and a couple even asked for autographs.

Bryan stayed in the background, smiling, and proud of his sister. She turned to introduce him to someone and he was gone. She then scanned the diminishing crowd of children and spotted him with an arm around a little boy who appeared to have been crying. She marveled. It was like the guy had radar for children in need.

"We actually know a little second-grader from your school and we are wondering if she is here today," Livy said to one of the teachers standing by. "Her name is Josette Martine."

"Anita, that little Martine girl...she was in your class, wasn't she?" One of the teachers said to another one standing to her left.

"Not anymore, unfortunately. It's for the best, actually. I received word that she was taken into state custody. She was hardly ever here before that, to tell you the truth. She missed most of the days of school before they took her. We had just started the year and she came only three or four times in the three weeks I had her in my class. The last day I remember seeing her, she had bruises all over her. I made her go to the nurse." Anita took Livy's elbow, led her a few feet away and spoke softly. "The nurse told me that she had been in her office many times at the end of the last school year with the same kinds of bruises. She also thought that she wasn't getting much to eat. She must have called child welfare about six or seven times. But they never did anything about it. They didn't send anyone to talk to her or her teacher or anything. I don't think they had ever sent anyone over to check out the home situation. Then the next thing I knew, she was removed from my class because she had been taken by the state. I was so relieved. After talking with the nurse, I was afraid for her life. She was the dearest little thing."

Livy recoiled when she heard the teacher say, "was". She probably didn't mean it that way but it made Livy tremble to think of the possibility of tiny little Josie dying at the hands of some monster. Why hadn't she listened when Josie told her how frightened she was? Why didn't she realize that Josie wouldn't take off her jacket because her mother wanted her to hide those bruises? Was it because deep down she didn't want to see what was happening? If Josie went back home, would anything be different?

Anita, realizing that she had said too much, excused herself. The other teachers approached and shook Livy's hand and thanked her again for her encouragement to their students. For the most part, these caring teachers seemed sincerely dedicated to their little charges. Livy thanked them for all they did for the kids and for letting her come. They begged her to make it an annual event.

What had Livy and Bryan learned? That Josie was not here, at this school. She was definitely better off in state custody than at home. They had been wondering about that one. They now knew that fighting for Josie was desperately important. They still didn't know anything more about Frankie. He was in middle school and that would be such a pivotal time for any child. Knowing that kids form so much of their identity at his age, Bryan was adamant about finding him. He would be searching for independence as well as some kind of "home base". Bryan said some kids this age would find the family ties they lacked in a gang. So far, Frankie's gang had consisted of some pretty good kids on the playground and a big white grinning dude from Idaho... if they could just keep it that way.

CHAPTER 19

It was a brisk morning in mid-November and Livy fought to stay awake in her third parenting class that week. She hadn't been sleeping well and these 8:00 a.m. classes were a challenge to get enthused about. Not because she didn't acknowledge that she needed them, but because they were taught by staff psychologists who couldn't have been more boring. Getting semi-literate and heavily accented Ukrainian street sweepers to read from the manual might have been an improvement over this guy. She settled in for another session of copious note taking, if only to stay conscious. The rule was no cell phones in class but Livy left hers on vibrate, just in case. She was supposed to be at work by now and Barbara promised to call her if anything pressing came up. Fifteen minutes into the class something came up, but not at work.

"Hello?" Livy whispered as she leaned way over her knees to keep from disturbing the class.

"Ms. Thomas? This is Sylvia at the child welfare office and we need you to come down here right now."

"Didn't I sign the roll or something? I am at the child welfare office right now, in the parenting class." Maybe they were just checking to see if she cheated and left her phone on.

"Could you step outside? They need to talk to you." She sounded deadly serious.

Livy excused herself and made her way out to the hallway. Two women and one gentleman were already waiting for her at the door. They had wasted no time.

"Ms. Thomas, we need to speak to you regarding Josie Martine." The man stated. He extended his hand to shake hers. "By the way, I'm Dr.

Langford and this is Mary Crawford and Daria Nelson." They all shook hands and exchanged pleasantries. Luckily, the woman from the playground episode was not there.

"I've been hoping to see her, find out how she is, anything at all, and I don't seem to get anywhere."

"So I take it that you are still interested in her case?"

"I'm interested in *her*. Is there a possibility that she could be placed with me?"

"You are taking the classes currently?" One of the women asked.

"Only a couple left. Has something happened?"

The group closed up their little circle to counsel with each other. At last they turned to Livy. "Since the child has asked for you by name, we think we can expedite matters in this case. We need to act quickly because she will need a place to go in the next couple of weeks. Would that be something you could work out?" The woman asked.

"It's what I've been working toward. I can't believe it!"

"Would you like to see her?"

"Of course I would. You have no idea how much I've worried about her. Is she here? And what about her brother, Frankie?"

Dr. Langford led her over to a vacant room. The two women followed and closed the door behind them. "We have some upsetting news for you. You might want to sit down."

Of course, such a set up made Livy doubly anxious. "What's happened? Where are they?"

"Francois has run away from his placement and we have been unable to locate him. We are fairly certain that he has taken up with a neighborhood gang and has been a courier for some older youths dealing drugs. The last time the social worker spoke with him, he had a wad of cash two inches thick in his pocket that he couldn't explain. He disappeared a couple of days later," Daria explained.

"Tell me you didn't take the cash away from him and then send him on his way? You know that someone was going to come looking for it. He'd be— " She was in total panic mode now.

"We're not stupid, Ms. Thomas. We were working with the police to devise a plan to get him out of the situation safely. But now he's taken off and we are very concerned, naturally," Dr. Langford said. He drew a deep breath and loosened his tie. "But we really need to talk about Josie."

"Is she alright? Tell me she's all right. Did that 'animal' come back?" Livy asked in dread without a breath.

"She's fine Ms. Thomas. It's just that she isn't going to be able to stay with the family she's been with up until now. They are taking in some severe abuse cases and it's better for everyone if Josie can find another arrangement. We can let you have some trial visits and if you still want to take her, we'll get the paperwork signed and make it happen. How does that sound?"

"It sounds great!" This was surreal.

"We thought we would start by letting you take her for Thanksgiving Day. We know that you are a very busy executive and in the limelight and all. It will probably take you a week or two to line up a nanny or someone to help you care for Josie. But we assume you do have Thanksgiving Day free, am I right?"

"Yes, of course. Thank you, so much! We will give her the best Thanksgiving a kid ever had!"

The agency had a rule against cohabitation for foster parents and Daria looked concerned. "Who's 'we', exactly? You're not living with someone, are you?"

"Oh no." She almost laughed at the suggestion. "It'll be just me and the doorman. We're like...well, we're friends and he's the one who introduced me to Josie in the first place."

The agency crew gave each other confused looks and then Daria extended her hand and said, "Well, you can look forward to having her on Thanksgiving then. Now, we'll just go over a few details here..."

****

Squinting in the sudden glare of the sunshine, Livy stepped out of the building and dug blindly in her purse to retrieve her ringing cell phone. It was Bryan calling.

"So...do you have something to tell me?" He asked excitedly.

"How did you find out?"

"I have my sources, you know."

"Oh Bryan! I'm so happy, but I'm so scared. What if I do everything wrong?" She was laughing with excitement and panicking at the same time.

"Livy, just by asking that question you're showing that you have only her interests at heart. How far wrong can you go? You love that little child."

She thought about it for a moment. *I do love her. I really do.*

"So, are you free, Bryan? I need you to go with me over to the apartment to pick up a few things that she's asked for, like her doll. The apartment manager is expecting me."

They hopped the subway and soon found themselves at the apartment complex. Livy hadn't been back since DFS had taken the kids. Seeing the place made her realize that she had missed the rest of the boys as well. Bryan had continued his visits and Livy had just maintained that she was too busy with everything going on at work.

They crossed the familiar playground and the sounds, sights and smells brought back the real reasons why Livy had not returned. Hopelessness and despair seem to hiss from the neighborhood like a snake lying in wait. They arrived at Building C and knocked on the manager's door.

Herbert Colby answered the knock with a mostly toothless smile. "Oh, it *is* you. I wondered when they told me Olivia Thomas would be coming by if it was you. I seen you on TV the other day. What you doin' with a kid from the South Bronx?"

When they declined to explain he invited them in and gestured to a small pile of belongings he had gathered in front of his desk. "Not much left of the little girl's things. The place was ransacked pretty bad within a day or two. I just found 'dese things here: a few shoes, some underwear, and a blanket. I didn't find one of them dolls. Guess somebody stole that first off."

"What about the boy's things?" Bryan asked.

"Even less of those. What I got is still down in the storage closet. You want it too?"

"Maybe later," Bryan answered. "Do you ever see Frankie—that's the brother—have you seen him hanging around?"

"Ever' now and again, I see him. –Wid 'dose gang boys. I seen him."

"If you do get the chance, tell him we want to see him... Bryan and Olivia. We want to talk to him," Bryan said.

They gathered up Josie's belonging into a small trash bag and headed back to the subway station. From the shadows, Frankie watched and followed, Josie's doll in hand, hidden in a bag.

CHAPTER 20

When Livy at last showed up for work, it was well after her appointed return time from lunch. She was a big shot now and recently promoted to Vice President of New Products Marketing, so what was a few hours time, especially when it was used for a good cause?

The intercom on her phone crackled and then buzzed. She picked it up. "Livy Thomas."

"Miss Thomas, would you come into my office, please?"

He didn't identify himself but by extension number Livy knew it was Mel. Otherwise she might not have recognized the voice. He sounded cold and irritated. Maybe a few hours did matter.

Miss Thomas? He hasn't called me that since our first interview about working here. She racked her brain for every possible explanation as she made her way down the hallway to Mel's office. *Everything is going so well. What's gone wrong?*

When she arrived at Mel's plush corner kingdom, his assistant, Ron, greeted her coolly and with tangible discomfort. "Have a seat, Ms. Thomas. He'll let us know when they are ready for you."

Just then, Kyle exited the office and looked at Livy with the look she suspected he gave his children when they had sorely disappointed him...anger mixed with sorrow. Not Kyle too! He was one a very select few people at the office whom Livy counted as friends. Mel was another. What had happened? "Livy, I tried to warn you." He lowered his eyes to his shoes and left the outer office.

Tried to warn me about what?

Ron's phone rang and he picked up. "Yes, sir. She's here. I'll send her right in."

Livy suddenly felt a familiar wave of grief and disappointment that she had so often experienced as a child. It always followed that "you screwed up again and I don't want to see your face anymore" scenario that dotted her growing up years. Her days as empress seemed to be over, big time.

She stood up, smoothed out her suit jacket, took a deep breath and entered the office. She would not lose it. She would not cry or break down in any way.

Mel and Joy Jameson were there along with two other members of the board. Bob Farrell was also present. *What is he doing here?* None of them looked very friendly. They were seated in a semi-circle around Mel's side of his massive mahogany desk. There was a lone chair facing them on the other side.

Where's the barbeque sauce? Prepare to be grilled.

"Have a seat Miss Thomas," Mel ordered.

I won't relinquish what little high ground I have. I will not be pinned or cornered. "I think I'd rather stand." Her defenses were definitely up.

"Suit yourself, *Livy.*" Joy sarcastically punched out the first use of her nickname. Joy never called her Livy. "This won't take long."

"We would like you to empty out your desk and be gone by 4:00 p.m. this afternoon. Otherwise, we will have the police escort you from the premises under arrest," said Hemmings. He was the silver-haired 80-year-old crony of the founding father, who had tried to grab Livy's backside at every meeting. No one ever took him seriously except Joy; he was damned serious now.

Livy did her best to stay composed, showing neither fear nor anger. "May I ask what this is about?"

"As if you don't know!" Joy blurted out.

"I'm sorry, but I don't know what is happening."

"I'm sure you noticed that Fitz was just here. He left this file with the computer entries, (traced to your computer), dummy invoices to retailers that don't exist, padded expense sheets and it seems that dolls have been disappearing, as it were, out the back door. Taking advantage of Black Market sales of your own project! Embezzlement of hundreds of thousands of dollars funneled through fake charities. That's what this is about!" Mel's voice had escalated several decibels in fury and now softened in disgust. "I saw such promise in you! I mentored you! I championed your ideas and believed in you, sometimes taking your side and your opinion over Joy's. How could you stab us in the back this way? Your seven-figure bonus on this wasn't going to be enough for you? Why Livy, why?"

Joy answered for her. "Because people of her ilk are never satisfied. They'll take you for all they can get."

"There has to be a mistake. I wouldn't sabotage my own project. You know how hard I've worked, how committed to its success I've been. There's some other explanation. I wouldn't do this, Mel! You know me! I wouldn't do it!"

"I never would have thought so, Livy, until with a little digging by Farrell here, we found out that you have a criminal record—one that includes grand larceny and attempted murder. Funny how you neglected to mention that on your job application."

Livy swallowed hard. "I was a juvenile. That was supposed to be expunged!"

"As he said, it took some digging, but when you throw in the possibility of hundreds of thousands of dollars going missing, files start to open up and all kinds of dirt surfaces," Farrell explained.

"See? She doesn't even deny that she has a record," Joy put in.

"No, but you don't know the circumstances. I was in the wrong place and I was...."

"Just like you are now. There's no place for you here." Joy triumphed in spitting out the words.

"You two!" Livy hissed, referring to Bob and Joy. "You have always been against me. You made this up to get me out of here."

"It was your buddy Kyle who brought it to our attention. For such an odd duck, he really is an astute accountant. He said he tried to go to you first, but you wouldn't reply to his emails or answer his voice messages, you've been out of the office most of the time for days—you were obviously avoiding him. He felt he had to come forward," Mel said.

"I never answered them because I never got them. I've spent the last few days on a personal problem and I have to admit I haven't spent much time in my office or looking at emails. What do you mean, to warn me? I don't understand. Come forward about what?"

"To hope you could explain yourself and these discrepancies. Fitz

140

doesn't want to believe you're capable of this either."

"You said 'either.' See, Mel? You don't want to believe it. You know there's something else going on here."

Hemmings stood and took the floor. "This product is one of the most successful undertakings this company has ever produced and has given us the market share and public acclaim that we've waited for. Not since Joy's father's *rocko-repeater* in the 50's have we had the number-one seller for a Christmas season and—"

"I gave you that product," Livy protested.

"And your greed will not take it away. We will not press charges if you tender your resignation, effective immediately and arrange to return the money... and the dolls. The company doesn't want to lose the respect that we've gained. We don't want some dirty scandal right now. I'm sure you can see this will be best for everyone," Hennings said.

"So, I'm just supposed to admit guilt, print you up some phony funny money and just go on my way? I don't have it! I didn't do it!" Livy turned to walk from the room.

"You should have seen this coming, Mel. I told you she was trash and that I didn't trust her," Joy said. "You can dress her up in a suit, stick some diplomas in her hand, give a chance, but she's still trash."

Livy faced her. "You've always hated me and never had the guts to say why."

"You hated me too, don't deny it."

"I didn't hate you; you're not worth the energy. But I do hold you in utter contempt and I'll tell you exactly why. I think you have as much business sense as Homer Simpson and about as much class as Coney Island Cuisine. I think you are a suspicious, conniving phony who's really afraid of her own shadow. Why? Because you know everything you ever got you had handed to you on Daddy's silver platter...even him!" Livy threw her gaze pointedly at Mel.

"I knew it was Mel you wanted all along! You've always tried to get your nasty little black claws into him!" Joy stood and leaned over the desk threateningly. Her poisoned words were almost whispered, "We're on to you, Livy. I know this is all your doing."

"Ladies, please. Let's not cat fight!" Farrell was enjoying this.

Livy kept at Joy. "I'd like to see you try to make it in the real world. You'd be home eating bonbons and disorganizing the garden club in a week!"

She stopped to see what if anything Mel would say to all of this. He made no response but Hemmings raised a hand to take control. "That's enough. We won't be giving you a reference, Ms. Thomas. So, please enjoy the wonderful world of fast food or an exciting career in hotel maid service. We want you out by four o'clock. Mel, do you have anything else to say?"

Those words brought Mel back from wherever he had been. He seemed momentarily lost in thought. "Uh...no. You're excused, Ms. Thomas. Just go. We'll be in touch." Under his breath Livy heard him say to Joy, "Why did you have to make that ugly racist remark?"

She started for the door and then turned to face them. "I DO HATE YOU. I HATE YOU ALL!" She walked out and slammed the door.

****

A half hour later, Mel sat uneasily at his desk. It just didn't feel right. He knew Livy and while she was ambitious and anxious to get ahead, she never seemed the type to betray the company this way. It felt personal. She had betrayed *him*.

Joy knocked at his door and at first just stuck her head in. When he didn't seem to object, she approached his desk. "I know how hard this is for you, Mel. But I really did try to warn you about her. I didn't want to bring this up in front of everyone, but you might find this interesting. Do you know why your 'wonderful Olivia' was willing to join in a crime spree? She was young, desperate and *pregnant*." Joy handed him a photo Farrell had found while gathering dirt on Olivia.

"What's this?" Mel asked. He took the photo and saw Livy hugging a little girl.

"She's her kid, Mel. Bob found it in her desk. I'd bet money on who our little Hannah is. Seems she's dumped her on some relative or somebody in the projects. Can you believe it? That somebody was helping her clean us out. Get over it Mel. She's just not as wonderful as you thought, is she?" She came up behind him and put her arms around his neck. She whispered seductively in his ear, "Let's go home, darling. Let me help you try to forget all of this."

142

CHAPTER 21

Livy walked stoically past Ron's desk and managed to get all the way to her office on some borrowed power outside her own. She felt like a water hose with the water pressure suddenly turned off. When she got to her office, Barbara was already clearing out the secretarial area. "They just sent me a memo telling me what was going on. They said that I was welcome to apply for some other in-house position, but I can't work for them now. You wouldn't do this, Livy. I know you wouldn't. What are you going to do?"

Livy only shook her head. She opened her inner office door and once inside, locked it behind her. She collapsed into the chair in a heap of anger and despair.

Now the pressure that had escaped her muscles found her chest and lungs and she realized that she had been holding her breath for quite some time. She let it out in a mournful barking sound. Then the breaths came shallow and quick and she was hyperventilating. She didn't know what to do. She couldn't calm down.

Who would do this? Who could do this? Why didn't I check those emails? Maybe then I could have... what? I still couldn't explain it. But I might have been prepared for what was coming.

For the last several days she had been busy concentrating on Josie and Frankie, and had not been paying too much attention to work or much of anything else. The child welfare representatives would never let her take the kids now. Before, they would have said that she worked too much. Now they would just conclude that she was unfit. Where would they go? Who'd take care of them now?

She sat up and marveled at herself. She was in one of the worst crises of her life and here she was, worried about someone else—two kids at that. At least she was an accused criminal with a heart!

At last, she pushed herself to stand up and walk around the room. Using the boxes that someone had left for her, most likely Barbara, she began to gather her things. She picked up the photo of herself with Senator Harrington and let out a wry laugh. *Oh yes, Senator, I'd love to meet you for lunch. Say my place? Prison cafeteria at 1:00 sharp? The bigger your dreams, the more likely they are to turn to horrific nightmares.* She took the diplomas from the wall and laid the Senator shot on top. She lingered at the photo of herself receiving the award for "Rookie of the Year, 2002" from Mel. He looked so proud of her. She remembered feeling so thrilled to have pleased him enough to make him beam at her like that. There was no spouse or family member there to share in her moment of triumph and that look of total delight from Mel was precious to her. His obvious pleasure at her success on the night of the *Hannah Gala* was so fulfilling and emotionally satisfying. She'd surely never see that approval from him again. She gently added the award photo to her pile and laid all of it in the box. She just wished she could crawl inside of it as well and just hide or disappear altogether.

I'm done! It's over. Everything I've worked for my whole life...ruined! How can they do this to me?

A knock at the door interrupted her reflections. It was Barbara. "Ms...Thomas...Livy? Bryan, your friend, is here to see you. He called while you were in Jameson's office and I told him to come right over...that you needed him. Is that okay?"

Another knock. "Livy, It's me. Can I come in?"

Livy dragged herself to the door and unlocked it. As soon as Bryan had crossed the threshold he took her in his arms. For a moment she let him really hold her; she barely had the strength to keep herself standing. Then she pulled away, angry and frantic again.

"Oh Bryan! Now I'm an embezzler, a liar and a cheat! How could they think that? How can they do this to me?"

"You're none of those things. Barbara said they fired you and they're threatening police action. What happened?"

"I honestly don't know. Kyle, our account...their accountant, found some discrepancies, money deficits, doctored invoices, missing shipments of dolls. It was all carefully hidden in some phony charity but they traced it somehow back to me. They say I have to pay it back or go to jail. How can I do that? I don't have it. He said it's hundreds of thousands of dollars!" She dumped the file they'd given her into his hands. "Hundreds of thousands of dollars, Bryan! What am I going to do?"

"Someone obviously hacked into your computer and used you as a front in case they got found out. So the proof is circumstantial. They don't have a motive, right? Why would you do it? You have too much to lose to pull something like this. They'd never win in court."

"They don't want it to go that far. They want to duck the scandal. They just want me to pay up and go away."

"And if you don't just go away?"

"Of course I'm not just going to roll over and let them do this to me. Right now I feel like burning this place down! But if I push it, I don't know if I even have the money to get a lawyer. I've been spending like there's no tomorrow. Now maybe there won't be."

"What about Garrett, your old...." Bryan began.

"No! They dug up my past... the things I always tried to hide from Garrett. They're things that now even make Kyle and Mel, those I considered friends and allies, they even believe that I'm capable of doing this. Garrett might too. I can't tell him this."

"Can you tell me?" Bryan asked.

"No, Bryan. I don't want you to think—"

"Don't you know by now that there is nothing that will change how I think about you or how I feel? You can tell me anything, Livy."

"Can I? We'll see." Livy sat down and remained silent for a few moments as she decided where to begin. She twisted her long black locks as she began her story.

"I was about 16, starting my junior year. I was with a foster family, the Lewis family, probably the best I'd had." She looked at Bryan for a reaction but he didn't seem surprised at all. He'd probably figured it out by himself a long time ago. "They are the ones I meant when I said I thought I had a family. I thought we were almost there. I don't know that we 'loved' each other exactly, but the arrangement worked, I was starting to feel comfortable there and I figured I'd stay with them at least until I was released from the system. At last, I sort of belonged somewhere. I had started to call them mom and dad; I thought they might even adopt me.

"Well anyway, I had this boyfriend, Freddie. I loved him like only an idiot teenaged girl can. He was so cute in a greasy, sleazy kind of way. Freddie knew that I was desperate for love and he used that as a tool to get me to do anything he wanted me to. 'If you love me, you'll…. do this. If you love me, you'll do that.' What he was really saying was, 'I won't love you unless or until you do.' He pushed and pushed until he'd taken my…" Livy looked at her sweet and pure little brother and tried to find the right words. "…Until he had taken what was left of my innocence. Most of it, along with my self-respect, had been stolen by others long before. The very next day I saw him laughing and flirting with some other girl, just to let me know that I had to keep putting out 'cause he had others waiting in line. I swear, he could charm the skin off a pig. Rules didn't pertain to him. He got away with everything. He made me do his homework. And I did it. Can you believe that? He could always convince the convenience store guys that he was old enough to buy beer and cigarettes…or they'd give it to him even if they didn't believe him. He was so slick.

"My foster parents could see exactly what he was. 'Slick white trash' is what they called him. They tried to forbid me from seeing him. I pretended to obey but I continually sneaked out my window in the middle of the night to be with him and they knew it. They threatened to kick me out… send me back to the system if I disobeyed again. By now it was more complicated, though. I was pretty sure I was pregnant. I wanted my baby and my Freddie and that's all I could see, all I could think about. I was so stupid! I was such an idiot! I told him they were going to kick me out and asked him to just take me away with him.

"We made this plan. We'd lay low for about a week. We'd act like we broke up. The Lewis' were so happy at that thought they almost danced. But the plan was that on Sunday Night, while they attended Bible Study, he would come for me.

"The only problem was we were both supposed to come up with some money. How could we run off with no money? I didn't have any. I tried asking for some money to buy a stereo—a hundred bucks—but of course they said no. I actually went and got a job at some burger place and worked about two days. I just walked out when I figured out I wouldn't actually get paid for another two weeks.

"So Sunday comes and I still don't have any money. I had like 12 dollars. I knew Freddie'd be so mad at me. I was desperate. I had to find some money and so I went into their bedroom. I found some money in a drawer and I found a heart-shaped diamond necklace and some matching earrings that he, Dad Lewis, had given her for their anniversary. I don't know what I was thinking. I took it all.

"When Freddie came, he didn't have any money at all. He said he used what he had to buy the truck he showed up in. So then he stops at one of his favorite convenience stores where they always give him the goods and this time the guy said no.

"And so I'm waiting out in the truck, watching. He starts pounding his fists on the counter and screaming that they always give him the stuff and when the guy still won't, he pulls out a gun and robs the store. He goes totally berserk and pistol-whips the clerk unconscious... bleeding all over the place. Then Freddie comes running out towards my side of the cab, waving the gun and yelling, 'Scoot over and drive!' So I did, but I didn't know where I was going. He said he knew people in Texas. We'd start over in Texas...change our names... these people would help us.

"I slammed on the brakes. 'Freddie! You stupid! You robbed a place that knows who you are!'

"He says, 'I told you, we'll go to Texas and start over. Anyway, this guy was new. He doesn't know me.' 'But the camera will,' I tell him. We have to go back. We'll take a little rap, a slap on the wrist. They'll just give us probation or something. That's better than going to prison. What if the guy dies?'

"He says that we're juveniles and that they wouldn't do anything to us anyway and screams at me to get going.

"I scream back at him, 'I'm not going to have our baby in jail!'

"Oh! He blows a gasket. 'What? What baby? Weren't you smart enough to use something?'

"'No. I guess not. Were you?'

"So then he tells me to get out. 'Just get out of the truck, you stupid girl.' And when I refused he picked up the gun off the seat and says 'Open the door, you little slut!'

"So naturally, I did. But I made one last attempt. 'You said you loved me, Freddie.'

"And he gets this really cold, hard look on his face and says, 'I never did. You know I'd say anything to get what I wanted. And I don't want no baby! Now get out!' With that he lifted up his big fat boot and kicked me as hard as he could out of the cab and into the dirt.

"By the time I walked the five miles back home, the police were waiting for me. The Lewis' were going to press charges and I was also an accessory to grand theft auto, armed robbery and attempted murder."

"He stole the truck? He took the money and jewelry too?" Bryan finally got a word in.

"Of course he did, and of course they caught him. He said the whole thing was my plan. I got sentenced to the juvenile detention center until I was 18 and then the case would be re-evaluated or I could agree to go to a boarding school for problem kids and be handled there until I was of age. Of course, I chose the school option. It was the weirdest thing; I ended up liking it there, I think because I knew they couldn't send me anywhere else. I kept writing to the Lewis's and begging their forgiveness. I asked if I could come home for Christmas."

"How did that work out?" Bryan queried.

"He said, 'Dad? I'm not your dad and you can't come here for Christmas or ever again. You have no home here... not anymore.'"

"That must have hurt."

"But I could understand how they felt. I really screwed up everything. But then somehow, the worst thing that could ever happen became the best thing. Mrs. Tolbert, my English teacher, for some reason, she liked me. She said I had a keen imagination and that I was a good writer. Some of the other faculty just dismissed me as a criminal brat but she was always kind to me. I think maybe she even "loved me" in a teacher sort of way, and that has given me something to cling onto through all these years. She stayed in touch until she died a couple of years ago."

"What about the baby?"

"There wasn't any baby." Livy paused and looked at Bryan for his reaction to all she had revealed. "I was mistaken, fortunately. I learned a big lesson about that. I just kept wondering what would have happened if I did bring a child into that mess. Would I ever want the child to know her despicable father? Would I want to keep it in a detention center and limit both of our possibilities for any future? Did I want that responsibility? I hadn't even been able to take care of myself, let alone anyone else. No, there was no baby. I made up my mind right then that I would never bring a child into that kind of situation. It's probably not even an issue because after that and all that happened to me as a kid, I've never since trusted a man to touch me ... you know, that way. But if I ever did have kids, I would be married, for one thing, and able to care for them for another. But I'm not sure that I would know how. I've never been part of a loving home. How can I create one? I guess that's why I went so ballistic on Jimmy that day. Can you imagine Jimmy as a father?"

"Jimmy *is* a father," Bryan confided.

"Oh no, and see? On it goes. People think that I don't like kids. That's not it. They make me uncomfortable. The ones in trouble break my heart and bring back so much pain. I know their suffering and I feel helpless to take it away. The spoiled rotten ones make me want to shake them and wake them up to all they have. And the happy ones, all snuggled in a loving father's arms are the hardest of all. I resent them for having what I never could find. They have someone who wants them, someone who loves them. They have a hero."

"So what made you what you are today? Well, let's say what you were yesterday. I realize today is a little difficult."

"I had to repeat my junior year so I had more than two full years there. Mrs. Tolbert helped me believe in myself. She helped me schmooze the coach into letting me play basketball. It turned out that I was pretty good. She had me believing that I was smart, too. If anyone else had told me that I would have laughed in his face."

"So it was just that easy?"

"Oh yeah, right. Heavens no. She had to figuratively slap me upside the head a few thousand times to get me to stop feeling sorry for myself. I finally saw that she was right. I could choose to be the victim and live in a world of excuses, or I could take charge and change my life."

"How?"

"It was a whole lot of hard work. She tried to teach me that no matter what the rest of the world thought, there was one person who loved me enough to die for me: Jesus. He would see me through; Jesus could get me through. She told me to imagine her and/or Jesus at my side all the time. I was supposed to feel their support and love in whatever I was trying to do. I felt like I had someone cheering me on and to tell the truth, I didn't want to screw up with Jesus sitting beside me, you know?   I haven't thought about that for a long time."

"So you were a believer then?"

"Well, the more confident I became, the more I started to feel like I didn't need anyone, especially God. I got the basketball scholarship and it was like, 'I got it covered, Lord. You weren't there when I needed you before and I can take it from here.' Then I blew out my knee and needed Him again for a while. Then my grades earned me an academic scholarship and I was pretty cocky and sure I could make it without Him. I was always so angry with God for letting me go through a childhood like mine that I started thinking that my successes and achievements were in spite of Him, not because of Him. I was going to show Him and everyone else..."

"Show Him what?"

"That I deserved better... that I was worthy of... I don't know, show Him what I was made of."

"He knows. He *made* you."

"Really?" Livy laughed sarcastically. "I always imagined that some poor unfortunate girl in the backseat of a Chevy made me. Everybody seems to wish I'd never come to this planet. Everyone except you, I hope."

"You've sure made this a better planet for me and those kids and this company, too! We'll get all this straightened out. We'll fight it!"

She reached for his hand. "Bryan, I'm so tired. I just want to go home."

"Let's get a cab. I'll take you home right now. Do you have your stuff?"

"Not home to my apartment. I want to go somewhere where someone is glad to see me come home. I want someone to hold me and to say, 'They can't do this to you! Nobody messes with my little girl!' I want a daddy. I've always sort of assumed my mother was dead or that she couldn't keep me, but I always wondered about my father. I thought if he just knew that I existed or where I was, he would come for me and take me home. I just wanted to go home." She was now sitting cross-legged on the floor, rocking. She would not cry, she bottled it all up.

"I'm always happy to see you come home." Bryan walked over behind her and sat down. He gingerly wrapped himself around her and joined in the motion.

She didn't push him away but instead sank into him and soaked up all the comfort he could offer. "Oh Bryan, whenever I'm with you my heart is home."

****

Barbara called for a taxi and helped Bryan and Livy carry various piles and boxes down to the street. They naturally passed several staff members on the trip through the halls and down the elevator. No one knew what to say. Some were definitely aware of the situation while others were shocked to see Olivia Thomas, the creator of the product of the year, obviously leaving in a hurry for good.

The last thing Livy heard as she neared the door was Marcie Jones' voice echoing across the reception lobby, "Hey! Here comes our new Vice President. Oops! There goes the new Vice President!" Bob and Marcie were there by the door, happily ready to usher her out into oblivion. Bob had never quite forgiven Livy for her successes, her promotion and more specifically for rebuffing his once-constant come-ons. She even had reported him for sexual harassment. Marcie hadn't reported him and had actually encouraged him. In her mind, they were a couple, a team. She believed she would move up into Bob's job now that he would get Livy's promotion. He had other ideas.

Barbara held the door for Livy and Bryan as they carried their items outside to the waiting car. Farrell sauntered up to Barbara and laid his hand on her lower back, a little too low, and whispered, "So...uh...Barbara, why don't you come work for me now? I'll be moving

Matheson into that office now as he moves up into my job. He's bringing his secretary up with him. So you could come on over to mine. I hear you're *very good* and you might be just what I need to spice up my new office."

It was the first time Marcie Jones had heard Farrell's actual plan and that it didn't include her. "To hell with you! And this whole company too!" She took off in a huff. *How dare he do this to me?*

He didn't even acknowledge her outburst.

Barbara smiled sweetly as she removed Bob's roaming hand and replied, "I could never work for a snake like you."

"I guess even a snake would be too drastic a leap up from your last job. I understand," Bob replied in mock sympathy.

Barbara picked up her heavy box lying next to the door, pretended to lose her grip and dropped it right on his foot. "I'm so sorry! It slipped."

Marcie Jones had slipped back to her office and picked up the phone. Within minutes she had contacted *Inside Success* magazine and had been put in touch with Kent Duckworth.

Jones reached over and locked her door. She spoke softly, almost seductively, "Yes, Mr. Duckworth? I understand you did the article on Olivia Thomas of JTC for your magazine there."

"Yes, I did. Who is this?"

"I'm not saying. You're looking to do a follow up article; that's the buzz I hear. I have some information that you might find interesting...for a price, of course."

"I'm listening and if I like what I hear, we can talk price. What ya' got?"

"I'll tell you this much as an appetizer. The much heralded Ms. Thomas just got herself fired." Jones smirk could be heard on the phone. "Of course it's very hush hush with *Hannah* being such a big splash."

"Fired? Wonder Woman? You're kidding. Why?" Duckworth asked in shock.

"No more until I know you're paying enough to not make me hang up and call another rag."

"So why are you telling me? Aren't you afraid you'll get fired as well for letting this major cougar out of the bag?"

"I don't need them. I already have another project of my own. But you're helping me with a little venture capital, right?" she said.

They haggled and came to an agreement on what this bombshell might be worth and Jones continued. "This isn't going to be announced publicly so you already have a scoop, right there. But the really good stuff is the 'why'. I don't know all the details yet, but it seems that she has been dipping into the company till a bit more than was agreed to. Got a little full of herself, I guess, and figured she deserved it."

"Well, I can certainly see why they would want to keep this hushed up with all their high flying sales of that doll. Their stock prices have gotten a bit inflated and this will definitely burst that bubble. So how did all of this go down?"

"It seems that she has been funneling everything through those supposed charities.

You remember, the winner was anonymous and the winnings were supposed to go to charity? Turns out they're bogus and they've received not only that money but a whole lot more and black market dolls to boot!"

"Oh my! This *is* good stuff."

"Now I don't know this for sure, but it seems to me that if the charities are bogus, then wouldn't it make sense that the contest was fixed?"

"It follows. And so...who is baby *Hannah?*"

"I don't know. But if I had to guess, I'd say she was Olivia's own kid that she keeps in a closet somewhere or she's dumped on a relative or something. Just came in real handy for this tidy scam."

"You know, I knew there was more to this woman than she was telling. I could just feel that she was hiding something when I interviewed her." Duckworth tapped his hand excitedly on the desk. "You're sure about all this? She's fired in disgrace?"

"Positive. I just saw her crying and fuming as she left with all her files and junk from her office. Game over."

CHAPTER 22

Bryan and Livy arrived at the apartment after the usual Manhattan traffic battle. She entered her key code in the door and wondered how long she'd be able to keep this nice place. It was perfect. The furniture was high-end and chosen by a highly recommended designer. The art was impressive and the taste displayed was impeccable. It was as tidy and clean as a hospital O.R. It wasn't really a home; it was a portfolio, a body of evidence of her worth. But there was no soul here, no warmth except for one crayon drawing of Josie's displayed on the fridge.

Where will I go? What will I do? How do I get out of this one? I've gotta be strong. I can't break down again.

Bryan put the boxes down by the closet and headed for the kitchen. He filled the teapot and searched the cupboard for the chamomile tea. He watched at the stove as she picked up the award photograph of her and Mel and carried it across the room to the huge window. She stood mesmerized overlooking her million-dollar view and breathing it in as if for the last time. When the kettle whistled, he poured her a cup and added honey, just how she liked it. He sat next to her on the floor and patted the carpet in invitation for her to sit down with him while they drank.

She sat down, took a sip and smiled at him for getting it just right. "Thank you. I was just wondering. Where did your mother come up with that story about the peasant and the battlefield?"

"From some experiences she had and from my dad. He was the one to pick her up off the battlefield and they've been out there working in it ever since. Sometimes it goes well, sometimes not so well. But in the end, they will win. Why do you ask?"

"Because I'm feeling like we're casualties in someone else's war right now — me and Josie, that's all." She was staring at the award photo now lying at her feet.

"You really care about what he thinks about you, huh?"

"More than anything in the world." She was silent for a few moments and continued to gently brush dust off of the framed picture. Finally, she decided to go ahead and confide in Bryan once again. "You know people kind of wonder what someone like me, someone not entirely comfortable with kids, is doing working at a toy company."

"It is kind of an interesting question."

"Well, you know how you said that if this whole thing did go to court, there was no motive and none of it would hold up?" Bryan nodded and she continued. "They might be able to find a motive if they do some more digging."

"What motive, Livy?"

"He is the reason that I came here. Not just for a job, I came to find him." She was looking at the photo.

"Him? Mr. Jameson?"

"When I was dating Garrett, and we were practically engaged, he took me home to meet his folks. They were really an impressive family. His dad was a big-shot lawyer and his mother was a professor of something or other at Temple University. I just felt so uncomfortable with them. I knew they thought that I was not worthy of their son. They kept asking about my background. Where did I grow up? Who were my parents? 'Oh, you don't have any parents? No one at all? How dreadful, how sad.' They looked down their noses at me; I could feel it. I couldn't tell them anything of my real story because they wouldn't be too thrilled to find out their son was marrying someone who had been charged with robbery and assault. And all the rest wouldn't play so well, either, do you think?

"Garrett didn't know much of my history either and asked me that night why I was being so evasive and I couldn't tell him. He was angry that I wouldn't open up. But I felt if I did tell him he wouldn't love me anymore and if I didn't tell him he'd feel that I was dishonest and that I was hiding things from him. I loved him so much and it about killed me when I told him that very night that it wouldn't work... that we couldn't get married.

He kept coming back and trying to get me to change my mind but I sent him away. I pushed away the only man who ever loved me. He never understood why."

"So you came here to...?" Bryan seemed confused.

"So I went back to the beginning. I needed to know, I had to know, who I was. I went back to the orphanage where I spent my early years to find out anything I could about my identity. In the meantime, someone had left a letter for me, just in case I did come back to find out about my parents. They said only that they had left me there when my mother died and that they prayed for me every day and hoped that I had a wonderful life. There was a birth certificate that revealed my mother's name, Margarita Sotomayor of the Dominican Republic, and that she was deceased, and my father's name, Melvin Edward Jameson of New York. There was no signature on the letter. I don't have any idea who left it, but no question, the letter was for me, little Linda who was left at the convent on Christmas Eve in 1978."

"Oh Livy! Melvin Jameson is your father!"

She nodded and stared out the window and spoke as if the memory were clearly painted there, "So as I was finishing Business School, I searched Mel out and arranged an interview with his company. I had to go through three meetings before I got to him. I was so nervous! Here he was the handsome, successful man and everything I had searched for my whole life was hinging on that moment. But then as we talked and got going... It just felt right from the beginning. I knew that he was impressed with me and as he laid out his vision for my role in the company..." The excitement of the memory still danced in her eyes. She stretched out her hands in the air. "I could just see it clearly, like it was my destiny. I would come to work for him, make him proud and then I would tell him who I was. I would belong somewhere, to someone. I'd have a father at last. I could go back to Garrett and his parents with a family, all successful and worthy." Her hands dropped to her lap. "But of course Garrett had given up and married Shelly after a year or two.

"And then there was Joy. She's always hated me. That's why I was so excited about the success of this doll. More than the money or the promotion, it was that I knew he was happy with me and she would even have to admit

156

that I was worth something. Maybe she could accept me. But no, she only got worse. And now.... I can never tell him. If he finds out now, with this embezzlement and everything, he'll think I planned all of this; they'll think I wanted to get revenge for his not keeping me when my mother died. I don't even know what happened. I don't even know if he knows a daughter exists. I don't think now is the time to tell him, do you?"

"No wonder you're so devastated."

"You should have seen his eyes. There was such disappointment and fury in them. He hates me now. He was practically shaking with rage as he handed me that file."

Bryan took her hands in his. "It's not over yet. You can prove your innocence and then be back on track with him."

"But how could he possibly believe that I would do this to him?"

You didn't do it. We just have to prove to him that you're a victim of this just like he is."

"How Bryan? Where do I start? He was my everything, my destiny." She was now embracing the photograph like a teddy bear.

"Maybe your destiny is just shifting a little."

"You might say that. I was flying so high. But what goes up—"

"I mean maybe God has other plans for you, Livy. Not that he wanted this to happen, but now it does open up some interesting possibilities."

"What kind of possibilities?"

"You are here for a reason, Livy. You have some glorious purpose; I know it. You have not only survived rejection and neglect and everything else that life could throw at you, but you thrived. You achieved. You have the strength to make it through this one too. You made it through the darkness and came out into the light."

"And don't forget, I'm right back in that darkness again."

"This is only a temporary set back. You can do it again. But you have to acknowledge the source of the light...and that's God. He was that voice inside you that said, 'you can do it. You can make it.' He was the voice even when it came from Mrs. Tolbert or Julie or Garrett. You have to acknowledge that God did not leave you completely alone. He sent teachers who believed in you, a coach to push you and I'm sure you can think of others."

"Like you. I should thank God for you. What would I do without you?"

Bryan deliberately dodged the compliment. "And like your boss, your father, despite what's going on right now, he has always seen your potential."

"The hope of having my father is what kept me going. Now I have nothing, nothing at all."

"I hate it when I get all preachy, but you have to pray. You have to say, 'Okay, Lord, I acknowledge your hand in my life. In the good and in the bad.' Then ask him what he wants you to learn and what to do now. Turn it over to Him and leave it in His hands. Ask Him how you can hold up the light for some other little soul trying to make her way through the darkness."

"You mean Josie. What do I have to offer her now? She needs so much more than I have to give and who knows what is going to happen? I can't be you, Bryan. Sometimes you are just so good that you make me want to gag." She noticed his slightly hurt reaction and laughed a little to show she was kidding... somewhat. "And besides, I don't know how to pray."

"Just talk to Him like you would to that Daddy you always wanted. Just tell him everything and then don't forget to listen. Then wait and see how you feel."

"For you, Bryan, I'll try. After you're gone tonight, I'll try."

He kissed her on the forehead. "Not for me; do it for you."

CHAPTER 23

"So...about Josie..." Bryan abruptly changed the subject. "You're still going to see her on Thanksgiving, aren't you?"

"Can you believe it? I almost forgot about that in all that's happened." Livy brightened at first and then remarked dejectedly, "They would never let me have her now."

"They don't know anything about all this stuff... yet. –The family services people, I mean. Let's at least have a kickin' Thanksgiving before all of that gets crazy. We can figure out how to cook a turkey!"

"I thought turkeys were your friends and you couldn't eat them," she answered dismissively. He wasn't having much success in brightening her mood.

"I've never actually been introduced to the ones at the grocery stores. I think I can deal with those."

"I'm no cook, you know that."

"Come on Livy! We can look forward to that one day and make it happy for the kids. That'll get you through this. Maybe we can find Frankie, too. Let's make it a day to remember for them! Let's make turkey shaped cookies and pie and of course, mashed POTATOES."

She was warming up to the idea. "Oh! Bryan, I know it isn't Christmas yet, but can we do a widow run? Do you think that Martha and Lucile, are those their names? ...Do you think they are still there?"

"I'm sure they are. I visited with them not too long ago. But I don't know about a widow run on Thanksgiving; that's not the accepted tradition." He wrinkled his brow teasingly shaking his head.

"Please? Only this year I play the mom and I don't have to wear pajamas and a robe! The kids can do that!"

"Lucille will be so pleased to see how well you're doing."

"Yeah, if she only knew. I'll be joining them in the park any day." Livy remembered how embarrassed she was at her appearance last Christmas and yet realized now that trotting and singing joyfully around the park on Christmas morning was one of her most treasured memories. "No, wait. WAIT!" she exclaimed. "I have a better idea! Let's invite Lucille and Martha over for Thanksgiving Dinner and that would be better than a meal at the shelter, right? But then, I want the real thing, the *real* widow run. I'm trying to show a little faith here. –Faith that all this mess will get cleaned up by then. So Bryan..." she mustered her courage to ask, "Will you take me home for Christmas? I want a real Idaho Christmas with hash browns and hot chocolate, a widow run and everything."

When she looked at Bryan's face she felt like Oliver Twist holding his bowl and brazenly asking for more gruel. She once again felt like a motherless child hoping against hope that someone would take her in and want her. Bryan was quiet and looked as if he were struggling for the way to tell her what she feared most: that once again, she was not wanted at the family Christmas table.

"You said I'm family, now, remember? I want an Idaho Christmas...we'll take the kids and make it special for them. Do you think they would let me do that? Do you think that it would be all right with Mom and Dad?"

"Livy, I've been meaning to tell you..." Bryan lowered his eyes to avoid Livy's gaze.

A foreboding silence hung in the air. Livy lifted Bryan's face and searched his eyes and read the story clearly. "Don't you say it, Bryan Kimball. Don't you dare say it!" Livy's heart sank into a familiar abyss. She knew what was coming and she was trembling.

Bryan found his tongue. "Mom and Dad would love to have you, I'm sure, all of you, but—" He just couldn't say it, not today of all days.

She said it for him. "You're leaving. Am I right? You're leaving me."

He was slow to answer. Finally, he pursed his lips, took a deep breath and said, "You knew that I was temporary, that eventually I would get an assignment for projects somewhere else and I would have to go. I've been here almost a year and that's the maximum."

"When? When do you have to go?" she demanded.

"Probably before Christmas, maybe soon. I'm not sure how it's all going to happen. It's not settled yet and there are two or three possible places that I'd be sent. I just know that it'll be soon and I have to go."

"No, Bryan. Not now, please. I need you... more than ever."

"You know that even if I go you're still my sister and my love for you does not change. I can't always be right here with you but I can always love you."

"Please, can't you wait until after the Holidays? You missed Christmas with your family last year; can't it wait until you take us home for Christmas?"

"I don't know. You of all people know how hard this time of year is for lonely kids, troubled kids. It's when I feel most needed by them, when I feel like I can make a difference."

"What about me? You can make a difference for me and two troubled kids right out there in Idaho! What about Jimmy and Jamal and the rest? Who will write their stories? What about *my* story?"

"I have been writing your story. It's the most important one," Bryan confessed.

"What? That's what I am? That's all? I'm one of your projects? That's why you want me to open up and 'share' with you because I'm part of some thesis project?"

"No, I really care about you and you know it!"

"Do I? Do you? All this has been research?"

"You're the whole reason I've stayed this long. Livy, I'm still here just to be with you because I love you!"

"Oh Really? If you love me then take me with you. I don't have anything holding me here now."

"Livy, I can't. It doesn't work that way. But I want you to go home to Blackfoot with or without me."

"Oh, right!" She was angry now and went looking for her coat and purse.

"Livy! Where are you going?"

"I'm leaving *you*!" she replied angrily as she headed for the door.

"Leaving me? This is your house. I know you're upset, but where are you going?"

"Upset? Why would I be upset? I'm not upset; I'm just determined. You can work it out. *We* are going to Blackfoot for Christmas and you can just figure out how."

"But it's not up to me...Please try to understand."

Livy was having none of it. She had lost enough for one day and this was one battle that she intended to win. "You can work it out. I know you can. Like I'm sure we are just going to show up in Blackfoot without you. 'Hey folks! We're here! Ho, Ho, Ho. You don't know us but Bryan said we could come.' Nope. You are going to take us home and if you *really* care, you can figure out how." She abruptly walked away from him. "Right now, I'm going to the *Crate & Barrel* because I saw they had some cute bunk beds; I can get one for Josie to sleep on." Bryan trailed right behind.

"Livy, please. I know that you're upset but..."

"You said that. I'm so far beyond upset; you have no idea!" She slammed the door in his face and ran for the elevator that was just closing.

When she got downstairs she stopped for a moment to button up her coat and was just opening the outside doors when Bryan stepped out of the adjacent elevator. "Livy wait."

She was down the stairs and would be heading across the street where she would catch the bus to the store. She turned back to Bryan, who was standing on the stairs. She called out, "No matter what, Bryan. We are having Christmas in Idaho!"

Glancing quickly across the street to check for the marker of the bus stop, she spotted Frankie. He carried Josie's doll in his arms. His eyes met hers and he gave a slight smile and held up the doll, communicating that he thought she could get it to his sister. Someone in the periphery whistled for him and he seemed to panic, dropped the doll and ran. "Frankie!" Livy was so frantic to catch him, to protect him that she darted into the street after him. –Right into traffic and the path of the oncoming bus.

It was then that she heard the brakes screaming and caught a glimpse of Bryan running down the stairs toward her. Suddenly he was practically tackling her, heaving her out of the way of the speeding bus coming right at her. More sounds of screeching brakes from the bus and nearby cars shattered the icy afternoon air. Then she heard a terrible thud just before she hit her head on the lamppost in the median. All went black.

****

Kent Duckworth had worked at record speed. He had a preliminary article written up for the magazine but he was not going to wait for publication. Under the company byline, he would go straight to CNN. By 6:00 p.m. much of the nation had heard of scandal brewing at Joy's Toys and that America's little sweetheart and the charities were all a fraud. Olivia Thomas was a fraud, caught red handed. From there, Duckworth went on to receive invitations to appear on FOX, MSNBC, and other media as well. He made it a point to include highlights from his conversations with his inside-source who had confirmed that the company now believed that "Hannah" was Ms. Thomas' own child. It was in the middle of an interview on Satellite Business News with hostess Jessica Barnes that new information surfaced.

"And so it would seem, Jessica," Duckworth was saying, "that the whole contest was a setup, a scam for personal gain…"

She interrupted Duckworth in mid-sentence. "I have just been handed some information on a related story. This must correlate with what you're telling us, Kent. According to reports just coming out, Olivia Thomas has just been taken to General Mercy Hospital in critical condition after an apparent suicide attempt. Witnesses say that she threw herself in front of a speeding bus. Would you like to comment on this story? I assume that you were not aware of this situation until this very moment."

The news hit him like a brick. "Oh Dear Lord! I was absolutely unaware. I'm stunned. Naturally, when someone is seeing their whole world tumbling down around them it's got to be very upsetting. But this is just tragic. I met with Ms. Thomas months ago for interviews and she seemed to be a strong and self-assured person. Even with all that's coming out, it's hard to believe that this has happened."

He hoped that she was not somehow pushed into this frame of mind because his damaging story was breaking.

It seemed Jessica had read his mind. "I'm just now hearing in my earpiece that this happened around 6:30 pm this evening, just about the time that this story was starting to air. Do you think that the public humiliation of this scandal drove her to this?"

"I doubt that she was sitting around watching news reports and then suddenly ran out into traffic. I'd bet she had no idea that anyone even knew her secrets at that point." He was saying what he hoped was true. "She just knew that her high-flying success had come to a bitter crashing end."

CHAPTER 24

Three and a half weeks later

Ron looked up to see Mel entering the office. It was 2:30 p.m. and he was just arriving. Ron knew where he'd been. "Any change, Mel?" He noted that Mel looked like he hadn't shaved or perhaps even slept for a day or two.

"Still no change, as of this morning. I had to get out of there. I actually ended up wandering through the stores trying to make Christmas get my mind off of her. It was all fluff and stuff and so meaningless. Joy thinks I'm crazy sitting there day after day. I'm hoping for a miracle, I guess. The doctors tell me that there's not much hope of her coming out of it and that I might just have to accept it. At some point they are going to give up on her and just let her go."

"But you're not ready for that yet, are you? After all that happened, all she did, why?" Ron asked.

"Why do I care? Because I guess I feel like I drove her to this. I worked alongside her for four years, Ron. I mentored her, taught her every-thing I knew and she soaked it up like a sponge. Then she turned around and taught me a thing or two. How could I not care? She has no one, Ron. No family. I haven't seen any friends or boyfriends," Mel tried to straighten his rumpled collar and tie. "I'm the one they are going to ask to pull the plug. She put *my* name on her emergency contact list, for heaven's sake. Somebody has to care."

"Yes, but she screwed up. She stabbed you in the back; you said it yourself. She got greedy. People like that tend not to have too many friends and for good reason. You're a better man than I to be so forgiving.

I've got to admire you for that."

"I don't know, Ron. I just don't know. Something tells me she didn't do it. It felt so right when I hired her. How could I have been such a poor judge of character?"

Ron didn't answer and began leafing through the files and messages strewn across his desk. "Oh, Mel, that woman called again—the one that says that she has some very important information for you. How did she even get your direct line? I told her to put it in an email and that I would make sure that you got it. –Hers and the six thousand others that have been pouring in. She's very anxious to give you her take on the scandal, I think."

"Isn't everyone? Doesn't she leave a name or a number or even a hint about what she wants to tell me? Something? Caller ID?"

"No, she's using a calling card and she says what she has is for your eyes and ears only. She won't tell me anything. I get the sense that she feels like she's in danger or that you are. She's probably just a nut case. And now, having said that, I should tell you that I did give her your personal email, not the public one. She won't sell it or give you a computer virus, I don't think..."

"Thanks, Ron. When I find she's a stalker and a spammer, I'll know who to blame."

****

Livy opened her eyes. Wintry afternoon sun shone dully through the blinds at a window and even this pale light caused her to squint. Unable to focus, it took her several minutes to identify the black box hanging in the air as a television suspended from the wall on a metal arm in front of and above her bed –her hospital bed.

Even more blurry than her vision was her mental state. At first she couldn't remember who she even was. When her identity had at last come into focus, she then couldn't quite clear her mind and remember what had happened and why she would be there in that hospital. She felt a heaviness in her body that gave her the terrifying impression she was paralyzed. She had to struggle with all her mental might to force her limbs to move. With some intense effort, she raised her right foot, just slightly, and then her left.

She felt a stabbing pain as she flexed her right hand and jostled the IV inserted there. Becoming aware of some discomfort in her abdomen, she tried to raise her head slightly to find the source. She couldn't quite lift her head from the pillow. She lowered her eyes and was able to see what she guessed was a feeding tube protruding from her belly. *What happened? Why am I here? How long...?* Her mind was an indistinct jumble of flashes. Thus she continued for hours, frightened that she might remain imprisoned in this confused and disabled state forever. Hospital workers came in and out of the room but she couldn't find her voice to speak to them. She could blink; she could move her toes and her hands, but only minimally.

Slowly, over time, the first vague memory began to trickle across her consciousness, and then another and another. She could see Mel, angry at his desk; she saw herself in shock and pain. She felt it to the very bone. But what was it about? She could not cross that hurdle in her mind. There was something else, something terrible trying to break through and at last it did.

Bryan! Where was Bryan? The last images before she blacked out flashed through her mind. She saw Bryan running down the stairs, heard him yelling her name, and then experienced again the terrible slow-motion horror of that bus slamming into one of the dearest creatures God had ever put on this earth. He couldn't be gone! Yet she knew he was. He could not have survived that impact. The horrifying sound of the brakes screaming and the slamming thud that followed resounded again and again in stereo in her head.

No, no! Don't let it be true—God please! What was she saying? Bryan had just begun to open the possibility to her that there really was a God and then He does this? That God takes Bryan away—wonderful, good-to-the-bone Bryan? Why? What kind of God could do that? Not the kind and loving Father Bryan had almost convinced her existed. How ironic that his death would be just the thing to refute everything he'd been trying to teach her. Poor, innocent, deluded Bryan! An endless string of empty tomorrows stretched out before her. How could she go home and never again be greeted by his cheerful, goofy smile and that silly top-hat? Who would make her laugh until her cheeks and her sides ached? What kind of God would take away the very last thing, the last person that she had to hold on to? To confide in? And what about all those kids he had helped and loved? And who loved him in return?

She wanted to scream. She wanted to rip the tubes out of her arms and run down the hall and yell, scream and beat on something. The anger and grief was building inside like a volcano. Livy's scarred and battle hardened heart burst and her whole body shook with loud wrenching sobs. She had found her voice.

Just then, the door to her room opened and a nurse bustled in, rolling some kind of contraption on a cart. Startled by the noise from the bed, she nearly upended the thing. "You're awake! You've come back to us!" She exclaimed in surprise. "Don't cry, Honey. You're back!" The chubby, older, African-American woman rushed toward the door. "I'll get the doctors. Sweetie, you stay with us now. We'll be right back. Doctor...!"

Horrified at being caught in such a state, Livy tried to put it all back inside, all the rage and all the anguish. She could barely stop the sobs and shaking. Unable to even wipe her tearstained face, because both arms were tethered to IV's, she managed to turn her face to the pillow just as an entourage of doctors and nurses streamed through the door, poking and prodding and asking her to perform such basic tricks such as reporting the number of fingers they were holding up and wiggling her toes and trying to bring her forefinger to her nose with eyes closed, and identifying the current president of the United States. After these and other more complicated tests and the scans they immediately took her to undergo, they tentatively pronounced with relief and amazement that she would be fine. She would need therapy and extensive rehab, but there appeared to be no long-term brain damage. Something of a miracle, they said.

Maybe not brain damage, but there was damage all right. She knew that in some ways, she would never be fine again. She would never be whole again.

The sweet, waddling nurse wore a nametag that read, "Betsy Granger" and she stood at Livy's shoulder stroking her hair as orderlies wheeled her back to her room. She spoke gently and said, "You've been sleeping about three and a half weeks now, dear. You had pretty severe head injuries and they kept you in a medically induced coma for the first fifteen days. They do that to reduce swelling and stress on the brain. But then, they gradually tried to bring you out of it and ...well I've watched you in your coma all this time and had about given up hope on your waking up. Somebody some-where has been praying for you," she said, bending down close to Livy's ear, "and I have too!" She added the last part in a whisper not meant for the rest of the group to hear. As she got Livy's bed situated and the IV's in place, she reached for a tissue and gently wiped her patient's face. "I thought for sure you'd miss Christmas, or that we'd lose you all together."

Gradually, the other medical team members left and Livy was alone with Betsy.

"Is there anyone that you'd like me to call?" Betsy asked.

She had to work hard to make the words come out right. "Do you know if there was a young man who was brought in at the same time as I was? He was involved in the same accident." Holding onto the faint hope that perhaps Bryan had made it, Livy challenged silently, *"Here's your chance, God."*

"If he was, he wasn't assigned to this floor. Do you know his name? I could check and see if he was admitted."

It took Herculean effort for Livy to say his name aloud without again bursting into tears. She pursed her lips hard until she felt she had control. "His name was Bryan, Bryan Kimball. He was about twenty-two." She heard herself saying, "was."

"Do you have any other information that you could give me that might help?"

"Well, his parents are Jake and Marilee Kimball and they live in Blackfoot, Idaho."

"I'll see what I can find out. In the meantime, do you want to see Mr. Jameson? He's been here almost every day and for hours at a time. He was listed as your person to

contact in case of emergency on your insurance papers. The paper-work didn't list any next of kin, but this guy sure has been worried about you. Sometimes he just came in and held your hand and sometimes he would talk to you. I kept an eye on him, though. He's already been here today and I'm sure he'll be back tomorrow, if not sooner. Do you want to see him? All those reporters and looky-lou's keep trying to find a way to see you but I scare 'em off pretty well. I may not look it, but I can be trouble." Livy could believe it and almost found a smile when she imagined Nurse

Betsy driving off the trespassers with anything handy, including bedpans. Betsy left the room to make the calls.

Did Livy want to see Mel? It was like trying to piece together a dream when she'd been awakened in the middle of it. If Mel was angry with her, why was he here all the time? What was it all about? Joy haunted the dream. She was there and Hemmings and Farrell and…and…suddenly the clouds parted and the whole scene repeated in colorful detail. She'd been fired, disgraced, and humiliated in front of everyone in the office. Reporters? Looky-lou's? The whole world had heard? She remembered enough to know everything she had worked for was gone.

CHAPTER 25

Mel gathered his messages and the files from Ron and opened the door to his inner office. "Did Kyle call?"

"There's something in the pile from him. You really ought to reconsider the voicemail idea. It's all the rage, you know," Ron chided him.

Mel replied in his best computer voice, "You have 68 unheard messages... No, I don't think so. That's what I pay my trusted assistant to wade through."

He entered his personal office and sat down at his computer. Holding his breath, he pulled up the latest sales and order figures and the picture was grimmer than he had expected. The scandal couldn't have come at a worse time. JTC had just begun production on the next run of Hannah dolls, the boy version and the Hannah sequel, Playtime Polly, soon to be unveiled. Orders from retailers were drying up as the public showed its disgust over the bogus charities, the questionable contest and the rest of the fiasco. So far however, they hadn't returned great numbers of the dolls already purchased. There were just too many of them already wrapped and waiting under the tree or popping up in Santa lists. The intercom buzzed. "Kyle is here to see you. I told him that you were not in the mood for the reindeer antlers right now, was I right?" Ron asked.

Kyle popped his head in the door and looked for approval to enter still wearing the headband with the jingle-belled antlers and Mel rolled his eyes.

"Well, somebody around here has to try to revive the Christmas spirit," Kyle protested. "It feels more like Halloween or the *Nightmare before Christmas.*"

"Well, this company just might be the ghost of Christmas past. Have you seen these figures?"

"I compiled those figures. It's what I do."

"So what's up? Did you follow up at the bank on that hunch you had?"

"I did and I found some interesting things, just as I thought I would. There was activity on the charity accounts and more company money transfers attempted after you fired Livy. That would be sort of gutsy, don't you think, to be found out and just keep stealing? Then, after a day or so, according to bank records, the money disappears, transferred into off-shore accounts or Swiss banks. By the time we told the authorities and they froze the accounts, they were empty. But then, dolls for sale on E-bay shot up, before the story broke and the price fell. I had some people that I know buy some from a few different sellers and most of them had serial numbers matching the missing shipments. They say, 'thank you for the dolls,' by the way."

"I can't take you seriously when you are wearing those things." Mel reached up and grabbed the antlers from off Kyle's head. "Okay, so she didn't act alone. We never said that she did. An accomplice was always a real possibility."

"But what does your gut tell you? Mine says hacker. These transfers were made through Thomas' computer but using backdoor codes that I'm not even sure that she knew. She was great with business but she always had the IT guys in there helping her with some glitch or another. She was no computer whiz."

"So maybe one of those IT guys was in on it with her?" Mel was playing devil's advocate.

"Yeah, so they put their heads together and decided to leave a trail that leads back to her, a well-hidden trail, but a trail nonetheless. An IT guy, a talented one with access to a few master codes could get into any computer in the company. Yours or mine, for example, have a lot more sensitive information and more access to money than hers did. Why leave a calling card? And to put her name on the invoice approvals, how stupid could she be?"

Mel was hearing from Kyle what his own gut had been telling him as he sat there at her bedside everyday. "Well, Fitz, you're the one who brought this to me with all fingers pointing at Olivia Thomas," Mel said, shifting some of his own feelings of guilt onto Kyle.

"True. But I wanted you to confront her about it, get to the bottom of it, not to fire her that very day. She might just possibly be a 'fall-guy...girl', whatever." Kyle had tossed the guilt right back into Mel's court.

"When Joy saw the files you brought us, she went ballistic, beyond postal! She wanted Livy out. She and Farrell had already dug up the dirt on her past to try to get me to change my mind about the promotion. I did feel misled or deceived. I was really disappointed in her. They got old Hemmings on the bandwagon and the other board members and then your file really clinched it. But if she didn't do it, why would she try to kill herself?"

"Uh...maybe because everything she worked for had just been vaporized in one fell swoop? Maybe because Jones and Farrell and that Duckworth guy made sure the whole world thought that she was a low down cheat and a fraud? Or, here's a lovely thought. Maybe she was pushed."

"Oh Dear God!" Mel meant it as a prayer. "Kyle, get that reporter, Duckworth, on the phone and tell him to get digging, that the real story may not be what he reported. This time, tell him to make sure he's got all the facts."

Kyle nodded, grabbed his reindeer headgear and charged out the door.

Mel logged into his private email account to find six unopened messages. One from Joy, marked urgent, implored him not to forget to pick up his tux for their annual Christmas dinner soiree for dozens of their most elite and most boring friends. This year they'd have something to talk about! They'd be consoling him and sympathizing, all the while relishing the dirt. "Not tonight," he sighed. "I'm really not in the mood."

Searching for the email mystery message Ron had mentioned, Mel found an obvious candidate. The subject line read, "Open immediately. Confidential information."

At first, as he read, he dismissed the letter as just another consumer stating her outrage at the turn of recent events. But when he got four or five lines into the email, the color drained from his face and his hands began to shake. Mel's entire world took on a new perspective. Everything had changed. And when he called the number she gave, it was clear what had happened at Joy's Toys and who baby Hannah really was.

Mel got out of the cab in front of his brownstone luxury townhouse and asked the driver to wait. He dodged caterers and a florist as he raced up the stairs to the front door. Joy was in the dining room, choosing between two centerpieces and asked Mel's opinion. He didn't answer and set off straight up the stairs to the bedroom. With a grunt, he pulled a large suitcase from the closet and opened it across the bed. He knelt at his dresser and from the very back of his bottom drawer he removed a locked leather-bound journal. He stood up and felt underneath the upper right sock drawer, located the key that was taped there and yanked it out. Opening the journal for the first time in more than five years, he felt his legs go weak when he saw her face. He sank to the floor and sat for a few moments studying the photograph. One word, one name, escaped his lips: "Daisy."

CHAPTER 26

When Mel Jameson and his roommates landed in the Dominican Republic to let off some steam between first and second years at the Harvard Business School, he had no intention of doing anything that could be remotely considered serious or life altering. The tropical beaches, soft breezes, the seemingly inexhaustible supply of alcohol and scantily clad, enticing women promised the kind of freedom and irresponsibility he'd been dreaming of since prep school. So for just this summer, Mel was anxious to drown out the past, postpone the future and explore the here and now in an endless round partying and sleep.

Not that life had been that bad, nor did the future look bleak and forbidding. Raised in a privileged, old-money family; he had been given all the advantages, and to his credit, hadn't wasted them. A hard-working, involved student he had excelled in his studies, played the expected sports with enthusiasm and grace, and explored options and opportunities that came his way. His parents were proud, if distant and old-fashioned-ly formal in their do-what-is-expected-of-you way. They approved when he began dating Joy Parker, the daughter of a manufacturing tycoon who had made his fortune in the toy market. (He had named his company after his daughter— Joy's Toys.) During this last year of business school, Mel would do the expected thing and ask to spend the rest of his life with Joy. Joy would do the expected thing and ask her father to offer Mel a future with Joy's Toys. Mr. Parker would scrutinize Mel's impressive scholastic record, notable pedigree and family fortune and do the expected thing by welcoming Mel as part of the literal and business family. That was the plan. It was a done deal. But that was later. This was now.

This would be his summer of abandon. The grind of school was on hold, a predictable June wedding awaited. He had only this moment to do the unexpected: no plans, no responsibilities, only a determination to enjoy a perpetual bachelor party of booze, babes and beaches before real life enveloped him. He counted on his buddies to keep the party going. What he hadn't counted on was Daisy Sotomayor.

Margarita Guadalupe Elena Sotomayor Reyes, like her name, was long and complicated. It was not only her height, a lanky 5'10", that distinguished Margarita from the other employees at *Susurro del Mar Resort*. Her drive and ambition distinguished her as well. Orphaned by Hurricane Carmen, Margarita vowed not only to raise her brother Carlos, but also to raise their station in life. At fourteen, determined to stay in school, Margarita had come to the resort looking for night work. The only opening was in the laundry where the supervisor was always seeking someone desperate enough to put up with the hot, tedious and often backbreaking work. Margarita stuck it out for two years. It was a definite step up when Margarita graduated to cleaning toilets and making beds.

Observing the lavish and carefree lifestyle of the wealthy American guests, Margarita saw a future that she dared to want for herself and Carlos. She watched Ramon, the front desk manager, charm guests with articulate and effortless English and realized that a command of that language was the key to her quest for a better life.

In the break room one afternoon, she mustered the courage to approach Ramon. He was flattered and impressed. He generously provided the tapes and books that he had used and often took time to practice with her. By the end of the summer, Margarita had earned his praise, his respect and the position of night clerk at the front desk. By the next May, she was night manager.

In her post at the front desk, she was a beautiful and logical target for bad pick-up lines and unwanted attention from vacationing frat boys. She got so deft at fending them off that they could feel flattered and put down all at the same time. Some, like Mel's buddies, Matt and Steve, took it as a challenge to try and try again. Rather than discouraged they were inspired to new heights of creative flirtation. They couldn't resist the temptation that her name presented. "Like the drink, you intoxicate me." "Are you a salty

Margarita? I'd like just a little lick to find out..." Their puns got more suggestive with every try and she was quickly tiring of them. She was about to have them thrown out of the hotel when Mel happened along and casually advised them to back off and stop acting like jerks.

Several days later, after a long day of bodysurfing and girl chasing of his own, Mel desperately wanted a drink. Seizing this golden opportunity, Matt suggested Mel call down and request the *front desk special Margarita*. "Mel, say, 'you know what I mean, the long, salty sexy Margarita that's served up right in your room.'"

Mel innocently fell right into their trap and in five minutes there was knock at the door. Matt and Steve positioned themselves to watch. The door opened and there stood a gorgeous bikini clad maiden with a tall margarita on a tray. She also wore her nametag on the strap of her bikini top. In her most sultry voice she asked, "Is this what you had in mind?" Mel's jaw dropped and before he could say, 'Oh! Yes!" she threw the drink in his face. "Towel?"

The next night he appeared at the desk with a bouquet of daisies. Having heard about the incident with the drink, Ramon nonchalantly mentioned to him with a snicker that Margarita was also the Spanish word for daisy.

"I'm sorry for the behavior of my friends and myself last night. They set me up. Can we start over?" Extending his hand and a bouquet of daisies, he continued, "I'm Melvin Jameson and from now on I promise only to associate you and your name with these lovely delicate flowers. Please accept my apologies...?"

She heaved an annoyed sigh and gave him a wary glance. He tried again.

"Please?" One by one he began to pluck the petals. "She forgives me...she forgives me not. She forgives me...she forgives me not..."

She finally smiled. "I forgive you, *Male Bean,*" which was how her pronunciation of his name came out. She accepted the flowers and an invitation for lunch the following day. From then on he was Bean and she was Daisy.

Almost overnight, Daisy and Mel were inseparable. Would she mind showing him around the island, and Boca Chica? What were the restaurants she recommended? Could he take her and her brother out for a seafood buffet? Soon, no excuses were needed to get together. Mel was feeling and doing things he never had imagined before, totally unexpected things. He was definitely not a morning person, yet when she was off work at 4:00 a.m. he would often find himself waiting for a pre-dawn walk in the moonlight or a sunrise swim.

When, after some weeks they found a secluded spot on the far side of the island and made love for the first time, Mel was surprised at his lack of "mission accomplished" feelings that would have accompanied previous conquests. He felt he was the one surrendering...not to her seduction, but to feelings of true tenderness and a longing for closeness. Though he knew the affair was wrong, every moment without her seemed empty and long, only a bridge to their next meeting. When mid-August came he had to stand back and counsel himself that this was just a summer fling. Well, wasn't it? She was merely forbidden fruit and therefore had extra appeal. They were not falling in love; that was not part of the plan. He was practically engaged, after all. He was leaving this place and this girl forever.

He had to begin thinking about returning to Boston and to his future wife, Joy. To buck the plan now would throw both families into turmoil. He knew that as wonderful and beautiful as Daisy was, she would never be accepted by his family. She was a gorgeous blend of Hispanic and Black, like most Dominicans, and his parents would never hear of his marrying someone of another race.

But there was something about Daisy. She had spark and substance. She was not merely a silly island girl infatuated with the rich boy from the States in the way so many of the girls there had been. Sweet and spiritual, she believed that God had saved her from that hurricane for her to do something good with her life. She had a destiny. She was smart and self-educated and had ambitions that rivaled his own. Few of the girls at Harvard had shown such determination. She wanted to go to Florida, study business and someday own a resort herself. And Mel believed she could do it, too.

He suddenly wondered if *he* could do anything on his own. He believed in himself and yet here he was living on his father's money, going to his mother's chosen college (her father, grandfather and great-grandfather had all gone to Harvard), about to marry the boss's daughter and set out on someone else's long appointed track to "success" forever. What if he were to break those chains, leave the expected things behind, marry Daisy and live on an island? What might they be able to create together? What did he want? Who was he, really?

In the end, he was a creature of his upbringing and generations of expectations. He would take the road most traveled, the sure thing, and the conciliatory thing. He would return to Boston, finish his MBA and marry Joy next June. He would break Daisy's heart and perhaps his own.

As the days went by, he knew he had to say something. It was like the continual splurge before one begins a diet. *Just one more day*, he'd rationalize; *I need one more delicious moment with her, one more sunrise, and one more time to be lost in her arms and in her eyes. After the weekend, then I'll do it. I'll break it off.*

They had talked about his schooling in Boston and she was aware that he would be returning soon, but he had avoided the question as to whether he would be leaving with or without her. She had dropped some little hints that he had carefully ignored. Would he return? That question was always left unanswered by a sudden change of subject. An obvious tension was building between them.

One breezy morning while walking through the tourist marketplace, he acknowledged that the dreaded time had come. As he wandered through the little shops he found a silversmith making and selling silver jewelry. His cross pendants were especially lovely and Mel asked if he ever made a custom piece for someone. Mel's gringo Spanish was terrible and the craftsman understood little English but somehow they were able to communicate on what Mel had in mind. He paid him to fashion a beautiful cross with a filigree daisy in the center. It could be ready the next day. This delicate tribute would be the perfect gift for her to remember him by.

He made a date for lunch and got a reservation at the nicest restaurant in the city. They shared a marvelous romantic lunch of coconut shrimp with rice and key lime pie. Mel was even allowed to have a *Margarita*. Daisy was having *Bean* dip after all. Margarita interpreted this wonderful lunch as possibly a set up for a proposal of marriage. She had even confided to Ramon that she thought today might be the day. Everything at the restaurant was so perfect. Candles set the mood, the bouquet of daisies made a statement of love, and Mel was especially charming and attentive. Things suddenly got very quiet as he contemplated how to proceed with what he had to say.

Margarita thought she saw his hands shake just a little and she smiled to herself about his shyness. *Doesn't he know I'll say 'Yes'?* She tenderly took his hand and asked, "Is there something that you want to say to me, Bean?"

He couldn't formulate the words. There is no easy, painless sentence one uses to break someone's heart. After an uncomfortably long silence, Mel spoke. "Daisy, I have something for you. I had it made special. It's something that I hope you will wear and that you will think of me when you do." He pulled a small box from his pocket. It was not a ring box. He opened it for her.

Her face showed that she was touched and delighted. "Put it on me, will you please?"

He stepped behind her and fastened the clasp. "I want this pendant to say that I know that you come straight from the heart of God; he loves you and made you so nearly perfect that you leave the rest of us ...in the dust." He stepped to her side and turned her face to him and kissed her lightly. "I'm so grateful that he allowed me to spend this time with you. I'll never ever forget this summer, you know that don't you?"

These were not exactly the words that she hoped to hear. "I love the cross, thank you. But what are you trying to say, 'Male Bean'?" She was trying to articulate his name the best she could.

He laughed a little and then said, "I will always smile when I think of how you say my name. I will remember all those little things that make me love you." He had moved back to his side of the table and mustered the nerve to go on. "You know that I have to be going home, very soon."

"What will you take with you to help you remember?" She paused waiting for him to seize the opportune moment. He let it pass and she prompted, "Can you take me with you?"

He shook his head sadly.

"But next year, you will come back, won't you? When you are finished with your school, you'll come back, right?" Daisy asked hopefully.

"No, I won't be back." He kept his eyes on a pea that he chased around his plate with a fork. "But this has been the most beautiful summer of my life because of you."

"Is that all that I am to you?" She took the fork from his hand and let it drop loudly onto the china. "Just someone you spent a summer with and now you go back where you came from and pretend nothing happened here? Is that what you are telling me?"

"No. I never thought—"

"No, you never thought. I would expect this of those stupid friends of yours, but not from you. I am just a cheap souvenir. Not even that. Souvenirs you take home with you and then eventually you throw them away. But you are throwing me away now."

"No, no, Daisy, my sweet, wonderful Daisy. You know that you are much more than that to me. You know that I love you but that our lives, our destinies, are so far apart. You have such marvelous plans for your life; wonderful dreams and I know you will make them come true!"

"When I fell in love with you, you became my destiny. You will always be part of my plans. Didn't I become part of yours?"

"Daisy, before I came here, before I ever knew that I could love someone like you, there were lots of plans…lots of expectations and responsibilities. I have commitments to my family and to… someone…"

"To a …girl? You're engaged?"

"It hasn't been made official but we're planning to be married in June, after I am out of school. I didn't know that something like this could happen. I love you, Daisy, but I can't marry you. I can't stay here. I belong to a whole other life back home. Do you understand that I didn't just flash into existence the day I landed in the Dominican Republic?"

"Do you think that I will just flash *out* of existence when you leave the Dominican Republic? I am real. What you had here was real. You can change the future, you can choose to change things."

"I can't. I've played it all out in my mind. I want to stay but I have to go."

"You are a coward, Male Bean!" She spit the name out with a vengeance this time. "Is that the right word, coward? You are afraid to do what you want and you only care about what other people will think. I thought that you were a man. You are less than a boy. You are more of a fool than your jerk amigos and I'm so sad that I was fooled into thinking that you were different. You looked like a man! You loved like a man! But you are someone's little child! I was just a silly toy!"

She threw the rest of his Margarita in his face and stormed out of the dark restaurant and into the afternoon sun.

She ran all the way up the palm-lined hill to the resort. She fingered the cross pendant as she tried to hold back the tears that would advertise to Ramon just how wrong she had been. She wanted to go back and throw the necklace at Mel but she couldn't. It would be all that she had from him, the only reminder of a wonderful summer, a wonderful love. Maybe he would go home and see that he belonged with her after all. Maybe then he would find the courage to follow his heart.

****

Mel gently placed the photo back into the journal, locked it and tucked it into the side pocket of his suitcase. He added enough clothes and toiletries to get him through the next few days until he could send for the rest of his things. He just needed to get out of there. He zipped up the bag and headed down the stairs and through the crowd of decorators, food servers, and the cleaning crew and of course, Joy.

"Did you get the tux? And I hope you picked the better one this year. Turn around and let me look at you. It was so..." She had finally caught a glimpse of his face. The cold expression there chilled her very soul. Then she saw the suitcase. "Mel...Mel? What's going on? Where are you going? Our guests will be here in less than an hour. Mel! Don't leave like this! What's happened? You can't do this to me!"

He continued out the door and down the stairs toward the waiting taxi with Joy trailing frantically behind. "Don't I at least deserve an explanation?"

He kept his eyes on the taxi and said coldly, "Like the one I got all those years ago? Like that?"

"Please, Mel. Our friends will be here soon; can't you stay and we'll talk about this later tonight? What am I supposed to say to them?"

He finally turned and looked at her. "Tell them whatever you like. The truth never mattered to you before, so why bother with it now?" He tossed the suitcase in the back, got in the cab and said to the driver, "Hyatt Regency, please."

Shortly after checking in, Mel received a call on his cell. It was from General Mercy Hospital.

"Mr. Jameson? You asked us to notify you if there was any change in Miss Thomas' condition..."

CHAPTER 27

Nurse Betsy ambled into the room, approached Livy's bedside and began attaching another bag to the IV drip.

"What's that?" Livy inquired. "It's lethal, I hope."

"It's just a little something to help you handle the stress and to relax. But it's not supposed to make you too sleepy. We want you alert for a little while yet. Don't want you slipping away again." She put down the side rail and helped Livy to slide over somewhat on the mattress so that there was room to sit beside her on the edge of the bed. "Honey, I made some calls. It seems that your Bryan wasn't brought to this hospital or the others in the area. That could mean that he either didn't need to go to the hospital or that he was pronounced...at the scene. I felt like you needed to know, so I called Idaho. I was able to get a number for his folks in Blackfoot. When they answered, I think it was his mother, I said that I was inquiring about Bryan Kimball and she said," Betsy paused, took Livy's hand and continued, "—she said, 'Are you a friend of his?' and I said that I was calling from New York on behalf of a friend and she said, 'We're so sorry to have to tell you, but Bryan has passed away.' She said to please thank you for your friendship with their son and that they are so sorry to have to give you the bad news. She was so caring. I apologized for troubling them at a difficult time and passed along your love and sympathy for their loss. I'm so sorry, Darlin'. Did I do the right thing?"

With some effort, Livy turned her head and looked out the window into the overcast sky. "You did. I had to know. Did you give them my name?"

"No, I just felt kind of awkward and wanted to get off the phone as quickly as I could. You can call them again when you feel stronger if you like. But at least now you know and don't have to torture yourself wondering. Was he really special to you? Were you close?"

"More than you can imagine. And to think at this time last year, when I first met him, I thought he was a little pest, a hick. Oh, I would do anything to see that pest coming through that door. He was like my..." She shook her head. "No, he *was* my little brother. And it's all my fault!" Livy fought to hold back the flood of tears but the dam broke and they gushed over hers cheeks anyway.

"If I tried to hug you right now, I'd smash you, but if I could, I'd take you in my arms and rock you like a baby," Betsy said and gave a slight sad laugh.

"I wish that someone could. Oh how I wish."

Betsy squeezed Livy's hand and then went to check on other patients in the ICU.

Despite what Betsy had said, the drug in the IV was making Livy drowsy. She kept slipping in and out of a dream. Bryan was there, telling her it was all going to work out and she'd be all right. He'd kissed her on the forehead like he had so many times before. "When you feel alone, just think of me," he said. "I'll always be there."

She kept mixing dream and her surroundings. The many flowers around the room were now part of a funeral setting for Bryan. They were all there: "Mom and Dad", Carolyn and Jackson, Stew, Michael and Clayt, Leslie, Elizabeth, even Becky, and sweet little Sarah, whom Bryan had not even had the chance to meet in person, and the other siblings. And all the rest, including grandparents, cousins, nieces, nephew, in-laws, clergy from church and all the people who must have loved him so, were all there. She had missed it. They were sad, yet smiling and celebrating a life well lived. She couldn't even say good-bye. Her subconscious couldn't help contrasting the picture with the scene of her own possible funeral. In the dream, she had died too, and she saw that no one was there to mourn her. Reporters told the tale in a 10-second sound bite, but no one really cared. "Olivia Thomas, much celebrated then disgraced former employee of Joy's Toys, died this morning. Now on to other news...In Toledo today, a new sandwich was invented..."

She tossed back and forth despite her entanglements and cried, "No one is there. No flowers. There aren't any flowers."

"No flowers? Sweetie, look at this place!" Betsy declared. "There are more flowers than I've ever seen. He brings some every time he comes. You're dreamin' up a storm. Now wake up! You're not supposed to go to sleep for a while. Do you want to see him or don't you?"

"See him?"

"Mr. Jameson. He's right outside the door and he's brought even more flowers. Shall I let him in or not?"

Did she want to see him? What does he want? Now that her memory was clearer, she wasn't at all sure that she ever wanted to see him. The thought of his betrayal at the office encounter made her want to retreat back into the darkness from which she had just emerged.

But her lips moved and she said, "Let him in, I guess. I'll see him." She kept her eyes closed, putting off seeing his face.

Betsy propped open the door, just in case Livy needed her, and motioned to Mel to come in.

"I'll be right outside, darlin'." She pushed the cart back into the hall-way.

Mel walked in carrying daisies in a small vase of daisies. He ambled slowly to her bed and dragged a chair alongside to sit close to her. He whispered, "Olivia, it's me, Mel. You have no idea how relieved I am to hear that you are awake. They tell me that you are going to be fine. I'm so, so glad. I want to tell you—"

Livy spoke calmly to the ceiling. "Tell me what? That you're so relieved that I get to go to jail after all? That you're glad that I didn't die so that I can enjoy the wonderful world of fast food? That even though I've cheated you and embezzled from JTC, it's okay if I live, that I have your permission?"

"No. I wanted to help you. Livy, I'm sorry. I can imagine how you must have felt, but to throw yourself into traffic?"

"I didn't throw myself in front of that bus; you and your company are not worth that. I just...I don't know. I can hardly remember what happened. I woke up here and I guess, unfortunately for you, I'm not dead."

"I thank God that you're not. I thank God that by some miracle you lived though the impact and that you're awake again. I'm not a praying man as a rule, but I've been by your bedside everyday doing just that—praying. I didn't even know how to pray or if God would listen to me. But you're here and you're going to make it. That's all I know."

"Well, just so that you know, it was Bryan that saved me, not you or God." Livy exclaimed. "If it hadn't been for him, I would have been crushed by that bus and it would be all over and no one would have cared. How ironic that the person who had so many loved ones, the one who meant so much to so many, is gone and I'm still here. What for? What am I here for?"

"What? Who is Bryan? What did—?"

"I can't talk about him right now or I will totally lose it. Let's talk about going to jail." She still stared at the ceiling.

"No, Olivia, no. I'm so sorry. I know that you're innocent and that you had nothing whatsoever to do with all that happened. Please, can you forgive me? I should have known better. I know you. That wasn't you at all. Please look at me and say that you forgive me."

"What changed your mind? Do you feel sorry for me?"

"Everything inside me told me that it was all wrong. The whole thing just nagged and nagged at me and I wanted to get the chance to tell that I believed you. Then, just today actually, I found out the truth. I think I know pretty much what happened and it had nothing to do with you."

She softened a little. "If you had just listened to me..." She stiffened again. "Let me guess. It had something to do with Joy."

She finally looked at his face, searching for his reaction.

"I just couldn't believe that she would do something like that to her own company. And she wouldn't have except that she was being black-mailed. I guess she used her position to maneuver everything to point to you if someone found that the numbers didn't add up. That was unforgivable. Livy, I'm so sorry that I took her word and blamed you." Mel explored Livy's eyes for signs of forgiveness.

"She was blackmailed? How? Why?"

"I wanted to be the one to tell you. I'm sure the whole world will know soon enough but I want you to get it from me." Placing the daisies on the floor, he stood up, wiped the sweat from his brow, and began his story. He

186

awkwardly started with the summer vacation in the Dominican Republic when he was in graduate school and explained that he had had an affair even though he was, for all intents and purposes, engaged to Joy. He knew then that it was wrong. It wasn't fair to either of the women or even to him. But it happened.

"What I didn't know at the time was that Daisy had gotten pregnant. I married Joy even though I was torn by my feelings for Daisy. Well, the child was born, somewhere in the U.S., I guess. –A little girl. I didn't know anything about it, and then when her mother died, she was brought to me. She was still just a baby. Daisy's brother Carlos and his girlfriend brought her. Only, I wasn't there at the time. I was away on business and they brought the baby to the house and it was not a pleasant surprise for Joy. You can understand; she was hurt and angry and just after having a miscarriage...it was more than she could bear."

Mel awkwardly stammered through the next words. "Things were different then, attitudes were...well...She couldn't find it in her heart to raise my half-black child while she couldn't even have a baby of her own. She paid those people, handsomely I gather, to get rid of my little daughter and to never let me know that she was ever born. She paid them to get rid of my child, my little girl. She's kept that secret from me for thirty years now. So when your contest came up, it was a perfect opportunity for Carlos to come out of the woodwork and blackmail Joy into fixing the contest and..."

"Joy fixed the contest?" The realization came slowly. "What? You mean that picture of *Hannah—she's your baby*?" Livy's mind was swimming through disbelief.

He nodded and stared at the floor. "If she didn't win, Carlos would expose everything. If Joy didn't keep paying he'd tell the world all about who our little doll baby really was. Joy didn't want me to know what she had done, let alone the whole world. And you know the rest."

A shrill, shaking voice rang out from the doorway. "No, she doesn't know the rest, Melvin. Why don't you tell her the rest? I'd like to hear how it sounds when you say it."

Joy had quietly come in, unnoticed while Mel was speaking.

"Joy! How long have you been standing there?" Mel asked.

"Long enough to hear your version of the story and it makes me ill.

Tell her the best part, Mel. It's my favorite part! Tell her or I will."

She paused and waited for him to start talking. He looked utterly lost.

She began again. "Olivia, he left out just one tiny little detail. He did know that his precious little Daisy was pregnant. He knew because she came to the states looking for him to tell him the good news. She tried to get his parents to stand up for their future grandchild and to make Mel marry the poor girl. But they wouldn't hear of it. They were having no part of a black child and its island trash mother. What would their social circle say? What about his great job at JTC? And what about our engagement? To them, and probably to him, it wasn't a marriage; it was a merger. How could he throw that away for this...this...little mistake? They convinced Mel that there was an easy way out and he agreed. They paid the girl big money to have an abortion and just disappear. How much was it, Mel? What was disposal of your kid worth to you? How much was it worth to her?"

In anguish, Livy looked to Mel to deny it but he didn't. He was pulling petals off the daisies.

"How much?" Joy was relishing his humiliation.

"I don't know."

"Oh come on, Mel. You knew. Was it ten thousand? Twenty thousand? What was it worth to you and the folks to get rid of her? For a little island slut, ten bucks plus the cost of the procedure might do, huh?"

Mel stood, shouting with rage, "It was a hundred thousand dollars. My parents had more money than they knew what to do with. I knew she could make her dreams come true and then some in Boca Chica with that kind of money. I wanted her to be happy, to..." He stopped short. "What about you? How much did you pay Carlos to get rid of the baby? You can't act so pure. You don't even know what became of her. They could have killed her for all you cared."

"Oh yes, you cared so much that you never checked to see if Daisy went through with it. She couldn't flush your kid down the toilet but *you* could and you never looked back." Joy was crying as she spoke. She turned to Livy. "I didn't want the baby, but *he* wanted her dead! The world would love to know all about 'Mr. Toyman.', about the 'JTC-loves-kids-man!'"

Mel's face reddened and he yelled, "You have no idea what you're talking about. A thousand times I literally cried over that day. And when we tried to have a baby and couldn't, that day stung even more. I have been haunted by that trip to the clinic more than anything in my life. I wanted to undo it. But I couldn't. I thought it was all over that afternoon. All these years, I find out that I could have had my child, my only child; I could have had some peace but you kept that from me."

Livy finally interrupted and she was visibly shaken. She asked Mel, "So do you know now, what happened to her? What the low-lifes did with her?"

"No, but I intend to find out. All Carlos' old girlfriend told me was that she left her at a convent. She doesn't want me to know where the baby went; I'd just mess up her life. The woman said if she had *wanted* me in her life she would have come to me by now. But I'll find her, somehow."

Livy couldn't help but give a bitter laugh. "This is all very enlightening, but why me, Joy? Why did you have to try to destroy me?"

"Because every time I see you, I think of *her*... that other woman. You're young, beautiful, and black and Mel has always thought you were so wonderful. It was like a knife in my heart, seeing you together. I don't know if there was anything going on or not but you were a constant reminder that he had loved her and had a child with her. I thought if you were blamed then Carlos would see the jig was up and leave us alone. You'd be gone and we could just go on with our lives." Joy turned and faced Mel now. "I know what I did was wrong but I did it to protect you and JTC. I did it for us! I was just so desperate. He was going to broadcast it to the whole world. And now he probably will."

He gave her his back and looked at Livy. "I've left Joy, Olivia. Of course that means that I'll be leaving the company as well, or what's left of it after all this. But if you can forgive me Livy, we, you and I, can start something new. I've always wanted to be in on the beginning of something. We'll build a new company from scratch. I'd love to have you join me if you can forgive me."

Livy thought for a moment and said, shaking her head, "No, Mel. I think you should stay with Joy. You deserve each other. Both of you get out of my room. Get out of my life!"

Mel was stunned. "I know all this comes as a shock, but I hope when you're feeling stronger and ready to face the world again, you'll change your mind. I'll make sure that you get your share of the doll revenues. You know how much I believe in you, Livy. Through it all, deep down I believed in you."

"And I believed in you. But everything I believed was a lie. Now get out! Both of you! Just go! And I think that's there's probably a cell available for you, Joy, at Riker's Island, now that I won't be using it. Enjoy the wonderful world of orange jumpsuits, won't you? But I don't know how you'll get those four hour pedicures that you're used to."

Betsy bustled into the room with a hypodermic needle in her hand and pointed it at Joy. "Now you scoot! She said get out; don't you understand English? And you too, Mr. High and Mighty, on your way!"

Mel tossed the mangled daisies in the trash and started to leave. At the door, he turned back. "I don't know what else to say. I hope you'll reconsider."

When he saw Betsy moving ominously towards him, he stepped up his pace to the elevator, down to the lobby and out of the building. Once outside, he drifted through the cars in the hospital entry circle and hailed a cab. For now, he would go to the Hyatt. But where would he go after that? He had no home, no parents, no children and soon, no wife and no company. He would begin again, but how? Where?

Joy stood in the hallway in stunned confusion. At home, guests were probably eating her food and drinking her wine, oblivious to the drama. She had not called any of them, hadn't told the caterers to lock up or to turn people away. She couldn't go home and face them now. She wandered out into the frigid December air just as a light snow began to fall. She had not brought a coat. After twenty-three blocks, she slipped on the snow-slick sidewalk and put her knee through her stockings. The scrape was bleeding. Her elegant black designer dinner dress had ripped from the hem to her waist and she sat there in the slush, numb, bleeding and dejected on the path. A heavy-set homeless woman with red hair happened along with her shopping cart and advised, "You'd better get into a good shelter tonight. You don't have enough meat on your bones to keep a cricket warm." Leaving Joy a ratty, filthy blanket, she continued on her way.

Back in the room and turning to Livy, Betsy said, "Are you all right, now? You didn't need those people here tonight of all nights, causing you so much pain. It's good that I gave you that stress medication; you might have really gone after that woman. Heavens! I might have gone after her."

Betsy got up and fished in the nightstand and at last produced a little plastic bag that contained the few things Livy had when she was brought in. There was a ring, a bracelet and the beautiful little daisy-cross that she had worn, well hidden, on an extra-long chain, most all her life. Betsy took the pendant out and lovingly put it around Livy's neck.

She held up the cross and said, "There is someone who can hug you. You just let *Him* hold you, baby." She got another tissue and wiped away Livy's remaining tears. "It's okay. You can just sleep now. It will help you heal."

She tiptoed to the door and quietly slipped out.

When Betsy had gone, Livy struggled to open the clasp of the necklace to take it off, but could not move her hands well enough to get any dexterity. Finally, in anger and frustration, she yanked it off and broke the link that held the clasp. It tumbled to the sheet beside her. At last, Livy slipped into sleep.

CHAPTER 28

September, late 1970's

Just days after Mel had left, Daisy discovered that she was pregnant. After Mel had only been gone three weeks, Daisy packed up her brother, Carlos, and followed Mel to Boston. She called for him at his apartment but Mel refused to see her claiming that it would be too painful to have to say good-bye yet again. She went to his parents on Long Island, looking for allies. Surely they would want their son to do the honorable thing, the responsible thing, and marry the girl who carried their grandchild. Mel was summoned home to resolve the situation.

This was the first he'd heard of the baby. Daisy nearly persuaded him to come away with her and to be a father to their child. He had always loved children and wanted several. What more excuse did he need? His feelings for Joy, while affectionate, had grown more out of expectation and duty than out of passion or true love.

Would the world end if he were to marry Daisy? His parents made it clear that the world he had always known would indeed come to an end if he did not follow the long decided upon plan. He would no longer be welcome as part of the family and he certainly would lose his promised position with Joy's Toys. His parents would never accept Daisy or her half-black child as part of their family. They reminded Mel that it was the 1970's and now it was safe, easy and legal for them to simply get rid of the little inconvenience. Nothing could be simpler. Mrs. Jameson knew of a clinic that had a reputation for being very discreet. They knew Daisy, poor thing, would be devastated and they would do what they could to ease her pain. $100,000 ought to numb it, they reasoned. In the Dominican Republic, that kind of money could set her up in business for life. In the 1970's, it could set up anyone anywhere for life. She could provide a good lifestyle for herself and for her brother as well. It was almost ideal, a chance of a lifetime.

"This is the least you can do for the girl after using her in this irresponsible way," they scolded. "Let her go back where she belongs and live like a queen. You'd never be happy with her, Melvin. As for that child, we wouldn't have a thing to do with it. And don't think we'll just get over it in time. You'll be turning your back on your family forever. Don't throw your future away because of one foolish summer indiscretion."

Daisy listened and watched as they discussed her and her unworthy offspring as if she were not human and had no more feeling than a piece of furniture they were thinking of discarding. Mel made a few weak attempts to stand up for her but got very little chance to say a word. Getting nowhere, he was easily defeated. So it was decided. It would be best for everyone concerned. Daisy would be gone, baby would be gone, and that would be the end of that.

Mel and Daisy agreed that he would go with her to the clinic and stay with her until he was assured that she was alright, all had gone well and that the child was no more. The money would be deposited in an offshore account that she could access as soon as she was safely and permanently out of their lives.

The couple rode silently in the back of the Jameson limousine and it seemed to take forever to get to the clinic that Mrs. Jameson had contacted. When they arrived, Mel tenderly held her hand and helped her to register with admissions and paid in cash for services. She couldn't look at him. She could barely raise her gaze from the floor. How could he ask her to do this? Did their baby and their time together mean nothing to him? How could she ask it of herself? He stayed and held her hand. He brushed her hair from her tear stained face.

"It's better this way. You will have a wonderful life." He was trying to convince himself as well. "You and I...it would never work. We are from two totally different worlds. But I do love you, Daisy. What I felt for you was real."

"Then why...?" She broke down in sobs.

"Please don't cry. Daisy, I can't stand to see you cry. Some things are just not meant to be. "

"But some things just *are.*"

A nurse approached and politely broke the tension. She guided them to an exam room where she explained that Daisy would be examined and then taken by gurney to her "procedure"—Such an innocuous word for so devastating an event. Daisy wondered how the nurses and other staff members could be so casual and pleasant. For them, it was just the beginning of another day at work while it was the end of everything for Daisy's baby. As they helped her onto the gurney, Mel kissed a tear from her cheek. He accompanied her down the long pink hallway to the surgical center. It was hung with black and white photographs of peaceful landscapes. –Scenes from a lifeless world.

"Please just go, Mel. I can't bear to see your face when this is all over."

"Daisy, I want to know that you're alright. I'm sorry. I'm so, so sorry."

"Please do this for me. I don't want you to be here when I come out. I don't want to say goodbye again. Please, just go."

He squeezed her hand and watched them wheel her down the long hall and out of his life. By now he had tears of his own. He walked out into the cold fall morning. He tried to console himself. She would be fine. He would have other children. Joy would never know and they would have a good life together. Hopefully, this horrible feeling inside would pass and life would go on. At least his would.

Daisy was all prepped for the abortion. She lay on her back, feet in stirrups staring at the ceiling. She waited alone for the nurse to bring the doctor and for them to begin their work.

"How will I feel when it's through? Will I feel better?" she wondered. "Will I feel free to go on and begin an exciting new future? I'll be rich. I'll make the dream of owning my own resort come true. Carlos will be well provided for... But will this hurting in my empty heart and the void in my empty arms haunt me for the rest of my life?"

She touched the cross necklace that Mel had given her.

A quiet, tender voice from her very core spoke to her, "This baby comes straight from the heart of God, too. She is my gift and *my* child." Daisy knew she couldn't do it. She had lost Mel. She didn't want to lose the baby as she was losing him. Part of him was growing inside her and she had come to love that little someone as she had loved him.

No puedo. No lo puedo hacer. I can't! I can't do this!

She pulled the IV from her arm, along with everything else that tethered her. She pulled the hospital gown closed and ran down the hall to the room where she had left her clothes. It was only when she emerged dressed and ready for escape that a nurse confronted her and assured her "everyone goes through this", that "things will work out for the best", that "she would feel better when it was over" and of course that "it wouldn't hurt a bit."

It wouldn't hurt a bit? Who was she kidding? My baby will be dead and how could that not hurt?

She gathered up Carlos and all she had brought with her to start her new life in America and headed for Miami. Her grandmother's two sisters, Balbina and Eugenia lived there and they would take her in and help her with her pregnancy.

She passed the next seven months preparing for her baby and trying to keep her brother out of trouble. The latter was not an easy task. He had fallen into what amounted to a gang and she suspected that he was involved in drugs and violent activities. Miami was full of such opportunities for a boy of 17. Daisy never told him about the Jameson money which now waited in an account in the Cayman Islands. She had merely said that they had paid her to have an abortion and that she couldn't do it. If he found out, she knew that he would find a way to get at that cash and would use it to buy drugs or for some other malevolent purpose. Daisy would not touch it either; it almost felt cursed. It was blood money that only represented death and the disgust she felt for Mel's parents. *Someday though, someday that money will belong to my child and she will use it for something wonderful. It will be washed clean when it belongs to the very one once marked for death.*

Daisy, Margarita to everyone except Mel, was thrilled to deliver a beautiful 7 pound 8 oz. baby girl on March 24th. She was a gorgeous blend of the races. She had huge black eyes and curly black lashes. She had milk-chocolate skin and a perfect little nose and full pink lips. She was born with lots of wavy dark brown-red hair and was 22 inches long, very long indeed for a girl. Mel was 6 ft. 4 inches tall and she would be tall like him, like both of them. When she'd grown a bit and when her teeth came in, she learned to use an adorable smile to get most anything she wanted, especially from two doting elderly aunts. She had total command of Margarita's heart and could even charm the ever more hardened Carlos, somewhat. She was the happiest and most beloved of children.

In the months that followed, Daisy worked hard to provide for Carlos and for her little Linda. Leaving Linda in the care of her aunts, she went to work in one of the high- end Miami Beach resorts. She won recognition for her hard work and abilities. She received promotions and raises and held to her dream of one day being in charge.

She had befriended a young girl by the name of Maria Elena Patino, 'Patti', who worked in resort housekeeping. They had become very close and Margarita openly confided in her new friend. Patti knew all about Linda, who and where the father was and how he never knew that his child was indeed born. Margarita used to share her dream that Mel would soon tire of his loveless marriage and realize he still longed for his island sweetheart. He would come looking for her and he would be so thrilled to find her. She would describe to Patti what it would be like when he swept her up in his arms, begged her forgiveness and wept with joy when he saw his little daughter was alive and so beautiful.

Early on, Patti confided to Margarita that she was attracted to Carlos and Margarita was torn as to whether to warn Patti or to encourage her interest. She knew many a floundering man had been saved by the love of a good woman. But the ruin of many a good woman had come from loving an evil man. Had Carlos crossed that line? Was he floundering or was he truly lost? Margarita prayed that somehow she and Patti could save him. Patti was strong enough to have survived living with her father, a talented photographer and an abuser when drunk. Her mother had left them for another man when Patti was only six. When Patti was fifteen, her father moved in with a new girlfriend and left Patti pretty much on her own in their trailer home. She had taken care of herself for three years now. She was mature for 18. Carlos returned her interest and they began spending a lot of time together. Eventually, she all but moved in with Carlos and family. Margarita hoped the four of them could leave this place and begin again in a new and safer environment.

Margarita feared that Carlos was in increasing danger. That meant all of them, including the elderly aunts and the baby, were in danger, too. The gang members he had become involved with were violent drug dealers who used this young inexperienced boy to run their errands. He was a drug courier and sometimes carried messages to those who dared to challenge his superiors for market share in this territory or that. He began to play both sides of the fence. He was Black *and* he was Hispanic and he worked the middle ground between the rival gangs. He began skimming a share for himself off the top. He knew the danger and almost reveled in the excitement of it. No more subservience to a "big sister." Now he was a man; he could prove it. He had started packing a gun and other weapons. He usually carried his own stash of one illegal substance or another as well. He had Patti using marijuana and other drugs now and alcohol too, facts that she had hidden from Margarita out of shame.

Margarita and Patti planned to move to Orlando. Just this once, Margarita would use some of the "blood money" to save their lives. She found the account number that had been given her and withdrew just enough to leave some with the Aunts along with a letter of explanation, and a sufficient amount to begin a new life in a new place. They packed just what belongings they needed for the trip and Margarita hid $15,000 in the bottom of Linda's diaper bag. They waited for a night when Carlos would come home wasted or drunk. He would simply wake up in a new life and would realize it really meant the safety and freedom that was best for all of them. They could all begin again, again.

They did not have to wait long. On December 21, within three days of finishing their preparations, Carlos did his part and came home high on something. He was not ready for sleep, however. He was wild and ranting about "something going down" and how "those guys are gonna pay."

They tried to calm him down and get him to go to bed but he would have none of it. They knew that regardless of Carlos' condition, the time had come to make their move. The Oldsmobile was packed and ready for their journey. Patti carried Linda out to the car and strapped her into her car seat. She started the car, backed it out to the street and left it running while she came back to assist Margarita in getting Carlos out to the car.

He raged and yelled and threatened to go for his gun because "he was going to get those guys." The two women managed to force him into the back seat and shut the door. Patti climbed into the driver's seat and Margarita ran towards the passenger door. They were almost on their way.

It was then that the previously invisible black sedan sped up the street towards them. The blinding headlights suddenly flashed and two rifles bolted out of the open windows. Shots exploded into the night. One bullet blasted through the windshield missing Patti by inches and lodging in the upholstery of the back seat next to Carlos. Another sailed right over little Linda's head and through the back window. Several pelted the front windows of the house. Two more found a human mark. Margarita lay bleeding in the street under the open passenger door.

By this point, Carlos had lunged from the car into the street and was struggling to get a shot off. He was too stoned to handle the weapon. By the time he had it out and pointed in the right direction, the sedan was long gone. He screamed curses and obscenities into the night as if they alone could bring the perpetrators down. He turned to see Patti cradling his sister in her arms, praying, *"Hail, Mary, full of grace. The Lord is with thee. Blessed is the fruit of thy womb, Jesus. Be with us now and at the hour of our death. Our Father, who art in heaven..."* She was holding Margarita's daisy-cross pendant almost as if it were a rosary. Blood seemed to gush from wounds in her chest and from the groin.

"No! Not Margarita, no!" Carlos shouted incredulously and then he began to cry, loud and hard.

Alone in the car, the baby trembled. Somehow she knew Mommy was hurt, Mommy was going away. "Ma ma ma," she sobbed.

Margarita knew there was nothing to be done. Life was slipping away into a red puddle in the street. She called out in a weak voice, "Patti, how can I leave my little Linda motherless as well as fatherless? How can this be? How can life be so unfair?"

"You'll be all right, Margarita. Carlos! Call an ambulance!"

He stood motionless, unhearing, unbelieving. Finally he ran into the house.

"Take her from here Patti, please, promise me. Take her to her father. He can't turn her away now. Even *she* can't turn her away now," Margarita whispered.

"But he didn't want her, Margarita."

"Please Patti! He needs to see her. She needs her father. Please do this for me."

"Hold on Margarita! She needs you. She loves you."

But Patti knew Margarita was dying. She knew it was true that Linda belonged with her father and if he only saw her, held her in his arms, he couldn't help but love her. Even the grandparents would have to love her.

"Everything you need is in my purse and in her bag. I have his address and a birth certificate and money. Take this money for yourself. But there's more, an account number is there, and promise me it will go to Linda, please Patti. Don't tell Carlos about the money. Promise me, Patti!"

Carlos came running out of the house with Aunt Balbina who immediately took Margarita from Patti's arms. She covered her in a blanket and gently rocked her.

Patti held onto Margarita's hand and whispered, "I promise. I'll take her. I'll make sure she's okay."

Carlos dragged her away. He was almost sober now. "Get in the car. The ambulance is coming and that means the police are too and we gotta go. Those bastards may be stupid enough to come back, too. We have to go. Get in and drive!"

"But Margarita!"

Aunt Balbina whispered, "You can't help her now. Go! Que se vayan! Get out of here!"

She held Margarita close until the ambulance arrived. The EMT pronounced Margarita Guadalupe Sotomayor Reyes dead at the scene. Balbina couldn't explain to the police why her grand niece was outside in the street after midnight and no, she did not know the whereabouts of her grand nephew. She hoped she never would.

Patti drove for the first half hour in silent anger and grief. Neither of them knew what to say. She wanted to scream at Carlos for bringing home the violent garbage he had filled his life with. Margarita was dead because of him. But he knew all of that already. He was sweating, rocking back and forth and breathing heavily. He reminded Patti of her father when he was trying to come to grips with what he had done to her or her mother in one of his drunken rages. She knew that like her father's, Carlos' remorse was real but she wondered if like her father, Carlos would fail to learn anything from it. If this didn't wake him up, nothing would.

The prospect of change didn't look too likely when Carlos rifled through his jacket pockets and pulled out joints and crack cocaine. "What are you doing? Carlito! Carlito, Carlito! Haven't you had enough of that? Don't you see what it's done?"

"I know, Baby, I know. But I just gotta calm down; then I can get myself together, I promise. I'll leave it forever. I promise. I will."

"Look at me!"

He kept his eyes on the joint he was trying to light.

"Carlos! I want you to look at me before you get high again. I want you to see that I am covered in your own sister's blood because of what you've done! Now look!"

He gave her a quick glance and went back to his rocking as he took his first long drag.

She grabbed the joint from his shaking fingers, took a drag of her own and then threw it out the window. "Now look behind you! Do it and keep looking this time!" He turned around and she said, "That is your niece, your own flesh and blood; she now has no mother...because of you! She is traumatized and scared out of her mind."

"I know, because of me! I feel terrible about it. I loved Margarita; she took care of me. She was the only person who ever loved me since...Mami and Papi died. But what do I do? What can I say? I can't bring her back. I wish I could, but I can't. What do you wan' from me, Baby?" He broke down into sobs. "What do you wan' from me?"

"For one thing, I want you to live, Carlos. You know if you ever go back there, they will kill you."

"No, I will kill them first."

"No, Carlos. They tried to kill you tonight and they will try again. I hope your Aunts keep the place crawling with cops for a good long time."

"So where are we going? You had some plan to go somewhere, there are suitcases and food and everything in here. What were you plannin' to do?"

"We were going to take you away and start over. Margarita made a deposit on a place in Orlando and we were going to have a new life there.

With all that new Disney stuff going in that place, we'll be able to get jobs easy. Real jobs, Carlos. Not dealin."

"So you two just decided to what? Kidnap me? I don' get no say in nothin'?"

"You had to get out of there. I just wish we could have gone before this happened."

He couldn't really argue with that. They drove in silence again until Carlos noticed that they were on I-95 instead of on I-75. "Hey! I thought we were goin' to Orlando?"

"We have a little errand to run first." Patti looked over her shoulder at Linda who had cried herself to sleep.

"She's not coming to Orlando?" Carlos asked and Patti shook her head. "Good! I don't know what to do with a kid. So what ya' doin'? Where ya' takin' her?"

"Margarita wants her to go to her father. He deserves to know that he has a child and she deserves a father."

"That dirt bag? I should have killed him two years ago, for my sister's honor. We are driving to New York? Now? Tonight?"

"That's what she wanted and that's where we are going. It's almost Christmas and who can turn away a needy child at Christmas? This is the perfect time."

They took their time driving North up the East Coast freeway. They spent a night in an expensive hotel in South Carolina. Carlos slept like the dead that night and nearly the whole next day as well. The hotel was happy to supply a little portable crib for Linda and she had her own space in what the hotel called the sitting room. Patti dug out a couple of Linda's toys from the trunk of the car and happily plopped down on the floor and played with her for a couple of hours. A very cheerful child by nature, Linda gleefully soaked up the peek-a -boo smiles and affectionate hugs that Patti offered. Soon, the two of them were frolicking in the hotel pool, exchanging splashes. While feeding, changing, bathing and dressing this little girl, Patti got just a taste of motherhood and found herself enjoying the flavor. It wouldn't be hard for someone to bond with this little one, Patti was sure. She would be fine; the father would instantly fall in love with her as Patti was falling even now. Did the wife have any idea at all? What kind of person was she? Could she find room in her heart for this little surprise?

Patti used some of the money from the diaper bag to pay the bill and Carlos got curious. He grabbed the bag and when he saw what was inside he asked where all that cash had come from.

"This was the money that Mel's parents gave her to go away. She never wanted to use it but this was a crisis and she put it in there for all of us to start over. I just thought we could splurge a little here and let off some steam after everything that's happened. Obviously, you needed to rest. She thought maybe with a little seed money, we could all get a house," Patti explained as she fastened the belts of the car seat for Linda. She didn't mention there was much more where that cash had come from.

Carlos' mind would not rest after this discovery. He had plans for the money as soon as they got rid of the kid. "I'm ready to roll, how 'bout you? Let's hit the road." He put his arm around Patti and opened the passenger door. "I'll drive, honey. I'm feelin' much better now."

They arrived at their destination on Long Island, New York, late in the evening of the 23rd. The house was unbelievable. It was a dignified ivy-covered Tudor that seemed to take up a full block. All around it stood a stone and iron rail wall and at the driveway were huge iron gates. The grounds seemed a fairyland of white with twinkling lights shining through a thin layer of new fallen snow and silvery silhouettes of reindeer grazing gracefully among the trees. Linda would have it made and Carlos envied her. He took one more drag on his joint to get up his nerve.

For some reason, the gates were open and Carlos drove right up the circular driveway to the front entrance. It was nearly eleven when they knocked on the massive door. Carlos and Patti were surprised when a frail young woman in a bathrobe answered the door instead of a butler. Not one to wait for an invitation, Carlos barged right in pulling Patti in right behind him. She was carrying the sleeping child in her car seat.

"Excuse me!" The young woman began. She seemed angry and wary, but not frightened. "Who are you? I don't remember asking you in."

"Are you Mrs. Jameson? Mrs. Melvin Jameson?"

She nodded. "What's this about? What do you want?"

Patti put the seat down and stepped forward. She glanced over her shoulder at Carlos with exasperation. With a little more finesse, Patti began, "We are sorry to arrive so late. We have important business with your husband. If you could ask him to come down please, we need to speak with him." Patti knew this woman was the person who would require the winning over. "We've come a long way and our business is very important."

"My husband is asleep."

"Well, get him up. This is important, like she said." Carlos barked.

"You still haven't told me who you are."

"I am Carlos and this is my girlfriend, Patti. Now, where is Melvin?"

"What is the nature of your business with my husband?" She gave him a look of utter contempt. "He doesn't deal with the likes of you!"

"Oh, he doesn't? Do you see this little darling over here?" He gestured to the child asleep in the car seat. "She is a Christmas present for the mister and for you, too. She is his child."

"She is not!"

"I assure you, Mrs. Jameson, she is. If you'll just wake your husband, he'll be able to explain it all to you."

"He's not here. He is on a business trip with my father and won't be back until tomorrow."

"Then you will have a nice surprise waiting for him when he comes home. You can say "Oh Sweetie, it's Christmas Eve and look what Santa brought!'"

"I don't believe you. Where is the mother? What proof do you have?"

"Why don't you ask Mel's parents about their grandchild, the one they paid good money to get rid of."

Joy Jameson turned pale and had to sit down. Just recovering from a very recent miscarriage, she was shaking and this news made her too weak to stand.

Patti sat down next to her. "I know this is coming as a shock to you, one your weren't ready for, but you will love this little girl if you just give her a chance. She really is the sweetest thing. Her mother was Carlos' sister. Her dying wish was that her child be raised by her father. 'Take her to her father.' Those were practically her last words."

"Really, that is very sad for you but we can't take this...this...kid. I can't pass her off as mine ...she's not even white."

"Oh yeah? Well, she's half-white," Carlos interrupted.

"I'm not raising some Black child as my own."

"People adopt mixed-race children all the time. No one needs to know... the rest." Patti said.

"Not people in my world."

"Don't you think that Mel should have something to say about this?" Patti asked.

"Does he even know?" Joy asked.

"No, I told you," Carlos said as if speaking to an idiot. "He paid Margarita to get rid of it. He thinks of it as a problem that just went away. Money can do anything, right? It made it...her...just go away. But as you can see, she couldn't go through with the abortion. Margarita wanted his baby."

"If anyone is going to give my husband children it will be me and not some Black, Hispanic slut!"

"How dare you! I think my sister is the only one who had any honor at all in the situation. She took responsibility for her actions."

"She took money for her actions. What does that make her?"

Patti jumped in. "She loved that child and she loved Mel. She couldn't throw part of him away. What did he do? He just went on his merry way as if nothing had happened." She got up and walked over to the car seat. "Just look at her. Her name is Linda. It means lovely and that's what she is. She is innocent in all of this. How it all happened is not her fault. Please just look at what a beautiful little angel she is. I know that you could love her...if you gave her a chance. Please!"

Joy turned away and wouldn't look at her. "No. I can't do it. I know that I can't. She'll never be mine. I'll always think of my husband with her mother and I'll resent her. I will never love her. Is that what you want?" She was adamant. She turned to Carlos. "Our family owns a toy company. We have money. I can pay you and you can raise her in your family where she belongs. You are her flesh and blood, why can't you take her?"

"How much money are we talking here?" Carlos asked and Patti couldn't believe that he would make a deal with this woman.

"Carlos, don't you think that he...Mel, should have some say in the matter?" Patti asked.

Carlos saw this as his bargaining chip. "Oh yes, definitely. He needs to know and we can stay right here until he comes home. What do you say, Mrs. Jameson?"

"No! As Mel already showed by paying for an abortion, he doesn't want her baby. I don't want the baby. I want to be the one to give him children. Take the money, keep her, put her up for adoption; I don't care. Just take her away."

"I don' know. It costs a lot to bring up a child these days."

"I told you; I will give you money. I can get $50,000 right now from the safe."

"Tell you what. You have a lot of nice things here and you know if $50,000 just suddenly turns up missing, someone's going to ask a lot of questions. –Ones that you will not want to answer. So if I take... say this nice camera over here..." He picked it up and handed the state-of-the-art Nikon to Patti, "and this silver tray over here and some jewelry. I'm sure you have some that you wouldn't miss much, right?"

"What are you talking about? I'm not going to give—"

"See, tha' way you can say it was a burglar. You have insurance and no one will think too much about it. And you did leave that big gate wide open. How careless of you."

"And when the police ask and I describe you?"

"You didn't see anything. You were resting and didn't hear anything either. You just got up to find the safe was missing some cash and then you noticed other things...blah, blah, blah. You definitely don't want to say it was me, because when I talk to the police I will tell them how it really went down and they'll ask your husband to come and identify me. And maybe you'll have your little Christmas present after all. We have met, you know," Carlos warned.

"Just take it all and go. Don't try to contact us again or I *will* have you charged with extortion." She turned and left the room to go to the safe.

Carlos turned to Patti with a triumphant smirk. "What do you thin' about that, Patti?"

Part of her wanted to say that they both made her somewhat sick but instead she pleaded, "We can give her a good home, Carlos, with this kind of money, no matter where it came from. We can live nice and start over and really give her a life...Margarita wouldn't want her to stay with that ...that, that New York witch."

Joy returned to the room with cash in hand. "And this will be the end of it?"

"I don't know. He's getting off too easy. Margarita wanted Linda to be with her father. I promised we'd bring the *nena* to her father." Carlos said just to rub it in.

Joy sat down again, shaking with her head in her hands.

Patti stepped over to the car seat and touched Linda's little hand. "She deserves better, Carlos. This woman doesn't want her. Her father wanted her dead. How could we leave her with these people? She deserves to be loved, Carlos. We can take her. We can love her."

And so the money and goods changed hands and the child did not. The light snow had turned into a full blizzard. The Oldsmobile backed out of the driveway at high speed. Patti realized over the hours on I-95 that she and Carlos could never be the kind of parents that Linda needed. And so, on Christmas Day of 1978, Linda Sotomayor began her long and lonely journey in search of a home, in search of a father, in search of love. Her next stop was St. *Thomas* of Aquinas convent in North Carolina and then St. Anthony's Home for children. There, the nuns chose a new last name for her. Now she would be Linda Thomas—for the saint.

CHAPTER 29

The doctors in charge of Livy's case decided she could return home for Christmas. She would, however, need in-home care on a three-times-per-day schedule to make sure she did not relapse or miss any necessary therapy or medication.

When Livy got home from the hospital, Rachel, her aide, got her situated in her bedroom with everything she needed: the TV, lots of DVD's, books, snacks and anything else she could think of to keep her occupied. After checking Livy's vital signs, giving her a shower and several medications, Rachel left for the evening. Livy didn't want to be in bed, snacking and watching TV. She had cheated death and wondered why. Lying here, of no use to herself or anyone else, was the last thing she needed.

Once again, her apartment showed no sign of the approaching holiday; no mirth or merriment was evident here. She got up from her bed and went to the hall closet. Behind the boxes from her office she found the 18-inch tree and the little nativity scene that Bryan had brought her last year. She lovingly displayed them in front of the nine-foot window. As she plugged in the lights, bittersweet memories of an Idaho-style family Christmas and an Idaho young man flooded her heart. Had a year really passed? She returned to the closet and took out the *Tiffany's* gift box she had intended to give to Mel for Christmas. Thousands of times she had imagined the reaction on his face when he opened it. That long-anticipated moment was lost forever. Now the lovely package would only be good for decoration under the tree.

She studied each piece of the Nativity scene and smiled when she picked up a little lamb. She could vividly recall one Christmas from when she was about six and savored just a taste of Christmas spirit when she thought of it. She was still at the Catholic group home then, and got to be in the pageant. She remembered being dressed as a little lamb with a big cowbell around her neck. The collar was a bit too loose and when it was her turn, she clanged and clanked up the aisle and the audience laughed. She ran to the front crying and hid behind a shepherd. Of course she thought they were laughing at her because she was silly and because of that dumb bell. But they laughed because she was so cute.

Afterwards, she asked Sister M why she had to wear it and the nun hugged her and answered, "You wear that so that Jesus will always know where you are. That way, little lamb, you will never be lost."

After that, she wouldn't take it off and she let the bell ring loudly and proudly all evening long. (She held onto it for two years after that, until someone at a shelter finally stole it from her belongings.) After the pageant, a sweet, funny-smelling old Santa gave her the doll she would cling to for the next seven years and through many different homes. She called her doll Hannah. But this "Hannah" had never felt so lost.

More than four weeks had gone by since she had heard anything about Josie and Frankie. She longed know where Frankie had gone that night. Had they found him? Was Josie safe? Would she have any kind of Christmas? Maybe she could see the kids. She wobbled on shaky legs to the kitchen and found the last crayon drawing Josie had made for her still displayed on the fridge. There she found the number she had scribbled for child welfare services and she picked up the phone and dialed. Sylvia connected her to Daria, the caseworker, who broke the news.

"It's good to hear that you are going to be alright, Ms. Thomas. You must realize, however, that when we heard, well, when everyone thought that you...had serious criminal and legal problems, and then you had that terrible...accident, we naturally took you off the parenting candidate list. You understand; I'm sure. Besides, it doesn't matter now," Daria stammered.

"What do you mean it doesn't matter?" Livy asked.

"As you already knew, Francois ran away from his placement. And now Josette is back with her—"

"You sent her back to her mother? How could you do that? Do you know what kind of danger she was in? What abuse and neglect was going on?"

"Madeline did everything we asked of her. We had no choice."

"Everything...like what?" Livy demanded.

"She went through her sixty-day rehab for the cocaine and she has been in job training. She has vowed to stay off the street. She did what we asked and she wanted her daughter back. What else could we do? She kept her end of the bargain; we had to keep ours."

"What about Josie? What about your responsibility to her?"

"She was happy to be with her mom again. She loves her, Ms. Thomas."

"Of course she does. But whatever happened to laws and punishment? Prostitution is illegal. Drugs are illegal. Neglect and child endangerment are illegal. The woman gets a pass and the reward of getting Josie back? Are you people insane?"

Daria was angry now. "She spent some time in jail and she went to lock-down rehab. And as I just told you, Ms. Thomas, you are not a candidate for fostering or anything else right now, so none of this is any of your business. We are closely monitoring the situation. That's all you need to know."

"Let me tell you something *you* need to know. The only reason Josie is alive is because she had Frankie. He protected her and took care of her. Now he is gone. What is she going to do when things get bad again? Who is going to feed her when her mother leaves again for days at a time? Who will hide her from that goon who repeatedly beat her and her mother last spring and again in the fall?"

"She can call on us. She knows that. She'll be fine. I'll make sure she is."

"Oh, I feel so much better now." Livy said bitterly. "Can I at least see her during the holidays?"

"It sounds to me like you would try to do more than just see her. Don't make us seek an injunction or a restraining order against you. You are not approved to be meddling in this case. You're obviously unstable. I'm warning you; just back off. It seems that you have enough problems of your own to deal with. You are not needed here. Good afternoon and Merry Christmas!" Daria curtly signed off and hung up.

Livy shouted at the dial tone, "This is not over yet!" She stood trembling, supporting herself at the kitchen counter, and she pondered Daria's statement.

"You are not needed here." Because she had always heard that, she had always felt it. Livy had said as much herself. That Christmas morning, a year ago, she had told Bryan, "A kid (meaning herself) is too much trouble. They poop, they cry, they smell, they get into everything and poke their little noses into places where they don't belong, they're inconvenient and expensive...who wants to mess with all that?" The phrases joined a cacophony of others she had heard throughout her life. "You aren't wanted here." "There's no room for you." "I'm sorry; this family will not work out for you." "I don't know why we bother with you! Go back to wherever it was you came from." "Your Daddy took one look at you and threw you in the trash can." "No, you can't come *home* for Christmas. You have no home here." And most recently, "There's no place for you at Joy's Toys. Enjoy the wonderful world of fast food!" Again, she heard Joy's voice, "I didn't want the baby, but *he* wanted her dead!"

I am not needed or wanted anywhere. Why was I born? Why didn't Mel just get his wish that I would never be born? Bryan said I was here for a reason. He saved me for a reason. What possible reason could there be, Bryan?

She knew he would be missed this Christmas and every Christmas from now on. A family in Idaho was missing Bryan terribly, like she was. While it was true that his work had kept him from making the trek last Christmas, she knew he would have been with them this year, if it had been at all possible... even if she had to force him. The kind of love and closeness that he had described would be calling to him like a beacon, especially at Christmas, his favorite holiday.

She could almost see Marilee Kimball, knee deep in some yuletide project or another, wiping off her hands on an apron and opening the door to see Bryan standing there. (It would be just like him to surprise them.) She would hug the daylights out of him and just when he was about to faint from lack of oxygen, she would let loose of him and yell, "Hey Jake! Hey kids! It's Bryan! He's home for Christmas!" Livy was designing in her mind, an image of what she, herself, would like to experience—just once.

Livy knew them all and really did feel part of them somehow. They shared the pain that she now felt in a way that no one else could comprehend. They would share the love and the sense of loss she felt so keenly for their son and brother. Did they even know that she existed? Had he told them of the sister that he had so boldly claimed as part of the family? Maybe they already knew about her and would love to embrace her as one of them.

And then she knew she just had to be with them now. It was Christmas and a terrible time for a total stranger to descend upon the Kimballs, but she had to be there. She had to tell them how much their son and brother and uncle and everything else Bryan was, had meant to her and how much she had come to care about them through him. She loved them because she loved him. She hoped that their common feelings of love and grief would bring them to a relationship beyond that of strangers.

But she couldn't make herself call them. She might say all that needed to be said on the phone and that would be that. They might say they didn't *need* her to come; it wasn't *necessary.* Wanting desperately not to hear those words, she made up her mind to just show up at their door. She would actually be with them, be a part of them. She had to just go and hope that they would let her stay to share memories of Bryan and his 'Kimball Christmas' with them.

She pulled out her day planner and turned to the listing for her travel agent. He had gotten her to Paris, Tokyo, and London. Certainly, he could get her to Blackfoot, Idaho. She picked up the phone and dialed.

There was no flight available, so close to the holidays, to the nearest airport in Idaho Falls, so she made a reservation for Salt Lake City on December 23rd and a hotel reservation for that night. She booked a rental car for the three-hour drive to Blackfoot.   She couldn't tell Rachel, her aide. Rachel would tell the doctor and Betsy would probably show up and chain Livy to the bed. No, she would be the perfect patient for the next few days and then that morning, when Rachel had gone, she would leave a vague note and make her escape.

CHAPTER 30

Things went according to plan and she was able to endure the flight better than she expected. She landed at Salt Lake, picked up her rental car at the terminal and drove to the beautiful *Grand America Hotel.* The luxurious lodgings were her Christmas present to herself. She awoke to a beautiful winter morning. The sky was crystal clear and the mountains surrounding the Salt Lake Valley were brilliantly white with new snow. It was cold enough to see her breath but it wasn't downright freezing. She gathered her courage, bundled herself up in her powder blue parka and dramatically flung the ends of the scarf Bryan had given her around her neck and over her shoulders in an act of resolve.

It will be fine. I will like them and they will like me and we'll all talk about Bryan. Maybe they will invite me to stay for Christmas and then...then life will go on. What if they hate me? After all one could say that it's my fault that he is...gone. I must be nuts! The brain damage must be worse than the doctors thought.

The courteous young parking attendant at *Grand America* placed her larger suitcase into the trunk and she kept her carry-on/purse with her upfront. The hotel valet had instructed her on navigating the complicated on-ramps, off-ramps, exits and overpasses locals affectionately dubbed "the spaghetti bowl" that would take her to I-15 North. Map in hand, she was on her way.

She was surprised at how pretty it was, especially after she had passed through the major cities and was out in the country among the small towns and farms. There weren't the thousands of trees she would have seen in the East, but the snow-covered countryside had a rural simplicity that was both charming and inviting. After two hours she crossed the Idaho border and uttered a cheerful "Thank you," as she read the *Welcome to Idaho* billboard signed by the governor. *I will enjoy my stay, sir.* The determined pledge was mostly for her own benefit.

Pocatello was the first city of any size that she came upon after crossing the state line. She had been on the road for nearly three hours and though that she should probably stop for gas and a snack. It had been hours since she had eaten and she didn't feel like she could crash a grieving family's Christmas (a family of strangers at that) on an empty stomach. She needed, as they say, intestinal fortitude. The doctor had warned her that while she may not have much appetite, it was important to remember to eat.

At the junction of interstates, she turned into the Gem State Truck Stop and parked her rental near the gift shop entrance. She would have a little lunch and get herself ready to face what was to come.

She found *The Trucker's Mama's Kitchen* café and waited for the hostess to seat her. A cute blonde of about 20 finally approached and escorted her to a table near the window and gave Livy a menu. As she looked it over, she wondered how many truckers had just had coronaries after eating at such places. The glossy photos displayed stacks of pancakes, six or seven high with loads of butter, accompanied by ham and bacon and sausage *and*, of course, deep-fried hash browns. The lunch page advertised triple cheeseburgers with a full pound of beef smothered with the restaurant's proprietary secret sauce, all guaranteed to clog an artery in five minutes or less or your meal was free. Well, something like that. Livy ordered a fruit plate and a cup of coffee. When it came, she slurped up the coffee and mostly played with the fruit.

As Livy was forcing herself to eat a chunk of banana, a little girl of four or five at the booth in front of her kept peeking around her Daddy to steal a look at Livy. Livy played along and pretended not to notice and then slyly made a silly face at her. The little girl giggled and whispered something in her Daddy's ear. Not so discreetly, he turned around and glanced at Livy for himself. After he whispered something back, she replied loudly, "It is *too* the dolly-lady!"

"No, Honey," the big man said. He wore a plaid flannel shirt and a baseball cap with a large "I" on it and with his sun-weathered freckled face, he looked just like what Livy thought an Idaho potato farmer should look like. "Leave her alone. It's not nice to stare. I think that lady you're talking about is in a coma or brain-dead or something." He tried to hush his deep voice but Livy heard every word.

Livy piped up. "You're both right. I am the dolly-lady and I am brain dead. I must be, to be doing what I'm doing. I'm Olivia Thomas and you are—?" She extended her hand across the booth without getting up.

"I'm Ray Proctor," he returned as he tried and failed to extend his hand over the booth-back and across the table. He made a little waving gesture instead. He was obviously embarrassed.

"Daddy, see? It is her." The child fished in the corner of her seat and produced a *Hold-Me-Hannah* whom she informed Livy, was really named Suzy. "She's sleeping now so I haf' ta talk softly. I really love her. Thank you for making her. She's my best birthday ever!" She held up five chubby little fingers. "I turned five and my name is Wendy."

"I'm sorry about the brain-dead remark." Ray fingered the brim of his baseball cap. "The last we heard, it was looking pretty bad for you. We followed the story for a while after Wendy picked up on it. They showed you and the whole doll connection and since she is enthralled with her Suzy, Wendy was very interested. It's amazing how that doll captivates her—that face and how it keeps her busy and all. By the way, we entered Wendy's picture in your contest, you know."

"Really? She should have won. She's a beautiful child, Ray."

"So...uh...how did all that play out, anyway?" Ray asked awkwardly.

"I didn't do what they said, if that's what you mean. Don't hold your breath for JTC to come out and make a big explanation and an apology, though."

"So you are alright now then?"

"Some might say yes and then again..."

"What in the world brings you out to little old Pocatello, Idaho, for Pete's sake?"

"It's a long sad story I just can't go into. I'm actually on my way to Blackfoot. Is it far from here?" Livy asked, happy to change the subject.

"Heck, no. It's just up the road apiece. –Half hour or so. I'm from Blackfoot myself. What ya' gonna do there?"

"Well," Livy hesitated and decided to go on. "Do you know the Kimballs?"

"Jake and Marilee Kimball?"

Livy nodded.

"Jake and Marilee Kimball? My heck, yeah! Their farm is just up the road; they are my neighbors. Everybody knows the Kimball family. They make up a quarter of the town... well, pert' near. That's where you're going?"

"What do you think of them?"

"They are somethin' else." Ray smiled and shook his head.

Livy's heart sank just a little. "Do you mean they are weird?"

"Not weird, they're amazing! Marilee's just a regular woman, I guess, but seems to handle more than any of us can even imagine. Like this one time? I was at the next check stand at the grocery store and she's got like six kids with her. You know, some are in the cart and some running around and stuff. Well, this woman comes up behind her and says, 'you know, there is such a thing as birth control. How can you possibly take good care of that many kids?' As if she could have actually borne all those different kinds a' kids! She didn't even know that there was a bunch more at home and at school. And Marilee answers back without missing a beat and says, 'Thank you! You're absolutely right. Which one would you like to take care of? Go ahead, pick one. I sure could use the help.' That shut her up fast. And yet Marilee, she's just...she's still..." Ray took off the cap and pushed his thick brown hair back as if it would help him find the right word.

"She's just, still what?" Livy really wanted to know what to expect from these people. Bryan, of course, wasn't objective; to him they were perfect.

"Well, I guess she's so good with kids 'cause she still is one. She's a big kid. Jake's even more that way. He's hardly ever serious," Ray laughed.

Wendy had been staring at Livy with a puzzled face. "Will Suzy grow up to look like you 'cause you made her?" Wendy asked Livy as she placed Suzy back in her little seat.

"Suzy will always be your baby, won't she? And if she did grow up, I bet she would look like you. See? She has pretty blonde hair like yours," Livy said.

"Mommy says she made me out of Maalox. Is that good?"

"Must be, because look how beautiful you turned out!"

Wendy leaned close, staring at Livy for a moment and then pronounced, "You are pretty."

"Thank you, Wendy."

"Are you black?" Wendy asked with childlike directness.

"Umm, that's a good question. I'm part black."

"Part black? Which part?" A light bulb seemed to turn on in her little head and her face lit up. "Do you have black feet? Is that why you came to our town?"

Livy tried not to laugh but couldn't help it. "Maybe that *is* why I came to Blackfoot. Actually, my feet are black but are part white too, is that okay?"

"Oh sure, it's okay. I just wondered."

Ray, a bit chagrinned, chuckled a little, too. "I guess we don't have enough diversity around here."

Just then, the waitress approached Livy's table with her check and exclaimed as she looked out the window, "Oh my goodness! Look at it comin' down out there!"

"What? Snowing?" Livy looked out into the white frenzied air. "It was sunny when I came in!" Livy cried in panic.

"Yes, ma'am. It's December in Idaho and it does tend to do that from time to time. Snows back East, don't it?" Ray could tell Livy was very nervous about it. He was about to offer some assistance but she was too quick for him.

Up and out of her booth almost faster than the waitress could finish her bill, Livy dashed to the cashier to pay and then out to the white blob her rental car was quickly becoming. She thought perhaps she could get to Blackfoot before the snow began to accumulate on the road. While it certainly snowed in New York, Livy had never driven in it there. She always took subways, taxis and busses. Most of her driving experience had been in Florida and conditions there never resembled anything like this. She started the car and the frightful last leg of her journey.

At first, harmless flurries of snow danced in the air and melted on the car-warmed asphalt. But with every passing moment, the darkness pressed in heavier around her and the winds raged more threateningly. Soon, harmless flurries turned to a frenzy of giant flakes of blinding white and the road was swallowed up in wet, slick snow. It had come up behind her like a giant stalking animal and had overtaken her. There was nothing much between here and Blackfoot and there was no turning back.

She knew her exit number but most of the signs were now covered in snow and unreadable. According to Map Quest, she would drive 19.7 miles from the last Pocatello exit to her destination ranch exit. It might as well be a hundred. She was creeping along at about five miles per hour now and her white knuckled hands strangled the wheel in a death grip. More experienced snow-drivers and those Livy assumed to be less encumbered by common sense, raced by, swerving, on all sides. She'd have to speed up some or this twenty-minute drive would become a two-hour nightmare or worse. She gave the gas a little push and immediately began to fishtail. *Turn into the skid and avoid sudden braking*, the Internet snow-driving tips had said. She corrected slightly, resisted the urge to brake and continued, terrified.

When the odometer clicked off the appropriate number of miles, and when fifty minutes that seemed like hours had passed, Livy thought she spotted the remote exit. From here, it would only be another 4.2 miles to the Kimball farm. She carefully moved to the right and followed the exit, which immediately became a downhill slope. At the bottom of the hill she could make out a partially hidden stop sign at the cross street. As instructed by the tips, she tried to pump the brake to gradually stop but suddenly launched into a spin. Instinct took over and she was braking for all she was worth. The car was totally out of control and then suddenly careening backwards at great speed, it sailed trunk first into a deep ditch across the intersecting road. A violent jolt marked the car's abrupt stop with the rear end at the bottom of the ditch and the front end sticking straight up. The front wheels didn't touch the ground. Livy was lying back against the seat, staring straight out the windshield into the white sky of the blizzard. Because the impact was in the rear, the airbag did not deploy, thankfully.

Mentally, she did an inventory of her body. She concluded that she was okay; she had no broken bones and she had blessedly not hit her head. She may have had just a little whiplash from the rough impact but nothing other than that. Now, however, she was trembling. Although the shaking was not from the cold, but from the panic and the ordeal she had just experienced, it did bring to mind a disturbing thought. With the winds and the blizzard raging on, it was probably colder than twenty degrees outside the car and the temperature was rapidly falling inside. The car had stopped running and when Livy's shaking hand turned the key, the engine did manage to start. She tried to feel whether the heater still worked. It wouldn't matter anyway. The interior air was quickly filling with carbon monoxide. The blow to the back end must have damaged the exhaust system.

She immediately stopped the engine. Opening the door to breathe some cleaner air, Livy was stung by little ice-blades and the freezing cold. She leaned out and looked down to see several jagged rocks jutting up through the snow below. There was no way to jump and avoid further injury. A growl of metal against rock sounded as the car began to lean precariously toward the driver's side. Livy didn't have time to completely close the door. The rocks did it for her in rough and ruthless fashion as the car slammed down on its side upon them, catching a good portion of her hair in the jammed door and giving her what felt like a good swift kick in the face and shoulder. The point of a sharp rock protruded through the shattered window just an inch or two from her face and it was edging its way further in as the side of the car settled down upon it. The seatback suddenly jerked forward and locked; her right arm was pinned between her chest and the wheel. She could barely breathe.

Her quivering was now uncontrollable as the very real possibilities of more injury and/or freezing to death loomed before her. She was quite sure that she was not visible from the interstate above. Probably, half an hour went by and no other vehicles had passed or were in sight. This remote exit most likely didn't get much traffic at any time, let alone in a blizzard.

Nurse Betsy had said what a great thing it was that she had awakened and wouldn't miss Christmas. Now she would miss it but no one would miss her. No one knew where she was or what her destination had been.

She remembered with half a hopeless smile, Fitz talking about nearly missing Christmas last year. Kyle Fitzgerald always like to decorate his office for all the holidays and Mel had allowed it, provided everything was back to its normal state after the holiday had passed. On Christmas Eve,

Kyle hired some homeless guys, down the block, who carried the proverbial "will work for food" signs, to repaint his office. He painted the doors bright red and added peppermint stripes to the interior walls and doors. He figured the men would enjoy a little Christmas Eve cash and they were happy to take the job. They had painted the interior doors, and not wanting to get paint on the fancy knobs, they removed them. They would come back in a day or two to replace them and to finish up.

Kyle had groused about having to work so late the day before Christmas and was about to leave when nature's urge suddenly struck. He took the chance "to go" because he was heading straight for his church on Long Island to see his kids in the Nativity pageant. Out of habit, he stepped into his office bathroom and let the door close behind him. After taking care of business, he realized that without the knob, he could not open the door. He yelled and kicked but most people on his floor had left hours before and no one heard him. His wallet, keys and cell phone were on the desk. He took off his jacket, sat down on the floor and settled in to miss Christmas.

Meanwhile, at the church, Kyle's wife Debbie refused to let the pageant committee start the show without him. He was to videotape it for everyone and he would be crushed to miss seeing the kids. She became more and more alarmed when he answered neither his office nor cell phones. She called the hospitals, his favorite bar, and the highway patrol and got nowhere. Finally, after a couple of hours of delay, and after the audience had sung every carol in the hymnbook, one of the Wise Men had the brilliant idea that Kyle might have had a heart attack while opening his holiday-inflated Visa bill at his desk in the office. It was the best explanation they had so far, so two Wise Men, an angel and an innkeeper set off to the city for the rescue. They finally persuaded the skeptical security guard to take them up to Kyle's office and to let them in. Feeling somewhat relieved when they didn't find him in a heap behind his desk, they checked the window ledge to see if he was poised to jump. No Kyle. Their voices awakened him from dozing in the bathroom and he yelled for them to get him out. The security guard managed to round up the necessary tools and they were able to take the door off. By 9:30 p.m. he was happily settled in behind the video camera and the pageant began. A few of the children were hungry and cranky but the show did go on. It was three hours late but it made a nice little segue right into the midnight service.

If Livy had been stuck in a bathroom on any one of twenty Christmases no one would have missed her, she was sure—not for days and days. She would have survived by drinking the water in the tank. And now, this Christmas, no one was looking for Olivia Thomas. No one would call the highway patrol or the hospitals.

Wouldn't it be strange if after all she had been through, all the trials she had overcome, and the miraculous recovery, she ended up frozen and forgotten in a snow-inundated ditch in the middle of nowhere in Idaho and only 4.2 miles from destination? She was utterly helpless and dependent on a miracle...again! For years and years, she had been out to prove that she didn't need anything or anyone. She had learned to get what she wanted to get, to go where she wanted to go and do it all on her own. Now there was absolutely nothing she could do to save herself. The car was not visible from the interstate above and not one vehicle had passed on this deserted country road. Now, when she needed someone, people suddenly had the common sense to stay off the roads! She pounded her left fist on the door in anger. The jagged rock inched closer to scraping her immobilized face.

Did she care at this point if she lived or died? Did anyone else care? The darkness of the winter day crowded upon in her and she felt the temperature dropping fast with the sun's departure. All she would have to do would be to free her hand, start up the car, breathe deeply, and go to sleep. There were worse ways to go. Everything she cared about was gone. And yet as she searched her feelings she found she wanted desperately to live. *But what for?*

"Ask God how he wants to use you," Bryan had said.

Ask God? Then it was as if she could hear God asking, "Livy, what does it take to get your attention? When will you admit that you need me?"

She answered back aloud, "When will you admit that you've forsaken me? My whole life you've left me to struggle and suffer alone. Where were you then? Where are you now?"

It wasn't much of a prayer. She realized that she really didn't know how to pray, but that if she was going to have this conversation, she had better learn. She began a little more humbly and in complete panic:

"Please God, I have no one left to turn to, no way to help myself. You win. I can only turn to you. So I hope that if you are there, you will hear me and if you care, you'll listen. I know that I've been rebellious and almost hated you at times because of my childhood. I've been so angry with you for taking away everyone I ever loved until I felt I could never risk loving again. Then Bryan helped me love again and now he too, is gone. The kids are out of reach. Mel and all he meant to me...gone." She softened somewhat. *"Bryan said to acknowledge your hand in everything in my life, but that's not quite the same thing as blaming you, is it? Forgive me; don't hate me. If you save me now, I'll have to acknowledge your hand in it. Please help me live. Do you have a plan for me? Is there a reason for me to stay? If you show me the way, I will try to follow. Can you forgive my sins and my anger and can you ease my pain? Jesus saves, they say. Can he save me now? One way or the other, save me, rescue me, please. —Whether in heaven or on this earth, save me, please God. But I want to live, and I want my life to mean something to someone."*

Bryan had said that she had to have the faith to say what she said next, and she really had no choice... *"Thy will be done. In Jesus' name I pray, amen."*

Still, no cars appeared on the road. But she was beginning to calm down and was almost resigned to her possible fate. As two hours passed, the temperature continued to drop and her hands and feet were numb, and yet she was not afraid; she was at peace. Her weak body's response to the cold was a desire for sleep. When she could fight it no longer, she surrendered to its call. After a time, she was aware of being warm and well and she felt herself being drawn up and away from the frigid car and toward a warm and wonderful being of light and love. She drew closer and closer until she saw his face and felt his arms around her... a familiar face and familiar arms. They were Bryan's!

He smiled at her, kissed the top of her head and said, "Hang on, Sis. You're almost there. You're almost home."

She held him tightly and whispered, "I told you Bryan, when I'm with you my heart is home. Is this where I'll stay? With you? Let me stay with you. Is this home?"

CHAPTER 31

"Not yet, my dear Livy. There is so much for you to do. Hold on. You're almost there."

He was fading away. "Bryan—!"

Suddenly, the screeching of a saw cutting away at the metal of the passenger door above her shattered the peaceful silence. But she had been with Bryan; had she only dreamt it?

"Hang on," the big man called out. "We're almost there." Grating and growling sounds of the metal door being wrenched from its hinges followed. The stranger reached down to her but couldn't pull her out because her hair held her fastened to the door. He pulled up and out and called to his son, "Clayton, get that rope from the back of the truck and start on the winch, and Jackson, you get Josh out here with the pocket knife from the glove box."

In a few moments, a little boy of about six or seven descended toward her, face first, while his dad held him by the feet. He held the open knife in his hand.

"Hi, I'm Josh," he said as casually as if they had met in the park in spring.

With that he began sawing away at her hair with the same stylistic finesse he used on the sheep he regularly sheared. When she was sufficiently shorn and freed from the door, he reached down and found the seat belt release and the seatback recline lever. The chair bolted violently backwards and so did Livy. Suddenly, Josh ascended back up and out of the door hole. Clayton was busily tying the rope around the frame of the car door while Jackson hooked up the winch. Soon the car was abruptly hauled up from the ditch. The father reached in and pulled Livy from the ravaged vehicle and carried her toward the truck. She felt a sudden wave of nausea overtake her and she quickly turned to her right and vomited on the uncut side of her hair and all over the stranger's boot.

"Thank you," she murmured. "I mean, I'm sorry."

"That's alright. I'm just glad we found you before you froze to death. I'm Jake Kimball by the way."

"I knew you were; you had to be." Livy smiled weakly. He was just as Bryan had described. –A large man with large hands, a weather-beaten kind face and a deep friendly voice. Under his stocking cap she could see wisps of graying blonde hair. She said, "I'm Olivia."

"I knew you were; you had to be," Jake repeated. Livy dared to hope that Bryan had told them something about her but couldn't imagine how they knew she was here. She was too weak to ask.

Jackson bundled up the rope and put away the saw, attached a bandana to the mangled car and was climbing into the cab. Jake got Livy into the backseat, laying her across the bench with her head on little Josh's lap and covering her with a blanket. Clayton reached into the backseat of the car, got her purse and brought it to her.

"She stinks like barf, Dad," Josh said and wrinkled up his slightly reddened little brown nose.

"You've stunk like that a few times yourself, bucko," Jake replied with a laugh as he took some snow and cleaned off his boots. He started for the driver's side. He turned his head to Livy and asked, "Do you think you need to go to the hospital?"

"No hospital please. I've been there, done that. Please, could you just take me to your home?"

"Sure thing, but our son David who's just graduated from med school, is home for the holidays and we'll have him check you out. If he says hospital, you'll go, okay?"

Livy nodded and they began their 4.2-mile journey to the Kimball farm.

CHAPTER 32

Proceeding carefully, the truck labored up the snow-bound country road and finally reached the long driveway leading to the charming old farmhouse. "We're home now, Olivia. Don't try to walk. We'll get 'ya inside."

With considerable effort she sat up and marveled at the little winter wonderland before her. She must be dreaming of heaven again. Icicles hung like stalactites from the gingerbread trim around the veranda of the stately old house. The icicles encased the Christmas lights and provided a misty prism for Christmas colors to shine through. The effect was magical as the aura reflected onto the frosted trees and the bushes in holiday splendor.

Marilee was already at the door, holding it open as Jackson carried a blanket- wrapped Livy into the house. "So you found her then?" Marilee commented on the obvious. She was just as Livy had pictured her in some ways. She wore an apron dusted with flour from Christmas baking. She exuded mothering and caring. But she bore no physical resemblance to Bryan at all. She had dark hair with a few strands of white, dark eyes and a light bronze complexion. Bryan must have taken after his blonde blue-eyed father.

Jake answered, "Yeah, we found her in that ditch by the freeway exit. –And not a moment too soon. She never would have made it out of there herself. She's probably dipping into hypothermia. We'd better..."

"Let's get her into a tub of warm water," Marilee suggested.

"First, let's let David look her over."

David, the eldest son, married, father of one, and about to start his internship in Seattle, stepped up and examined Livy. She examined him as well. He was the overachiever, Bryan had told her, a perfectionist. She would be in good hands. After checking her vital signs and examining her as best he could, he explained that she mostly needed warming, food and rest. From what he could tell, going back outside onto questionable roads in freezing weather in search of an emergency room was definitely not what the doctor would order.

Livy was vaguely aware of Jackson carrying her into the bathroom off the main hallway. Marilee was already filling the tub.

"Sweetheart, come and give me a hand with her, would you please?" Marilee called out to the beautiful dark-eyed teen watching from the hall. She must be the "gorgeous one" with the cruel tongue that Bryan had talked about. She was a foster-daughter trying to decide whether to accept the invitation to become a permanent member of the family. She'd been with them since deciding to give up her baby for adoption. Her parents had thrown her out and the Kimballs had taken her in.

With very little of Livy's own power, mother and daughter managed to get her out of the blanket and her wet cold clothes down to her underwear. They helped her to step into the warm water that felt scalding hot to her frozen flesh. She gasped at its sting. Gradually they helped her sit and lie back while they gently massaged her limbs. After a few moments, the burning subsided and she was able to relax.

"Honey," Marilee said to Becky, "run upstairs to my dresser and in the top drawer you'll find a wrapped package with your name on it. It's new underwear. I was going to give it to you in your Christmas stocking, but I think she needs it more. Also, get my just washed green flannels from the laundry basket in my closet, okay?"

All the while, Marilee cooed a soothing banter of comforting phrases as if bathing a baby. "This should help you feel better. There now, let's give those pretty little toes a rub and get them nice and warm. Now, how's that feel? Are you doing alright?" She filled in the gaps with soft humming.

Livy's proud, independent nature resisted the helplessness and humiliation of being treated like a baby. But the humble, wounded inner child drank it in and felt this was what it must be like to be loved and cared for by angels. Marilee then, careful not to get shampoo in her eyes, gently washed and conditioned Livy's ravaged hair.

"Mom, I can't find the pajamas in that basket," Becky called out.

"Come stay with Olivia for a moment. I'll find them."

Becky helped Livy to stand up and dry off and Livy ventured, "You're Becky, right?" The girl nodded in bewilderment and Livy explained, "I knew your brother, Bryan, in New York. He described you perfectly."

"You knew Bryan? What did Bryan tell you about me?" she asked cautiously.

"He said you were the gorgeous one. He was certainly right about that."

"That's what he said...after all the awful things I called him...he called me the gorgeous one? What else did he tell you?"

"Well, he said you didn't always appreciate him trying to scare the guys away and you were hurting pretty badly at the time—"

"I was hurting but that was no excuse for how I treated him. When you hurt someone like that, over and over and then they die...it feels just awful. Especially someone like Bryan," Becky added with an edge of emotion in her voice.

"He'd forgiven you, long ago. I could tell. Imagine how *I* feel. It was because of me—"

Just then Marilee returned with green flannels in hand. "I found them all folded and put in my drawer. I must be losing my mind. Here you go, Olivia. You can put these on."

Soon, Livy was warmed, bathed, clothed and coiffed. (Becky had helped her even out Josh's sheep shearing job.) She was seated in a large easy chair facing the fire. The room, the whole house she supposed, was *Christmas Incorporated.* The old parlor had very high ceilings, allowing for a tall, full, ponderosa pine, which smelled heavenly. On it was every kind of ornament imaginable, from the very classy to the child's handmade masterpiece. Loads of presents, many obviously wrapped by childish hands, had it surrounded. The archways between rooms were decked with boughs of homemade holly along with red and green paper chains. The other smells of the season wafted through the air: fresh baked gingerbread, the smell of the fire and something else...soup!

Marilee pushed through the swinging dining room door with a tray of soup, crackers, orange slices and chamomile tea. "Becky and the girls thought that I should come up with something a little fancier than chicken noodle soup, but to me, there's nothing better when you've come in from the cold. Don't you think so?"

She laid the tray over Livy's lap.

"This is wonderful, just perfect. Thank you," she replied lifting her cup to take a sip of tea.

Jake and three very tall teenage and older boys came barreling into the room in some kind of wrestling mode. One of the guys, probably Clayton, if she remembered right, was up on the back of the biggest one, Jackson, not jousting, but as if trying to take him down. Without warning, Clayton went flying up and over Jackson and above the couch and landed on his back on the beanbag chair right next to Livy's feet. The thud rattled the entire room and shook the Christmas tree. Livy steadied her soup and her tea but was not surprised by what she saw. She had been warned. She could imagine a bouncing Bryan right in the thick of the rough housing.

"Boys! This is neither the WWF nor the NFL. You could have spilled that hot liquid all over her. Save your tackling for the football field. Now stand up and introduce yourselves to Olivia," Marilee lovingly scolded.

Jackson was suddenly all chivalry and honor. With a hand on his heart he said, "Jackson Kimball, m'lady, at your service." He came around and knelt at her feet. He gestured to his brothers. "And these are my knaves, Clayton the bold and Stewart the dwebe."

The brothers were on their feet and offering slight polite bows. Stewart slyly and lightly kicked Jackson in the back of the head while he had the standing advantage. It didn't faze him a bit. They all sat back down.

"I'm sorry," Jake said. "I should have calmed them down before I brought them in. I get a little caught up in their bedlam sometimes, too. They really are good guys, though, trust me." He sat down in a big recliner to the left of the couch.

"Oh, I know they are." She finally asked, "How did you know who I was and how to find me?"

"Our neighbor, Ray Proctor, called and said that he had met you in Pocatello and you were on your way here. He said you seemed terrified of the storm and he was concerned about you. He and Wendy had gone to pick up a special gift he had some shop make for Emily, his wife, you know. He didn't even make it home and so he called from a motel and asked if

227

you got here all right." Marilee explained. "When you still hadn't arrived after a couple of hours, we were very worried."

Livy was incredulous. "He was *concerned* about me? You were *worried?* And when I didn't arrive, you came out in that blizzard mess after me; you just showed up like the freakin' red cross! Is everyone in Idaho this good? This nice?" Livy asked, thinking of Bryan.

"Well," Jake said from across the room, "we have to look out for each other in a rural community like this. It's just what you do. You take care of each other."

"Yes, but I'm just a stranger."

Jake smiled and shook his head. "Not anymore. After all, you upchucked on my boots; so you're practically family. And you can't get much stranger than this crowd, right, guys?"

Livy looked around the room, which had gradually filled with Kimballs of varying ages, sizes and races already dressed for the family Christmas pageant. Becky 'shepherded' Sarah and Leslie, dressed as angels and Elizabeth in her Biblical garb into the room. When little Sarah saw Livy was of darker skin like hers, she lit up and went over to sit on the floor beside her and laid a comforting hand on Livy's arm.

Livy knew all their names and their stories. The curiosity in the sea of eyes made it clear they wanted to know her story and how the infamous doll-lady had ended up in their living room.

Elizabeth, a ten-year-old already dressed as *Mary* for the family Nativity, and according to Bryan, suspicious of everyone until trust was built, voiced the thoughts of all when she asked pointedly, "Well?"

"You are Elizabeth, aren't you? I can tell."

"I know who I am but I'm asking about you."

That was Elizabeth all right. Bryan had described her to a tee. He thought that she would grow up to be either a lawyer or an interrogator for the FBI. She was a no nonsense kind of person and Livy knew she'd better answer, or else!

Livy really felt too weak and tired to go into it all at this moment but there they were, waiting for an explanation. She took a deep breath and asked, "Didn't *he* tell you about me?" They gave her confused stares.

She sighed with tired trepidation and searched for the right way to begin. Why had Bryan told her, *'they love you already'* when he hadn't said a word?

Marilee intervened with, "We don't have to give her the third degree. She's been through a lot. Maybe she just needs to get some rest. We can talk in the morning." She stood up to help Livy upstairs. "Boys, go get the barn ready for the Nativity." And gesturing to the little twins, asked, "Where are my wise men? Have you got your props?"

The boys reluctantly started for the door.

Elizabeth pressed on. "She can tell us why she's here and then she can rest."

Marilee looked at her with embarrassment and scolded, "Leave her alone, Bethie. You're being rude."

"It's okay," Livy said. "Elizabeth is right. I probably won't be able to rest until I explain myself." Livy said.

Now the little detective *was* suspicious. "Explain what? And how do you know my name?"

"I know all your names. I know all about you."

"What's her name?" Elizabeth gestured to Sarah.

"That's your newest sister, Sarah, from Ethiopia."

Elizabeth was floored and gasped, "Mom, she's a spy. Why does she know all about us?"

"She's not a spy and…" Marilee began but seemed a little nervous, herself.

"It's because of Bryan…I met him in New York and…you're sure he never mentioned me in a phone call or anything?"

"Bryan? No, don't think so. We heard from him quite often when he was in New York but he didn't tell us much about what he was doing. He mostly was homesick and wanted us to tell him what was going on at home," Jake said.

"I know I must have offended him all those times I tried to brush him off. But now, I just can hardly imagine never seeing him again. I couldn't help but love him. I just couldn't help it and I don't know if I ever will meet someone like that again. And I'm not sure I will let myself care about someone so much that it hurts like this when they are gone. I've shut most people out for years, but Bryan would not give up."

"Maybe he just forgot to tell us. He could practically forget his name sometimes and then with other things…he could remember stuff that happened and things people said down to the smallest detail. But you know, he never held a grudge. With all the horrible things that some of the kids at school said to him and worse, the things they did, he never held a grudge. Those things, he seemed to forget easily," said Marilee.

"He would go on being nice to them and forgive and forgive," Leslie added.

Livy glanced at Becky who looked away.

"Anyway, I never met anyone like him. I resisted being friends with him at first, like I always do, but he was persistent and he made me love him …he taught me so much. I felt like he was my little brother."

Jake interjected, "You know, a lot of people told us they felt that way. So you knew our Bryan?" He shook his head and looked a bit puzzled. "I'm sorry, you two just seem like an unlikely pair."

"I know this may sound strange, but he sort of *adopted me* as part of the family."

"That sounds just like Bryan."

She decided to go on. "And after everything that's happened to me…I just don't know what to do now, without him."

"I know, Livy. I know. We weren't sure we could ever live without him. None of us could imagine it," Marilee said.

Livy finally managed to ask, "But how do you deal with it? You all seem to be holding up very well. I'm the one who is a basket case. How do you do it?"

"We are doing something that I think will help us get through Christmas a little easier this year. See that pile of presents over there?" Jake pointed to a group of small gifts stacked on the floor next to the Christmas tree. There was a piece of card stock folded and standing on top that read, "FROM BRYAN".

"In each of those boxes is some act of kindness that someone has done for another member of the family. They're supposed to be the kinds of things that Bryan would have done, like paying compliments, giving hugs, doing someone's chores or reading to the little ones," Jake explained.

"The person who does the kindness writes it on paper, wraps it up in a box and gives it to the person but as a tribute to Bryan." The pile is growing and little things are happening that almost make it feel like he's here with us," Marilee added. "I think it helps, don't you, kids? And of course, it helps that we know that we'll see him again; this life is not the end." Marilee, too, was getting choked with emotion. "Without that, our faith in Jesus Christ, I don't think I could handle it at all."

"Bryan was always trying to teach me about that kind of faith and most of the time I didn't listen. But I'm listening now. I'm starting to believe that God cares about what happens to us." She thought about her prayer and Jake appearing just in time to keep her from freezing to death and of her dream of Bryan telling her to hold on.

"I never had much of a family and Bryan kind of convinced me I could be part of his and he told me all about you. –How you open up your hearts and your home. He made you all so real and so wonderful. And he told me the story of the battlefield. I feel like I've been languishing out there my whole life." She stopped and tried to regain control of her emotions. "But now he's gone and after all I've been through lately, I just *had* to come… I didn't have anywhere else to go. I've been thinking about all of you so much in these last few weeks. I thought maybe I could belong here…he made me…love you all like he did. I know this sounds so stupid and that I should have called first and asked if I could come but …I just needed to be here for Christmas…I'm sorry… I couldn't bear it if you told me not to come…" She broke down.

Sarah was all angel now and flew to Livy's arms. "Sure you can come! We all needed to come here to belong, to be home," she sobbed as she hugged the daylights out of the newcomer. "You can come for Christmas or anytime you want!"

"If Bryan said you're family, you're family!" Jake said reassuring her. "Of course you can stay with us."

Livy looked to Marilee for confirmation. She smiled and nodded.

"Really," Jake added. "Our home is your home, okay?"

Olivia absorbed the hug and Jake's loving words with a giant sigh of relief as if all her life she had been holding her breath in anticipation of this moment.

Little Sarah put her hand on her head to offer Livy her halo. "You can be an angel, too! You can wear my costume."

Livy's tears turned to laughter. "I don't think it would fit but I can't wait to see you little cherubs do your part." She replaced Sarah's halo squarely on the angelic head. The hug had left it hanging over one ear.

"Well, okay, then," Elizabeth pronouced as she joined in the hugging.

No one else knew exactly what to do or say; they were letting it all sink in when some sudden crashing and banging upstairs broke the spell.

"Mom!" yelled Josh and Jesse from the upstairs hall. "We can't find the Frankenstein and Fur!"

Marilee got up from the couch, laughing. She called back, "That's Frankincense and Myrrh. I think it's in the costume closet in the basement. Jake, go help them get ready, okay?"

Jake escorted the Bethlehem boys out of the room. After listening to the twins tromping down the back stairs, Marilee turned to look thoughtfully at Livy. "So... *he* didn't send you? And *how* did you know about Sarah?" she asked quietly.

"What?" Livy asked absently as she tried to wipe up the soup that Elizabeth's excited hug had spilled in her lap.

"Nothing," Marilee said unconvincingly. "Never mind."

Just then, from the porch there arose the clatter of eight heavy winter boots prancing across the wooden planks. As they trooped in, Jackson announced in a voice big enough to be heard by all the ears in the sizeable family and probably those in the neighboring farms as well, "The barn's ready. Let's get this show on the road!"

David and his wife Pam proudly held up their six-month-old William, wrapped in "swaddling clothes."

"We've got the Baby Jesus. Doesn't he look great?" Pam bragged.

He was an adorable little boy with fat pink cheeks, chestnut colored curly hair and twinkling brown eyes. They had bundled him up in a snowsuit and then wrapped him in ace bandages. The fat little mummy wiggled and wrangled 'til he managed to get his little arms free. They then went off to change their own clothes.

Elizabeth, sure that now Livy was one of them and could be trusted, jumped to her feet and pulled up her blue robe to reveal her little legs. "See?" she confided. "I have to wear my long underwear and my snow boots underneath."

Sarah followed her lead and showed her black leggings and hot pink boots. "You can be our lantern partner!"

Livy looked puzzled and Marilee stepped in. "We make our procession to the stable in Bethlehem, otherwise known as the barn, and the little ones pair off with an older child to help them carry their lanterns." She turned back to the girls. "Sorry, my little darlings, but I don't think it's a very good idea for Olivia to go back out in the cold just yet. We'll leave her right here snuggled up by the fire until we get back."

"Oh no you won't!" Livy said stubbornly. "I didn't come all this way to miss the most important part of Christmas. I'm going out there even if it means coming down with pneumonia in the morning!" She really was feeling stronger and more alive than she had since ...well, for a very long time.

Marilee snagged Leslie by the sleeve. "Run and get those rice bags you made me last year and put them in the microwave. Becky, get the comforter off your bed and Bethie get the knitted hat that Grandma made you." Off they all went to do as they were told and Marilee shrugged her shoulders and turned to Livy, "All right. I guess you're coming, by popular demand. Boys, go set up that old barn heater. We'll be ready in a little bit."

She got up and walked to the door and called, "Jake, could you get the twins busy on the pageant and then come in here? We need to talk with Olivia for a moment." Now Marilee had Livy alone in the room, and without turning to look at her, she said, "Please, Olivia, tell me the truth. You're sure *he* didn't track me down and send you here to find...? Was it really because of Bryan that you came?"

Livy was completely confused. No one had sent her. No one even knew she was here. "Who else would have sent me?"

Marilee turned and studied Livy for a few moments. She tried again, shaking her head, "It's just so strange...that someone like you and someone like my sweet Bryan would...please... You're sure *he* didn't send you here?"

"He? Who? Why is it strange?"

Satisfied that Olivia was not holding anything back, Marilee took her tray away and led her by the hand to the couch and then she reached for one of many scrapbooks on a bookshelf. She sat down next to Olivia, opened the album to a page of Kimball baby pictures and laid it on Livy's lap. The very first photo on the page took Livy's breath away. It was the contest-winning photo; it was Hannah.

CHAPTER 33

"You? You sent in the anonymous photo that won the contest? I can't believe for one second that you were involved in blackmailing Joy. But—"

"I took that picture, but I didn't send it in. But I know who did. The only other person that had a copy was Carlos Sotomayor. Does that name mean anything to you?"

Trying to disguise her shock, Livy answered knowing more than she let on, "Jameson mentioned that name."

"I knew the minute the scandal broke that he was behind the thefts and the phony charities and everything else. I knew exactly what had happened and how he had blackmailed that woman. The contest opened up the perfect opportunity, a scam made in heaven, or hell more likely, just for him. When she, Joy Jameson, let it be insinuated publicly that the baby was your child, I knew she had started that rumor and had blamed you to cover her involvement. I wanted to come forward right away, but I was afraid that Carlos would come after my family. He promised me once that he would kill me if I got in his way. Believe me, he tried. I was also afraid for the girl, her name was Linda—afraid that Carlos might find her and ruin her life. But there you were, in the hospital on the brink of death with these terrible lies being told about you. I had to tell Mr. Jameson the truth. I owed him that much and I owed it to you since you were taking all the blame."

Livy traced the lovely little baby face with her finger. "So *you* left her at the convent. All of these other children you've taken in; but you left *her* there," she said so quietly that Marilee almost didn't hear.

"I was a different person then. I don't want the kids to know the story, at least not all of it, until they're all older. I told Bryan just a little because he asked and asked and it had everything to do with him."

"Please tell me, I have to know."

"Jake is the only person who knows the whole story. I don't feel—"

"Please. I have to know."

Marilee wasn't sure why but she awkwardly began her story. "My last name was Patino and somehow that got me the nickname of Patti with my friend Margarita...the baby's mother. He called her Daisy."

She told the story... about Mel and Daisy and how they fell in love. She explained how a heartbroken Daisy left the Island to plead with him to stay with her and be a father to their child...how his family had controlled him and pushed their plan and paid for the baby to be aborted and for Daisy to just disappear.

"Margarita told me how she felt when she was lying there waiting for the doctor to come to perform the abortion. She was overcome with a sick, horrible feeling. She just couldn't go through with it.

"Suddenly that baby inside of her became real and precious and *Linda*...a Spanish word for lovely or beautiful. She named her right then. –Her angelita Linda. She felt God telling her the baby was a gift from Him, straight from Him. Margarita always felt that little Linda would grow up to do something very special, to be someone wonderful."

When Marilee shared the part about Carlos' gangs and the story of Daisy's tragic death, she still had to fight back her emotions.

"I promised her that her brother Carlos, who was my... boyfriend at the time, and I would take baby Linda to her father. We took our time driving up the coast from Florida and over the next three days, I fell totally and completely in love with that child. Margarita had been sure, and now I was too, that if he saw her and held her, his heart would melt; he would have to love her. But he never got the chance. That woman practically vowed to make Linda's life miserable and convinced us that he wouldn't want to have anything to do with this 'unworthy baby' either. After all, he had agreed to the abortion. She screamed, 'You keep her! Put her up for adoption; leave her on the side of the road! I don't care. Do what you want with her, just take her away.'"

Jake had come in during the conversation and sat down next to his wife. He took her hand.

Marilee smiled a little, as she looked at the beautiful little face. "I really had started making plans to keep her. I could just picture it. I would dress her up, put her hair in braids and we'd go back to church again. I'd give up drugs, and Carlos and I... we'd get married and have more kids. I had such lovely plans. But Carlos' ideas were very different from mine. And he had no shame in sharing them with me in detail. First of all, he would use her to milk every dime out of that woman in exchange for keeping the secret from her husband. He finally settled on keeping her around for any and all other despicable purposes. The horrible thing was that she was his niece, his blood, not mine. He would be legally able to get custody of her and I was just his strung out girlfriend, an addict with a ninth grade education. What did I have to offer her? Who would listen to me? He could charm anybody and put on a show like an academy award winning actor. But for the very first time, I was clearly seeing the real Carlos, or what he had become. He had turned purely evil.

"When I came upon that lovely little convent and orphanage, and Carlos was sound asleep, I knew what I had to do. I had to leave her in God's hands and not in mine and definitely not in Carlos'. Leaving her there was the hardest thing I ever did in my whole life. I took that picture there at the door of the church. When she reached for me like that I longed to pick her up and give her the world. But I had nothing. And that image has stayed with me all these years. It's the moment that changed my life.

"I left her with some money, a picture of her mother and the cross with the daisy on it that Mr. Jameson had designed for Margarita. I wanted her to know somehow that she had been loved and treasured by her mother and by me. I was sorry to have failed her; so sorry that I wasn't able to protect her and give her the love and care that she needed but I hoped that there at the convent someone would help her find all those things—that she'd be adopted. I promised Linda and myself, that from that moment, I would get ready. I would change my life so if ever another child needed me, I would be there for her or him as I couldn't be there for Linda."

"What happened when Carlos woke up?" Livy asked.

"It was hours later and we were far from the convent. He was furious and I wouldn't tell him where I left her, no matter how much he yelled. He threatened to kill me, but still I wouldn't tell him. He dragged me out of the car and beat me until I think he thought that I was pretty much dead. I nearly was. At first, I think he was going to leave me there to die but he decided to try again to get the information when I regained consciousness. He was patient. Carlos carried me to the car and pressed on to temporary digs in my father's old trailer home in Miami. I guess with a new windfall of cash and stolen jewelry, he wasted no time in going out to fence the goods and cash in. When I woke up alone, I used my dad's dark room there and developed the two photos I'd taken of the baby at the church. The shots of little Linda reaching up for love and affection were heart wrenching. I had failed Margarita. I failed my little angel child.

"I knew that sooner or later, he would come looking for me back there and finish what he began. So on the back of one of Linda's photos, I wrote: *Always remember me. Always remember my mother* and tucked the picture into Carlos' wallet that he had left on the nightstand. Then I limped the five blocks or so to the freeway entrance and hitched a ride West. I'd always assumed my mother had gone to Seattle and perhaps I could find her there.

"I got as far as a rest stop in Idaho Falls before I was too sick with drug withdrawals, and too bruised and broken to go on—out of money and all out of hope. That's where Jake found me and he took me home to his family. They took me in and re-introduced me to God and with His help, put me back together. It took a couple of years and a whole lot of love and prayer." She laid her head on Jake's shoulder. "Jake took a big chance on me," she said as Jake kissed her cheek.

Now Marilee was touching the beautiful little face as she continued, "So you see, that's why she is here with all our children. In a way, she's our first child and she is definitely the reason we are the family that we are. She's the reason I am where I am, who I am." Her hand danced across the other little faces. "They are the fulfillment of my promise to her."

"Bryan told me that Jake had picked you up off the battlefield, but I had no idea," Livy said as she got up and locked the door to the room. "I just want to make sure that we get to be alone for just a few more moments. I thought it was crazy before but now it all makes sense. I know why Bryan led me here," Livy said breathlessly. "I don't know how he knew…I don't know how he knew."

Sitting in puzzled silence, the mom and dad waited for Livy to go on.

"You left Linda at the St. Thomas of Assisi Convent on Christmas hoping she'd be adopted. Well, she never was. She went into foster care at about age six, and she went from home to home for the next ten years. Around the time she turned 20, it was you who left a letter and a birth certificate at the convent in case she ever came looking for clues to her identity, right? It was you…wasn't it?"

Marilee nodded, totally astonished. "How could you possibly know this? Not from Mr. Jameson. When we spoke, he said she never contacted him."

Livy came back around the couch, knelt in front of Marilee and took both of her hands. "That's because I never told him who I was. I know what happened to Linda because I *am* Linda."

Marilee gasped in utter amazement. "You are my Linda, my sweet, beautiful little Linda?" With tears streaming down her face she squeezed Livy hands. "I've always dreamed that someday I'd find you again, that I would know you're alright. It's like a miracle… an answer to a million prayers. Oh, my angel Linda, I'm so, so sorry. Can you ever forgive me?"

"You said you were a totally different person then, but I'm still the same; I'm still reaching," Livy said. And without hesitation Livy lovingly reached out her Hannah arms for Marilee's embrace. "I'm home… Mom. I'm home where I belong."

Marilee pulled her to her feet and they held each other, weeping.

Livy reached her hand out to Jake to invite him to join them.

"It *is* a miracle that somehow Bryan found you and brought you home," Jake said, joining their arms. They remained there for several moments, not wanting to let each other or this feeling go.

"You were never adopted, never had a family?" Marilee finally asked.

"No. I never fit anywhere…until Bryan made me feel that somehow I could belong here."

"And you never told your father who you were?" Jake asked.

"I searched him out while I was in business school and managed to get a job at his company just so that I could be near him. I'd always longed for the father I knew was out there somewhere. I respected Mel, even came to love him but I never dared to tell him who I was for fear of more rejection. I was going to prove myself capable and acceptable and then I would tell him." Her tone turned cold. "But because of Joy... I was never acceptable to her...I couldn't say anything. Then he fired me; he believed me *capable all right,* capable of crime and betrayal. And it broke my heart. And then when I found out, when he told me himself, that he'd paid to have his child aborted and everything, I was glad he didn't know."

Marilee sat back down, overcome with wonder and happiness and with regret as well. "I'm so sorry, Olivia, my little Linda. I'm so sorry for everything."

Livy sat down beside her. "I understand. You did the only thing you could do. And you risked your very life to protect me. Now you've taken a risk again, for me." She rested her head on the mother's lap. "I now know that I was loved, I wasn't just thrown away."

"You most certainly were loved... by Margarita, by her aunts, by me...and even Jake, too. I never stopped loving you and praying for you to this very day." Marilee caressed Livy's hair and began, "And because of you, we had the wonderful gift of our beloved Bryan and all the rest, too. You know, it was directly because of you that we adopted Bryan."

"Adopted? For some reason, I thought that Bryan was your own...I just assumed."

"We had David and Carolyn by that time. Then we heard about this young girl we knew in Idaho Falls, who was considering an abortion."

"Why wouldn't she want to keep Bryan?"

"She was young and her boyfriend had taken off. She was terrified of the responsibility and expense that a baby like Bryan would bring. Naturally, we thought of little Linda, and we begged the girl to go on with her pregnancy and promised we'd adopt the baby. She was so relieved and agreed to let us have him."

Jake picked up where Marilee left off. "I remember so clearly the day we first saw him at the hospital. There was something so special about him, something in his eyes. Although we couldn't bring him home for a couple of months, he was all ours from that very moment."

"A couple of months? Why? Was he sick?"

"He had to have surgery for his enlarged heart. He had two more surgeries before he was nine," Jake answered.

"I really never dreamed ...he just seemed so healthy."

Livy remembered him piggy-backing her all over Manhattan and the jousting adventure in the park. Her mind and heart were reeling.

"He was like that," Jake said. "Bryan never let on. He always wanted to be rough and tough like the rest of the boys."

"I can't imagine our family without the blessing of having had Bryan among us. You knew him; you know how he was. He was our little peacemaker, so forgiving and loving...and..." Marilee's voice trailed off just a little, choked with emotion

Jake finished, "And now because of Bryan, we have our Linda, home where she belongs."

"When he was little, I used to show Bryan this picture and tell him how Angelita Linda was his special angel who made sure that he got to come to our family. I'd catch him looking at her all the time," Marilee recalled. "Somehow he must have recognized you from the photo. I can't imagine how he could have."

"Wait a minute...oh my goodness," Jake said. "Speaking of recognizing from the photo, it was a while ago, but I think I found a picture of the two of you together; a clipping that was with Bryan's New York stuff. Of course, it was you. Why didn't I think of that before? I stuck it in here somewhere."

He was going through the albums on the shelf.

Livy was confused. She couldn't remember any pictures being taken with Bryan. She'd wished she had one. She decided it must have been one snapped by a photographer at the gala event for Hannah, since Jake had said *clipping*.

He brought over a scrapbook and sat down beside her. He took her hand and spoke slowly and softly. I found this after he died. –Must have been taken just before he came home."

"Came home?"

He was again thumbing through the scrapbook, looking for the clipping.

CHAPTER 34

"Ah! Here it is!" He was unfolding it.

And there it was, a clipping from the New York Post. It was a photo taken by the company publicity crew that had accompanied Livy to the children's shelter more than a year before. There were the stacks of JTC toys and then Livy and next to her was the volunteer elf with Down's syndrome. The caption read, "JTC executive Olivia Thomas, along with one of Santa's own elves, sharing holiday cheer with the kids at the Harlem Interim Shelter." On the back of the clipping was scribbled, "Angelita Linda."

"I remember that young man; the kids adored him...but where's Bryan?"

Jake almost laughed. "What do you mean, where's Bryan? He's right there."

He pointed at the Downs-syndrome elf.

"What? This is Bryan? No. I remember this boy. He walked up to me and said something like, 'It's you! I knew you'd come and Jesus said you'd come.' It sort of freaked me out. But Bryan wasn't—That's not how I knew Bryan."

"Well, that's our son," Jake affirmed in a puzzled tone.

"This one? Why was *he* in New York?"

"Well, when his siblings started doing church service missions like the humanitarian one James is on right now, Bryan wanted to do something as well. They don't usually send out handicapped young people but he really wanted to do his part."

Jake looked to Marilee and she continued, "They found something perfect for Bryan. They sent him with a group doing a special children's mission. It was hard for him to be so far away from the family and it was hard for us to let him out of our sight, but he was very proud to go and serve."

"He went to hospitals and shelters and simply held the babies and played with little children. Sometimes babies are in intensive care for a long time and their parents can't be with them every day so Bryan would be there and he would just lovingly hold the babies. Once in a while a very ill child would die in his arms," Jake added.

Marilee went on, "He went to shelters where children were brought when they were abused, before they found foster homes, and he would hold them or play with them. He would make them feel they were loved, like they were just one more brother or sister in our family. He said he going there to be the arms of Jesus; he would love them the way Jesus would if he were there," she recalled.

Livy remembered the marvelous effect he had on those children that day and the effect he had on her. "That's just what he did. He loved them and shared in their happiness and joy."

The health care specialists and the social workers were wary of him and the whole idea at first, but when they saw the way the kids responded to him, they were amazed and then he was in great demand. Many of them, when they heard of Bryan's death, called and told us what a difference he had made and how much love he brought. A few even came out for the funeral. You see, it didn't surprise us when another acquaintance of Bryan's from New York wanted to share with us how much he had meant to them," Jake continued. "But this isn't the Bryan you knew?" When she shook her head he asked, "Then, how did you meet *your* Bryan?"

"He was my doorman at my apartment building. He met me at the door every night. He had to be yours! He talked my ear off sometimes about Idaho and all of you and—"

"Well, that part sounds like Bryan." Marilee said with a befuddled smile. "But he wasn't like Bryan is there in the photo?"

Livy exclaimed, "NO! But he *was* Bryan! I wish you could have seen him! He was tall and handsome and wise and funny. He was beautiful to me. He was working with kids and writing their stories. He took me to the playground and introduced me to Josie and the rest. He was real and he was perfect! I should know what he was like; I spent most all of the last twelve months with him!"

"Twelve months? But he..." Marilee started.

"Now Olivia, please don't take this wrong, but are you sure that you haven't got things a little mixed up with the head injury and all?" Jake asked.

Livy stood up and protested, "No, I'm not confused about this. Yes, I had a head injury but without Bryan I would have died in that accident! Why is it that no one is making that connection? Why doesn't anyone see that? November 21st, you have to remember that day." She studied their perplexed faces and adamantly continued. "He told me that he had to leave New York, to leave me, and I was so angry because I couldn't let go of another person that I had come to love. I wasn't paying attention to what I was doing. And then I saw Frankie and I just ran out into the street after him—right into traffic. That bus hit Bryan because I wasn't looking where I was going and he ran out there to push me out of the way! It was all because of me!" She turned away to face the fire.

Marilee stood up and went to Livy's side, putting an arm around her and leading her back down onto the couch. Marilee spoke calmly. "No, honey no. It wasn't your fault. It couldn't be." She looked to Jake to fill in the rest.

He took her hand and spoke slowly and softly. He didn't die in an accident in New York. He came home and just days later he was rough-housing with the boys and his big old heart just gave out on him. He died December 3rd of *last* year. None of us could ever forget *that* day." Jake said.

"Last year? Things like this don't happen," she cried. None of it made any sense. "How could this be? *My Bryan* brought me an Idaho Christmas last year; we did a widow run! He told me he wished he could be home for Christmas and just had to share a Kimball-style Christmas morning with me. Though I tried to resist, I let him into my heart and he really became my brother. He taught me how to love again. He was the inspiration for the doll; he was there in my triumphs and there when it all came crashing down. He said mine was his most important case study. It was real, all of it. I know it was! And I didn't spend the last year hallucinating or with a...a spirit...as my best friend."

For a few moments, the parents sat in silence as understanding, little by little, swelled within them.

"Of course it was real," Jake finally said. "Not a spirit, exactly...but—"

"But what...?"

"He was our Bryan, all right," Jake said slowly with a nod, his big hand wiping a tear from his cheek "Listen to yourself, Olivia. 'He brought me home, he taught me to love, he was there in my triumph, he was my brother, he saved me.' Don't you see? He found you that day at the shelter. He said Jesus knew you would come. He knew you were *his* angel and when he got the chance, he became yours."

Livy's glance went to the clipping sitting beside them on the cushion. "But what about...?"

Smiling through brimming eyes, Marilee supplied, *"Our* Bryan is *your* Bryan now. Our sweet, loving and handicapped Bryan is beautiful and tall and perfect. He was always perfectly beautiful to us. We knew him from the inside out. He isn't handicapped anymore because our spirits aren't handicapped, Olivia. They are made in the image of God. Perhaps Bryan's challenges and problems on earth were only experiences that prepared him for greater things. You see he would understand what it is like for people who feel inadequate, those who have been treated cruelly and have experienced rejection and pain. He suffered all of those things. He knows exactly how it feels. And it looks to me like Bryan came back out onto the battlefield and brought you home. You're home, Sweetheart. Your angel saved your life and he brought you home."

Livy tried out the words on her tongue. "My angel...you have to understand how strange this sounds to me. I've gone through life only halfway believing in God or angry with a God who would let a child grow up as lonely and rejected as I was. Why would God suddenly send an angel to me of all people?"

"Maybe it wasn't suddenly at all. If anything, this shows us there are probably angels around us all the while, guiding us, supporting us and we just don't know they are there. You said Bryan knew about Sarah but we weren't even sure we could have her until after our Bryan died. He couldn't have known her name and that she really came unless he was watching over us. Can you imagine how much joy that brings us? He's with us. We haven't lost him at all and neither have you."

She let the thought settle into her very soul. She remembered his words there in that beautiful place of light and love, *"Hang on sis! You're almost home."* She remembered the terrible day of the shootings and how Bryan somehow knew they had to be away from that playground. She realized how he always seemed to show up just when she needed him. She remembered his love and felt it again.

After a few moments of the Kimballs' embrace and sweet, warm, confirming peace, Livy abruptly sat up. "I have to go back. There are two more little souls out there that I have to rescue. I don't know how I can, but I know I have to. Then we'll be back, if that's all right."

"If it's all right? Promise you'll come back. We just found you. We can't lose you again. Please come back." Marilee pleaded.

"I promise. I'll bring them back." With a bitter tone she added, "I don't have any reason to stay there."

"Forgive him, Olivia." Marilee gave her an encouraging touch on the arm. "Your father, I mean. You've made mistakes and heaven knows I have. But people can repent and change. And they can learn. I know from talking to him that he has been suffering over his mistakes, one in particular, for years and years. I know he'll want to know who you are and that you forgive him."

"I don't know if I ever can forgive him. He wanted me dead; he wanted me out of his life forever. He didn't believe in me or care about me, even after all I did to prove myself to him. How can I ever...?"

Someone had been knocking on the door intermittently for a few moments and Livy finally noticed it consciously when she heard Elizabeth, Leslie and Sarah asking to come in. Livy got up and opened the door for them.

"Mom and Dad...and Olivia...we're all ready. We're waiting for you!" Sarah cried excitedly and took Olivia's hand.

CHAPTER 35

In a surprisingly short time, the Kimball family was assembled on the back porch and lined up on the steps with their eight glowing lanterns. Solemnly, the children lifted their lanterns and took the hand of a partner. The girls had decided that Elizabeth would be Livy's partner on the way out and Sarah would get her for the return trip. 13-year-old Michael would be the trade off. Bethie confidently slid her white-gloved hand into Livy's. "Oh! Look how beautiful!" she whispered.

It was beautiful indeed. The storm had lifted, leaving behind a picture postcard winter scene. The star-filled sky was now crystal clear, a full moon shedding light on the soft blanket of new fallen snow. Jake and Marilee clasped hands and began to sing. The children joined in and the old melody echoed through the peaceful night.

Oh come all ye faithful,
Joyful and triumphant.
Oh come ye, oh come ye to
Bethlehem.

Once inside the barn, the boys carefully hung the lanterns around the charming makeshift stage. The "actors" eagerly hurried to the back corner of the barn to await their moments of stardom. Jake and Marilee settled Livy into a cozy nest in the hay.

The Kimball Players had everything ready to go in what seemed like mere moments. It was clear that this was a well-rehearsed and oft repeated tradition. The little cardboard buildings of Bethlehem appeared and the homemade pageant began. An angel (a.k.a. Leslie) appeared in radiant white and called to Mary (Elizabeth). "Behold, you have found favor with God and shall bear a son and call his name Jesus." And little Elizabeth, more Elizabeth than Mary, answered in her usual skeptical way, "Oh yeah? How can this be? I'm not married to a man."

And the little angel answered, "The Holy Ghost will come upon thee and the power of the Highest shall overshadow thee ...that Holy child which shall be born of thee shall be called the Son of God." And the angel added with a touch of reproach, "With God, nothing is impossible."

Marilee narrated from the viewpoint of an older Mary reflecting back upon these events and said, *"How could this be? I could not understand. How could I bear a son when I knew not a man?"*

It was as if Livy was hearing the Christmas story for the very first time. She had never really thought about what an inconvenient baby Jesus was. His mother was young, unmarried, and was engaged to someone who was not the father of her child. How could anyone be prepared for such a responsibility? No one could possibly understand her circumstances and if her Joseph hadn't believed her angel story, he might well have had her stoned.

"This miracle from the Lord, I humbly received. But asked just one miracle more... Please, let my Joseph believe."

Elizabeth approached Michael, playing Joseph, and she acted out telling him of her baby and pleading with him to believe her. He turned his back to her.

Marilee continued, *"This news, like a sword pierced his heart, to think I, our vows had betrayed. But more bitter still, was the thought of the stone. He would put me privately away."*

What that poor girl must have gone through! Livy thought. *Mary would be shunned, disgraced and sent away from everyone and every- thing she knew. What faith she had to have, to trust and hope that God had a plan.*

He did. The angel came to set Joseph straight.

Next, Joseph led little pillow-stuffed Mary through Bethlehem on a Donkey, played by a Shetland pony named Zach. Old Zach struggled and stubbornly pulled backwards refusing to proceed as Michael directed.

Finally, he irreverently bucked Mary off onto the hard ground where she bravely remained, crying softly as Joseph tried his luck at various inns. At each inn he was turned away and the door shut in his face. He was told they must seek shelter in a stable, (a cow's stall.)

Livy could only imagine Joseph's shame at only being able to provide this humble shelter for his wife at the birth of her babe, God's son.

"How can this be? No room for to stay. I must cradle my King in a manger of hay?"

And then again, Livy marveled that this wonderful, glorious child was not welcomed with a baby shower and celebration but instead, with "no vacancy" signs. *You are not wanted here. There is no room for you. We see your need, but we don't care.*

Then suddenly the bright-as-daylight milking lamp flashed on shining down from the loft onto shepherds and real sheep huddled fearfully below.

Sarah spoke in her beautiful African (almost British sounding) English. "Fear not: for, behold I bring you tidings of great joy which shall be unto all people...For unto you is born this day, a Savior, which is Christ, the Lord. Ye shall find the babe, wrapped in swaddling clothes and lying in a manger."

Jackson, the technical director, swung the light up and over to reveal other angels in the loft. Everyone joined in singing "Angels We Have Heard on High." The 'star' then led the angels and the three wise kings, who had joined in the procession, to the stall.

While attention was focused on shepherds, wise men and angels, little Mary traded her padding pillows for baby William in the manger. The light shone down on the little Holy Family. Mary beamed at the baby with loving pride. Joseph stood watch nearby. Gradually, the worshippers arrived. "Magi Josh" tripped on Jesse's velvet robe, tossing the Frankincense into the air. "Joseph" made a nimble catch without ever breaking character.

"A marvelous star, and its light filled the sky. And angels were singing a glorious lullaby. Sent by the angels the shepherds drew near, seeking the Lamb of God. And Magi, in search of the King of Kings, by his simple majesty were awed."

Livy too, pondered these things in her heart as if they were brand new to her. *Only lowly shepherds and mysterious wise men from far away lands rejoiced and knelt at the manger. So vehemently did King Herod want this child not to be, that he killed hundreds of babies, newly born, yet to be born and even those up to two years old. How could this happen? Tiny children, innocent children!*

Marilee read on, the light now focused only on her. **"My miracle grew and he walked among men, teaching of love purified. But most would not hear and most would not see... And my son was crucified. He looked on me as he hung on that tree saying, 'Woman, behold thy son. Into my Father's hands I go; it is finished. His work is done.'"**

Jesus preached life-changing, world-changing sermons, healed the sick and raised the dead and yet was still rejected by his own...by his own! He knows how I feel. He understands how I feel because he's been there before. And he was the Son of God... He didn't have to do these things. He went through it all for us, for me... So he would know how I feel. And he suffered and died so He could take away my pain and my guilt. –Do for me what I could never do for myself –forgive me, heal me, rescue me. He can take it all –my anger and my sins, the abuse and all of it. He can heal it all.

Then Jackson pointed the light up to the corner of the barn, as if to heaven itself. Marilee swallowed hard, looked first to Livy and then to the light and said, **"How can this be? I don't understand. I saw Him die; yet before me He stands. This miracle Lord, I humbly receive! Just one miracle more...Let the whole world believe!"**

And Livy did believe it; she knew it. *How could I, of all people, turn Him away? He just wants what I've wanted all along... room in the heart for him to come, to be welcomed, and to be loved.*

The family concluded by singing a song that Livy had never heard that ended with these words:

And so like dear Mary, each one for his part
Must ponder these glorious things in his heart.
Will we embrace them and will we receive
All of God's wonders and will we believe?

We all shall raise a song of praise

And sweet Hosannas we'll sing.
Each knee shall bend and tongue confess
That Jesus Christ is the King.

The last four lines of the song were sung over and over as a round and as they sang of knees bending, the family knelt, one by one at the manger where little baby Jesus lay, forming a circle around him. All had gone to the manger except Livy who now felt herself almost unconsciously drawn forward. She found her way through the others and knelt right in front of "baby Jesus" and gave him her burdens, her anger, her sins, her gratitude and her whole heart. It was as though light was slowly filling her being from her head to her toes, warm, bright and the most beautiful feeling she had ever experienced. Everything and everyone around her appeared bathed in light, most especially the baby.

And then, in his most perfect way, the little baby Jesus reached for Livy just exactly the way little Hannah did in the photo—begging her to love Him, and to let him love her. His little arms seemed to ache for her embrace as hers did for him. She gathered him up and hugged him with everything her soul had to give and he seemed to soak up every bit of her affection as he pressed his little head against her heart.

In that moment, she felt other, unseen arms around her and a love that she had never experienced before in her life—the love that she had always yearned for... and it was real, enveloping her, warming her, nourishing her. She knew she was in the Savior's arms and she would never question His love or His awareness of her again. Nothing else mattered now. *He* was her father and she was His child—God's child.

Sarah, feeling the same spirit of love, came to Livy, dropped to her knees and put her little arm around Livy's back. Then Becky, then Leslie and Elizabeth, and one by one, all the family members were linking arms all around Livy, tears running down their cheeks. She couldn't see him, but she knew somehow Bryan was there too, smiling and joining in the embrace.

CHAPTER 36

Christmas morning dawned well before the sun actually rose to touch the sky. Michael and Clayton were out milking cows around 4:00 a.m. and when they finished, just before 5:00 o'clock, they felt it their duty to wake everyone else. "Let's get the party started!"

Perhaps they needed as early a start as this to tackle Christmas for 19! Marilee marched everyone to the kitchen for warm cinnamon rolls and cocoa before the demolition began.

After plugging in the Christmas tree lights, Jake fiddled with the tripod and then found the perfect angle for capturing the pandemonium on video.

Santa had brought some refurbished toys and bicycles, inexpensive dolls and clothes for them and some '80's-sized' boom boxes for the older boys. There were lots of gently worn baby clothes for William. But the real fun and joy came with opening the presents the kids had found or made for each other. They had found some real treasures at the Youth Ranch Thrift Store and at the Deseret Industries. Not one guessed his or her gift correctly, even after considerable shaking. And, best of all, they had created some homemade masterpieces sure to be treasured (and laughed about) for years to come. Livy remembered Bryan's glee in watching her unwrap his simple gifts.

One by one they began to open the gifts they had given in Bryan's name. They were the sweetest gifts of all. There were lots of hugs and lots of laughs as each child explained his gift and how it related to what Bryan might have done.

There was one gift left from the pile that no one had noticed before. Elizabeth picked it up. "It says, 'For Livy' on it," she said and handed over the small box.

Livy took it, giving Elizabeth's red hair a tussle. "Did you wrap me up something, Elizabeth? You didn't have to."

Elizabeth shrugged. "I didn't do it, honest."

Holding it where Jake and Marilee and all could see, Olivia ripped away the paper from the box and totally forgot to shake and guess. She lifted the lid and inside she found her tarnished, rusted old cowbell on a collar. Livy stared at Elizabeth in wonder and awe. "How—? Where did you—?"

"I didn't do it, honest," the little girl repeated as she peered into the box. "And I wouldn't give you a dumb cowbell!" She seemed almost insulted at the insinuation. Under the bell was the daisy-cross pendant Livy had broken and discarded at the hospital.

Marilee exclaimed, "It's your mother's cross!"

The chain was wrapped around a note. The words written there were familiar and sweet. *"You see, little Lamb, Jesus and I will always know where you are. Merry Christmas, Livy. Welcome Home. Love, Bryan."*

Jake, Marilee and Livy, standing frozen for a moment in the magic and the miracle, gradually became aware of a low rumble of voices building around the room as it grew louder and louder. "Widow run! Widow run! Widow RUN!"

EPILOGUE

Mel had wandered the streets of Manhattan on Christmas Eve. He'd observed the frantic last minute shoppers and envied their sense of purpose. They obviously had people to buy for, places to go, homes where families and friends waited for them. In the hotel, he had watched all the in-room movies of interest to him and had absently "read" two novels. Dreading the uncomfortable stares from the employees, he had avoided the office. There was much to do. There were offers on the table to buy out the company. But he couldn't force himself to go there. Not yet. And he couldn't stand being in the hotel a minute longer.

Kyle had invited him to his home to spend Christmas Eve and for Christmas dinner but Mel had declined. It wouldn't do to have an employee share his hospitality out of pity. He had sent his regards and his Christmas greeting to Kyle's wife, Debbie, and the kids. Part of him was longing to be in a home full of children, another part resisted, the part haunted by the realization that he had lost his only child... not just once, but lost her again when Joy sent her away.

Now he again wandered aimlessly on Christmas Day. This time the streets were nearly deserted. Sounds of distant church bells floated illusively through the air along with tiny flakes of blowing snow.

After an hour of walking, he came upon a small Episcopal Church. People were streaming out the door, still humming the carols from the Christmas Service. Many smiled happily and wished him a Merry Christmas; and he returned their good wishes as he leaned on the gate of the churchyard. He hadn't been in a church in years. His mother had told him that his people were Episcopalian but he didn't remember going more than two or three times on Christmas Eve and to a couple of funerals at their parish church. But still, he had believed. And he believed now. He believed that God had heard his prayers for Livy. God had healed her and brought her back from the edge. *Couldn't He heal me, too? Help me figure out what to do?* He wondered.

Pulling his collar up around his neck, he walked on, staring at the sidewalk, oblivious to the world around him. In a half-hour or so, he looked up to find himself in front of a door that read, N.Y. D.C.F.S. Children's Shelter.

Not knowing why, he went in and immediately wished he hadn't. There were children running everywhere. Some were fussing and crying and some were fighting with other kids. A few played quietly alone. Cheap toys lay strewn around the floor. Sitting in a big chair was a volunteer Santa who tried to get the children to sing *Frosty the Snowman* with him. Most weren't interested, even when he offered them candy canes. Hard as he tried, he couldn't bring any Christmas delight to these kids.

One of the social workers recognized Mel when he came in.

"Mr. Jameson! How nice of you to come! We really missed JTC this year." Then she awkwardly added, "I know its been a tough time for your company this Christmas. But it's good to have you here, toys or no toys. Would you like some punch?"

He shook his head. The annual event had gotten lost in the mess at JTC. He had empty hands and a heart full of guilt.

He remembered Livy's description of her PR event at the shelter the year before. It had been the day after Thanksgiving; the day was chosen for its shopping significance. Saying it all felt contrived and that she was hopeless with kids, she begged him to send someone else. But then afterwards, she'd told him about the sweet retarded elf and how he had brought such love and happiness to the children and how much it had touched her.

A movement to his left caught his eye. There he was! It had to be the elf Livy had described. The young man with Down's came up to Mel and said, "Merry Christmas, Melvin. I knew you'd come. He knew you'd come and here you are."

Mel was unnerved. *He called me by name.*

"They just want to be loved... and to be worth a few moments of your

254

precious time. You just have to get down there and play with them. Just be a kid again; that'll do it."

Mel motioned at himself with his hand and raised his eyebrows as if to ask, "Who me?"

The elf smiled and nodded.

He wasn't sure why, but he did as the elf suggested. Mel shed his camel hair coat and his silk tie, pulled his shirttails out and got down on the floor with a small boy who was playing with a cheap little truck. Making some terrific engine noises, Mel joined the youngster's world and grabbed a little *Hummer* for himself. Soon, another little guy jumped into the fray with his army jeep and then another and another until a full scale vehicle deployment was underway. Explosions and battles raged to the tune of Mel's sound effects. Now the little girls sauntered over with their dolls, wanting a piece of the action. Even ole' Santa sprang from his chair, a slightly broken police car in hand. He sang out a dandy siren wail. One little blonde girl, with the vestiges of last week's pigtails, put down her dolly and managed to maneuver herself into Mel's arms. He held her with one arm and piloted a small helicopter with the other. He was having a blast. From time to time he looked up to see the elf smiling approvingly on the scene. Christmas had come to the shelter, and to Mel, at last. Before this moment, if anyone had told him he would be on the floor playing with children, in his suit, in a shelter, he never would have believed it.

He completely lost track of the hour, probably because for the first time in ages, he had nothing on his schedule. The social workers and a couple of volunteers appeared and began rounding up the kids and herding them through the backdoor into the kitchen. One of the staff, whose nametag read Julie Burns, remarked, "Mr. Jameson, you are a wonder. You have such a way with children; you've been great! Please come back anytime. –With or without toys!"

"I will. You know, I think I will."

"I know this is silly to ask a man like you, but would you like to join us for dinner?" She paused, waiting for an answer. "Oh, never mind. I'm sure you're very busy, but I thought I'd ask. It's okay. But thank you so much for coming by." With that she ushered more children into the dining area.

Mel was tempted to stay for dinner. But right now he was intrigued with the elf leaning up against the wall. Brushing the dust from the floor off his suit pants, he pulled himself up and walked over to the young man.

"She just needs to be loved and wanted, that's all," the elf stated.

Mel's eyes searched the room and he spotted the little pigtailed girl. She turned and waved at him as she exited through the kitchen door.

"No, not her. She did all she could to prove herself to you, to make you proud. You know who I mean."

He wasn't sure he did.

Jangling a large set of keys, the children's center director charged through a corner office door and called to Mel. He turned to face her.

She said, "If you won't be joining us for dinner then...I'm sorry...you'll need to go. I have to lock the front door now. I don't mean to be rude. We really are so thrilled that you came."

"I'm glad too. More than you could ever know."

When he turned to follow her to the door, he saw the elf was gone. "Uh...I wanted to ask you about that Down's syndrome fellow. He was here..."

She seemed to search her mind for a moment and then said, "Oh sure. He was here last year and the children just loved him. We all did. We miss him! You know, seeing you down there on the floor with the kids, it was almost like having Bryan back again. You know what I mean?"

He picked up his coat and tie and vaguely gestured to where the elf had stood. "What? No, he was just—"

"He was here on some church sponsored Children's ministry for about six weeks... from a little before Halloween to the first of December, I think. At first, we were a little concerned about his...handicap, but not for long; he was amazing. It was so sad when we heard that he passed away just days after he went home to Idaho."

"Passed away?" Mel asked in disbelief. "No, it couldn't be. He was just—"

"I know. We couldn't believe it either. I guess his heart just stopped. I suppose he had some kind of condition where it could give out, just like that." She snapped her fingers to illustrate. "So awfully sad; a sweet boy like him! Well, good night and Merry Christmas, Mr. Jameson." She opened the door for him and locked it behind him.

256

Crazy. He must be crazy. He was having a conversation with an elf nobody else had seen, who just happened to have died over a year ago. *No, thought Mel, denying the possibility of his own insanity, he had to have been there.* Mel guessed he could not have gone far. He searched up and down the street, left and right, for signs of the illusive elf, but to no avail. Leaning forward, his hands on his knees, he took a deep breath of frigid air, then slapped his cheeks and closed his eyes and then popped them open again, all to make sure he was not dreaming. But when he opened them, he saw the young man was across the street watching him.

His eyes focused on the apparition, and taking a step forward, Mel called out, "You're not really there, are you?"

Mel had stepped right in the path of a woman rushing down the sidewalk and she collided with him. "Well excuse me!" she exclaimed. "Of course I'm really here. Are you blind or just nuts?"

She hurried on, glancing back over her shoulder in disgust.

The elf was amused but Mel wasn't.

"You mean Livy? Is that who you are talking about?" Mel yelled across the road. The elf nodded but Mel continued, "She doesn't want anything to do with me."

"Well, she has a Christmas present for you." Shrugging his shoulders, the elf turned and walked down the street. He faded from view.

"Taxi!" Mel flagged down the sedan and jumped inside calling out Livy's address to the driver. "I know she won't see me," he muttered aloud. "What am I doing following a hallucination? Never mind, driver. Take me to the Hyatt!"

****

He'd tried to forget the whole elf experience over the last four days, but he couldn't. He kept staring out his 35th floor window at the falling snow and he couldn't get the elf and Livy out of his mind. He decided to try to see her.

Traffic was light on that afternoon, a few days after Christmas. The taxi pulled up in front of Livy's building in record time but he still found he wasn't ready to face her or that elf. Mel took his time getting out of the cab. He paid the driver extra for Christmastime's sake; he took a moment to straighten his tie and tuck in his shirt, checked his silver hair in the rearview mirror. He was stalling, worried about what might be in store for him there.

Mel spotted the fellow sitting on the steps of the apartment building. But now he was dressed as the doorman, top hat and all. Ushering Mel inside, he said, "I thought you'd eventually show up here. Come with me." They got in the elevator and instantly arrived at the 19th floor. Then they were at her door and without so much as a key, or a code, or a turn of a knob, the door just opened.

"Olivia!" Mel called out. "Livy it's me, Mel. Are you here? Are you alright?"

"She's not here," Bryan informed him. "She's gone home."

"Gone home? Home where?" Mel considered the possibilities and gasped. "You're not an angel... are you?" Mel couldn't believe what he was asking but went on anyway. "You didn't come to take her home to... to heaven? She's not dead, is she?"

"No, not that home." Bryan smiled. "She went home to my house, in Idaho. It's a place where people like me and little children are looked upon as precious gifts from God. If only people could see those little souls as He sees them, things might be different. It's like Wordsworth said, 'Trailing clouds of glory from our feet do we come, from God who is our home...'"[1]

After quoting the poem, the young man began to transform before Mel's eyes. He grew taller, stronger and broader. He grew handsome and in his blue eyes, intelligence and wisdom shone brightly. He glowed with health and vigor. Mel recognized him as the fellow that Livy had brought to the gala. But he didn't stop there. His metamorphosis continued until he became a brilliant and magnificent being, beyond description. He exuded light and love, knowledge and goodness. Mel couldn't help but feel the urge to weep and to kneel before this wonderful, glorious personage.

He was on his way to his knees when Bryan smiled and shook his beautiful head of longish golden hair. "Don't kneel, Mel. It's embarrassing. Save that for God. Aren't you going to open your present?"

He motioned to the little tree in front of the window and the beautifully wrapped gift that lay under its tiny boughs.

258

Melvin wobbled on weakened legs to the little Christmas tree and picked up the gift. He tore away the paper to reveal a beautiful double-sided Tiffany Crystal frame. Taped to the outside was a folded piece of parchment paper with the words:

For the man who has everything...almost.

Inside, the note said,

November 3rd
Dearest Mel,
I've wanted to share this gift for a very long while but the timing had to be perfect. With the success of our Hannah project, I felt like it was now or never. I hope that you will be happy about it. You may have wondered why someone like me ended up at your toy company. It was no accident; I sought you out. I came here especially to be with you, because you are my father. It felt so right from the start and I know you felt it too. So, Merry Christmas to the man who has everything ... the man who is everything to me.
Love, Olivia

He opened the frame to find a beautiful photo of Daisy on one side and a reduced birth certificate on the other. The state of Florida certified the birth of a baby girl, 7 lbs 8 oz. born March 24, 1977 to Mother: Margarita Elena Guadelupe Sotomayor Reyes of the Dominican Republic and Father: Melvin Edward Jameson of New York.

This time the angel being didn't stop him from falling to his knees. "Oh Livy! No wonder she hates me!" Mel exclaimed as his hands shook and his heart sank. "She came to find a father and only found more rejection...more than she ever imagined. How did I not see it? Can she ever forgive me?" He looked to the angel. "Can God forgive me?"

"They both love you very much, so I imagine they will. She has to know that you really feel she's everything you ever could have wanted in a daughter, because she is." He reached down and helped Mel to his feet and then his brightness began to dim. He was fading away, smaller and fainter until he became a little trail of light that disappeared into the ceiling.

Mel called out to the empty room, "But where is she? What do I do now? What do I say when I find her?" He stood there for a few moments, waiting for answers. They didn't come.

He kept reading her note over and over.

"I sought you out... it felt so right from the start," she had said.

Why hadn't he seen it? How could he have doubted her?

"Who's here? Who's in there?" Livy's voice called nervously through the open door. "Rachel, is it you? Are you in there?"

Then she cautiously popped her head in and found Mel standing there with her gift in his hands.

"What are you doing here? How did you get in?" she asked coolly and dropped her battered suitcase at the door.

He didn't know how to explain what he had just experienced. "Uh...there was this elf...but then he was your doorman...and then he was...this, this..." He was still dizzy from the experience and the revelation.

"Angel?" Livy supplied with a knowing smile. "You saw my angel?" It felt so good to know that he was still close, still involved and watching over. "He was here? He brought you here?"

Mel was relieved and surprised that she didn't seem to question his sanity. He held up the frame and said, "He brought me here to find this and I don't know what to say. I can understand why you never wanted to see me again. I can only imagine how much all of this has hurt you..."

"Mel, you will never know how much all of this has hurt me, all that this has cost me throughout my whole life. I always thought that if I just found my father he would be so happy to have me. –Like I had been taken away from him and he just needed to know where I was, who I was... and then he would swoop in and save me from everything and be my hero. There wasn't a day when I didn't think about finding my hero, not a day when I didn't want to make him proud. But then I found out it was just easier for him if I was dead."

"I know this will never be enough, but I'm so, so sorry, Olivia. I'm also so honored to know that you are my daughter. You are everything I would have ever dreamed my child to be and even more. You are the second chance I never believed I'd have. Please, please tell me that you won't hate me forever." He looked down at the frame in his hands and then held it out to her. "This is the most perfect gift I've ever received in my whole life."

Livy sat down by the little Christmas tree, closed her eyes and uttered a silent prayer. She remembered the wonderful feeling she'd felt while kneeling at the manger and she now realized there were still some things that she had not left at Jesus' feet. There was something inside of her that didn't want to lay the anger down and release it. She prayed for help to let it go, and for God to set her free from this last painful load of anger, resentment and disillusionment.

"You know," she said, "I found my family while I was in Idaho. I discovered where I really belong." She glanced up to see bitter disappointment on Mel's face. Then she looked at the delicate manger scene that Bryan had given her and picked up the Mary figure, cradling the Christ Child in her arms. She kept her eyes on it and before she spoke, she uttered a prayer inside and the warm peace of His grace flowed through her again. His grace was for Mel, too. God could heal what Mel could never change or undo or restore.

"I found my *real* Father there, a couple of them actually... I guess I might have an opening for one more."

She looked into his eyes and could see into his yearning, suffering soul. She reached her hand out to him and he took it in both of his. And then it just wasn't nearly enough and she was in his arms.

"We can start fresh, Olivia. –Like none of this ever happened." He wished it could be so with all his heart.

"Not exactly, Mel. But we can learn from all that's happened." She gently pulled away from his embrace. "I do want to take you up on something you said, though."

"What? Take me up on anything you want."

"You said that together we could build something new, from scratch."

"I remember. I want that, if you do."

"I want to do something for children: neglected, unwanted or abused children. I don't want to sell anything; I want to give something to them, something permanent to hold onto... to the kids who need so much more than a new doll."

"Whatever you want. We can use our share of the Hannah revenues."

"And in addition, I understand that there's an account in the Cayman Islands with money my mother wanted me to have."

"It's still there?"

"According to my source, it is. I want to buy this big chunk of land. We can study the prototypes that are already in existence. There's the *Idaho Youth Ranch, the Alpine Academy,* and this wonderful place called *Hope Meadows.* We could build someplace like that. But to start with, there are these two kids...Josie and Frankie. No matter what, we have to find them and rescue them. Can you help me do that?"

"Whatever you say, Olivia. How can we fail? We've got angels on our team."

"We have to *be* the angels first. They'll fill in the gaps when we've given it our all. Before I acknowledged God's hand in my life, I never recognized that there were angels along the way. But they were there: My dear Sister M., Mrs. Tolbert, my English teacher, my friend Julie, my coaches, some of my social workers and others too. All of them were human angels sent to guide me through the dark."

"You know, my dearest girl, you make me so proud!" Mel said and squeezed her hand.

When she looked at his face and into his eyes, it was all there—the love, the pride and the joy of finding her at last—everything she had wanted to see as she had imagined this day all her life. "That's all I needed to know," Livy said. After a moment, she asked, "Can you tell me about my mother?"

"She was so much like you...I don't know why I didn't see it before...gorgeous and smart and ready to take on the world."

He was happy to share wonderful memories of a beautiful, extraordinary woman, memories he'd never been able to share with anyone before. It was sweet release.

They got around to fixing some lunch and brainstormed some ideas for their project. They left many of the pressing questions unasked and unanswered for another day. They were on the cusp of a new year and a new chapter of their lives. They would have plenty of time to catch up.

At last, Livy got up, cleared the dishes and noticed the phone message light blinking. She dialed her access number. There must have been twenty-five messages in the queue. A few of them were from Julie but most all of them were from Garrett.

****

Mel had completely forgotten that he had asked Fitz to get Kent Duckworth to follow up on his story about Livy's role in the scandal at JTC. Kent was driven by his own guilt to discover Livy's secrets, what had made her who she was. This editorial appeared in Newspapers across the country on New Year's Day.

Who is Hannah?
By Kent Duckworth
Inside Success Magazine

Who is Hannah? That question is more end than beginning of this story. I set out to find answer to this and other questions surrounding the JTC toy scandal. Would Olivia Thomas cheat the company and was she blackmailed into doing it? Many questions remain but now we know she didn't do it. But what I found in the meantime reached much deeper and brought up many more questions than answers and many disturbing images that most Americans don't want to think about.

We love to see faces of beautiful and happy children as was evidenced by the success of the JTC contest. The nation was mesmerized by those adorable little dimpled faces and what they promised in the way of a happy future on the horizon. Nothing epitomized our responsibility to that rising generation more than the hopeful and longing face and outstretched arms of Hannah. We all loved her. We all wanted to give her everything that her pleading pose and sweet face demanded: Love, nurture, care, a childhood of innocence and joy, and a bright future. We had absolutely no idea.

Hannah's picture has slight multi-colored tints in the background. I know now that those colors are rays of light coming from a stained glass window in a church located in North Carolina. Hannah was abandoned at St Thomas of Aquinas convent on December 24, 1978. No one I spoke to knew why. It was a mystery to the nuns who discovered her crying there in front of that beautiful window. It was a mystery to those who cared for her at St. Anthony's home for needy children. She was so beautiful, so sweet and loveable.

Those first years at St. Anthony's were happy years. A much beloved, elderly sister by the name of Sister Marian Margaret was barely able to talk to me about the day the state came and took the little six-year-old away.

It was obvious that the child had been loved and cared for there. The state had other plans for her. I don't mean to criticize the motives of the state, only the results. Judges with good intentions, armies of lawyers and advocates for children, advocates for religious institutions, opponents of any mixing of church and state funding, all thought they were fighting for the same goal: the good of the children. In the end, the children are the casualties of their fight.

At six, our Hannah entered "the system." By the time the state decided that no one was going to magically appear and claim Linda (her real name) and she was declared to be eligible for adoption, she had long since passed the most appealing baby years when children are easily adopted. Her uncertain race also was a factor. At that time, fewer homes were open to mixed-race children than might be today. By the time she was nine, she had been through more changes of placement than most of us have changes of clothes. And in between the placements came the group shelters where she was bullied, beaten, mentally and sexually abused and where she certainly lost that hopeful expectation of loving arms. She also found abuse in some of the homes where she was placed. Perhaps hardest of all, the dream of being adopted was three times within reach only to be snatched away. She didn't know why. Her child mind couldn't understand the complexities of adult circumstances. She only knew that again, she would not have a place at the table, a place to call home, the loving face of a mom, or the safe, protective arms of a dad.

She stopped hoping and turned to anger. Why couldn't she have what all the other kids had? Classmates mocked her and at one school she became known as *Foster Fanny*. She figured she was unlovable; she must be. She must be no good. She was the kid that no one wanted and she concluded that there must be a reason. By now, she didn't want anyone else, either. The risk of being rejected yet again would be unbearable. And yet, she wasn't nearly as damaged as some of the children who come through the system.

She ran away on occasion and tried to make it on her own at the age of fourteen. She lived on the streets for seven months before once again being rounded up and assigned to yet one more home that wasn't home. They were a kind and patient family and she tried to fit in. Things were going well until a young punk ruined it all. He managed to involve her in his criminal exploits in the name of that illusive love that she had been searching for all her life. In her need to be loved, she went along for the ride. His destination: robbery and assault. She went first to jail and then to a juvenile detention boarding school.

It was there, at Mountain Valley Academy, that things began to change. Things had to change or she would have found herself incarcerated when she turned eighteen. What a difference a caring teacher can make. Enter one Mrs. Roberta Tolbert: hero, angel. She saw in Linda what others had missed behind the labels of "delinquent", "foster kid" or "unwanted" or "damaged goods". Mrs. Tolbert dared to see the seeds of amazing potential that lacked only the proper sunlight and water to sprout and grow. Mrs. Tolbert would be that light and little successes along the way would be the water. And grow and blossom Linda did.

Life and sparkle began to shine from Linda's eyes again when at last someone believed in her inherent worth. Creativity, drive and passion were reborn when opportunity and encouragement made them welcome. Success built upon success and confidence blossomed, a beautiful flower emerging from once barren soil. How rare a miracle this was! Certainly, God played a part as other angels began to appear. Teammates, coaches, friends and professors all contributed to Linda's wondrous transformation.

A new life would bring a new name: *Olivia*. Mrs. Tolbert suggested it because she would *live* this new life to it's fullest. *Thomas* was for the Saint, namesake of the convent where she was found and found love. She would graduate with honors from both the University of South Florida and from the Wharton School of Business. Olivia Thomas would land a Madison Avenue job, right out of graduate school. She would create not just a toy, but also a phenomenon. How interesting that each doll, despite the many versions and distinctions, is first and foremost made in the image of her creator, each one capable of doing marvelous things!

No one from her childhood circles would have kept a scrapbook of her baby pictures so she didn't recognize the face in the picture as herself. This particular baby picture was taken the day, the moment she was left at St. Thomas of Aquinas Convent. The person who left her there must have taken it. Even with all that happened, I believe that it was meant to be shown to the world. She's a reminder of little ones all around reaching up to us for attention, love, and care, and to show us just how beautiful they are. It's as if she has been left on all our doorsteps. What will we do?

I began with the question; who is Hannah? And now I have far too many painful answers. Hannah is the face of the child staring up from a child pornography website on the Internet. Hannah is the terrorized and then raped and murdered subject of an *Amber Alert*. Hannah's are the cries of the child left neglected, unwashed and unfed by a drug-addicted mother. Hannah's are the wounds of a child beaten and abused by her mother's latest temporary boyfriend. Hannah is the weapon wielded in a painful divorce to inflict the greatest pain on a now-despised ex-spouse. Hannah is the inconvenient souvenir of a forbidden affair. Hannah is the product of impulse procreation, brought into existence because someone thought it might be nice to have a baby just as it might be nice to accessorize with matching shoes and purse. With buyer's remorse, shoes and purse go to the Goodwill; the child goes through hell or worse to a trashcan, never allowed to breathe. Hannah is everywhere. Hannahs are legion. Hannah belongs to all of us and reaches out to every heart. Hannah is our future. Hannah is our shame or she can be our opportunity and our inspiration for miracles. She is the clarion call for angels everywhere to open their hearts, their arms and their homes to just such a child. Will we hear the call?

1. Ode. Intimations of Immortality from Recollections of Early Childhood.
By William Wordsworth 1770-1850. Arthur Quiller-Couch, ed. 1919. The Oxford Book of English Verse 1250-1900. # 536

ACKNOWLEDGMENTS

I would like to express my appreciation to all those who have encouraged me in the creating of this story. First, thank you to Jane Bennion for not laughing at me when I suggested that I'd like to write a book. Without your ideas and your holding my hand and guiding the way, it never would have happened. I'd like to express special thanks to Leslie Donaldson for believing in my story and in me. You're *my* angel in the background, helping me to believe in myself. Thank you to my longsuffering husband, Ed, and our children for your patience in putting up with all the experimental versions of the story and having to listen to and evaluate every one. In addition to those mentioned in the dedication, other families, such as the Jacksons with their sweet Becca, Trisha and the Nielsens, Johnny and the Taylors, the Loosli's, the Dobbman's, the Crowe's, Keith and Karen Anderson, the entire Whiting clan, Bob and Carolyn Allen are such great examples of taking the risk to open hearts and truly love. And of course, my own dear parents, Ray and Elaine Habenicht, Mom and Dad Snow, and all our siblings have all inspired me to believe in the power of a good family and to want to cheer its preservation and protection.

I acknowledge the true soldiers in the battle for the souls of the little ones at risk: the loving foster parents and adoptive parents who open their hearts and homes. They are truly rescuers sent from above. I praise the social workers who struggle to help these children in impossible situations. In writing this story I am not saying that those working in the "system" are generally at fault. The situation is inherently difficult and most all of those involved are sincerely there to help children. There just aren't enough good homes and options to go around. I salute the mentors who take an interest and show the way.

And of course, there are the children. My own children have blessed my life and taught me so much. I have been humbled in the realization of what a better parent I could have been. Still, I delight in seeing the people Sean, Jeff and Stephanie are becoming in spite of me. The many students I've taught over the years have inspired me with a love for the pure innocence and the heavenly nature of children. (Yes, even the challenging ones.) They have touched my heart and soul and changed me to the core.

And finally, I sincerely express my gratitude to my God and my Savior Jesus Christ who make every good thing possible. God sends us a vitally important stewardship, children. Let us suffer the children to return unto His loving embrace by way of our own.

RESOURCES FOR HELPING CHILDREN

Alpine Academy: (Part of Youth Village)

The Village changes the lives of troubled children and families and offers residential care in Treatment Foster Homes and in Group Homes. The Village also offers in-home help through Families First, an intensive program that teaches parents valuable skills. Other programs include Parenting For Success classes, therapy, and privately funded higher education grants for Village graduates.

One of the Group Homes is the Village's Alpine Academy, which provides residential treatment for teenage girls from all over the country. Located in rural Tooele County, Utah, Alpine Academy provides a small, family-style environment with an emphasis on individualized treatment and academic excellence, using the Teaching-Family Model, the treatment model used in all Village programs. **Help One Child, Help Generations to Come.**

http://www.youthvillage.org

Hope Meadows:

Hope Meadows is a unique residential community – a five-block small-town neighborhood where neglected and abused children who have been removed from their biological parents for their safety, find a permanent and caring home, as well as grandparents, playmates and an entire neighborhood designed to help them grow up in a secure and nurturing environment. Hope Meadows is a place where children, adoptive parents and surrogate grandparents develop supportive relationships capable of healing the hurts of abuse and neglect - **a place where three generations care for and learn from each other.**

www.generationsofhope.org

Idaho Youth Ranch:
The Idaho Youth Ranch provides troubled children and families a bridge to a valued, responsible and productive future. To this end, we help each child find the hope, vision, courage and will to succeed. We provide stability, opportunity and security. We encourage growth and offer a chance to develop confidence, independence, esteem and respect. We teach values, responsibility and self-discipline in honest, caring environments. We believe in family, work, accountability, education and responsible behavior. **We are a catalyst for change**.

www.youthranch.org

Foster Care Alumni of America:
FCAA successfully advocates for opportunities for people in and from foster care, working toward improvements in practice and policy in child welfare. We build the capacity of our members and the foster care system through our strength in numbers and our deep expertise gained by experience.

www.fostercarealumni.org

Girls and Boys Town:
Girls and Boys Town is America's largest privately funded organization serving severely at-risk, abused, abandoned and neglected children. The nonprofit, nonsectarian organization provides these children with a safe, caring, loving environment where they gain confidence to get better and learn skills to become productive citizens. Now 90 years strong, Girls and Boys Town continues to carry on Father Flanagan's mission to bring help, healing and hope to America's children.

www.girlsandboystown.org

Share Your Story
Hannah's Reach blog... If you would like to comment or share your story of "angels" who have changed your life or your experience with helping a child, go to...

Hannahsreach.com